"MICHAEL CRICHTON AND PETER BENCHLEY, MOVE OVER. I COULDN'T PUT *RIPTIDE* DOWN. IT'S NONSTOP ACTION AND ADVENTURE FROM A TERRIFIC TEAM."
—**David Morrell**, author of *Double Image*

"THESE GUYS ARE MASTERS AT SCARING THE HELL OUT OF PEOPLE."
—*Tampa Tribune*

"AN AMAZING THRILLER; IT OUT-CRICHTONS CRICHTON in its grasp of technological detail, and far surpasses him in character and suspense. Steven Spielberg, where are you?"
—**Stuart Woods**, author of *Dead in the Water*

"A HOLD-YOUR-BREATH EXCITING TALE filled with all the twists that could come with the most wicked of common sins—greed."
—*St. Louis Post-Dispatch*

"A HIGHLY SATISFYING SEA ADVENTURE . . . *RIPTIDE* PULLS YOU IN AND DOESN'T LET YOU GO. . . . Has been compared to the adventure stories of Michael Crichton. It is that and more. . . . This is one to remember."
—*Maine Sunday Telegram*

more . . .

"Machine-gun pacing, startling plot twists, smart use of legend, scientific lore, and the evocative setting carry the day. . . . AN EXCITING ADVENTURE TALE THAT'S BOUND TO BE ONE OF THE MOST POPULAR OF THE SUMMER READS."
—*Publishers Weekly*

"UNSTOPPABLE SUSPENSE AND MYSTERY. . . THRILLING ADVENTURE!"
—*Kirkus Reviews*

"A RIPPING GOOD YARN. . . . Non stop action adventure . . . The red-hot authors of Reliquary score another big winner."
—*Library Journal*

"SOLID GOLD. . . . ONCE YOU START READING *RIPTIDE*, IT WON'T LET YOU GO. . . . Preston and Childs expertly deliver a thrilling adventure story that matches any novel written by Michael Crichton, Peter Benchley, or even Robert Louis Stevenson."
—*New Mexican*

"TAUT AND COMPELLING. . . . An excellent read for those who enjoy a good mystery and are tired of detectives and politicians."
—*Chattanooga Free Press*

"INTRIGUING . . . EXCITING."
—*Southern Pines Pilot* (NC)

RIPTIDE

DOUGLAS PRESTON
AND LINCOLN CHILD

WARNER BOOKS

A Time Warner Company

Lincoln Child dedicates this book to his daughter, Veronica

Douglas Preston dedicates this book to his brother,
Richard Preston

WARNER BOOKS EDITION

Copyright © 1998 by Douglas Peston and Lincoln Child
All rights reserved.

Cover design and illustration by Tony Greco

Warner Books, Inc.
1271 Avenue of the Americas
New York, NY 10020

Visit our Web site at
www.warnerbooks.com

 A Time Warner Company

Printed in the United States of America

Originally published in hardcover by Warner Books.
First International Paperback Printing: May, 1999
First United States Paperback Printing: July, 1999

10 9 8 7 6 5 4 3 2 1

Acknowledgments

We owe a great debt to one of Maine's finest doctors, David Preston, for invaluable help with the medical aspects of *Riptide*. We also wish to thank our agents, Eric Simonoff and Lynn Nesbit of Janklow & Nesbit; Matthew Snyder of Creative Artists Agency; our superb editor, Betsy Mitchell, and Maureen Egen, publisher, of Warner Books.

Lincoln Child would like to thank Denis Kelly, Bruce Swanson, Lee Suckno, M.D., Bry Benjamin, M.D., Bonnie Mauer, Chérif Keita, the Reverend Robert M. Diachek, and Jim Cush. In particular, I wish to thank my wife, Luchie, for her support, and for her stringent (and sometimes astringent) criticism, over the past five years, of four novels-in-progress. I want to thank my parents for instilling in me, from the beginning, a profound love for sailing and salt water that continues to this day. I also wish to acknowledge the shadowy company of centuries-dead buccaneers, pirates, codemakers and codebreakers, dilettantes, and Elizabethan intelligence agents, for providing some of the more colorful archetypes and source material in *Riptide*'s arsenal. And, lastly, I want to give a long-overdue thank-you to Tom McCormack, ex-boss and mentor, who with enthusiasm and perspicacity taught me so much about the art of writing and the craft of editing. *Nullum quod tetigit non ornavit.*

Douglas Preston would like to express his appreciation to John P. Wiley, Jr., senior editor of *Smithsonian* magazine, and to Don Moser, editor. I would like to thank my wife, Christine, for her support, and my daughter Selene, for reading the manuscript and offering excellent suggestions. I want to express my deepest gratitude to my mother, Dorothy McCann Preston, and to my father, Jerome Preston, Jr., for keeping and preserving Green Pastures Farm so that my children and grandchildren will be able to enjoy the real place that figures as one of the fictional backdrops to *Riptide*.

We offer our apologies to Maine purists for reconfiguring the coastline and moving islands and channels about with brazen abandon. Needless to say, Stormhaven and its inhabitants, and Thalassa and its employees, are fictitious and exist only in our imaginations. Similarly, though there may be several Ragged Islands found along the Eastern seaboard, the Ragged Island described in *Riptide*—along with the Hatch family that owns it—is a completely fictitious object.

Such a day, rum all out:—Our company somewhat sober:—
A damned confusion amongst us!—Rogues a-plotting:—
Great talk of separation—so I looked sharp for a
prize:—Such a day took one, with a great deal of liquor on
board, so kept the company hot, damned hot; then all things
went well again.

> —From the logbook of Edward Teach,
> aka Blackbeard, ca. 1718

Applying twentieth-century solutions to seventeenth-
century problems affords either absolute success or absolute
chaos; there is no middle ground.

> —Orville Horn, Ph.D.

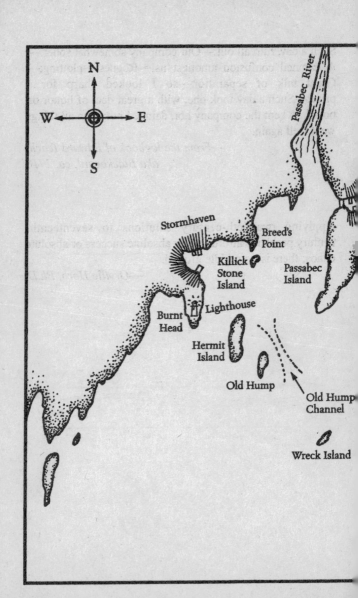

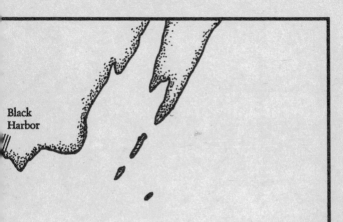

Black
Harbor

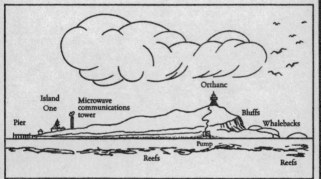

Orthanc

Island
One

Microwave
communications
tower

Bluffs

Pier

Whalebacks

Pump

Reefs

Reefs

Ragged Island

Prologue

On an afternoon in June 1790, a Maine cod fisherman named Simon Rutter became caught in a storm and a strong riptide. His dory overloaded with fish, he went badly off course and was forced to put in at fogbound Ragged Island, six miles off the coast. While waiting for the heavy weather to pass, the fisherman decided to explore the deserted spot. Inland from the rocky bluffs that gave the islet its name, he found a massive old oak tree with an ancient block and tackle dangling from one low-slung limb. Directly underneath it the ground had subsided into a depression. Although the island was known to be uninhabited, Rutter found clear evidence that someone had visited many years before.

His curiosity aroused, Rutter enlisted the aid of a brother and returned one Sunday several weeks later with picks and shovels. Locating the depression in the ground, the men began to dig. After five feet they hit a platform of oak logs. They pulled up the logs and, with increasing excitement, kept digging. By the end of the day, they had dug almost twenty feet,

*passing through layers of charcoal and clay to another oak
platform. The brothers went home, intending to renew their
digging after the annual mackerel run. But a week later, Rutter's brother was drowned when his dory capsized in a freak
accident. The pit was temporarily abandoned.*

*Two years later, Rutter and a group of local merchants de-
cided to pool their resources and return to the mysterious
spot on Ragged Island. Resuming the dig, they soon reached
a number of heavy vertical oak beams and cross-joists,
which appeared to be the ancient cribbing of a backfilled
shaft. Precisely how deep the group dug has been lost to history—most estimates assume close to one hundred feet. At
this point they struck a flat rock with an inscription carved
into it:*

> *First will yᵉ Lie*
> *Curst shall yᵉ Crye*
> *Worst must yᵉ Die*

*The rock was dislodged and hoisted to the surface. It has
been theorized that the removal of the rock broke a seal, because moments later, without warning, a flood of seawater
burst into the pit. All the diggers escaped—except Simon
Rutter. The Water Pit, as the flooded shaft became known,
had claimed its first victim.*

*Many legends grew up about the Water Pit. But the most
plausible held that around 1695, the notorious English pirate Edward Ockham buried his vast hoard somewhere
along the Maine coast shortly before his mysterious death.
The shaft at Ragged Island seemed a likely candidate.
Shortly after Rutter's death, rumors began to circulate that
the treasure was cursed, and that anyone attempting to plunder it would suffer the fate threatened on the stone.*

Numerous unsuccessful efforts were made to drain the Water Pit. In 1800, two of Rutter's former partners formed a new company and raised money to finance the digging of a second tunnel, twelve feet to the south of the original pit. All went well for the first hundred feet of digging, at which point they attempted to dig a horizontal passage beneath the original Water Pit. Their scheme was to tunnel up from underneath the treasure, but as soon as they angled in toward the original pit, the passage rapidly began filling with water. The men barely escaped with their lives.

For thirty years, the pit lay fallow. Then, in 1831, the Bath Expeditionary Salvage Company was formed by a downstate mining engineer named Richard Parkhurst. A friend of one of the original merchants, Parkhurst was able to gain valuable information about the earlier workings. Parkhurst decked over the mouth of the Water Pit and set up a large steam-driven pump. He found it impossible to drain the seawater. Undaunted, he brought in a primitive coal-drilling rig, which he positioned directly over the Pit. The drill went well beyond the original depth of the Pit, striking planking as deep as 170 feet, until the drill was stopped by something impenetrable. When the drilling pipe was removed, bits of iron and scales of rust were found jammed in the torn bit. The pod also brought up putty, cement, and large quantities of fiber. This fiber was analyzed and found to be "manilla grass" or coconut fiber. This plant, which grows only in the tropics, was commonly used as dunnage in ships to keep cargo from shifting. Shortly after this discovery, the Bath Expeditionary Salvage Company went bankrupt and Parkhurst was forced to leave the island.

In 1840, the Boston Salvage Company was formed and began digging a third shaft in the vicinity of the Water Pit.

After only sixty-six feet, they unexpectedly struck an ancient side tunnel that appeared to lead from the original Pit. Their own shaft filled instantly with water, then collapsed.

Undaunted, the entrepreneurs dug yet another, very large shaft thirty yards away, which became known as the Boston Shaft. Unlike earlier tunnels, the Boston Shaft was not a vertical pit, but was instead cut on a slope. Striking a spur of bedrock at seventy feet, they angled downward for another fifty feet at enormous expense, using augers and gunpowder. Then they drove a horizontal passage beneath the presumed bottom of the original Water Pit, where they found cribbing and the continuation of the original backfilled shaft. Excited, they dug downward, clearing the old shaft. At 130 feet they struck another platform, which they left in place while debating whether to pull it up. But that night, the camp was awakened by a loud rumble. The diggers rushed out to find that the bottom of the Water Pit had fallen into the new tunnel with such force that mud and water had been ejected thirty feet beyond the mouth of the Boston Shaft. Among this mud, a crude metal bolt was discovered, similar to what might be found on a banded sea chest.

Over the next twenty years, a dozen more shafts were dug in an attempt to reach the treasure chamber, all of which flooded or collapsed. Four more treasure companies went bankrupt. In several cases, diggers emerged swearing that the flooding was no accident, and that the original builders of the Water Pit had designed a diabolical mechanism to flood any side shafts that might be dug.

The Civil War brought a brief respite to the diggings. Then, in 1869, a new treasure-hunting company secured the rights to dig on the island. The dig foreman, F. X. Wrenche, noticed that water rose and fell in the Pit in accordance with the tides, and theorized that the Pit and its water traps must *all be connected to the sea by an artificial flood tunnel. If the tunnel could be found and sealed, the Pit could be drained and the treasure removed safely. In all, Wrenche dug more than a dozen exploratory shafts of varying depths in the vicinity of the Water Pit. Many of these shafts encountered horizontal tunnels and rock "pipes," which were dynamited in an attempt to stop the water. However, no flood tunnel to the sea was ever found and the Water Pit remained flooded. The company ran out of money and, like those before, left its machinery behind to rust quietly in the salt air.*

In the early 1880s, Gold Seekers Ltd. was formed by a consortium of industrialists from Canada and England. Powerful pumps and a new kind of drill were floated out to the island, along with boilers to power them. The company tried boring several holes into the Water Pit, finally hitting pay dirt on August 23, 1883. The drill came up against the plate of iron that had defeated Parkhurst's drill fifty years before. A new diamond bit was fitted and the boilers were stoked to a full head of steam. This time the drill bored through the iron and into a solid block of a softer metal. When the corer was extracted, a long, heavy curl of pure gold was found inside its grooves, along with a rotten piece of parchment with two broken phrases: "silks, canary wine, ivory" and "John Hyde rotting on the Deptford gibbet."

Half an hour after the discovery was made, one of the massive boilers exploded, killing an Irish stoker and leveling many of the company's structures. Thirteen were injured and one of the principals, Ezekiel Harris, was left blinded. Gold Seekers Ltd. followed its predecessors into bankrupty.

The years immediately before and after 1900 saw three more companies try their luck at the Water Pit. Unsuccessful in duplicating the discovery of Gold Seekers Ltd., these companies used newly designed pumps in concert with randomly placed underwater charges in an attempt to seal and drain the waterlogged island. Working at their utmost capacity, the pumps were able to lower the water level in several of the central shafts by about twenty feet at low tide. Excavators sent down to examine the condition of the pits complained of noxious gases; several fainted and had to be hauled to the surface. While the last of the three companies was at work in early September 1907, a man lost one arm and both legs when an explosive charge went off prematurely. Two days later, a vicious Nor'easter howled up the coast and wrecked the primary pump. Work was abandoned.

Although no more companies came forward, individual diggers and enthusiasts still occasionally dared to try their hands at exploratory tunnels. By this time, the original location of the Water Pit had been lost among the countless flooded side shafts, holes, and tunnels that riddled the heart of the island. At last the island was abandoned to the ospreys and the chokecherry bushes, its very surface unstable and dangerous, shunned by the mainland townspeople. It was in 1940 that Alfred Westgate Hatch, Sr., a young, wealthy New York financier, brought his family to Maine for the summer. He learned of the island and, growing intrigued, researched its history. Documentation was spotty: none of the previous companies had bothered to keep careful records. Six years later, Hatch purchased the island from a land speculator and moved his family to Stormhaven.

As had so many others before him, A. W. Hatch, Sr., became obsessed with the Water Pit and was ruined by it. Within two years the family's finances had been drained and Hatch was forced to declare personal bankruptcy; he turned to drink and died soon after, leaving A. W. Hatch, Jr., at nineteen, the sole support for his family.

1

July 1971

Malin Hatch was bored with summer. He and Johnny had spent the early part of the morning throwing rocks at the hornet's nest in the old well-house. That had been fun. But now there was nothing else to do. It was just past eleven, but he'd already eaten the two peanut-butter-and-banana sand-wiches his mother had made him for lunch. Now he sat crosslegged on the floating dock in front of their house, looking out to sea, hoping to spot a battleship steaming over the horizon. Even a big oil tanker would do. Maybe it would head for one of the outer islands, run aground, and blow up. Now *that* would be something.

His brother came out of the house and rattled down the wooden ramp leading to the dock. He was holding a piece of ice on his neck.

"Got you good," Malin said, secretly satisfied that he had escaped stinging and that his older, supposedly wiser, brother had not.

"You just didn't get close enough," Johnny said through his last mouthful of sandwich. "Chicken."

"I got as close as you."

"Yeah, sure. All those bees could see was your skinny butt running away." He snorted and winged the piece of ice into the water.

"No, sir. I was right there."

Johnny plopped down beside him on the dock, dropping his satchel next to him. "We fixed those bees pretty good though, huh, Mal?" he said, testing the fiery patch on his neck with one forefinger.

"Sure did."

They fell silent. Malin looked out across the little cove toward the islands in the bay: Hermit Island, Wreck Island, Old Hump, Killick Stone. And far beyond, the blue outline of Ragged Island, appearing and disappearing in the stubborn mist that refused to lift even on this beautiful midsummer day. Beyond the islands, the open ocean was, as his father often said, as calm as a millpond.

Languidly, he tossed a rock into the water and watched the spreading ripples without interest. He almost regretted not going into town with his parents. At least it would be something to do. He wished he could be anywhere else in the world—Boston, New York—anywhere but Maine.

"Ever been to New York, Johnny?" he asked.

Johnny nodded solemnly. "Once. Before you were born."

What a lie, Malin thought. As if Johnny would remember anything that had happened when he was less than two years old. But saying so out loud would be to risk a swift punch in the arm.

Malin's eye fell on the small outboard tied at the end of the dock. And he suddenly had an idea. A really good idea.

"Let's take it out," he said, lowering his voice and nodding at the skiff.

"You're crazy," Johnny said. "Dad would whip us good."

"Come on," Malin said. "They're having lunch at the Hastings after they finish shopping. They won't be back until three, maybe four. Who's gonna know?"

"Just the whole town, that's all, seeing us going out there."

"Nobody's gonna be watching," said Malin. Then, recklessly, he added, "Who's chicken now?"

But Johnny did not seem to notice this liberty. His eyes were on the boat. "So where do you want to go that's so great, anyway?" he asked.

Despite their solitude, Malin lowered his voice further. "Ragged Island."

Johnny turned toward him. "Dad'll kill us," he whispered.

"He won't kill us if we find the treasure."

"There's no treasure," Johnny said scornfully, but without much conviction. "Anyway, it's dangerous out there, with all those pits."

Malin knew enough about his brother to recognize the tone in his voice. Johnny was interested. Malin kept quiet, letting the monotonous morning solitude do his persuading for him.

Abruptly, Johnny stood up and strode to the end of the dock. Malin waited, an anticipatory thrill coursing through him. When his brother returned, he was holding a life preserver in each hand.

"When we land, we don't go farther than the rocks along the shore." Johnny's voice was deliberately gruff, as if to remind Malin that simply having one good idea didn't alter their balance of power. "Understand?"

Malin nodded, holding the gunwale while Johnny tossed in his satchel and the life preservers. He wondered why they hadn't thought of doing this before. Neither boy had ever been to Ragged Island. Malin didn't know any kids in the town of Stormhaven who ever had, either. It would make a great story to tell their friends.

"You sit in the bow," Johnny said, "and I'll drive."

Malin watch Johnny fiddle with the shift lever, open the choke, pump the gas bulb, then yank the starter cord. The engine coughed, then fell silent. Johnny yanked again, then again. Ragged Island was six miles offshore, but Malin figured they could make it in a half hour on such a smooth sea. It was close to high tide, when the strong currents that swept the island dropped down to nothing before reversing.

Johnny rested, his face red, and then turned again for a heroic yank. The engine sputtered into life. "Cast off!" he shouted. As soon as the rope was uncleated, Johnny shoved the throttle all the way forward, and the tinny little eighteen-horsepower engine whined with exertion. The boat surged from the dock and headed out past Breed's Point into the bay, wind and spray stinging Malin's face delightfully.

The boat sent back a creamy wake as it sliced through the ocean. There had been a massive storm the week before, but as usual it seemed to have settled the surface, and the water was glassy. Now Old Hump appeared to starboard, a low naked dome of granite, streaked with seagull lime and fringed with dark seaweed. As they buzzed through the channel, countless seagulls, drowsing one-legged on the rock, raised their heads and stared at the boat with bright yellow eyes. A single pair rose into the sky, then wheeled past, crying a lost cry.

"This was a great idea," Malin said. "Wasn't it, Johnny?"

"Maybe," Johnny said. "But if we get caught, it was *your* idea."

Even though their father owned Ragged Island, they had been forbidden to visit it for as long as he could remember. Their dad hated the place and never talked about it. Schoolyard legend held that countless people had been killed there digging for treasure; that the place was cursed; that it harbored ghosts. There were so many pits and shafts dug over the years that the island's innards were completely rotten, ready to swallow the unwary visitor. He'd even heard about the Curse Stone. It had been found in the Pit many years before, and now it was supposedly kept in a special room deep in the church basement, locked up tight because it was the work of the devil. Johnny once told him that when kids were really bad in Sunday School, they were shut up in the crypt with the Curse Stone. He felt another shiver of excitement.

The island lay dead ahead now, wreathed in clinging tatters of mist. In winter, or on rainy days, the mist turned to a suffocating, pea-soup fog. On this bright summer day, it was more like translucent cotton candy. Johnny had tried to explain the local rip currents that caused it, but Malin hadn't understood and was pretty sure Johnny didn't, either.

The mist approached the boat's prow and suddenly they were in a strange twilit world, the motor muffled. Almost unconsciously, Johnny slowed down. Then they were through the thickest of it and ahead Malin could see the Ragged Island ledges, their cruel seaweed-covered flanks softened by the mist.

They brought the skiff through a low spot in the ledges. As the sea-level mist cleared, Malin could see the greenish tops of jagged underwater rocks, covered with waving seaweed; the kind of rocks so feared by lobstermen at low tide or in heavy fog. But now the tide was high, and the little motorboat slid past effortlessly. After an argument about who was to get his feet wet, they grounded on the cobbled shore.

Malin jumped out with the painter and pulled the boat up, feeling the water squish in his sneakers.

Johnny stepped out onto dry land. "Pretty neat," he said noncommittally, shouldering his satchel and looking inland.

Just up from the stony beach, the sawgrass and chokecherry bushes began. The scene was lit by an eerie silver light, filtered through the ceiling of mist that still hung above their heads. A huge iron boiler, at least ten feet high, rose above the nearby grass, covered with massive rivets and rusted a deep orange. There was a split down one side, ragged and petalled. Its upper half was cloaked by the low-lying mists.

"I bet that boiler blew up," Johnny said.

"Bet it killed somebody," Malin added with relish.

"Bet it killed two people."

The cobbled beach ended at the seaward point of the island in ridges of wave-polished granite. Malin knew that fishermen passing through the Ragged Island Channel called these rocks the Whalebacks. He scrambled up the closest of the Whalebacks and stood high, trying to see over the bluffs into the island.

"Get down!" Johnny yelled. "Just what do you think you're gonna see in all this mist? Idiot."

"Takes one to know one—" Malin began, climbing down, and received a brotherly rap on the head for his troubles.

"Stay behind me," Johnny said. "We'll circle the shore, then head back." He walked quickly along the bottom of the bluffs, his tanned legs chocolate brown in the dim light. Malin followed, feeling aggrieved. It was his idea to come out here, but Johnny always took over.

"Hey!" Johnny yelled. "Look!" He bent down, picking up something long and white. "It's a bone."

"No, it isn't," Malin replied, still feeling annoyed. Coming to the island was his idea. *He* should have been the one to find it.

"It is, too. And I bet it's from a man." Johnny swung the thing back and forth like a baseball bat. "It's the leg bone off somebody who got killed trying to get the treasure. Or a pirate, maybe. I'm gonna take it home and keep it under my bed."

Curiosity overcame Malin's annoyance. "Let me see," he said.

Johnny handed him the bone. It felt surprisingly heavy and cold, and it smelled bad. "Yuck," Malin said, hastily handing it back.

"Maybe the skull's around here somewhere," Johnny replied.

They poked among the rocks, finding nothing but a dead dogfish with goggle eyes. As they rounded the point, a wrecked barge came into view, left from some long-forgotten salvage operation. It was grounded at the high-tide mark, twisted and pounded onto the rocks, buffeted by decades of storms.

"Look at this," said Johnny, interest rising in his voice. He scrambled out on the heaved, buckled deck. All around it lay rusted pieces of metal, pipes, busted gears, and nasty snarls of cable and wire. Malin began looking through the old junk, keeping an eye out for the gleam of a pirate doubloon. He figured that the pirate, Red Ned Ockham, was so rich he'd probably dropped a whole lot of doubloons around the island. Red Ned, who'd supposedly buried millions and millions in gold on the island, along with a jeweled weapon called St. Michael's Sword, so powerful it could kill any man who even looked at it. They said Red Ned had once cut a man's ears off and used them to make a bet in a dice game. A sixth-grade girl named Cindy told him it was really the man's balls that Red Ned cut off, but Malin didn't believe her. Another time Red Ned got drunk and cut a man open, then threw him overboard and towed him by his guts until the sharks ate him. The kids at school had a lot of stories about Red Ned.

Tiring of the barge, Johnny motioned for Malin to follow him along the rocks that lay scattered at the bottom of the bluffs on the windward side of the island. Above them, a high dirt embankment rose against the sky, roots of long-dead spruce trees poking horizontally from the soil like gnarled fingers. The top of the embankment was lost in the clinging mists. Some of the bluffs were caved in and collapsing, victims of the storms that slammed into the island every fall.

It was chilly in the shadow of the bluffs, and Malin hurried on. Johnny, excited now by his finds, was bounding ahead, heedless of his own warnings, whooping and waving the bone. Malin knew his mother would throw the old bone into the ocean as soon as she found it.

Johnny stopped briefly to poke among stuff that had washed up on shore: old lobster buoys, busted-up traps, pieces of weathered planking. Then he moved toward a fresh gash farther up the bluffs. A bank had recently caved in, spilling dirt and boulders across the rocky shore. He leaped easily over the boulders, then disappeared from view.

Malin moved more quickly now. He didn't like having Johnny out of sight. There was a stirring in the air: it had been a sunny day before they disappeared into the Ragged Island mist, but anything could be happening out there now. The breeze felt cold, as if weather was coming on, and the sea was beginning to break hard over the Ragged Island ledges. The tide would be close to turning. Maybe they'd better start back.

There was a sudden, sharp cry, and for a terrible moment Malin feared Johnny had hurt himself on the slippery rocks.

But then the cry came again—an urgent summons—and Malin scrambled forward, clambering over the fallen rocks and around a bend in the shoreline. Before him, a huge granite boulder lay at a crazy angle, freshly dislodged from the bank by a recent storm. On its far side stood Johnny, pointing, a look of wide-eyed wonderment on his face.

At first, Malin couldn't say a word. The movement of the boulder had exposed the opening of a tunnel at the foot of the bank, with just enough room to squeeze behind. A clammy stream of stale air eddied from the tunnel mouth.

"Cripes," he said, running up the slope toward the embankment.

"I found it!" Johnny cried, breathless with excitement. "I bet you *anything* the treasure's in there. Take a look, Malin!"

Malin turned. "It was my idea."

Johnny looked back with a smirk. "Maybe," he said, unshouldering his satchel. "But I found it. And *I* brought the matches."

Malin leaned toward the tunnel mouth inquisitively. Deep down, he'd believed his father when he said there never was any treasure on Ragged Island. But now, he wasn't so sure. Was it possible his dad could be wrong?

Then he leaned back quickly, nose wrinkling against the stale smell of the tunnel.

"What's the matter?" Johnny asked. "Afraid?"

"No," said Malin in a small voice. The mouth of the tunnel looked very dark.

"I'm going first," Johnny said. "You follow me. And you'd *better* not get lost." Tossing his prize bone away, he dropped to his knees and squirmed through the opening. Malin knelt also, then hesitated. The ground was hard and cold beneath him. But Johnny was already disappearing from sight, and Malin didn't want to be left on the lonely, fogbound shore. He squirmed through the opening after his brother.

There was the snap of a match, and Malin sucked in his breath unconsciously as he rose to his feet. He was in a small antechamber, the roof and walls held up by ancient timbers. Ahead, a narrow tunnel led into blackness.

"We'll split the treasure fifty-fifty." Johnny was talking in a very serious voice, a voice Malin hadn't heard before. Then he did something even more surprising: He turned and shook Malin's hand with a childlike formality. "You and me, Mal, equal partners."

Malin swallowed, feeling a little better.

The match died as they took another step forward. Johnny paused and Malin heard the scratch of another match, followed by a flare of feeble light. He could see his brother's Red Sox cap haloed in the flickering flame. A sudden stream of dirt and pebbles rattled down through the timbers, bouncing across the stone floor.

"Don't touch the walls," Johnny whispered, "and don't make any loud noise. You'll cave the whole thing in."

Malin said nothing, but unconsciously moved closer to his brother.

"Don't follow so close!" Johnny hissed.

They went forward along a downward incline, then Johnny cried out and jerked his hand. The light went out, plunging them into darkness.

"Johnny?" Malin cried, feeling a surge of panic, reaching out to grasp his brother's arm. "What about the curse?"

"Come on, there's no curse," whispered Johnny scornfully. There was another scratching sound and the match flared. "Don't worry. I got at least forty matches in here. And look—" He dug into his pocket, then turned toward Malin, a big paper clip held between his fingers. He stuck the lit match into one end. "How about that? No more burned fingers."

The tunnel took a gentle turn to the left, and Malin noticed that the reassuring crescent of light from the tunnel entrance was gone. "Maybe we should go back and get a flashlight," he said.

Suddenly, he heard a hideous sound, a hollow groan that seemed to erupt from the heart of the island and fill the narrow chamber. "Johnny!" he cried, clutching his brother again. The sound sputtered away into a deep sigh as another trickle of dirt fell from the timbers overhead.

Johnny shrugged his arm away. "Jeez, Malin. It's just the tide turning. It always makes that noise in the Water Pit. Keep your voice down, I said."

"How do you know that?" Malin asked.

"*Everybody* knows that."

There was another moan and a gurgle, followed by a loud creaking of timbers that slowly died away. Malin bit his lip to keep it from trembling.

A few matches later, the tunnel turned at a shallow angle and began sloping downward more steeply, its walls shorter and rougher.

Johnny held his match toward the passage. "This is it," he said. "The treasure chamber would be at the bottom."

"I don't know," Malin said. "Maybe we'd better go back and get Dad."

"Are you kidding?" Johnny hissed. "Dad *hates* this place. We'll tell Dad *after* we get the treasure."

He lit another match, then ducked his head into the narrow tunnel. Malin could see that this passage wasn't more than four feet high. Cracked boulders supported the wormy timbers of the roof. The smell of mold was even stronger here, mingled with seaweed and a hint of something worse.

"We're gonna have to crawl," Johnny muttered, his voice momentarily uncertain. He paused, and for a hopeful instant Malin thought they were turning back. Then Johnny straightened one end of the paperclip and stuck it between his teeth. The wavering shadows thrown by the match gave his face a ghoulish, hollow look.

That did it. "I'm not going any farther," Malin announced.

"Good," said Johnny. "You can stay here in the dark."

"No!" Malin sobbed loudly. "Dad's gonna kill us. Johnny, *please . . .*"

"When Dad finds out how rich we are, he'll be too happy to be mad. He'll save a whole two dollars a week on allowance."

Malin sniffed a little and wiped his nose.

Johnny turned in the narrow space and placed a hand on Malin's head. "Hey," he whispered, his voice gentle. "If we chicken out now, we may never get a second chance. So be a pal, okay, Mal?" He ruffled Malin's hair.

"Okay." Malin sniffed.

He got onto his hands and knees and followed Johnny down the sloping tunnel. Pebbles and grit from the tunnel floor dug into the palms of his hands. Johnny seemed to be lighting a whole lot of matches, and Malin had almost screwed up the courage to ask how many were left, when his older brother halted abruptly.

"There's something up ahead," came the whispered voice.

Malin tried to see around his brother, but the tunnel was too narrow. "What is it?"

"It's a door!" Johnny hissed suddenly. "I swear, it's an old door!" The ceiling angled up to form a narrow vestibule ahead of him, and Malin craned desperately for a view. There it was: a row of thick planks, with two old metal hinges set into the frame of the tunnel. Large slabs of dressed stone formed the walls to either side. Damp and mold lay over everything. The edges of the door had been caulked with what looked like oakum.

"Look!" Johnny cried, pointing excitedly.

Lying across the front of the door was a fancy embossed

seal made of wax and paper, stamped with a coat of arms. Even through the dust, Johnny could see that the seal was unbroken.

"A sealed door!" Johnny whispered, awestruck. "Just like in the books!"

Malin stared as if in a dream, a dream somehow wonderful and terrifying at the same time. They really had found the treasure. And it had been his idea.

Johnny grasped the ancient iron handle and gave an exploratory tug. There was a sharp creak of protesting hinges. "Hear that?" he panted. "It's not locked. All we have to do is break this seal." He turned and handed the matchbox to Malin, his eyes wide. "You light the matches while I pull it open. And move back a little, willya?"

Malin peered into the box. "There's only five left!" he cried in dismay.

"Just shut up and do it. We can get out in the dark, I swear we can."

Malin lit a match, but his hands shook and it flickered out. *Only four more,* he thought as Johnny muttered impatiently. The next match sprang to life and Johnny placed both hands on the iron handle. "Ready?" he hissed, bracing his feet against the earthen wall.

Malin opened his mouth to protest, but Johnny was already tugging at the door. The seal parted abruptly, and the door opened with a shriek that made Malin jump. A puff of foul air blew out the match. In the close darkness, Malin heard Johnny's sharp intake of breath. Then Johnny screamed *"Ouch!"*, except the voice seemed so breathless, so very high, it almost didn't sound like Johnny. Malin heard a thump, and the floor of the tunnel shivered violently. As dirt and sand rained down in the darkness, filling his eyes and nose, he thought he heard another sound: a strange, strangled sound, so brief that it might almost have been a cough. Then a wheezing, dripping noise like a wet sponge being squeezed.

"Johnny!" Malin cried, raising his hands to wipe the dust out of his face and dropping the matchbox in the process. It was so very dark, and things had gone wrong so suddenly, and panic began to overwhelm him. In the close, listening darkness came another noise, low and muffled. It took Malin a moment to realize what it was: a soft, continuous *dragging* . . .

Then the spell was broken and he was fumbling in the dark on his hands and knees, hands outstretched, searching for the matches, bawling his brother's name. One hand touched something wet and he snatched it away just as the other hand closed on the matchbox. Rising to his knees, choking back sobs, he grabbed a match and scratched it frantically until it flared.

In the sudden light he looked around wildly. Johnny was gone. The door was open, the seal broken—but beyond lay nothing except a blank stone wall. Dust hung thickly in the air.

Then wetness touched his legs and he looked down. In the spot where Johnny had stood there was a large, black pool of water, crawling slowly around his knees. For a crazy moment, Malin thought maybe there was a breach in the tunnel somewhere and seawater was leaking in. Then he realized the pool was steaming slightly in the flicker of the match. Straining forward, he saw that it was not black but red: blood, more blood than he ever imagined a body could hold. Paralyzed, he watched as the glossy pool spread, running in tendrils across the hollows of the floor, draining into the cracks, creeping into his wet Keds, surrounding him like a crimson octopus, until the match dropped into it with a sharp hiss and darkness descended once again.

Cambridge, Massachusetts
Present Day

The small laboratory looked out from the Mount Auburn Hospital annex across the leafy tops of the maple trees to the slow, sullen waters of the Charles River. A rower in a needle-like shell was cutting through the dark water with powerful strokes, peeling back a glittering wake. Malin Hatch watched, momentarily entranced by the perfect synchronicity of body, boat, and water.

"Dr. Hatch?" came the voice of his lab assistant. "The colonies are ready." He pointed toward a beeping incubator.

Hatch turned from the window, reverie broken, suppressing a surge of irritation at his well-meaning assistant. "Let's take out the first tier and have a look at the little buggers," he said.

In his usual nervous way, Bruce opened the incubator and removed a large tray of agar plates, bacterial colonies growing like glossy pennies in their centers. These were relatively harmless bacteria—they didn't need special precautions beyond the usual sterile procedures—but Hatch watched with alarm as the assistant swung the rattling tray around, bumping it on the autoclave.

"Careful, there," said Hatch. "Or there'll be no joy in Whoville tonight."

The assistant brought the tray to an uneasy rest on the glove box. "Sorry," he said sheepishly, standing back and wiping his hands on his lab coat.

Hatch gave the tray a practiced sweep with his eyes. Rows two and three showed good growth, rows one and four were variable, and row five was sterile. In an instant he realized the experiment would be a success. Everything was working out as hypothesized; in a month he'd have published another impressive paper in the *New England Journal of Medicine*, and everyone would be talking yet again about what a rising star he was in the department.

The prospect filled him with a huge feeling of emptiness.

Absently, he swiveled a magnifying lens over to make a gross examination of the colonies. He'd done this so often that he could identify the strains just by looking at them, by comparing their surface textures and growth patterns. After a few moments he turned toward his desk, pushed aside a computer keyboard, and began jotting notes into his lab notebook.

The intercom chimed.

"Bruce?" Hatch murmured as he scribbled.

Bruce jumped up, sending his notebook clattering to the floor. A minute later he returned. "Visitor," he said simply.

Hatch straightened up his large frame. Visitors to the lab

were rare. Like most doctors, he kept his lab location and telephone number under wraps to all but a select few.

"Would you mind seeing what he wants?" Hatch asked. "Unless it's urgent, refer him to my office. Dr. Winslow's on call today."

Bruce went off again and the lab fell back into silence. Hatch's gaze drifted once again toward the window. The afternoon light was streaming in, sending a shower of gold through the test tubes and lab apparatus. With an effort, he forced his concentration back to his notes.

"He's not a patient," Bruce said, bustling back into the lab. "Says you'll want to see him."

Hatch looked up. *Probably a researcher from the hospital,* he thought. He took a deep breath. "Okay. Show him in."

A minute later, footsteps sounded in the outer lab. Malin looked up to see a spare figure gazing at him from the far side of the doorframe. The setting sun was striking the man full force, modeling the sunburnt skin drawn tight across a handsome face, refracting light deep within a pair of gray eyes.

"Gerard Neidelman," the stranger said in a low, gravelly voice.

Couldn't spend much time in a lab or the OR with a tan like that, Hatch thought to himself. *Must be a specialist, getting in a lot of golf time.* "Please come in, Dr. Neidelman," he said.

"Captain," the man replied. "Not Doctor." He passed through the doorway and straightened up, and Hatch immediately knew it wasn't just an honorary title. Simply by the way he stepped through the door, head bent, hand on the upper frame, it was clear the man had spent time at sea. Hatch guessed he was not old—perhaps forty-five—but he had the narrow eyes and roughened skin of a sailor. There was something different about him—something almost otherwordly, an air of ascetic intensity—that Hatch found intriguing.

Hatch introduced himself as his visitor stepped forward and offered his hand. The hand was dry and light, the handshake short and to the point.

"Could we speak in private?" the man asked quietly.

Bruce spoke up again. "What should I do about these colonies, Dr. Hatch? They shouldn't be left out too long in—"

"Why don't you put them back in the refrigerator? They won't be growing legs for at least a few billion more years." Hatch glanced at his watch, then back into the man's steady gaze. He made a quick decision. "And then you might as well head home, Bruce. I'll put you down for five. Just don't tell Professor Alvarez."

Bruce flashed a brief smile. "Okay, Dr. Hatch. Thanks."

In a moment Bruce and the colonies were gone, and Hatch turned back to his curious visitor, who had strolled toward the window.

"Is this where you do most of your work, Doctor?" he asked, shifting a leather portfolio from one hand to the other. He was so thin he would have seemed spectral, were it not for the intensity of calm assurance he radiated.

"It's where I do just about all of it."

"Lovely view," Neidelman murmured, gazing out the window.

Hatch looked at the man's back, mildly surprised that he felt unoffended by the interruption. He thought of asking the man his business but decided against it. Somehow, he knew Neidelman had not come on a trivial matter.

"The water of the Charles is so dark," the Captain said. "'Far off from these a slow and silent stream/Lethe the river of oblivion rolls.'" He turned. "Rivers are a symbol of forgetfulness, are they not?"

"I can't remember," Hatch said lightly, but growing a little wary now, waiting.

The Captain smiled and withdrew from the window. "You must be wondering why I've barged into your laboratory. May I ask a few minutes of your indulgence?"

"Haven't you already?" Hatch indicated a vacant chair. "Have a seat. I'm about finished for the day here, and this important experiment I've been working on"—he waved his hand vaguely in the direction of the incubator—"is, how shall I put it? Boring."

Neidelman raised an eyebrow. "Not as exciting as fighting an eruption of breakbone fever in the swamps of Amazonia, I imagine."

"Not quite," Hatch said after a moment.

The man smiled. "I read the article in the *Globe*."

"Reporters never let the facts stand in the way of a story. It wasn't nearly as exciting as it seems."

"Which is why you returned?"

"I got tired of watching my patients die for lack of a fifty-cent shot of amoxycillin." Hatch spread his hands fatalistically. "So isn't it odd that I wish I were back there? Life on Memorial Drive seems rather tepid by comparison." He shut up abruptly and glanced at Neidelman, wondering what it was about the man that had gotten him talking.

"The article went on to talk about your travels in Sierra Leone, Madagascar, and the Comoros," Neidelman continued. "But perhaps your life could use some excitement right now?"

"Pay no attention to my grousing," Hatch replied with what he hoped was a light tone. "A little boredom now and then can be tonic for the soul." He glanced at Neidelman's portfolio. There was some kind of insignia embossed into the leather that he couldn't quite make out.

"Perhaps," came the reply. "In any case, it seems you've

hit every spot on the globe over the last twenty-five years. Except Stormhaven, Maine."

Hatch froze. He felt a numbness begin in his fingers and move up his arms. Suddenly it all made sense: the round-about questions, the seafaring background, the intense look in the man's eyes.

Neidelman stood very still, his eyes steady on Hatch, saying nothing.

"Ah," Hatch said, fighting to recover his composure. "And you, Captain, have just the thing to cure my ennui."

Neidelman inclined his head.

"Let me guess. Does this, by any freak of chance, have to do with Ragged Island?" A flicker in Neidelman's face showed that he had guessed right. "And you, Captain, are a treasure hunter. Am I right?"

The equanimity, the sense of quiet self-confidence, never left Neidelman's face. "We prefer the term 'recovery specialist.'"

"Everyone has a euphemism these days. *Recovery* specialist. Sort of like 'sanitary engineer.' You want to dig on Ragged Island. And let me guess: Now, you're about to tell me that you, and only you, hold the secret to the Water Pit."

Neidelman stood quietly, saying nothing.

"No doubt you also have a high-tech gizmo that will show you the location of the treasure. Or perhaps you've enlisted the help of Madame Sosostris, famous clairvoyant?"

Neidelman remained standing. "I know you've been approached before," he said.

"Then you'll know the common fate of those who've approached me. Dowsers, psychics, oil barons, engineers, everybody with a foolproof scheme."

"Their schemes may have been flawed," Neidelman replied, "but their dreams were not. I know about the tragedies that befell your family after your grandfather bought the island. But his heart was in the right place. There *is* a vast treasure down there. I know it."

"Of course you do. They all do. But if you think you're the reincarnation of Red Ned himself, it's only fair to warn you that I've heard from several others who already claim that distinction. Or perhaps you purchased one of those old-looking treasure maps that occasionally come up for sale in Portland. Captain Neidelman, faith won't make it true. There never was, and there never will be, any Ragged Island treasure. I feel sorry for you, I really do. Now, perhaps you should leave before I call the guard—I beg your pardon, I mean the security specialist—to escort you to the door."

Ignoring this, Neidelman shrugged, then leaned toward the desk. "I don't ask you to take it on faith."

There was something so self-confident, so utterly detached, about the Captain's shrug that a fresh flood of anger swept Hatch. "If you had any idea how many times I've heard this same story, you'd be ashamed for coming here. What makes you any different from the rest?"

Reaching inside the leather portfolio, Neidelman withdrew a single sheet of paper and wordlessly pushed it across the desk.

Hatch looked at the document without touching it. It was a simplified financial report, notarized, indicating that a company named Thalassa Holdings Ltd. had raised a sum of money to form the Ragged Island Reclamation Corporation. The sum was twenty-two million dollars.

Hatch glanced from the paper back to Neidelman, then began to laugh. "You mean you actually had the nerve to raise this money before even asking my permission? You must have some pretty pliant investors."

Once again, Neidelman broke into what seemed to be his trademark smile: reserved, self-confident, remote without arrogance. "Dr. Hatch, you've had every right to show treasure hunters the door for the last twenty years. I perfectly understand your reaction. They were underfunded and underprepared. But they weren't the only problem. The problem was also *you*." He leaned away again. "Obviously, I don't know you well. But I sense that, after more than a quarter century of uncertainty, maybe at last you're ready to learn what really happened to your brother."

Neidelman paused for a moment, his eyes still on Hatch. Then he began again, in a tone so low it was barely audible. "I know that your interest is not the financial reward. And I understand how your grief has made you hate that island. That is why I come to you with everything prepared. Thalassa is the best in the world at this kind of work. And we have equipment at our disposal that your grandfather could only have dreamed of. We've chartered the ships. We have divers, archaeologists, engineers, an expedition doctor, all ready to go at a moment's notice. One word from you, and I promise you that within a month the Water Pit will have yielded up its secrets. We will know *everything* about it." He whispered the word "everything" with peculiar force.

"Why not just leave it be?" Hatch murmured. "Why not let it keep its secrets?"

"That, Dr. Hatch, is not within my nature. Is it within yours?"

In the ensuing silence, the distant bells of Trinity Church tolled five o'clock. The silence stretched on into a minute, then two, and then five.

At last, Neidelman removed the paper from the desk and placed it back in his portfolio. "Your silence is sufficiently eloquent," he said quietly, no trace of rancor in his voice. "I've taken enough of your time. Tomorrow, I'll inform our partners that you have declined our offer. Good day, Dr. Hatch." He rose to go, and then just before the door he stopped, half turning. "There is one other thing. To answer your question, there *is* something that makes us different from all the rest. We've uncovered a small piece of information about the Water Pit that nobody else knows. Not even you."

Hatch's chuckle died in his throat when he saw Neidelman's face.

"We know who designed it," the Captain said quietly.

Involuntarily, Hatch felt his fingers stiffen and curl in toward his palms. "What?" he croaked.

"Yes. And there's something more. We have the journal he kept during its construction."

In the sudden silence, Hatch fetched a deep breath, then another. He looked down at his desk and shook his head. "That's beautiful," he managed to say. "Just beautiful. I guess I underestimated you. After all these years, I've heard something original. You've made my day, Captain Neidelman."

But Neidelman had gone, and Hatch realized he was talking to an empty room.

It was several minutes before he could bring himself to rise from the desk. As he shoved the last of his papers into his briefcase, hands still trembling a little, he noticed that Neidelman had left his card behind. A telephone number had been scribbled across the top, presumably the hotel he was staying in. Hatch brushed the card into the wastebasket, picked up his briefcase, left the lab, and briskly walked back to his town house through the dusky summer streets.

At two o'clock that morning, he found himself back in the laboratory, pacing before the darkened window, Neidelman's card grasped in one hand. It was three before he finally picked up the phone.

3

Hatch parked in the dirt lot above the pier and stepped slowly from the rented car. He closed the door, then paused to look over the harbor, hand still grasping the handle. His eyes took in the long, narrow cove, bound by a granite shore, dotted with lobster boats and draggers, bathed in a cold silver light. Even twenty-five years later, Hatch recognized many of the names: the *Lola B*, the *Maybelle W*.

The little town of Stormhaven struggled up the hill, narrow clapboard houses following a zigzag of cobblestone lanes. Toward the top the houses thinned out, replaced by stands of black spruce and small meadows enclosed by stone walls. At the very top of the hill stood the Congregational church, its severe white steeple rising into the gray sky. On the far side of the cove he glimpsed his own boyhood home, its four gables and widow's walk poking above the treeline, the long meadow sloping to the shore and a small dock. He quickly turned away, feeling almost as if some stranger was standing in his shoes, and that he was seeing everything through that stranger's eyes.

He headed for the pier, slipping on a pair of sunglasses as he did so. The sunglasses, and his own inner turmoil, made him feel a little foolish. Yet he felt more apprehension now than he'd felt even in a Raruana village, piled with corpses infected with dengue fever, or during the outbreak of bubonic plague in the Sierra Madre Occidental.

The pier was one of two commercial wharfs that projected into the harbor. One side of the wharf was lined with small wooden shacks: the Lobsterman's Co-op, a snack bar called Red Ned's Eats, a bait shack, and an equipment shed. At the end of the pier stood a rusting gas pump, loading winches, and stacks of drying lobster pots. Beyond the harbor mouth there was a low fog bank, where the sea merged imperceptibly with sky. It was almost as if the world ended a hundred yards offshore.

The shingle-sided Co-op was the first building on the pier. A merry plume of steam, issuing from a tin pipe, hinted at the lobsters that were boiling within. Hatch stopped at the chalkboard, scanning the prices for the various grades of lobster: shedders, hard-shelled, chickens, selects, and culls. He peered through the rippled glass of the window at the row of tanks, teeming with indignant lobsters only hours removed from the deep. In a separate tank was a single blue lobster, very rare, put up for show.

Malin stepped away from the window as a lobsterman in high boots and a slicker rumbled a barrel of rotten bait down the pier. He brought it to rest under a quayside winch, strapped it on, and swung it out to a boat waiting below, in an action that Malin had watched countless times in his childhood. There were shouts and the sudden throb of a diesel, and the boat pulled away, heading out to sea, followed by a raucous crowd of seagulls. He watched the boat dissolve, spectrally, into the lifting fog. Soon, the inner islands would be visible. Already, Burnt Head was emerging from the mists, a great brow of granite rock that leaned into the sea south of town. Surf snarled and worried about its base, carrying to Hatch the faint whisper of waves. On the crown of the bluff, a lighthouse of dressed stone stood among the gorse and low bush blueberries, its red and white stripes and copper cupola adding a cheerful note of color to the monochromatic fog.

As Malin stood at the end of the pier, smelling the mixture of redfish bait, salt air, and diesel fumes, his defenses—carefully shored up for a quarter of a century—began to crumble. The years dropped away and a powerful bittersweet feeling constricted his chest. Here he was, back in a place he had never expected to see again. So much had changed in him, and so little had changed here. It was all he could do to hold back tears.

A car door slammed behind him, and he glanced back to see Gerard Neidelman emerge from an International Scout and stride down the pier, erect, brimming with high spirits, a spring of steel in his step. Smoke wafted from a briar pipe clamped between his teeth, and his eyes glimmered with a carefully guarded but unmistakable excitement.

"Good of you to meet me here," he said, removing the pipe and grasping Hatch's hand. "I hope this hasn't been too much trouble."

He hesitated slightly before saying the last word, and Hatch wondered if the Captain had guessed his own private reasons for wanting to see the town—and the island—before making any commitment. "No trouble," Hatch replied coolly, accepting the brisk handshake.

"And where is our good boat?" Neidelman said, squinting out at the harbor, sweeping it appraisingly with his eyes.

"It's the *Plain Jane*, over there."

Neidelman looked. "Ah. A stout lobster boat." Then he frowned. "I don't see a dinghy in tow. How will we land on Ragged Island?"

"The dinghy's at the dock," Hatch said. "But we're not going to land. There's no natural harbor. Most of the island is ringed with high bluffs, so we wouldn't be able to see much from the rocks anyway. And the bulk of the island is too dangerous to walk on. You'll get a better sense of the place from the water." *Besides,* he thought, *I for one am not ready to set foot on that island.*

"Understood," said Neidelman, placing the pipe back in his mouth. He gazed up at the sky. "The fog will lift shortly. Wind quartering to the southwest, a light sea. The worst we can expect is some rain. Excellent. I'm looking forward to this first look, Dr. Hatch."

Hatch glanced at him sharply. "You mean you've never seen it before?"

"I've restricted myself to maps and surveys."

"I'd have thought a man like you would make the pilgrimage long ago. In days past, we used to get crackpots sightseeing around the island, even some attempts to land. I'm sure that hasn't changed."

Neidelman turned his cool gaze back to Hatch. "I didn't want to see it unless we'd have the chance to dig it." A quiet force lay beneath his words.

At the end of the pier, a wobbly gangplank led down to a floating dock. Hatch untied the *Plain Jane*'s dinghy and grabbed the starter.

"Staying in town?" Neidelman asked as he stepped nimbly into the dinghy, taking a seat in the bow.

Hatch shook his head as he started the engine. "I've booked a room in a motel in Southport, a few miles down the coast." Even the boat rental had been done by an intermediary. He wasn't ready yet to be recognized by anyone.

Neidelman nodded, staring over Hatch's shoulders toward land as they motored out to the boat. "Beautiful place," he said, smoothly changing the subject.

"Yes," Hatch replied. "I suppose it is. There may be a few more summer homes, and there's a bed-and-breakfast now, but otherwise the world has passed Stormhaven by."

"No doubt it's too far north, off the beaten track."

"That's part of it," Hatch said. "But all the things that look so quaint and charming—the old wooden boats, the weather-beaten shacks, the crooked piers—are actually the result of poverty. I don't think Stormhaven ever really recovered from the depression."

They came alongside the *Plain Jane*. Neidelman boarded the boat while Hatch tied the dinghy to the stern. He clambered aboard and was relieved to hear the diesel start up on the first crank with a nice, smooth rumble. *Might be old,* he thought as he eased out into the harbor, *but it's well kept up.* As they cleared the no-wake zone, Hatch throttled up and the *Plain Jane* surged forward, slicing through the gentle swell. Overhead, the sun was struggling through the cloud cover, glowing in the remaining mist like a cold lamp. Hatch gazed southeastward, beyond Old Hump Channel, but could see nothing.

"It's going to be chilly out there," he said, glancing at Neidelman's short-sleeved shirt.

Neidelman turned and smiled. "I'm used to it."

"You call yourself Captain," Hatch said. "Were you in the navy?"

"Yes," came the measured response. "Captain of a minesweeper cruising off the Mekong Delta. After the war I bought a wooden dragger out of Nantucket and worked Georges Bank for scallops and flounder." He squinted out to sea. "It was working that dragger that got me interested in treasure hunting."

"Really?" Hatch checked the compass and corrected course. He glanced at the engine hour meter. Ragged Island was six miles offshore; they'd be there in twenty minutes.

Neidelman nodded. "One day the net brought up a huge bolus of encrusted coral. My mate struck it with a marlin spike, and the thing fell apart like an oyster. There, nestled inside, was a small, seventeenth-century Dutch silver casket. That started my first treasure hunt. I did a little digging through records and figured we must have dragged over the wreck site of the *Cinq Ports*, a barque commanded by the French privateer Charles Dampier. So I sold the boat, started a company, raised a million in capital, and went from there."

"How much did you recover?"

Neidelman smiled slightly. "Just over ninety thousand in coins, china, and antiquities. It was a lesson I never forgot. If I'd bothered to do my research, I'd have looked up the manifests of the Dutch ships that Dampier attacked. They were mostly carrying lumber, coal, and rum." He puffed his pipe meditatively. "Not all pirates were as skillful as Red Ned Ockham."

"You must have been as disappointed as the surgeon who hopes for a tumor and finds gallstones."

Neidelman glanced at him. "I guess you could say that."

Silence fell as they headed seaward. The last wisps of fog disappeared and Hatch could clearly make out the inner islands, Hermit and Wreck, green humps thickly covered with spruce trees. Soon, Ragged Island would become visible. He glanced at Neidelman, looking intently in the direction of the hidden island. It was time.

"We've been chitchatting long enough," he said quietly. "I want to hear about the man who designed the Water Pit."

Neidelman remained silent for a moment, and Hatch waited.

"I'm sorry, Dr. Hatch," Neidelman said. "I should have made myself clear on that point in your office. You haven't yet signed the agreement. Our entire twenty-two-million venture stands on the information we've obtained."

Hatch felt a sudden surge of anger. "I'm glad you have so much faith in me."

"You can understand our position—" Neidelman began.

"Sure I can. You're afraid I might take what you've discovered, dig up the treasure myself, and cut you out."

"Not to put too fine a point on it," Neidelman said. "Yes."

There was a brief silence. "I appreciate your directness," said Hatch. "So how's this for a reply?" He swung the wheel, heeling the boat sharply to starboard.

Neidelman looked at him inquiringly as he gripped the gunwale for support.

Coming about 180 degrees, Hatch pointed the *Plain Jane* back toward port and throttled up.

"Dr. Hatch?" Neidelman said.

"It's quite simple," said Hatch. "Either you tell me all about this mysterious find of yours, and convince me you're not just another nut, or our little field trip ends right now."

"Perhaps if you'd be willing to sign our nondisclosure agreement—"

"For Chrissakes!" Hatch cried. "He's a damn sea lawyer as well as a sea captain. If we're to be partners—an ever-receding possibility—we'll have to trust each other. I'll shake your hand and give you my word, and that will be sufficient, or else you lose all hope of ever digging on the island."

Neidelman never lost his composure, and now he smiled. "A handshake. How quaint."

Hatch held the boat steady as she roared ahead, eating through the remains of wake laid down just minutes before. The dark bluff of Burnt Head came gradually into focus again, followed by the rooftops of the town.

"Very well then," Neidelman said mildly. "Turn the boat around, please. Here is my hand."

They shook. Hatch eased the engine into neutral and let

the *Plain Jane* coast for a long moment. At last, engaging the throttle again, he nosed her seaward, gradually accelerating once more toward the hidden rocks of Ragged Island.

A period of time passed in which Neidelman gazed eastward, puffing on his pipe, seemingly in deep contemplation. Hatch stole a glance at the Captain, wondering if this was some kind of delaying tactic.

"You've been to England, haven't you, Dr. Hatch?" Neidelman said at last.

Hatch nodded.

"Lovely country," Neidelman went on, as coolly as if he was reminiscing for pleasure. "Especially, to my taste, the north. Ever been to Houndsbury? It's a charming little town, very Cotswolds, but all in all rather unremarkable I suppose, if it weren't for its exquisite cathedral. Or have you visited Whitstone Hall in the Pennines? The Duke of Wessex's family seat?"

"That's the famous one, built like an abbey?" Hatch said.

"Exactly. Both delightful examples of seventeenth-century ecclesiastical architecture."

"Delightful," echoed Hatch with a trace of sarcasm. "So what?"

"They were both designed by Sir William Macallan. The man who also designed the Water Pit."

"Designed?"

"Yes. Macallan was a very great architect, perhaps England's greatest next to Sir Christopher Wren. But a far more interesting man." Neidelman was still gazing eastward. "In addition to his buildings and his work on Old Battersea Bridge, he left behind a monumental text on ecclesiastical architecture. The world lost a true visionary when he disappeared at sea in 1696."

"Lost at sea? The plot thickens."

Neidelman pursed his lips, and Hatch wondered if he was finally nettled.

"Yes. It was a terrible tragedy. Except . . ." He turned toward Hatch. "Except, of course, he was *not* lost at sea. Last year, we uncovered a copy of his treatise. In the margins were what seemed to be a pattern of spottings and discolorations. Our laboratory was able to confirm that the discolorations were actually notes, written in invisible ink, just now becoming visible through the corruption of time. Chemical analysis showed the ink to be an organic compound derived from vinegar and white onions. Further analysis dated this 'stain'—as invisible inks were then known—to approximately 1700."

"Invisible ink? You've been reading too many Hardy Boys stories."

"Invisible inks were very common in the seventeenth and eighteenth centuries," Neidelman said calmly. "George Washington used one for his secret dispatches. The colonists referred to it as writing with white ink."

Hatch tried to phrase another sarcastic response, but was unable to articulate a reply. Against his will, he found himself half believing Neidelman's story; it was almost too incredible to be a lie.

"Our laboratory was able to recover the rest of the writing, using a chemical wash. It turned out to be a document of around ten thousand characters written in Macallan's own hand in the margins of his book. The document was in code, but a Thalassa specialist decrypted the first half relatively easily. When we read the plaintext, we learned that Sir William Macallan was an even more intriguing architect than the world had previously believed."

Hatch swallowed. "I'm sorry, but this whole story sounds absurd."

"No, Dr. Hatch, it is not absurd. Macallan *designed* the

Water Pit. The coded writing was a secret journal he kept on his last voyage." Neidelman took a moment to draw on his pipe. "You see, Macallan was Scottish and a clandestine Catholic. After William III's victory at the Battle of the Boyne, Macallan left for Spain in disgust. There, the Spanish Crown commissioned him to build a cathedral, the greatest in the New World. In 1696 he set sail from Cadiz, bound for Mexico, on a two-masted brig, escorted by a Spanish man-of-war. The ships vanished and Macallan was never heard from again. It was assumed they were lost at sea. However, this journal tells us what really happened. Their ships were attacked by Edward Ockham. The Spanish captain struck his colors and was tortured into revealing the nature of his commission. Then Ockham put everyone to the sword, sparing only Macallan. The architect was dragged to Ockham in chains. The pirate put a saber to his throat and said—here I quote from the journal—*Lete God build his owen damned church, I have ye a newe commission.*"

Hatch felt a strange stirring of excitement.

The Captain leaned against the gunwale. "You see, Red Ned wanted Macallan to design a pit for storing his immense treasure. An *impregnable* pit, to which only Ockham would have the secret. They cruised the Maine coast, picked out Ragged Island, the pit was constructed, and the treasure was buried. But, of course, shortly thereafter Ockham and his crew perished. And Macallan, no doubt, was murdered as soon as the pit was finished. With them died the secret to the Water Pit."

Neidelman paused, his eyes almost white in the brightness coming off the water. "Of course, that's no longer true. Because the secret did *not* die with Macallan."

"Explain."

"Midway through his journal, Macallan switched codes. We think he did so specifically to record the secret key to the

Water Pit. Of course, no seventeenth-century code is a match for high-speed computers, and our specialists should have it cracked any day now."

"So how much is supposed to be down there?" Hatch managed to ask.

"Good question. We know the cargo capacity of Ockham's ships, we know they were fully laden, and we have manifests from many of the ships he attacked. Did you know that he was the only pirate to successfully attack the Spanish plate fleet?"

"No," murmured Hatch.

"When you add it all up, the most conservative estimate places the contemporary value of the treasure at"—Neidelman paused, a trace of a smile on his lips—"between 1.8 and 2 billion dollars."

There was a long silence, filled by the throbbing of the engine, the monotonous wheeling of the gulls, and the sound of the boat moving through the water. Hatch struggled to grasp the enormity of the sum.

Neidelman lowered his voice. "That is, not including the value of St. Michael's Sword, Ockham's greatest prize."

For a moment, the spell was broken. "Come on, Captain," Hatch said with a laugh. "Don't tell me you believe such a mossy old legend."

"Not until I read Macallan's journal. Dr. Hatch, it *is* there. Macallan watched them bury it with the treasure."

Hatch stared unseeing at the deck, his mind a turmoil. *This is incredible, almost beyond belief . . .*

He glanced up and felt the muscles of his gut tighten involuntarily. The countless questions that had risen within him suddenly evaporated. Across the expanse of sea, he could now make out the long, low fog that concealed Ragged Island, the same fog bank that had lain on the island more than twenty-five years before.

He heard Neidelman next to him, saying something. He turned, breathing shallowly, trying to quiet his beating heart. "I'm sorry?"

"I said, I know you have little interest in the money. But I wanted you to know that in the agreement I've proposed here, you would receive half the treasure, before expenses. In return for my undertaking all the financial risk, I will receive St. Michael's Sword. Your share would therefore be in the vicinity of one billion dollars."

Hatch swallowed. "You're right. I couldn't care less."

There was a long pause, then Neidelman raised his binoculars and examined the island of fog. "Why does it remain fogbound?"

"There's a good reason," Hatch said, grateful for the change of topic. "The island's powerful riptide deflects the frigid Labrador Current into the warm Cape Cod Current, and where they mix you get a large eddy of fog. Sometimes only a thin ring of fog surrounds the island, other times it's totally socked in."

"What more could a pirate ask for?" Neidelman murmured.

It won't be long now, Hatch thought. He tried to lose himself in the hissing of water racing along the chine, the briny scent of the air, the cool brass of the wheel against his palms. He glanced at Neidelman, and saw a muscle twitching in his set jaw. He was also experiencing a powerful emotion, of another though no less private kind.

The patch of fog drew closer. Hatch struggled in silence, willing himself to keep the boat pointed in the direction of the creeping fingers of mist, so strangely alien on a horizon that had otherwise grown clear. He eased down the throttle as the boat nosed its prow into the murk. Suddenly, clamminess surrounded them. Malin could feel droplets of condensation begin to form on his knuckles and along the back of his neck.

He strained to see through the fog. A dark, distant outline seemed to appear, only to vanish again. He cut the throttle further. In the relative quiet, he could now hear the sound of surf, and the ringing of the Ragged Island bell buoy, warning mariners away from its treacherous reefs. He swung the boat in a more northerly course, to bring it around the leeward end of the island. Suddenly, a ruined iron derrick loomed above the mists about two hundred yards off the port side, twisted by storms, streaked with rust.

With a short intake of breath, Neidelman swiftly raised the binoculars to his eyes, but the boat had plunged into another patch of fog and the island disappeared once again. A chill wind had picked up and a light drizzle began to fall.

"Can we get closer?" Neidelman murmured.

Hatch steered the boat toward the reefs. As they entered the lee of the island, the surf dropped along with the wind. Abruptly, they broke through the circle of mist and the island stood revealed in its entirety.

Hatch brought the boat parallel to the reef. In the stern, Neidelman kept the binoculars glued to his face, forgotten pipe clenched between his teeth, his shoulders darkening in the rain. Bringing the bow into the sea, Hatch threw the boat into neutral and let it drift. Then at last he turned toward the island to face it himself.

The dark, terrible outline of the island, so persistent in memory and nightmare, was now once again before him in reality. It was little more than a black silhouette etched hard against the gray of sea and sky: shaped like a peculiar, tilted table, a gradual incline rising from the leeward to sharp bluffs on the seaward coast, punctuated by a hump of land in the center. The surf pounded the bluffs and boiled over the sunken ledges that ringed the island, leaving a scurf of foam that trailed like the wake of a boat. It was, if anything, even bleaker than he remembered: windswept, barren, a mile long and eight hundred yards wide. A single deformed spruce stood above the cobbled beach at the lee end of the island, its top exploded by an old lightning strike, its crabbed branches raised like a witch's hand against the sky.

Everywhere, great ruined hulks of infernal machines rose from the waving sawgrass and tea roses: ancient steam-driven compressors, winches, chains, boilers. A cluster of weather-beaten shacks sat to one side of the old spruce, listing and roofless. At the far end of the beach, Hatch could make out the smooth rounded forms of the Whalebacks that he and Johnny had clambered over, more than twenty-five years before. Along the nearest rocks lay the shattered carcasses of several large boats, dashed and battered by countless storms, their decks and ribbing split and scattered among the granite boulders. Weather-beaten signs, posted every 100 feet above the high water mark, read:

WARNING!
EXTREME DANGER
NO LANDING

For a moment Neidelman was speechless. "At last," he breathed.

The moment stretched into minutes as the boat drifted. Neidelman lowered his binoculars and turned toward Hatch. "Doctor?" he inquired.

Hatch was bracing himself on the wheel, riding out the memory. Horror washed over him like seasickness as the drizzle splattered the pilothouse windows and the bell buoy tolled mournfully in the mists. But mingled with the horror was something else, something new: the realization that there *was* a vast treasure down there—that his grandfather had not been a complete fool who destroyed three generations of his family for nothing. In a moment, he knew what his decision had to be: the final answer that was owed to his grandfather, his father, and his brother.

"Dr. Hatch?" Neidelman asked again, the hollows of his face glistening with the damp.

Hatch took several deep breaths and forced himself to relax his desperate grip on the wheel. "Circle the island?" he asked, managing to keep his voice even.

Neidelman stared at him another moment. Then he simply nodded and raised the binoculars again.

Easing the throttle open, Hatch swung seaward, coming out of the lee and turning into the wind. He proceeded under low engine, keeping the boat at three knots, looking away from the Whalebacks and the other, more dreadful landmarks he knew would lie just beyond.

"It's a hard-looking place," Neidelman said. "Harder than I'd ever imagined."

"There's no natural harbor," Hatch replied. "The place is surrounded by reefs, and there's a wicked tiderip. The island's exposed to the open ocean, and it gets hammered by Nor'easters every fall. So many tunnels were dug that a good part of the island is waterlogged and unstable. Even worse, some of the companies brought in explosives. There's unexploded dynamite, blasting caps, and God knows what else beneath the surface, just waiting to go off."

"What's that wreck?" Neidelman said, pointing at a massive, twisted metal structure rearing above the seaweed-slick rocks.

"A barge left over from my grandfather's day. It was anchored offshore with a floating crane, got caught in a Nor'easter, and was thrown on the rocks. After the ocean got through with it, there wasn't anything left to salvage. That was the end of my grandfather's effort."

"Did your grandfather leave any records?" Neidelman asked.

"My father destroyed them." Hatch swallowed hard. "My grandfather bankrupted the family with this island, and my father always hated the place and everything about it. Even before the accident." His voice trailed off and he gripped the wheel, staring straight ahead.

"I'm sorry," Neidelman said, his face softening. "I've been so wrapped up in all this that I sometimes forget your personal tragedy. Forgive me if I've asked any insensitive questions."

Hatch continued gazing over the ship's bow. "It's all right."

Neidelman fell silent, for which Hatch was grateful. Nothing was more painful than hearing the usual platitudes from well-meaning people, especially the one that went *Don't blame yourself, it wasn't your fault*.

The *Plain Jane* rounded the southern end of the island and went broadside to the swell. Hatch gave it a little more throttle and plunged ahead.

"Amazing," Neidelman muttered. "To think that only this small island of sand and rocks separates us from the largest fortune ever buried."

"Careful, Captain," Hatch replied, putting what he hoped was a playful tone on the warning. "That's the kind of rapturous thinking that bankrupted a dozen companies. Better to remember the old poem:

> *Because, though free of the outer court*
> *I am, this Temple keeps her shrine*
> *Sacred to Heaven; because, in short*
> *She's not and never can be mine."*

Neidelman turned to him. "I see you've had time to do a little extracurricular reading beyond *Gray's Anatomy* and the Merck manual. Not many bonecutters can quote Coventry Patmore."

Hatch shrugged. "I enjoy a bit of poetry, here and there. I sip it like a fine port. What's your excuse?"

Neidelman smiled briefly. "I spent more than ten years of my life at sea. Sometimes there's precious little else to do but read."

A coughing sound suddenly broke from the island. It grew louder, turning into a low rumble and finally breaking into a throaty heaving groan, like the dying sound of some deep-sea beast. Hatch felt his skin crawl.

"What in blazes is that noise?" Neidelman asked sharply.

"Tide's changing," Hatch replied, shivering slightly in the raw, wet air. "The Water Pit is apparently connected to the sea by a hidden flood tunnel. When the rip current changes and the flow in the tunnel reverses, you hear that noise. At least, that's one theory."

The moan continued, slowly subsiding into a wet stutter before dying away completely.

"You'll hear another theory from the local fishermen," Hatch said. "Maybe you noticed that there aren't any lobster pots around the island. Don't think that's from any lack of lobsters."

"The Ragged Island curse," Neidelman said, nodding, a sardonic look in his eyes. "I've heard of it." There was a long silence while Neidelman looked down at the deck. Then he slowly raised his head. "I can't bring your brother back to life," he said. "But I can promise you this: we will learn what happened to him."

Hatch waved his hand, made speechless by a sudden overflow of emotion. He turned his face to the open pilothouse window, grateful for the concealing presence of the rain. Quite suddenly, he realized he could not bear to spend any more time at the island. He nosed the boat westward without explanation, opening the throttle as they once again entered the encircling mantle of mist. He wanted to return to his motel room, order an early lunch, and wash it down with a pitcher of Bloody Marys.

They broke through the mist into the welcoming gleam of daylight. The wind picked up, and Hatch could feel the droplets of moisture begin to evaporate from his face and hands. He did not look back. But the simple knowledge that the fogbound island was quickly shrinking into the horizon eased the constricting feeling in his chest.

"You should know that we'll be working closely with a first-rate archaeologist and a historian," Neidelman said at his side. "The knowledge we'll gain about seventeenth-century engineering, high seas piracy, and naval technology—perhaps even about Red Ned Ockham's mysterious death—will be of incalculable value. This is as much an archaeological dig as a treasure reclamation."

There was a brief silence. "I'd want to reserve the right to stop the whole show if I felt conditions were growing too dangerous," Hatch said.

"Perfectly understandable. There are eighteen clauses in our boilerplate land-lease contract. We'll just add a nineteenth."

"And if I become part of this," Hatch said more slowly, "I don't want to be a silent partner, looking over anyone's shoulder."

Neidelman stirred the dead ashes of his pipe. "Salvage of this sort is an extremely risky business, especially for the layman. What role do you propose to play?"

Hatch shrugged. "You mentioned that you'd hired an expedition doctor."

Neidelman stopped stirring his pipe long enough to look up and raise his eyebrows. "As required by Maine law. Are you suggesting a change of personnel?"

"Yes."

Neidelman smiled. "And you're comfortable taking leave from Mount Auburn Hospital at such short notice?"

"My research can wait. Besides, we aren't talking about all that long. It's already the end of July. If you're going to do this, it'll have to be over and done within four weeks—for better or worse. The dig can't continue into storm season."

Neidelman leaned over the side of the boat and knocked the dottle from his pipe with a single hard stroke. He straightened up again, the long dark line of Burnt Head framing the horizon behind him.

"In four weeks, it *will* be over," he said. "Your struggle, and mine."

5

Hatch parked the car in the dirt lot next to Bud's Superette. It was his own car this time, and it was strangely unsettling to be viewing his past life through the windshield of a vehicle so much a part of his present. He glanced at the cracked leather seats, at the faded coffee stains on the burled walnut of the gearbox. So familiar, and somehow so safe; it took a supreme effort to open the door. He plucked the sunglasses from the dash, then put them back. The time for dissembling was over.

He looked around the small square. More stone cobbles were peeping up through the worn asphalt of the street. The old newsstand at the corner, with its wobbly wire racks of comic books and magazines, had given way to an ice-cream shop. Beyond the square, the town fell away down the hill, as impossibly picturesque as ever, the slate and cedar-shingled roofs gleaming in the sunlight. A man walked up from the harbor in rubber boots, a slicker over his shoulder: a lobsterman coming back from work. The man glanced at Hatch as he passed, then disappeared down a side lane. He was young, no more than twenty, and Hatch realized the man wasn't even born when he had left town with his mother. An entire generation had grown up in his absence. And no doubt an entire generation had died, too. He suddenly wondered if Bud Rowell was still alive.

Superficially, Bud's Superette looked exactly as he remembered it: the green screen door that didn't shut properly, the ancient Coca-Cola sign, the weathered, tilting porch. He stepped inside, worn floorboards creaking under his feet, and pulled a cart from the small rack by the door, grateful for the emptiness of the place. Moving down the narrow aisles, he began picking up some food for the *Plain Jane*, where he'd decided to stay until the old family house could be readied for him. He poked around, dropping necessities into the cart here and there, until at last he realized he was just delaying the inevitable. With an effort he pushed the cart toward the front of the store and found himself face-to-face with Bud Rowell: large, bald, and cheerful, in a crisp butcher's apron. Many times, Hatch remembered Bud slipping him and Johnny forbidden red licorice sticks under the counter. It drove their mother crazy.

"Afternoon," said Bud, his glance moving over Hatch's face and then drifting to the car parked outside, checking the plates. It wasn't often that a vintage Jaguar XKE pulled into the Superette's lot. "Up from Boston?"

Hatch nodded, still uncertain how best to do this. "Yup."

"Vacation?" Bud asked, carefully placing an artichoke into the bag, arranging it with deliberation, and ringing it up on the old brass machine with his usual glacial slowness. A second artichoke went into the bag.

"No," said Hatch. "Here on business."

The hand paused. Nobody ever came to Stormhaven on

business. And Bud, being the professional gossip that he was, would now have to find out why.

The hand moved again. "Ayuh," said Bud. "Business."

Hatch nodded, struggling with a reluctance to drop his anonymity. Once Bud knew, the whole town would know. Shopping at Bud's Superette was the point of no return. It wasn't too late to just gather up his groceries and get out, leaving Bud none the wiser. The alternative was painful to contemplate: Hatch could hardly bear to think about the whispered revival of the old tragedy, the shaking of heads and pursing of lips. Small towns could be brutal in their sympathy.

The hand picked up a carton of milk and inserted it into the bag.

"Salesman?"

"Nope."

There was a silence while Bud, going even slower now, placed the orange juice next to the milk. The machine jingled with the price.

"Just passing through?" he ventured.

"Got business right here in Stormhaven."

This was so unheard-of that Bud could stand it no more. "And what kind of business might that be?"

"Business of a delicate nature," Hatch said, lowering his voice. Despite his apprehensions, the consternation that gathered on Bud's brow was so eloquent that Hatch had to hide a smile.

"I see," Bud said. "Staying in town?"

"Nope," Hatch said, taking a deep breath now. "I'll be staying over across the harbor. In the old Hatch place."

At this Bud almost dropped a steak. The house had been shut up for twenty-five years. But the steak went in, the bags were finally filled, and Bud had run out of questions, at least polite ones.

"Well," said Hatch. "I'm in a bit of a hurry. How much do I owe you?"

"Thirty-one twenty-five," Bud said miserably.

Hatch gathered up the bags. This was it. If he was going to make a home in this town, even temporarily, he had to reveal himself.

He stopped, opened one bag, and poked his hand in. "Excuse me," he said, turning to the second bag and rummaging through it. "Haven't you left something out?"

"I don't b'lieve so," Bud said stolidly.

"I'm sure you have," Hatch repeated, taking things back out of the bags and laying them on the counter.

"It's all there," Bud said, a shade of Maine truculence creeping into his voice.

"No, it's not." Hatch pointed at a small drawer just below the countertop. "Where's my free licorice stick?"

Bud's eyes went to the drawer, then followed Hatch's arm back up to his face, and for the first time really looked at him. Then the color drained from his face, leaving it a pale gray.

Just as Hatch tensed, wondering if he'd gone too far, the old grocer exhaled mightily. "I'll be damned," he said. "I'll be *God* damned. It's Malin Hatch."

The color in the grocer's cheeks quickly returned to normal, but his expression remained that of a man who has seen a ghost.

"Well," said Hatch. "How've you been, Bud?"

Suddenly, the grocer lumbered around the counter and crushed Hatch's right hand in both of his. "Look at you," he said, grasping Hatch's shoulders and holding him at arm's length, a huge grin lighting up his plump face. "To think you've grown up into such a fine, big young man. I don't know how many times I wondered what happened to you, wondered if we'd ever see you again. And by God, here you are, plain as day."

Hatch inhaled the grocer's scent—a mixture of ham, fish, and cheese—and felt both relieved and embarrassed, as if he were suddenly a boy again.

Bud gazed up at him a little longer, then glanced back at the licorice drawer. "You son of a gun," he laughed. "You still eating licorice? Here's one on the house." And he reached in, pulled one out, and slapped it down on the counter.

6

They sat in rocking chairs on the back porch of the store, drinking birch beer pop and gazing out over a meadow to a dark row of pines. Under Bud's probing, Hatch had related some of his adventures as an epidemiologist in Mexico and South America. But he had successfully steered the conversation away from his own reasons for returning. He didn't feel quite ready to start the explanations. He found himself anxious to get back to the boat, hang his portable grill over the taffrail, throw on a steak, and sit back with a sinfully dry martini. But he also knew that small-town etiquette required his spending an hour shooting the breeze with the old grocer.

"Tell me what's happened in town since I left," he said to stopper a gap in the conversation and forestall any probing questions. He could tell Bud was dying to know why he'd returned, but that Maine politeness forbade him to ask.

"Well, now," Bud began. "There've been some pretty big changes here." He proceeded to relate how the new addition was built onto the high school five years ago, how the Thibodeaux family home burned to the ground while they were vacationing at Niagara Falls, how Frank Pickett ran his boat into Old Hump and sank it because he'd had a few too many. Finally, he asked if Hatch had seen the nice new firehouse.

"Sure have," said Hatch, secretly sorry that the old wooden one-berth house had been torn down and replaced with a metal-sided monstrosity.

"And there's new houses springing up all over the place. Summerpeople." Bud clucked disapprovingly, but Hatch knew perfectly well there wasn't any complaining at the cash register. Anyway, Bud's idea of houses springing up everywhere translated to three or four summer houses on Breed's Point, plus some renovated inland farmhouses and the new bed-and-breakfast.

Bud concluded with a sad shake of his head. "It's all changed around here since you left. You'll hardly recognize the place." He rocked back in his chair and sighed. "So, you here to sell the house?"

Hatch stiffened slightly. "No, I've come to live here. For the rest of the summer, anyway."

"That right?" Bud said. "Vacation?"

"I already told you," Hatch said, trying hard to keep his tone light, "I'm here on a rather delicate business matter. I promise you, Bud, it won't be a secret long."

Bud sat back, slightly offended. "You know I wouldn't have any interest in your business affairs. But I thought you said you were a doctor."

"I am. That's what I'll be doing up here." Hatch sipped his birch beer and glanced surreptitiously at his watch.

"But Malin," the grocer said, shifting uncomfortably, "we've already got a doctor in town. Dr. Frazier. He's healthy as an ox, could live another twenty years."

"That's nothing a little arsenic in his tea wouldn't fix," said Hatch.

The grocer looked at him in alarm.

"Don't worry, Bud," Hatch replied, breaking into a smile. "I'm not going into competition with Dr. Frazier." He reminded himself that his particular brand of wit wasn't especially common in rural Maine.

"That's good." Bud gave his guest a sidelong look. "Then maybe it's got to do with those helicopters."

Hatch looked at him quizzically.

"Just yesterday it was. Nice, sharp, clear day. Two helicopters came by. Big things they were, too. Went right over town and headed out toward the islands. Seen them hovering over Ragged Island for quite a spell. I thought they were from the army base." Bud's look turned speculative. "But then again, maybe not."

Hatch was spared having to reply by the creak of the screen door. He waited while Bud lumbered inside to attend to the customer. "Business seems good," he replied when Bud returned.

"Can't hardly say that," Bud replied. "Out of season, population's down to eight hundred."

Hatch thought to himself that this was about the size Stormhaven had always been.

"Ayuh," Bud went on, "kids just up and leave now when they finish high school. Don't want to stay in town. They go off to the big cities, Bangor, Augusta. One even went so far as Boston. We've had five kids leave town in the last three years. If it weren't for the summerpeople, or that nudist camp on Pine Neck, I don't think I'd have two extra pennies to rub together."

Hatch merely nodded. Bud was obviously prospering, but it would have been impolite to disagree with him in his own store. The "nudist camp" he referred to was actually an artists' colony, located on an old estate in a pine forest some ten miles up the coast. Hatch remembered that thirty years before, a lobsterman pulling traps had seen a nude sunbather on their beach. The memory of a Maine seacoast town was long indeed.

"And how's your mother?" Bud asked.

"She passed away in 1985. Cancer."

"Sorry to hear that." Hatch could tell Bud meant it. "She was a good woman, and she raised some fine . . . a fine son." After a short silence Bud rocked back in his chair and polished off his birch beer. "Seen Claire yet?" he asked, as nonchalantly as possible.

Hatch waited a moment. "She still around?" he replied with equal nonchalance.

"Yup," said Bud. "Been some changes in her life. And how about you? Any family?"

Hatch smiled. "No wife. Not yet, anyway." He put down his empty bottle and stood. It was definitely time to go. "Bud, it's been great visiting with you. I think I'll go and fix myself dinner."

Bud nodded and clapped him on the back as Hatch pushed his way through into the store. He had his hand on the screen door when Bud cleared his throat.

"One other thing, Malin."

Hatch froze. He knew he'd gotten off too easily. He waited, dreading the question he knew was coming.

"You watch out with that licorice," Bud said with great solemnity. "Those teeth won't last forever, you know."

Hatch emerged on the deck of the *Plain Jane*, stretched, then looked around the harbor through slitted eyes. The town of Stormhaven was quiet, almost torpid under the heavy light of the July afternoon, and he felt grateful for the silence. The night before, he'd washed down the steak with a little more Beefeater's than he'd intended, and he'd woken that morning to his first hangover in almost a decade.

It had been a day of several firsts. It was the first day he had spent in the cabin of a boat since his trip down the Amazon. He'd forgotten how peaceful it could be, alone with nothing but the gentle rocking of the waves for company. It was also the first day he could remember without having much of anything to do. His lab was now closed down for the month of August, and Bruce the bewildered lab assistant had been sent off to write up initial results under the care of a colleague. The Cambridge town house was locked up, with instructions to the housekeeper that he would not be back until September. And his Jaguar was parked, as discreetly as possible, in the vacant lot behind the old Coast to Coast hardware store.

Before checking out of the hotel in Southport the day before, he'd received a note from Neidelman: a single sentence, asking him to rendezvous off Ragged Island at sunset this evening. That gave Hatch an entire day to himself. At first, he'd been afraid this meant a day alone with his memories. He'd thought of dragging out the watercolors he dabbled with on weekends and hazarding a sketch of the shoreline. But the intention fell away unpursued. Somehow, here on the water, he felt a torpid kind of peace. He had come home to Stormhaven. He'd even approached Ragged Island. He had gazed upon the beast and survived.

He checked his watch: almost 7:30. Time to get started.

He cranked the engine and was pleased to hear the big diesel turn over obediently. The deep vibration underfoot, the *blub-blub* of exhaust fumes, was like a siren song out of the past, at once sweet and painful. He put the boat in gear with a thrust of his hand and pointed the big bow in the direction of Ragged Island.

The day was clear, and as the boat cut through the water Hatch watched its shadow flitting on ahead of him, draped across the water by the afternoon sun. The ocean was deserted except for a lone lobster boat, hauling traps off the coast of Hermit Island. He had come on deck a few times during the day to scan the horizon, half-expecting to see activity of some sort in the direction of Ragged Island. Seeing nothing but sea and sky each time, he hadn't been sure whether he was disappointed or relieved.

Past the harbor, the air turned cool. But instead of throttling down and grabbing his windbreaker, Hatch found himself cranking the boat faster, turning his face into the wind, opening his mouth to the occasional salt spray as the *Plain Jane* slapped through the chop. It was somehow cleansing, alone out here; he felt almost as if the wind and water might begin to shake loose the accumulated cobwebs and dirt of a quarter century.

Suddenly, a dark shadow appeared ahead, low on the eastern horizon. Hatch throttled back, feeling the old, familiar trepidation return. The fog around the island was thinner today, but the outlines were still vague and forbidding, the derricks and winches protruding dimly like the ruined minarets of some alien city. Hatch turned the boat to port, keeping his distance, preparing to circle.

Then, on the lee side of the island, he saw an unfamiliar boat, moored perhaps a quarter mile offshore. As he approached, he could see it was an antique fireboat, built of rich brown wood, mahogany or teak. The name GRIFFIN was painted across its stern in severe gold letters. And below, smaller: MYSTIC, CONNECTICUT.

Hatch considered coming alongside, then changed his mind and cut the *Plain Jane*'s engine about a hundred yards off. The boat appeared empty. Nobody came on deck to acknowledge his arrival. For a moment he wondered if it belonged to some tourist or trophy hunter, but it was now almost sunset; the coincidence seemed too strong.

He stared curiously at the boat. If it was Neidelman's command craft, it was an unusual but practical choice. What the thing lacked in speed it made up for in stability: Hatch felt sure it would ride out any but the heaviest sea, and with fore-and-aft engines it would be highly maneuverable. The hose reels and monitors had been removed, freeing up a lot of deck space. The davits, tower, and searchlights had been retained, and a computer-controlled crane was retrofitted onto the stern. Hatch's eyes traveled up to the capacious pilothouse and flying bridge. Above, there was the usual cluster of electronic antennae, loran, and radar, along with additional gear not especially nautical: a microwave horn, satellite dish, air-search radar, and VLF antennae. *Impressive rig,* Hatch thought. He dropped one hand to the instrument panel, ready to give a blast of his air horn.

Then he hesitated. Beyond the silent boat, and beyond the mist-shrouded island, he could make out a deep throbbing sound, so low in pitch it was almost beneath the audible spectrum. His hand dropped away as he listened. In a minute, he was certain: a boat engine, distant but approaching fast. Hatch scanned the horizon until he picked up a smudge of gray to the south. As he watched, he saw a momentary flash as the setting sun hit some article of polished metal on the distant craft. *Probably a Thalassa boat,* he thought, *swinging up from Portland.*

Then, slowly, Hatch saw the smudge separate into two, then three, then six distinct shapes. He waited in disbelief as a veritable invasion fleet approached the tiny island. A huge sea barge steamed toward him, its dark red underbelly revealed as bow waves pulled back across the waterline. In its wake labored a tug, its bow-net mossy and glistening, a hundred-ton floating crane towed behind. Next came a brace of powerboats, sleek and muscular-looking, bristling with electronics. A supply boat followed, heavy with cargo and low in the water. From its masthead flew a small flag of white and red. Hatch noticed that the design on the flag matched the insignia he'd seen on Neidelman's portfolio cover, just days before.

Last came an elegant vessel, large and fantastically equipped. The name CERBERUS was stenciled on its bows in blue letters. Hatch gazed in awe over the gleaming superstructure, the harpoon gun on the foredeck, the smoked-glass portholes. *Fifteen-thousand tonner, minimum,* he thought.

In a kind of silent ballet, the vessels nosed up to the *Griffin.* The larger ships came to a stop on the far side of the fireboat, while the smaller craft came to rest beside the *Plain Jane*. There was a rattling of chains and singing of hawsers as anchors ran out. Gazing at the powerboats straddling his port and starboard sides, Hatch could see the occupants staring back. A few smiled and nodded. In the closest boat, Hatch noticed a man with iron-gray hair and a plump white face looking at him with an expression of polite interest. He wore a bulky orange life preserver over a carefully buttoned suit. Next to him lounged a young man with long greasy hair and a goatee, dressed in Bermuda shorts and a flowered shirt. He was eating something out of a white paper wrapper, and he gazed back at Hatch with a kind of insolent disinterest.

The last engine was cut, and a strange, almost spectral silence fell over the gathering. Hatch looked from boat to boat, and noticed that everyone's eyes were gravitating toward the empty deck of the fireboat in the center.

A minute passed, then two. At last a door in the side of the pilothouse opened and Captain Neidelman emerged. Silently, he walked to the edge of the railing and stood, ramrod-straight, gazing out at the company that surrounded him. The setting sun gave a burgundy cast to his sunburned face, and kindled his fair, thinning hair into gold. It was amazing, Hatch thought, how his slender presence projected out over the water and the circle of boats. As the silence gathered, another man, small and wiry, stepped unobtrusively out of the door behind Neidelman and remained standing in the background, hands folded.

For a long moment, Neidelman remained silent. At last he started to speak, in a voice that was low, almost reverent, yet carried easily over the water.

"We live in an era," Neidelman began, "when the unknown is known, and most of earth's mysteries have been solved. We have gone to the North Pole, scaled Everest, flown to the Moon. We have broken the bonds of the atom and mapped the abyssal plains of the oceans. Those who tackled these mysteries often endangered their lives, squandered their fortunes, and risked everything they held dear. A great mystery can only be solved at a high price—sometimes the highest price."

He gestured in the direction of the island. "Here—a mere hundred yards away—lies one of those great riddles, perhaps the greatest still left in North America. Look at it. It looks like nothing, a hole in a patch of dirt and rock. And yet this hole—this Water Pit—has sucked the living marrow from the bones of everyone who tried to plumb its secrets. Many millions of dollars have been spent. Lives have been ruined and even lost. There are those among us today that have felt firsthand just how sharp the teeth of the Water Pit can be."

Neidelman looked around at the company, gathered on the assembled boats. His eyes met Hatch's. Then he began again.

"Other enigmas of the past—the monoliths of Sacsahuamán, Easter Island's statues, the standing stones of Britain—cloak their meaning in mystery. Not so the Water Pit. Its location, its purpose, even its history is known. It lies here before us, a brazen oracle, daring to take on all comers."

He paused another moment. "By 1696 Edward Ockham had become the most feared pirate cruising the high seas. The ships in his treasure fleet were swollen with accumulated loot, sluggish, low in the water. The next storm, even an unlucky meeting with a man-of-war, could deal his fleet a mortal blow. He had held off hiding his treasure and he was now desperate. A chance encounter with a certain architect provided the answer."

Neidelman leaned on the rail, the wind stirring his hair. "Ockham seized that architect and charged him with designing a pit to house the treasure. A pit so fearfully impregnable that it would stymie even the most well-equipped treasure hunter. Everything went according to plan. The pit was built, the treasure stored. And then, as the pirate set out for another round of murder and depredation, providence struck. Red Ned Ockham died. Since that day, his treasure has slumbered at the bottom of the Water Pit, waiting for the time when technology and human resolve would finally bring it once again into the world."

Neidelman took a deep breath. "Despite the enormous value of this treasure, the best efforts of one man after another have failed to pluck anything of value from the pit. Anything but this!" And suddenly the Captain held his arm aloft, something gripped between his fingers. The light of the setting sun winked and played so dazzlingly across it that his fingertips seemed to burn. Murmurs of wonder and surprise rippled across the company.

Hatch leaned over the railing to get a better look. *My God,* he thought, *that must be the gold cored up by the Gold Seekers' drill over a hundred years ago.*

Neidelman held the curl of gold over his head, motionless, for what seemed a long time. Then he spoke again. "There are some who say there is no treasure at the bottom of the Water Pit. To those doubters, I say: Gaze upon *this.*"

As the dying sun lit water and vessel a dusky rose, he turned to face the forward windows of the *Griffin's* pilothouse. Picking up a small hammer, he placed the piece of gold against the roofline of the pilothouse and, with a single blow, drove it against the wood with a nail. He stepped away to face the company once again, the gold glittering from the superstructure.

"Today," he said, "the rest of Ockham's treasure remains at the bottom of the pit, unvexed by sun or rain, undisturbed for three hundred years. But tomorrow marks the beginning of the end of that long rest. Because the key that was lost has been found again. And before the summer is over, the treasure will sleep no longer."

He paused to survey the crowd of vessels. "There is much to do. We must remove the litter of past failure and make the island safe again. We must determine the location of the original pit. We must then find and seal the hidden underwater channel that allows seawater to enter. We must pump the existing water from the shaft, and secure it for the excavation of the treasure chamber. The challenge is vast. But we come equipped with technology more than adequate to handle the challenge. We're dealing with perhaps the most ingenious creation of the seventeenth-century mind. But the Water Pit is no match for twentieth-century tools. With the help of all who are assembled here today, we will make this the greatest—and most famous—salvage in history."

A cheer began to break out, but Neidelman silenced it with an open hand. "We have among us today Dr. Malin Hatch. It is through his generosity this endeavor was allowed to proceed. And he, more than anyone, knows that we're here today for more than just gold. We're here for history. We're here for knowledge. And we're here to make sure that—at long, long last—the ultimate sacrifices of those brave souls who came before us will not have been in vain."

He bowed his head a brief moment, then stepped back from the railing. There was a scattering of applause, a thin waterfall of sound skipping over the waves, and then in an instant the company erupted into a spontaneous cheer, arms lifted above heads, caps thrown in the air, a cry of excitement and eagerness and jubilation rising in a joyous circle around the *Griffin*. Hatch realized he was cheering too, and as a single tear trickled down his cheek he had the absurd feeling that Johnny was peering over his shoulder, watching the proceedings with wry interest, longing in his youthful way to finally be laid to rest.

8

A day later, Hatch stood at the helm of the *Plain Jane*, watching the preparations going on around him. Almost despite himself, he felt a sense of mounting excitement. At his side, two communications monitors—a closed-band scanner covering all the expedition's channels, and a radio tuned to the dedicated medical frequency—emitted occasional chirps and squawks of conversation. The ocean was calm, with only the barest swell, and there was a gentle off-shore breeze. The perpetual mist was thin today, gauzy linen loosely encircling the island. It was a perfect day for off-loading, and Captain Neidelman was making the most of it.

Although the *Plain Jane* was anchored in the same spot as the night before—just outside the Ragged Island reef—the landscape had changed dramatically. Setup had begun shortly after sunset and escalated at daybreak. The huge sea barge was now anchored two points off the eastern shore by massive chains, bolted into the rocky sea floor by Neidelman's dive team. As Hatch watched, the hundred-ton floating crane was being moored off the western end of the island, its long hydraulic rig hanging over the shoreline like a scorpion's tail, ready to pluck off the wrack of two hundred years of treasure hunting. Lying in its shadow was the *Griffin*, Neidelman's command ship. Hatch could just make out the Captain's stiff, narrow figure on the flying bridge, closely supervising the proceedings.

The large research vessel, the *Cerberus*, remained beyond the circle of mist, silent and still, as if not deigning to approach land. The two launches, named the *Naiad* and the *Grampus*, had dropped crews on the island early in the morning. Now the boats were busy offshore. From the pattern of the *Naiad*'s movements, Hatch could tell she was plotting the sea floor. The *Grampus* was taking readings of the island itself, using equipment he was not familiar with.

Hatch continued scanning the activity around him until his gaze fell at last upon the island itself. He still felt a kind of sickness in his gut when he looked at it. Perhaps it was a sickness that would never go away. But he had made his decision, and that in itself lifted a huge burden from his shoulders. Every morning now, he awoke more certain that his decision had been the right one. The night before, he'd even caught himself speculating over what he could do with close to a billion dollars. Then and there, he'd made up his mind: He would put all of it, every penny, into a foundation in his brother's name.

A sudden flicker of white on the island briefly caught his eye before disappearing again into the mists. Somewhere, he knew, crews were already on the move, locating old pits, roping safe trails, tagging ancient junk hidden by the tall brush for later removal. "Tall nettles," Hatch quoted to himself,

Cover up, as they have done
These many springs, the rusty harrow, the plough
Long worn out, and the roller made of stone.

Other teams, he knew, were taking corings from beams in
the countless cribbed shafts. These corings would be carbon
14 dated in the *Cerberus* lab to determine their age in an attempt to pinpoint which shaft was the original Water Pit. He
pulled out his binoculars and swung them slowly across the
terrain until he located one of the teams, pale apparitions in
the mist. They were spread out in a ragged line, moving
slowly, hacking away at the chokecherries with brush hooks
and axes, stopping occasionally to take photographs or
scribble notes. One man swept a metal detector in an arc
ahead of him; another probed the ground with a long, narrow instrument. At the head of the group, he noticed a Ger-
man shepherd, diligently sniffing the ground. *Must be
trained to smell high explosive,* Hatch thought to himself.

There were, all told, perhaps fifty people bustling on and
around the island. All Thalassa employees, and all highly
paid: Neidelman had told him that—outside of the core
half-dozen or so that would receive actual shares of the prof-
its instead of salary—the average worker would earn twenty-
five thousand dollars. Not bad, considering that the majority
would be gone from the island within a fortnight, once the
various installations were complete and the island stabilized.

Hatch continued scanning the island. At the safe northern
end of the island—the only area one could walk without
fear—a pier and dock had gone up. Beside it, the tug was
off-loading a welter of equipment: crated generators, acetylene tanks, compressors, electronic switching equipment.
Already onshore were orderly piles of angle iron, corrugated
tin, lumber, and plywood. A tough-looking little all-terrain
vehicle with bulbous tires was towing a trailerload of equip-

ment up the improvised path. Nearby, a group of technicians was beginning the work of wiring an island phone system, while another was erecting Quonset huts. By tomorrow morning, one of them would be Hatch's new office. It was amazing how fast things were happening.

Still, Hatch was in no hurry to set foot on Ragged Island. *Tomorrow's plenty soon enough,* he thought.

A loud clatter echoed toward him as a heavy piece of equipment was loaded onto the pier. Sound carried well across water. Hatch knew that, even without Bud Rowell's assistance, all of Stormhaven must now be buzzing with news of his return and the sudden flurry of activity on the island. He felt a little guilty that he hadn't been able to tell Bud the whole story two days before. By now, he'd certainly figured it out. Idly, Hatch wondered what people were saying. Perhaps some of the townspeople suspected his motives. If so, let them; he had nothing to be ashamed of. Even though his grandfather's bankruptcy had relieved his family of legal responsibility, his father had paid off—painfully, over many years—all the family's local debts. There had been no finer man than his father. And that fineness of character made his grotesque, pathetic end that much more painful. . . . Hatch turned away from the island, refusing to follow the line of thought any further.

He checked his watch. Eleven o'clock: the Maine lunch hour. He went belowdecks, raided the gas-powered refrigerator, and returned with a lobster roll and a bottle of ginger ale. Climbing into the captain's chair, he propped his feet on the binnacle and dug avidly into the roll. *Funny thing about sea air,* he thought to himself. *Always makes you hungry.* Maybe he ought to research that particular nugget for the *Journal of the American Medical Association.* His lab assistant Bruce could use a good dose of salt air. Or any air, for that matter.

As he ate, a seagull landed on the thrumcap and eyed him quizzically. Hatch knew lobstermen hated seagulls—called them wharf rats with wings—but he'd always had a fondness for the loudmouthed, garbage-swilling birds. He flicked a piece of lobster into the air; the gull caught it and then soared off, chased by two other gulls. Soon, all three had returned and were perched on the taffrail, staring him down with hungry black eyes. *Now I've done it,* Hatch thought, good-naturedly plucking another piece of lobster from the roll and tossing it toward the middle bird.

In an instant, all three birds tore into the air with a desperate beating of wings. Hatch's amusement turned to surprise as he noticed they weren't after the lobster, but were instead fleeing the boat as fast as they could, heading toward the mainland. In the sudden hush left by their departure, he heard the chunk of lobster hit the deckboards with a soft splat.

As he gazed after the birds, frowning, he felt a convulsive shudder pass under his feet. He leaped out of the chair, thinking the anchor cable had parted and the *Plain Jane* had run aground. But the cable was still taut. Except for the thin veil of mist that girdled the island, the sky overhead was clear; there was no lightning. Quickly, he scanned the surroundings for any unusual activity. Had they been dynamiting? No, it was too early for that. . . .

Then his eyes fell on a patch of ocean, just inside the reef about a hundred yards away.

In an area some thirty feet in diameter, the placid surface of the water had suddenly broken into chop. A roiling mass of bubbles crested the surface. There was a second shudder, another explosion of bubbles. As they died away, the surface of the water began to move counterclockwise: slowly at first, then faster. A dimple appeared in its center, almost immediately imploding into a funnel. *A whirlpool,* Hatch thought. *What the hell—?*

A burst of static on the scanner brought Hatch to the railing. There was hysterical shouting on the bands: first from one, then many voices. ". . . Man down!" broke through the riot of sounds. ". . . Get the rope around him!" cried another voice. Then: "Look out! Those beams are about to go!"

Suddenly, Hatch's private radio burst to life. "Hatch, do you copy?" came Neidelman's clipped tones. "We've got a man trapped on the island."

"Understood," Hatch said, firing up the big diesels. "I'm bringing the boat to the pier now." As a puff of wind blew shreds of mist from the island, he could make out a cluster of white-suited men near the island's center, scurrying frantically.

"Forget the pier," Neidelman broke in again, a fresh note of urgency coloring his voice. "No time. He'll be dead in five minutes."

Hatch glanced around for a desperate moment. Then he cut the engines, grabbed his medical bag, and pulled the *Plain Jane*'s dinghy alongside. Tearing the rope free of its cleat, he tossed it into the dinghy, then leaped over the side after it. The dinghy heeled crazily under his sudden weight. Half-kneeling, half-falling onto the stern seat, Hatch pulled at the starter rope. The outboard leaped into life with an angry buzz. Grabbing the throttle, he pointed the little boat toward the circle of reefs. Somewhere near the south end, there were two narrow gaps in the jagged underwater rocks. He hoped to hell he remembered where they were.

As the shoreline drew nearer, Hatch watched the water beneath the bow turning from a bottomless gray to green. *If only there was a bigger swell,* he thought, *I could see the rocks through the breaking water.* He glanced at his watch: no time to play it safe. Taking a deep breath, he opened the throttle wide with a flick of his wrist. The boat sprang forward eagerly, and the green outline of the submerged reefs grew lighter as the water became rapidly shallower. Hatch braced himself against the throttle, preparing himself for the impact.

Then he was past the reef and the ocean floor sank away again. He aimed the boat at a small pebbled area between the two Whalebacks, keeping the throttle wide open until the last second. Then he cut the engine and swiveled the outboard upward, raising the propeller above the wake. He felt the shock as the bow of the dinghy hit the shore and skidded up across the shingles.

Before the boat came to a halt, Hatch had grabbed his kit and was scrambling up the embankment. He could now hear the shouts and cries directly ahead. At the top of the rise, he stopped. Ahead stretched an unbroken mass of sawgrass and fragrant tea roses, swaying in the breeze, concealing the deadly ground below. This wild southern end of the island had not yet been mapped by the Thalassa team. *It's suicide to run across there,* he thought even as his legs began to move and he was crashing through the brush, jumping over old beams and skittering across rotten platforms and around gaping holes.

In a minute he was among the group of white-suited figures clustered around the ragged mouth of a pit. The smell of sea-water and freshly disturbed earth rose from its dark maw. Several ropes were wrapped around a nearby winch. "Name's Streeter," shouted the nearest figure. "Team leader." He was the same man who had stood behind Neidelman during his speech—a lean figure with compressed lips and a marine-style haircut.

Without a word, two of the others began buckling a Swiss Seat harness around Hatch.

Hatch glanced into the pit, and his stomach contracted involuntarily. Dozens of feet down—it was impossible to tell exactly how far—he could see the yellow lances of flashlight beams. Two roped figures were frantically working at a thick beam. Beneath the beam, Hatch was horrified to see another figure, moving feebly. Its mouth opened. Over the roar of water, Hatch thought he could hear an anguished scream.

"What the hell happened?" Hatch cried, grabbing a medical kit from his bag.

"One of the dating team fell into this shaft," Streeter replied. "His name's Ken Field. We sent a rope down, but it must have snagged on a beam. Triggered some kind of cave-in. His legs are pinned by the beam, and the water's rising fast. We've got three minutes, no more."

"Get him a scuba tank!" Hatch yelled as he signaled the winch operator to lower him into the pit.

"No time!" came Streeter's reply. "The divers are too far offshore."

"Nice way to lead the team."

"He's already roped," Streeter continued after a moment. "Just cut him loose and we'll haul him up."

Cut him loose? Hatch thought just as he was shoved off the edge of the pit. Before he could think, he was swinging in space, the roar of water almost deafening in the confines of the shaft. He dropped for a moment in near free fall, then the Swiss Seat jerked him to a rude halt beside the two rescuers. Swinging around, he found a purchase, then glanced down.

The man lay on his back, the massive beam lying diagonally across his left ankle and right knee, pinning him tightly. As Hatch watched, the man opened his mouth again, crying out with pain. One rescuer was scrabbling rocks and dirt away from the man, while the other was chopping at the beam with a heavy ax. Chips flew everywhere, filling the pit with the smell of rotten wood. Beneath them, Hatch could see the water, rising at a terrifying rate.

He knew immediately that it was hopeless; they could never chop through the beam in time. He glanced at the rising water and made a quick mental calculation: no more than two minutes before the man would be covered, even less than Streeter had guessed. He mentally reviewed his options, then realized there were none. No time for painkiller, no time for an anaesthetic, no time for anything. He rummaged desperately through his kit: a couple of scalpels long enough for a hangnail repair, but that was it. Tossing them aside, he began shrugging out of his shirt.

"Make sure his rope's secure!" he shouted to the first rescuer. "Then take my kit and get yourself topside!"

He turned to the other. "Stand by to hoist this man up!" He ripped his shirt in half. Twisting one sleeve, he tied it around the trapped man's left leg, about five inches below the knee. The other sleeve went around the fat part of the man's right thigh. He knotted first one sleeve, then the other, jerking them as tight as possible.

"Give me the ax!" he cried to the remaining rescuer. "Then get ready to pull!"

Wordlessly, the man handed him the ax. Hatch positioned himself astride the trapped man. Bracing his own legs, he raised it above his head.

The trapped man's eyes widened in sudden understanding. "No!" he screamed. "Please, don't—"

Hatch brought the ax down on the man's left shin with all his might. As the blade drove home, it felt to Hatch for a curious instant as though he was chopping the green trunk of a young sapling. There was a moment of resistance, then a sudden give. The man's voice ceased instantly, but his eyes remained open, straining, the cords of his neck standing out. A wide, ragged cut opened in the leg, and for a moment the bone and flesh lay exposed in the weak light of the pit. Then the rising water roiled up around the cut and it filled with blood. Quickly, Malin drove the ax home again and the leg came free, the water frothing red as it churned across the beam. The man threw his head back and opened his jaws wide in a soundless scream, the fillings in his molars shining dully in the glow of the flashlight.

Hatch stepped back a moment, and took several deep breaths. He clamped down hard on the trembling that was beginning in his wrists and forearms, then repositioned himself around the man's right thigh. This was going to be worse. Much worse. But the water was now bubbling above the man's knee and there was no time to waste.

The first blow hit home in something softer than wood, but rubbery and resistant. The man slumped to one side, unconscious. The second blow missed the first, cutting a sickening gash across the knee. Then the water was boiling around the thigh, heading for the man's waist. Estimating where the next blow had to fall, Hatch positioned the ax behind his head, hesitated, then swung it down with a tremendous effort. As it plunged into the water he could feel it strike home, slicing through with a crack and give of bone.

"Pull him up!" Hatch screamed. The rescuer gave two tugs on the rope. Immediately, it went taut. The man's shoulders straightened and he was pulled into a sitting position, but the massive timber still refused to release him. The leg had not been completely severed. The rope slackened once more and the man slumped backward, the black water creeping up around his ears, nose, and mouth.

"Give me your brush hook!" Hatch yelled to the rescuer. Grabbing the stubby, machetelike implement, he took a deep breath and dove below the surface of the surging water. Feeling his way in the blackness, he worked his way down the right leg, located the cut, and quickly sliced through the remaining hamstring muscle with the hook.

"Try again!" he coughed the moment his head broke the surface. The rope jerked and this time the unconscious man came bursting out from under the water, blood and muddy water running from the stumps of his legs. The rescuer went next, and then a moment later Hatch felt himself hoisted toward the surface. Within seconds he was out of the dark, damp hole and crouching next to the man in a swale of matted grass. Quickly, he felt for the vitals: the man was not breathing, but his heart was still beating, fast and faint. Despite his improvised tourniquets, blood was oozing from the savaged stumps of the legs.

ABC, Hatch recited under his breath: *airway, breathing, circulation.* He opened the man's mouth, cleared out mud and vomit with a hook of his finger, then rolled him on his left side, squeezing him into a fetal position. To Hatch's great relief a thin stream of water came from the man's mouth, along with a sigh of air. Hatch immediately began a stabilizing pattern: a ten count of mouth-to-mouth, then a pause to tighten the tourniquet around the left leg; ten more breaths; a pause to tighten the other tourniquet; ten more breaths; then a pulse check.

"Get my bag!" he yelled at the stunned group. "I need a hypo!"

One of the men grabbed the bag and began rummaging through it.

"Dump it out on the ground, for Chrissakes!" The man obeyed and Hatch fished through the scatter, pulling out a syringe and a bottle. Sucking one cc of epinephrine into the hypo, he administered it sub cu in the victim's shoulder. Then he returned to mouth-to-mouth. At the five count, the man coughed, then drew a ragged breath.

Streeter came forward, a cellular phone in his hand.

"We've called in a medevac helicopter," he said. "It'll meet us at Stormhaven wharf."

"The hell with that," Hatch snapped.

Streeter frowned. "But the medevac—"

"Flies from Portland. And no half-assed medevac pilot can lower a basket while hovering."

"But shouldn't we get him to the mainland—?"

Hatch rounded on him. "Can't you see this man won't survive a run to the mainland? Get the Coast Guard on the phone."

Streeter pressed a number in the phone's memory, then handed it over wordlessly.

Hatch asked to speak to a paramedic, then quickly began describing the accident. "We've got a double amputation, one above, one below the knee," he said. "Massive exsanguination, deep shock, pulse is thready at fifty-five, some water in the lungs, still unconscious. Get a chopper out here with your best pilot. There's no landing spot and we'll need to drop a basket. Hang a bag of saline, and bring some unmatched O negative if you have it. But get your ass out here, that's the most important thing. This'll be a scoop and run." He covered the phone and turned to Streeter. "Any chance of getting those legs up in the next hour?"

"I don't know," Streeter said evenly. "The water will have made the pit unstable. We might be able to send a diver down to reconnoiter."

Hatch shook his head and turned back to the phone. "You'll be flying the patient straight through to Eastern Maine Medical. Alert the trauma team, have an OR standing by. There's a possibility we may recover the limbs. We'll need a microvascular surgeon on tap, just in case."

He snapped the phone shut and handed it back to Streeter. "If you can recover those legs without risk of life, do it."

He turned his attention back to the injured man. The pulse was lousy but holding steady. More importantly, the man was beginning to regain consciousness, thrashing feebly and moaning. Hatch felt another wave of relief; if he'd stayed unconscious much longer, the prognosis would have been poor. He sorted through his kit and gave the man five milligrams of morphine, enough to give him some relief but not enough to lower his pulse any further. Then he turned to what remained of the legs. He winced inwardly at the raggedness of the wounds and the shattered ends of bone; the dull blade of the ax was nothing like the nice, neat saws of the operating room. He could see some bleeders, especially the femoral artery of the right leg. Sorting among the refuse of his medical kit, he grabbed a needle and some thread and began tying off the veins and arteries.

"Dr. Hatch?" Streeter asked.

"What?" Hatch replied, head inches from the stump, using tweezers to fish out a medium-sized vein that had already retracted.

"When you have a moment, Captain Neidelman would like to talk to you."

Hatch nodded, tied off the vein, checked the tourniquets, and rinsed the wounds. He picked up the radio. "Yes?"

"How is he?" Neidelman asked.

"He's got a fair chance of survival," Hatch said. "Provided there's no screwup with the helicopter."

"Thank God. And his legs?"

"Even if they recover them, I doubt there's much chance of reattachment. You better review some basic safety procedures with your team leader here. This accident was entirely avoidable."

"I understand," said Neidelman.

Hatch switched off the phone and looked toward the northeast and the nearest Coast Guard station. In three minutes, perhaps four, they should see the bird on the horizon. He turned to Streeter. "You'd better drop a marker flare. And get this area cleared, we don't want another accident on our hands. When the chopper comes in, we'll need four men to lift him onto the stretcher, no more."

"Right," said Streeter, his lips tightening.

Hatch saw that the man's face was unnaturally dark, blood throbbing angrily in a vein on his forehead. *Tough luck,* he thought. *I'll repair that relationship later. Besides, he's not the guy who's going to live without legs for the rest of his life.*

He glanced again at the horizon. A black speck was approaching fast. In a few moments, the dull thud of heavy rotors filled the air as the helicopter shot across the island, banked sharply, then approached the small group gathered around the pit. The backwash from the blades whipped the sawgrass into a frenzy and kicked dirt into Hatch's eyes. The door of the cargo bay slid back and a rescue platform came bobbing down. The injured man was strapped aboard and sent up, and Hatch signaled for the platform to be sent down again for himself. Once he was safely on board, the waiting paramedic shut the door and gave the pilot a thumbs-up. Immediately, the chopper banked to the right and dug its nose into the air, heading for the southwest.

Hatch looked around. There was saline already hung, an oxygen bottle and mask, a rack of antibiotics, bandages, tourniquets, and antiseptics.

"We didn't have any O negative, Doctor," the paramedic said.

"Don't worry," Hatch replied, "you've done okay. But let's get an IV into him. We've got to expand this guy's blood volume." He noticed the paramedic looking at him strangely, then realized why: shirtless, covered in a crust of mud and dried blood, he didn't look much like a Maine country doctor.

There was a moan from the stretcher, and the thrashing began again.

An hour later, Hatch found himself alone in the silence of an empty operating room, breathing in the smell of Betadine and blood. Ken Field, the wounded man, was in the next bay, being cared for by Bangor's best surgeon. The legs could not be recovered, but the man would live. Hatch's work was over.

He fetched a deep breath, then let it out slowly, trying to drain the day's accumulated poisons out with it. He took another breath, then another. At last he sank heavily onto the operating table, leaned forward, and pressed his balled fists tightly against his temples. *This didn't have to happen,* a cold voice was whispering inside his head. The thought of how he'd sat there on the *Plain Jane,* idly eating lunch and playing with the seagulls, made him ill. He cursed himself for not being on the island when the accident happened, for letting them proceed before his office and equipment were in place. This was the second time he'd been unprepared, the second time he had underestimated the power of the island. *Never again,* he thought, raging: *Never again.*

As calm slowly returned, another thought insinuated itself into his mind. Today was the first time he had set foot on Ragged Island since the death of his brother. During the emergency, there had been no time to think. Now, in the darkened operating theater, alone with his thoughts, it took all the self-control Hatch could muster to control the fit of shaking that threatened to overwhelm him.

9

Doris Bowditch, licensed Realtor, strode briskly up the front steps of 5 Ocean Lane. The old boards of the porch groaned beneath the unaccustomed weight. As she bent forward to try the front door key, a vast assortment of silver bracelets cascaded down her forearm with a jingling that reminded Hatch of sleigh bells. There was a brief struggle with the key, then she turned the knob and threw the front door open with a little flourish.

Hatch waited until she had stepped through the door, muumuu billowing out behind, then followed her into the cool, dark interior of the house. It hit him immediately, like a blow to the gut: the same smell of old pinewood, mothballs, and pipesmoke. Though he hadn't inhaled that scent for twenty-five years, it was all he could do not to step back into the sunlight as the intense scent of childhood threatened to bypass all his defenses.

"Well!" came Doris's bright voice as she shut the door behind them. "It's a beautiful old thing, isn't it? I've always said, what a shame it was shut up for so long!" The woman swept into the center of the room in a swirl of pink. "What do you think?"

"Fine," said Hatch, taking a tentative step forward. The front parlor was just as he remembered it, the day his mother had finally given up and they'd left for Boston: the chintz easy chairs, the old canvas sofa, the print of the HMS *Leander* over the mantelpiece, the Herkeimer upright piano with the circular stool and braided rug.

"The pump's been primed," Doris continued, oblivious. "The windows washed, electricity turned on, propane tank filled." She ticked off the items on long red fingernails.

"It looks very nice," Hatch said distractedly. He moved to the old piano and ran his hand along the fallboard, remembering the wintry afternoons he had spent struggling over some Bach two-part invention. On the shelf beside the fireplace was an old Parcheesi set. Next to it lay a Monopoly board, its cover lost long ago, the pink and yellow and green rectangles of play money worn and creased from countless contests. On the shelf above lay several grimy packs of cards, held together by rubber bands. Hatch felt a fresh stab as he remembered playing poker with Johnny, using wooden matches as chips, and the vigorous arguments about which was higher, a full house or a straight. Everything was here, every painful reminder still in place; it was like a museum of memory.

They had taken nothing but their clothes when they left. They were only supposed to stay away a month, at first. Then the month turned into a season, then a year, and soon the old house receded to a distant dream: shut up, unseen, unmentioned, but waiting nevertheless. Hatch wondered again why his mother had never sold the place, even after they'd fallen on hard times in Boston. And he wondered at his own, deeply buried, reasons for a similar reluctance, long after his mother's death.

He passed into the living room and stepped up to the bow window, letting his gaze fall on the infinite blue of the ocean, sparkling in the morning sun. Somewhere out on the horizon lay Ragged Island, at rest now after claiming its first casualty in a quarter century. In the wake of the accident, Neidelman had called a one-day halt to the operation. Hatch's eyes dropped from the sea to the meadow in the foreground, a green mantle that fell away from the house toward the shoreline. He reminded himself that he didn't have to do this. There were other places to stay that didn't come with the added burden of memory. But those places wouldn't be in Stormhaven; driving to the house that morning, he'd seen perhaps a dozen Thalassa employees clustered outside of the town's sole bed-and-breakfast, all eager to book the five available rooms. He sighed. As long as he was here, he had to do it all.

Dust motes drifted in the banners of morning sunlight. As he stood before the window, Hatch could feel time dissolving. He remembered camping out in that meadow with Johnny, their sleeping bags sprawled across the damp and fragrant grass, counting shooting stars in the dark.

"Did you get my letter last year?" the voice of Doris intruded. "I was afraid it had gone astray."

Hatch turned away from the window, tried to make sense of what the woman was saying, then gave up and moved back in time again. There in the corner was a half-finished needlepoint seatcover, faded to pastel. There was the shelf of his father's books—Richard Henry Dana, Melville, Slocum, Conrad, Sandberg's life of Lincoln—and two shelves of his mother's English mysteries. Below were a stack of tattered *Life* magazines and a yellow row of *National Geographic*s.

He drifted into the dining room, the Realtor rustling along in his wake.

"Dr. Hatch, you know how expensive it is to keep up an old house like this. I've always said, this is just too much house for one person . . ." She let the thought die away into a bright smile.

Hatch walked slowly round the room, his hand trailing on the drop-leaf table, his eyes roaming the Audubon chromolithographs on the walls. He passed into the kitchen. There was the old Frigidaire, trimmed in thick round pieces of chrome. A piece of paper, curled and faded, was still stuck to it with a magnet. *Hey Mom! Strawberries please!* it read in his own teenage hand. He lingered in the breakfast nook, the scarred table and benches bringing back memories of food fights and spilled milk; memories of his father, straight-backed and dignified in the midst of friendly chaos, telling sea stories in his slow voice while his dinner went cold. And then later, just he and his mother at the table, his mother's head bent with grief, the morning sun in her gray hair, tears dropping into her teacup.

"Anyway," came the voice, "what I wrote you about was this young couple from Manchester, with two children. A lovely couple. They've been renting the Figgins place for the last few summers, and are looking to buy."

"Of course they are," Hatch murmured vaguely. The breakfast nook looked out over the back meadow, where the apple trees had grown wild and heavy. He remembered the summer mornings when the mist lay on the fields and the deer came up from the woods before sunrise to eat apples, stepping through the timothy with nervous precision.

"I believe they'd pay upwards of two hundred fifty. Shall I give them a call? No obligation, of course—"

With great effort, Hatch turned toward her. "What?"

"I was wondering if you had any intention of selling, that's all."

Hatch blinked at her. "Selling?" he asked slowly. "The house?"

The smile remained on Doris Bowditch's face, undented. "I just thought that, you being a bachelor and all . . . it seemed, you know, impractical." She faltered a bit, but stood her ground.

Hatch repressed his first impulse. One had to be careful in a small town like Stormhaven. "I don't think so," he said, keeping his voice neutral. He moved back into the living room, toward the front door, the woman following.

"I'm not talking about right away, of course," she called brightly. "If you find the—the treasure, you know . . . Well, it couldn't possibly take that long, could it? Especially with all that help you have." Her expression clouded for a moment. "But oh, wasn't it awful! Two men being killed yesterday, and all."

Hatch looked at her very slowly. "Two men? Two men weren't killed, Doris. Not even one. There was an accident. Where did you hear this?"

Doris looked slightly bewildered. "Why, I heard it from Hilda McCall. She runs the beauty parlor, Hilda's Hairstyling. Anyway, once you get all that money you're not going to want to stay here, so you might as well—"

Stepping forward, Hatch opened the front door for her. "Thank you, Doris," he said, trying to muster a smile. "The house is in wonderful shape."

The woman stopped well short of the frame. She hesitated. "About this young couple. The husband's a *very* successful lawyer. Two children, you know, a boy and a—"

"Thank you," said Hatch, a little more firmly.

"Well, you're welcome, of course! You know, I don't think two hundred fifty thousand would be unreasonable for a summer—"

Hatch stepped out on the porch, far enough so that she would have to follow if she wanted to be heard. "Real estate prices are up right now, Dr. Hatch," she said as she appeared in the doorway. "But like I've always said, you never know when they'll drop. Eight years ago—"

"Doris, you're a love, and I'll recommend you to all my many doctor friends who want to move to Stormhaven. Thanks again. I'll be expecting your bill." Hatch quickly stepped back inside and shut the door quietly but firmly.

He waited in the parlor, wondering if the woman would have the audacity to ring the bell. But she only stood irresolutely on the porch for a long moment before returning to her car, the muumuu floating behind her, the irrepressible smile still plastered across her face. A six percent commission on two hundred and fifty thousand, Hatch thought, was quite a lot of money in Stormhaven. He vaguely remembered hearing that her husband was a drinker who'd lost his boat to the bank. *She can't possibly know how I feel,* he thought, managing to find some compassion in his heart for Doris Bowditch, Realtor.

He settled on the little stool in front of the piano and softly struck the first chord of Chopin's E-minor prelude. He was surprised and pleased to find the piano had been tuned. Doris had at least followed his instructions carefully: *Clean the house, get everything ready, but don't touch or move anything.* He played the prelude dreamily, pianissimo, trying to empty his mind. It was hard to comprehend that he had not touched these keys, sat on this stool, or even walked across these floorboards for twenty-five years. Everywhere he looked, the house eagerly offered up memories of a happy childhood. After all, it *had* been happy. It was only the end that was unendurable. *If only . . .*

He stepped down hard on this chill, persistent voice.

Two men dead, Doris had said. That was pretty imaginative, even for a small-town rumor mill. So far, the town seemed to be accepting the visitors with a kind of hospitable curiosity. Certainly it would be good for the merchants. But Hatch could see that someone would have to step in as community spokesman for Thalassa. Otherwise, there was no telling what bizarre stories might spring from Bud's Superette or Hilda's Hairstyling. With a sinking feeling, he realized that there was really only one person for the job.

He sat at the piano for another long minute. With any luck, old Bill Banns would still be editor in chief of the local paper. Sighing heavily, he stood up and headed for the kitchen, where a can of instant coffee and—if Doris hadn't forgotten—a live telephone were waiting.

10

The group that gathered around the antique maple table in the pilothouse of the *Griffin* the following morning was a far cry from the noisy, eager crowd that had encircled the boat with their cheers three evenings before. As Hatch walked in for the scheduled meeting, he found most of the small group looking subdued, even demoralized, after the accident.

He looked around at the nerve center of Neidelman's boat. The curving sweep of windows gave an unimpeded view of island, sea, and land. The pilothouse was constructed of Brazilian rosewood and brass, beautifully restored, with intricate beadboard ceilings. What looked like an eighteenth-century Dutch sextant stood in a glass case next to the binnacle, and the wheel itself was carved of an exotic black wood. Rosewood cabinets on either side of the wheel held a discreet array of high-tech equipment, including loran and sonar screens and a geo-positioning satellite grid. The back wall of the pilothouse housed a massive array of unrecognizable electronics. The Captain himself had not yet emerged from his private quarters below: a low wooden door, set into the electronics of the back wall, was closed. An old horseshoe hung upside down on a nail above the doorway, and a brass plaque on the door itself read PRIVATE in discreet but unmistakable letters. The only sounds in the room were the creaking hawsers and the soft slap of water against the hull.

Taking a seat at the table, Hatch glanced at the people around him. He had met a few of them informally the first night, but others remained strangers. Lyle Streeter, the crew foreman, looked pointedly away from Hatch's smile of greeting. Obviously, he was not a man who enjoyed being yelled at. Hatch made a mental note to remember that although every first-year resident knew that yelling, screeching, and cursing during a medical emergency was standard procedure, the rest of humanity did not.

There was a sound from below, then the Captain stooped through the pilothouse door. All eyes shifted as he walked to the head of the table and leaned on it with both hands, looking into each person's face in turn. There was a noticeable decrease in tension, as if everyone was drawing strength and control from his arrival. When Neidelman's eyes landed on Hatch, he spoke. "How is Ken?"

"Serious, but stable. There's a small chance of an embolism, but it's being monitored closely. I guess you know they couldn't recover the legs."

"So I understand. Thank you, Dr. Hatch, for saving his life."

"I couldn't have done it without the help of Mr. Streeter and his crew," Hatch replied.

Neidelman nodded, letting a silence build. Then he spoke, quiet and assured. "The survey crew was following my orders, taking every precaution I deemed necessary. If anyone is to blame for the accident, it is myself, and we have overhauled our safety procedures as a result. There can be sorrow at this unfortunate development. There can be sympathy for Ken and his family. But there are to be no recriminations."

He stood up and placed his hands behind his back. "Every day," he said in a louder voice, "we'll be taking risks. All of us. Tomorrow, you or I could lose our legs. Or worse. The risks are very real, and they are part of what we do. If it were easy to lift two billion from a watery grave, it would have been done years ago. Centuries ago. We are here *because* of the danger. And already, we've been dealt a blow. But we must not allow this to dampen our resolve. No treasure has ever been buried with such skill and cunning. It will take even more skill and cunning to retrieve it."

He walked to the nearest window, gazed out for a moment, then turned. "I'm sure most of you know the details of the accident by now. As his crew was moving across the island, Ken Field broke into a boarded-over shaft, probably dug in the mid-nineteenth century. His safety rope stopped his fall before he reached the bottom. But as he was being pulled out, his rope became caught in an exposed beam whose underpinnings were rotted by time. The tug of the rope dislodged the beam, triggering a cave-in and breaching the adjoining flooded shaft."

He paused. "We know what lessons can be learned from this. And I think we all know what our next duties must be. Tomorrow, we begin preparations for dye-testing the Water Pit in order to locate the hidden flood tunnel to the sea. We'll need to have the primary computer systems up and running by that point. The hardbody sonar array, the seismometers, tomographic systems, and the proton magnetometers must be assembled before work begins. The diving equipment should be inspected and ready to go by fifteen hundred hours. Most importantly, I want the tandem pumps up and ready for testing by end of day."

Neidelman glanced briefly at each in turn. "As my core

team, each person at this table will receive a share in the treasure instead of salary. You know that if we succeed, each of you will become enormously wealthy. That may not seem bad for four weeks' work, until you consider what happened to Ken Field. If any of you are contemplating leaving, now is the time to do it. You'll get the standard Thalassa compensation package, but no share. There will be no bad feelings, no questions asked. But don't come to me later, saying you've changed your mind. We're seeing this through, no matter what. So speak now."

The Captain turned to a cabinet and extracted an old briar pipe. He removed a tin of Dunhill tobacco from the cabinet, pinched out a bowlful and placed it in the pipe, tamped it thoughtfully, and lit up with a wooden match. All this was done with deliberate slowness, while the silence around the table deepened. Outside, the omnipresent Ragged Island mist had grown denser, curling around the *Griffin* with an almost sensuous caress.

At last, the Captain looked back and spoke through a wreath of blue smoke. "Very good. Before we adjourn, I'd like to introduce you all to the newest member of the expedition." He glanced at Hatch. "Doctor, I was hoping to have you formally meet my senior staff under more pleasant circumstances." He took in the group with a sweep of his hand. "As most of you know, this is Malin Hatch, owner of Ragged Island and partner in this operation. He will be our medical officer."

Neidelman turned. "Dr. Hatch, this is Christopher St. John, the expedition's historian." He was the plump-faced man Hatch had seen looking back at him from the launch two nights before. A shock of unruly gray hair topped his round head, and the man's rumpled tweed suit displayed the telltale traces of several breakfasts. "You'll find him an expert on all areas of Elizabethan and Stuart history, including piracy and the use of codes. And this"—Neidelman indicated the slovenly looking man in Bermuda shorts, who was picking at his nails with a look of intense boredom, one leg thrown over an arm of the chair—"is Kerry Wopner, our computer expert. Kerry is highly adept at network design and cryptanalysis." He stared hard at the two men. "I don't need to tell you the paramount importance of cracking the second half of the journal, especially in light of this tragedy. Macallan must not keep any more of his secrets from us."

Neidelman continued around the table. "You met our team foreman, Lyle Streeter, yesterday. He's been with me ever since our days cruising the Mekong. And here"—he pointed to a small, severe, prickly looking woman in sensible clothes—"is Sandra Magnusen, Thalassa's chief engineer and remote sensing specialist. At the end of the table is Roger Rankin, our geologist." He indicated a broad, hirsute brute of a man who sat in a chair that looked two sizes too small for him. His eyes met Hatch's, his blond beard parted in a spontaneous grin, and he tipped two fingers to his forehead.

"Dr. Bonterre," Neidelman continued, "our archaeologist and dive leader, has been delayed and should arrive late this evening." He paused a moment. "Unless there are any questions, that's all. Thank you, and I'll see you all again tomorrow morning."

As the group broke up, Neidelman came around the table to Hatch. "I've kept a special team on the island, preparing the net grid and the Base Camp," he said. "Your medical area will be stocked and ready by dawn."

"That's a relief," said Hatch.

"You're probably eager for some more background on the project. This afternoon would be a good time. How about coming by the *Cerberus* around fourteen hundred hours?" A thin smile appeared on his lips. "Starting tomorrow, things are liable to get a little busy around here."

11

At 2:00 P.M. precisely, the *Plain Jane*, moving slowly in the calm water, pulled free of the last tendrils of mist surrounding Ragged Island. Ahead, Hatch could see the white outlines of the *Cerberus* riding at anchor, its long, sleek superstructure low in the water. Near the waterline, he made out a boarding hatch, with the tall, thin shape of the Captain silhouetted within it, awaiting his arrival.

Cutting the throttle, Hatch angled in alongside the bulk of the *Cerberus*. It was cool and still under the vessel's shadow.

"Quite a little boat you've got here," Hatch called out as he came to a stop opposite the Captain. The ship dwarfed the *Plain Jane*.

"Biggest in Thalassa's fleet," Neidelman replied. "She's basically a floating laboratory and back-office research station. There's only so much equipment we can off-load to the island. The big stuff—the electron microscopes and C14 particle accelerators, for example—will stay on the ship."

"I was curious about the harpoon gun up in the bows," Hatch said. "Do you spear a blue whale every now and then, when the deckhands get peckish?"

Neidelman grinned. "That betrays the ship's origins, my friend. It was designed as a state-of-the-art whaler by a Norwegian company about six years ago. Then the international ban on whaling happened, and the ship became a costly white elephant even before it was fitted out. Thalassa got it for an excellent price. All the whaling davits and skinning machinery were removed, but nobody ever got around to dismantling the harpoon gun." He nodded over his shoulder. "Come on, let's see what the boys are up to."

Hatch secured the *Plain Jane* to the side of the *Cerberus*, then ran the gangplank across to the ship's boarding hatch. He followed Neidelman through the hatch and into a long, narrow corridor, painted a light gray. The Captain led him past several empty laboratories and a wardroom, then stopped outside a door marked COMPUTER ROOM.

"We've got more computing power behind that door than a small university," Neidelman said, a trace of pride in his voice. "But it's not just for number crunching. There's also a navigational expert system and a neural-net autopilot. In emergencies, the ship can practically run itself."

"I was wondering where all the people were," Hatch said.

"We keep only a skeleton crew on board. It's the same with the rest of the vessels. It's Thalassa's philosophy to maintain a fluid resource pool. If necessary, we could have a dozen scientists here tomorrow. Or a dozen ditchdiggers, for that matter. But we try to operate with the smallest, ablest team possible."

"Cost containment," Hatch said jokingly. "Must make the Thalassa accountants happy."

"Not only that," Neidelman replied, quite seriously. "It

makes sense from a security perspective. No point tempting fate."

The Captain turned a corner and walked past a heavy metal door that was partially ajar. Glancing in, Hatch could make out various pieces of lifesaving equipment attached to wall cleats. There was also a rack of shotguns and two smaller weapons of shiny metal he couldn't identify.

"What are those?" he asked, pointing to the stubby, fat-bellied devices. "They look like pint-sized vacuum cleaners."

Neidelman glanced inside. "Fléchettes," he said.

"Excuse me?"

"A kind of nail gun. It shoots tiny, finned pieces of tungsten-carbide wire."

"Sounds more painful than dangerous."

Neidelman smiled thinly. "At five thousand rounds per minute, fired at speeds over three thousand feet per second, they're plenty dangerous." He closed the door and tested the handle. "This room shouldn't be left open. I'll have to speak to Streeter about it."

"What the hell do you need them around for?" Hatch frowned.

"Remember, Malin, the *Cerberus* isn't always in such friendly waters as rural Maine," the Captain replied, ushering him down the corridor. "Often, we have to work in shark-infested areas. When you're face to face with a Great White, you'll quickly come to appreciate what a fléchette can do. Last year, in the Coral Sea, I saw one shred a shark from snout to tail in a second and a half."

Hatch followed the Captain up a set of steps to the next deck. Neidelman paused for a moment outside an unmarked door, then rapped loudly.

"I'm busy!" came a querulous voice.

Neidelman gave Hatch a knowing smile and eased open the door, revealing a dimly lit stateroom. Hatch followed the

Captain inside, tripped over something, and looked around, blinking, as his eyes became accustomed to the low light. He saw that the far wall and its portholes were entirely covered by banks of rack-mounted electronic equipment: oscilloscopes, CPUs, and countless pieces of dedicated electronics whose purpose Hatch couldn't begin to guess. The floor was ankle-deep in crumpled papers, dented soda cans, candy wrappers, dirty socks, and underwear. A ship's cot set into one of the far walls was a whirlpool of linen, its sheets strewn across mattress and floor alike. The smell of ozone and hot electronics filled the room, and the only light came from numerous flickering screens. In the midst of the chaos sat the rumpled-looking figure in flowered shirt and Bermuda shorts, his back to them, typing feverishly at a keyboard.

"Kerry, can you spare a minute?" Neidelman said. "I've got Dr. Hatch with me."

Wopner turned away from the screen and blinked first at Neidelman, then Hatch. "It's your party," he said in a high, irritated voice. "But you need everything else done, like, yesterday." He pronounced the word *yestidday*. "I've spent the last forty-eight hours setting up the network and haven't done jack shit with the code."

Neidelman smiled indulgently. "I'm sure you and Dr. St. John can spare a few minutes for the expedition's senior partner." He turned to Hatch. "You couldn't tell from appearances, but Kerry is one of the most brilliant cryptanalysts outside the NSA."

"Yeah, right," said Wopner, but Hatch could see he was pleased by the compliment.

"Quite a rig you've got here," Hatch said as he closed the door behind him. "Is that a CAT scan I see there on the left?"

"Very funny." Wopner pushed his glasses up his nose and sniffed. "You think this is something? This is just the backup system. They shipped the main rig off to the island yesterday morning. Now *that's* something."

"Are the on-line tests complete?" Neidelman asked.

"Doing the last series now," Wopner replied, shaking a lock of greasy hair from his eyes and swiveling back to the monitor.

"A team's completing the installation of the island network this afternoon," Neidelman said to Hatch. "Like Kerry said, this is the redundant system, an exact duplicate of the Ragged Island computer grid. Expensive way of doing things, but a real time saver. Kerry, show him what I mean."

"Yassuh." Wopner tapped a few keys and a blank screen winked to life overhead. Hatch looked up to see a wireframe diagram of Ragged Island appear on the screen, rotating slowly around a central axis.

"The backbone routers all have redundant mates." A few more keystrokes, and a fine tracery of green lines was superimposed on the rendering of the island. "Linked by fiber-optic cables to the central hub."

Neidelman gestured at the screen. "Everything on the island—from the pumps, to the turbines, to the compressors, to the derricks—is servo-linked into the network. We'll be able to control anything on the island from the command center. One instruction, and the pumps will fire up; another command will operate a winch; a third will turn off the lights in your office; and so forth."

"What he said," Wopner added. "Totally extensible, with thin OS layers on the remote clients. And everything's tweaked up the wazoo, believe you me, miniature data packets and all the rest. It's a huge net—a thousand ports in one collision domain—but there's zero latency. You wouldn't believe the ping time on this bad boy."

"In English, please," Hatch said. "I never learned to speak Nerd. Hey, what's that?" He pointed to another screen, which showed an overhead view of what appeared to be a medieval village. Small figures of knights and sorcerers were arrayed in various attitudes of attack and defense.

"That's *Sword of Blackthorne*. A role-playing game I designed. I'm dungeon master for three on-line games." He stuck out his lower lip. "Got a problem with that?"

"Not if the Captain doesn't," said Hatch, glancing at Neidelman. It was clear that the Captain gave his subordinates a fair amount of freedom. And it seemed to Hatch that—however unlikely—Neidelman was genuinely fond of this eccentric young man.

There was a loud beep, then a column of numbers scrolled up one of the screens.

"That's it," Wopner said, squinting at the data. "Scylla's done."

"Scylla?" Hatch asked.

"Yeah. Scylla is the system on board the ship. Charybdis is the one on the island."

"Network testing's finished," Neidelman explained. "Once the island installation is complete, all we have to do is dump the programming to Charybdis. Everything is tested here first, then downloaded to the island." He glanced at his watch. "I've got some odds and ends to attend to. Kerry, I know Dr. Hatch would like to hear more about your and Dr. St. John's work on the Macallan codes. Malin, I'll see you topside." Neidelman left the stateroom, closing the door behind him.

Wopner returned to his manic typing, and for a minute Hatch wondered if the youth planned to ignore him completely. Then, without looking away from the terminal, Wopner picked up a sneaker and hurled it against the far wall. This was followed by a heavy paperback book entitled *Coding Network Subroutines in C++*.

"Hey, Chris!" Wopner yelled. "Time for the dog and pony show!"

Hatch realized that Wopner must have been aiming at a small door set in the far wall of the stateroom. "Allow me," he said, stepping toward the door. "Your aim's not so good."

Opening the door, Hatch saw another stateroom, identical in size but completely different in all other ways. It was well lit, clean, and spare. The Englishman, Christopher St. John, sat at a wooden table in the center of the room, pecking slowly away at a Royal typewriter.

"Hello," Hatch said. "Captain Neidelman volunteered your services for a few minutes."

St. John stood and picked up a few old volumes from the desk, a fussy expression creasing his smooth, buttery face. "A pleasure to have you with us, Dr. Hatch," he said, shaking his hand, not looking at all pleased with the interruption.

"Call me Malin," said Hatch.

St. John bowed slightly as he followed Hatch back into Wopner's stateroom.

"Pull up a seat, *Malin*," Wopner said. "I'll explain the real work I've been doing, and Chris can tell you about all those dusty tomes he's been lifting and dropping in the back room. We work together. Right, old chum?"

St. John compressed his lips. Even out here on the water, Hatch sensed a certain air of dust and cobwebs about the historian. *He belongs in an antiquarian bookshop, not on a treasure hunt,* he thought.

Kicking aside the detritus, Hatch pulled a chair up next to Wopner, who pointed to one of the nearby screens, currently blank. A few rapidly typed commands, and a digitized picture of Macallan's treatise and its cryptic marginalia appeared on the screen.

"Herr Neidelman feels that the second half of the journal contains vital information about the treasure," said Wopner.

"So we're taking a two-track approach to break the code. I do the computers. Chris here does the history."

"The Captain mentioned a figure of two billion dollars," Hatch said. "How did he arrive at that?"

"Well now," said St. John, clearing his throat as if preparing for a lecture. "Like most pirates, Ockham's fleet was a ragtag collection of various ships he'd captured: a couple of galleons, a few brigantines, a fast sloop, and, I believe, a large East Indiaman. Nine ships in all. We know they were so heavily laden they were dangerously unmaneuverable. You simply add up their cargo capacities, and combine that with the manifests of ships Ockham looted. We know, for example, that Ockham took fourteen tons of gold from the Spanish Plate Fleet alone, and ten times that in silver. From other ships he looted cargoes of lapis, pearls, amber, diamonds, rubies, carnelian, ambergris, jade, ivory, and lignum vitae. Not to mention ecclesiastical treasures, taken from towns along the Spanish Main." He unconsciously adjusted his bow tie, face shining with pleasure at the recital.

"Excuse me, but did you say fourteen *tons* of gold?" Hatch asked, dumfounded.

"Absolutely," said St. John.

"Fort Knox afloat," said Wopner, licking his lips.

"And then there's St. Michael's Sword," St. John added. "An artifact of inestimable value by itself. We're dealing here with the greatest pirate treasure ever assembled. Ockham was brilliant and gifted, an educated man, which made him all the more dangerous." He pulled a thin plastic folder from a shelf and handed it to Hatch. "Here's a biographical extract one of our researchers prepared. I think you'll find that, for once, the legends don't exaggerate. His reputation was so terrible that all he had to do was sail his flagship into harbor, hoist the Jolly Roger, and fire a broadside, and everyone from the citizens to the priest came rushing down with their valuables."

"And the virgins?" Wopner cried, feigning wide-eyed interest. "What happened to them?"

St. John paused, his eyes half closed. "Kerry, do you mind?"

"No, really," said Kerry, all impish innocence. "I want to know."

"You know very well what happened to the virgins," St. John snapped, and turned back to Hatch. "Ockham had a following of two thousand men on his nine ships. He needed large crews for boarding and firing the great guns. Those men were usually given twenty-four hours, er, *leave,* in the unfortunate town. The results were quite hideous."

"It wasn't only the ships that had twelve-inchers, if you know what I mean," Wopner leered.

"You see what I have to endure," murmured St. John to Hatch.

"Terribly, *terribly* sorry about that, old chap," Wopner replied in a travesty of an English accent. "Some people have no sense of humor," he told Hatch.

"Ockham's success," St. John continued briskly, "became a liability. He didn't know *how* to bury such a large treasure. This wasn't a few hundredweight in gold coin that could be slipped quietly under a rock. That's where Macallan came in. And, indirectly, that's where *we* come in. Because Macallan kept his secret diary in code."

He patted the books under his arm. "These are texts on cryptology," he said. "This one is *Polygraphiae,* by Johannes Trithemius, published in the late fifteen hundreds. It was the Western world's first treatise on codebreaking. And this one is Porta's *De Furtivus Literarum Notis,* a text all Elizabethan spies knew practically by heart. I've got half a dozen others, covering the state of the cryptographic art up to Macallan's time."

"They sound worse than my second-year med school textbooks."

"They're fascinating, actually," St. John said, a flush of enthusiasm briefly coloring his tone.

"Was code writing common in those days?" Hatch asked curiously.

St. John laughed, a kind of seal bark that gave his ruddy cheeks a brief jiggle. "Common? It was practically universal, one of the essential arts of diplomacy and war. Both the British and Spanish governments had departments that specialized in making and breaking ciphers. Even some pirates had crewmen who could crack codes. After all, ships' papers included all kinds of interesting coded documents."

"But coded how?"

"They were usually nomenclators—long lists of word substitutions. For example, in a message, the word 'eagle' might be substituted for 'King George' and 'daffodils' for 'doubloons'—that sort of thing. Sometimes they included simple substitution alphabets, where a letter, number, or symbol replaced a letter of the alphabet, one for one."

"And Macallan's code?"

"The first part of the journal was written with a rather clever monophonic substitution code. The second—we're still working on that."

"That's *my* department," said Wopner, pride and a trace of jealousy mixing in his voice. "It's all on the computer." He struck a key and a long string of gibberish appeared on the screen:

AB3 RQB7 E5OLA W IEW D8P OL QS9MN WX 4JR 2K WN I8N7 WPDO EKS N2T YX ER9 W
DF3 DEI FK IE DF9F DFS K DK F6RE DF3 V3E IE4DI 2F 9GE DF W FEIB5 MLER BLK BV6 FI PET
BOP IBSDF K2LJ BVF EIO PUOER WBI3 OPDJK LBL JKF

"Here's the ciphertext of the first code," he said.

"How did you break it?"

"Oh, *please*. The letters of the English alphabet occur in fixed ratios, *E* being the commonest letter, *Q* being the rarest. You create what we call a contact chart of the code symbols and letter pairs. Bang! The computer does the rest."

St. John waved his hand dismissively. "Kerry is programming the computer attacks against the code, but I am supplying the historical data. Without the old cipher tables, the computer is hopeless. It only knows what's been programmed into it."

Wopner turned around in his seat and stared at St. John. "Hopeless? Fact is, big mama here would have cracked that code without your precious cipher tables. It just would have taken a little longer, is all."

"No longer than twenty monkeys typing at random might take to write *King Lear*," said St. John, with another brief bark of laughter.

"Haw haw. No longer than one St. John typing with two fingers on that Royal shitwriter back there. Jeez, get a laptop. And a life." Wopner turned back to Hatch. "Well, to make a long story short, here's how it decoded."

There was a flurry of keystrokes and the screen split, showing the code on one side and the plaintext on the other. Hatch looked at it eagerly.

> The 2nd of June, Anno D. 1696. The pirate Ockham hath taken our fleet, scuttled the ships, and butcherd every soull. Our man-of-war scandalously struck her colours without a fight and the captain went to his ende blubbering like a babe. I alone was spared, clapped in chaines and straightaway taken down to Ockham's cabin, where the blackguard drewe a saber against my

> *person and said, Lete God build his owen*
> *damned church, I have ye a newe commission.*
> *And then he placed in front of me the articalls.*
> *Lete this journal bear witnesse before God that I*
> *refused to sign . . .*

"Amazing," breathed Hatch as he came to the end of the screen. "Can I read more?"

"I'll print out a copy for you," said Wopner, hitting a key. A printer began humming somewhere in the darkened room.

"Basically," said St. John, "the decrypted section of the journal covers Macallan's being taken prisoner, agreeing on pain of death to design the Water Pit, and finding the right island. Unfortunately, Macallan switches to a new code just when they began actual construction. We believe the rest of the journal consists of a description of the design and construction of the Pit itself. And, of course, the secret for getting to the treasure chamber."

"Neidelman said the journal mentions St. Michael's Sword."

"You bet it does," Wopner interrupted, hitting the keys. More text popped up:

> *Ockham hath unburthened three of his ships in*
> *hopes of taking a prize along the coast. Today a*
> *long leaden coffin trimmed in golde came ashore*
> *with a dozen casks of jewells. The corsairs say*
> *the coffin holds St. Michael's Sword, a costly*
> *treasure seized from a Spanish galleon and*
> *highly esteemd by the Captain, who swaggerd*
> *most shamefully, boasting that it was the greatest*
> *prize of the Indies. The Captain hath forbidden*
> *the opening of the casket, and it is guarded by*
> *day and night. The men are suspicious of each*

other, and constantly make stryfe. Were it not for
the cruell discipline of the Captain, I feare every
one would come to a bad end, and shortly.

"And now here's what the second code looks like." Wopner tapped on the keys and the screen filled again:

34834590234582394438923492340923409856902346789023490562349083934
29086399812349012849123400494903412089509868907347605783568496324
09873507839045709234045895390456234826025698345875767087645073405 9
34038909089080564504556034568903459873468907234589073908759087 25
08723459035696590 87302

"The old boy got smart," Wopner said. "No more spaces, so we can't go by word shapes. All numbers, too, not a character to be seen. Just look at that fucker."

St. John winced. "Kerry, *must* you use such language?"

"Oh, I must, old *thing,* I must."

St. John looked apologetically at Hatch.

"So far," Wopner continued, "this puppy's resisted all of Chris's pretty little cipher tables. So I took the matter into my own hands and wrote a brute-force attack. It's running as we speak."

"Brute-force attack?" Hatch asked.

"You know. An algorithm that runs through a ciphertext, trying all patterns in the order of likelihood. It's just a matter of time."

"A matter of a waste of time," St. John said. "I'm working up a new set of cipher tables from a Dutch book on cryptography. What's needed here is more historical research, not more CPU time. Macallan was a man of his age. He didn't invent this code out of thin air; there must be a historical precedent. We already know it's not a variant of the Shakespeare cipher, or the Rosicrucian cipher, but I'm convinced some lesser-

known code in these books will give us the key that we need.
It should be obvious to the meanest intelligence—"

"Put a sock in it, willya?" Wopner said. "Face it, Chris old
girl, no amount of hitting the history books is gonna break
this code. This one's for the computer." He patted a nearby
CPU. "We're gonna beat this puppy, right, big mama?" He
swiveled around in his chair and opened what Hatch realized
was a rack-mounted medical freezer normally used for storing tissue samples. He pulled out an ice-cream sandwich.

"Anybody want a BigOne?" he asked, waving it around.

"I'd as soon eat takeaway tandoori from a motor stop on
the M-1," St. John replied with a disgusted expression.

"You Brits should talk," Wopner mumbled through a
mouthful of ice cream. "You put meat in your pies, for
Chrissake." He brandished the sandwich like a weapon.
"You're looking at the perfect food here. Fat, protein, sugar,
and carbohydrates. Did I mention fat? You could live on this
stuff forever."

"And he probably will, too," St. John said, turning to
Hatch. "You should see how many cartons he has stored
away in the ship's kitchen."

Wopner frowned. "What, you think I could find enough
BigOnes in this jerkwater town to satisfy my habit? Not
likely. The skidmarks in my underwear are longer than the
whole main street."

"Perhaps you should see a proctologist about that," said
Hatch, causing St. John to erupt in a string of grateful barks.
The Englishman seemed glad to find an ally.

"Feel free to take a crack, doc." Wopner stood up and,
twitching his behind invitingly, made a gesture as if to drop
his trousers.

"I would, but I've got a weak stomach," said Hatch. "So
you don't care for rural Maine?"

"Kerry won't even take rooms in town," St. John said. "He prefers sleeping on board."

"Believe you me," Wopner said, finishing the ice-cream sandwich, "I don't like boats any more than I like the damn hinterland. But there are things here I need. Electricity, for example. Running water. And AC. As in air-conditioning." He leaned forward, the anemic goatee quivering on his chin as if struggling to retain a foothold. "AC. *Gotta have it.*"

Hatch thought privately that it was probably a good thing Wopner, with his Brooklyn accent and flowered shirts, had little reason to visit the town. The moment he set foot in Stormhaven he would become an object of wonder, like the stuffed, two-headed calf brought out every year at the county fair. He decided it was time to change the subject. "This may sound like a stupid question. But what, exactly, is St. Michael's Sword?"

There was an awkward silence.

"Well, let's see," said St. John, pursing his lips. "I've always assumed it had a jeweled hilt, of course, with chased silver and parcel-gilt, perhaps a multifullered blade, that sort of thing."

"But why would Ockham say it was the greatest prize in the Indies?"

St. John looked a little flummoxed. "I hadn't really thought in those terms. I suppose I don't know, really. Perhaps it has some kind of spiritual or mythical significance. You know, like a Spanish Excalibur."

"But if Ockham had as much treasure as you say, why would he place such an inordinate value on the sword?"

St. John turned a pair of watery eyes on Hatch. "The truth is, Dr. Hatch, nothing in my documentation gives any indication of *what* St. Michael's Sword is. Only that it was a carefully guarded, deeply revered object. So I'm afraid I can't answer your question."

"*I* know what it is," said Wopner with a grin.

"What?" asked St. John, falling into the trap.

"You know how men get, so long at sea, no women around, St. Michael's *Sword* . . ." he let the phrase fall off into a salacious silence, while a look of shock and disgust blossomed on St. John's face.

Hatch opened the door on the far side of his parents' bedroom and stepped out onto the small porch beyond. It was only half past nine, but Stormhaven was already asleep. A delightful late summer breeze had gathered in the trees that framed the old house, cooling his cheek, teasing the hairs on the back of his neck. He placed two black folders on the weather-scarred rocker and stepped forward to the railing.

Across the harbor, the town dropped away, a bracelet of lights, tumbling down the hill in streets and squares to the water. It was so still he could hear the pebbles grating in the surf, the clink of mast lines along the pier. A single pale bulb shone from above the front door of Bud's Superette. In the streets, cobbles shone with reflected moonlight. Farther away, the tall narrow form of Burnt Head Light blinked its warning from the head of the bluff.

He had almost forgotten about this narrow second-story porch, tucked away under the front gable of the old Second Empire house. But now, from its railing, a host of memories crowded back. Playing poker with Johnny at midnight when his parents had gone to Bar Harbor to celebrate an anniversary, watching out for the lights of the returning car, feeling naughty and grown up at the same time. And later, looking down at the Northcutt house, waiting for a glimpse of Claire in her bedroom window.

Claire . . .

There was laughter, and a brief, quiet babble of voices. Hatch's eye came back to the present and traveled down to the town's bed-and-breakfast. A couple of Thalassa employees stepped inside, the parlor door closed, and all was silent again.

His eyes made a leisurely stroll up the rows of buildings. The library, its red-brick facade a dusky rose in the cool nocturnal light. Bill Banns's house sprawling and sagging delightfully, one of the oldest in town. And at the top, the large, shingled house reserved for the Congregational minister, a study in shadow, the only example of stick-style architecture in the county.

He lingered a moment longer, his gaze wandering out to sea and the veiled darkness where Ragged Island lay. Then, with a sigh, he returned to the chair, sat down, and picked up the black folders.

First came the printout of the decrypted portion of Macallan's journal. As St. John had said, it described in terse terms the architect's capture and forced labor, designing a hiding place for Ockham's loot that would allow only the pirate to retrieve the gold. Macallan's contempt for the pirate captain, his dislike of the barbarous crew, his dismay at the rough and dissolute conditions, came through clearly in every line.

The journal was brief, and he soon laid it aside, curious now about its second half and wondering how soon Wopner would have it cracked. Before Hatch left his cabin, the programmer had complained bitterly about having to do double duty as the computer technician. "Goddamn network setup, a job for plumbers, not programmers. But the Captain won't be happy until he whittles the crew down to just himself and Streeter. Security concerns, my left nut. Nobody's gonna steal the treasure. But you watch. By tomorrow, once the physical plant is in place, all the surveyors and assistant engineers will be gone. History."

"Makes sense," Hatch had replied. "Why keep unnecessary staff around? Besides, I'd rather treat a bad case of necrifying madura foot than sit in a cabin like this, staring at a jumble of letters."

Hatch remembered how Wopner's lip had curled in scorn. "Shows how much you know. A jumble of letters to you, maybe. Listen: On the other side of that jumble is the person who encrypted it, looking back, giving you the finger. It's the ultimate contest. You get his algorithm, you get his crown jewels. Maybe it's access to a credit card database. Or the firing sequences for a nuclear attack. Or the key to how a treasure is buried. There's no rush like cracking a code. Cryptanalysis is the only game worthy of a truly intelligent being. Which makes me feel mighty lonely in present company, believe you me."

Hatch sighed, returning his attention to the black folders. The second contained the brief biography of Ockham, given him by St. John. Leaning back once again to let the moonlight catch the pages, he began to read.

EXTRACT FOLLOWS

Document Number: T14–A–41298
Spool: 14049
Logical Unit: LU–48
Research associate: T. T. Ferrell
Extract requested by: C. St. John

COPY 001 OF 003

EDWARD OCKHAM SUMMARY BIOGRAPHY

T. T. Ferrell, Thalassa—Shreveport

1   Edward Ockham was born in 1662 in Cornwall, England, the son of minor landed nobility. He was educated at Harrow and went on to spend two years at Balliol College, Oxford, before being sent down by the college dons for unspecified infractions.

His family desired him to pursue a naval career, and in 1682 Ockham received his commission and shipped as a lieutenant with the Mediterranean fleet under Admiral Poynton. Rising
10   quickly and distinguishing himself in several actions against the Spanish, he left the navy to become captain of a privateer, having been granted a letter of marque from the British Admiralty.

After a number of choice prizes, Ockham apparently decided that he no longer wished to share his spoils with the crown. Early in 1685 he took up slaving, running ships from Africa's Guinea Coast to Guadeloupe in the Windward Islands. After almost two years of profitable
20   voyages, Ockham was trapped within a blockaded harbor by two ships of the line. As a diversion, Ockham set his ship afire and got away in a small cutter. Before escaping, however, he put all the slaves on deck to the sword. The rest of the four hundred slaves, shackled together in the hold, perished in the blaze. Docu-

mentary evidence attributes the nickname of
"Red Ned" Ockham to this deed.

Five of Ockham's crew were captured and returned to London, where they were hung at Ex-
30   ecution Dock in Wapping. Ockham, however,
escaped to the infamous pirate haven of Port
Royal in the Caribbean, where he joined the
"Brethren of the Coast" in 1687. *[Cf. Thalassa
document P6-B19-110292, Pirate Treasures of
Port Royal (Reputed)]*

Over the next ten years, Ockham became known
as the most ruthless, venal, and ambitious pirate
operating in the waters off the New World.
Many notorious pirate techniques—such as
40   walking the plank, use of the skull and
crossbones to strike fear into the hearts of ad-
versaries, and *rescate* (ransoming of civilian
prisoners)—can be traced to his innovations.
When attacking towns or ships, he was quick to
use torture on any and all in order to ascertain
where plunder might be hidden. Imposing both
physically and intellectually, Ockham was one
of the few pirate captains to demand—and be
granted—a much larger share of the spoils than
his crew.

50   During his reign as pirate captain, Ockham won
his victories with a rare blend of psychology,
tactics, and ruthlessness. When attacking the
heavily fortified Spanish city of Portobello, for
example, he forced the nuns from a nearby
abbey to place the siege engines and ladders

themselves, reasoning that the strong Catholicism of the Spaniards would constrain them from firing. His weapon of choice became the musketoon, a short-barreled weapon that fired a lethal spray of lead pellets. Frequently, under pretense of a parley, he would gather the town fathers of a besieged city or the commanding officers of an opposing ship before him. Then—raising the weapons in both hands—he would destroy the group with a double blast.

As his thirst for prizes grew stronger, Ockham's brazenness grew proportionately. In 1691 he tried an overland siege of Panama City, which ultimately failed. While retreating across the Chagres River, he saw a galleon in the nearby bay, heading for the open sea and Spain. When he learned that the ship was carrying three million pieces of eight, Ockham reputedly swore never to let another galleon escape his grasp.

In the years that followed, Ockham turned his attention ever more strongly toward Spanish gold, the towns that hoarded it, and the ships that carried it. So adept did he become at anticipating the shipments of gold that some scholars believe he was able to crack the ciphers of Spanish captains and envoys *[Cf. Thalassa restricted document Z-A4-050997]*. In a single month's plundering spree of Spanish settlements in the fall of 1693, each of Ockham's eight hundred crew received six hundred pieces of eight as their share of the booty.

As Ockham became more powerful and more feared, his sadistic tendencies seemed to gain ascendency. Reports of barbarous cruelty became legion. Frequently, after overwhelming a ship, he would cut off the ears of the officers, sprinkle them with salt and vinegar, and force the victims to consume them. Rather than keep his men in check when despoiling a town, he would instead whip them into a lustful fury and then let them loose upon the helpless populace, reveling in the acts of violence and abandon that resulted. When victims could not provide him with the ransom he demanded, he would order them to be roasted slowly on wooden spits, or disemboweled with heated boathooks.

Ockham's single greatest accomplishment came in 1695, when his small armada of ships successfully captured, plundered, and sank the Spanish *flota de plata* bound for Cadiz. The sheer volume of treasure he acquired—in gold bars and cakes, silver wedges and pigs, undrilled pearls, and jewels—has been estimated at over a billion dollars in face value alone.

Ockham's eventual fate remains a mystery. In 1697, his command ship was found off the Azores, drifting free, all hands dead of an unknown affliction. No treasure was found on board, and scholars of the period agree he had concealed it along the east coast of the New World sometime shortly before his death. Although many legends of varying credibility have arisen, the strongest evidence points to one of three potential sites: Île à Vache off Hispaniola; South Carolina's Isle of Palms; or Ragged Island, off the Maine Coast, seventy miles north of Monhegan.

PRINTOUT ENDS
SPOOL TIME: 001:02
TOTAL BYTES: 15425

Hatch throttled down the diesels of the *Plain Jane*, then dropped anchor twenty yards off the lee shore of Ragged Island. It was 6:30, and the sun had just topped the sea horizon, throwing a gauzy gold light across the island. For the first time since Hatch had returned to Stormhaven, the island's protective mist had lifted completely. He clambered into the dinghy and motored toward the navy-issue prefabricated pier at Base Camp. Already the day was warm and humid, and there was a certain heaviness in the air that presaged bad weather.

As he gazed across the scene, his old apprehensions began to ease. Over the last forty-eight hours, Ragged Island had grown comfortably unrecognizable. An enormous amount of work had been accomplished, more than he could have believed possible. Yellow "crime scene" tape had been strung around the unstable areas of the island, with safe corridors delineated for walking. The meadows above the narrow strip of shingle beach had been transformed from a place of deserted silence to a miniature city. Trailers and Quonset huts were arranged in a tight circle. Beyond, a brace of massive generators thrummed, wafting diesel fumes into the air. Beside them sat two enormous fuel tanks. Bundles of white PVC pipe flowed across the muddy ground, shielding date lines and power cords from the elements and unwary feet. In the midst of the chaos stood Island One, the command center, a double-wide trailer festooned with communications gear and transmitters.

Securing the dinghy, Hatch jogged along the pier and up the rough path beyond. Arriving at Base Camp, he walked past the Stores shed and stepped into the Quonset hut marked MEDICAL, curious to see his new office. It was spartan but pleasant, smelling of fresh plywood, ethyl alcohol, and galvanized tin. He walked around, admiring the new equipment, surprised and pleased that Neidelman had purchased the best of everything. The office was fully equipped, from a locked storeroom full of equipment and drug cabinets to an EKG machine. Almost too equipped, in fact: Among the medical supplies in the lockers, Hatch found a colonoscope, a defibrillator, a fancy electronic Geiger counter, and a variety of expensive-looking high-tech gadgets he couldn't identify. The Quonset hut itself was larger than it looked. There was an outer office, an examination room, even a two-bed infirmary. In the rear of the structure was a small apartment, where Hatch could spend the night during inclement weather.

Stepping outside again, Hatch headed for Island One, carefully avoiding the ruts and furrows left behind by the treads of heavy equipment. Inside the command center, he found Neidelman, Streeter, and the engineer, Sandra Magnusen, bending over a screen. Magnusen was like a small, intense bug, her face blue in the outwash of the computer terminal, scrolling lines of data reflecting on her thick glasses. She seemed all business, all the time, and Hatch got the distinct feeling that she didn't like most people, doctors included.

Neidelman looked up and nodded. "Data transfer from Scylla finished several hours ago," he said. "Just completing the pump simulation now." He moved aside to give Hatch a view of the terminal.

```
SIMULATION COMPLETED AT 06:39:45:21
RESULTS FOLLOW
===================DIAGNOSTICS===================
INTERLINK SERVER STATUS                OK
HUB RELAYS                             OK
SECTOR RELAYS                          OK
DATASTREAM ANALYZER                    OK
CORE CONTROLLER                        OK
REMOTE SITES CONTROLLER                OK
PUMP STATUS                            OK
FLOW SENSORS                           OK
EMERGENCY INTERRUPT                    OK
QUEUE MEMORY                           305385295
PACKET DELAY                           .000045
===================CHECKSUM VERIFICATION===================
CHECKSUMS FROM REMOTES                 OK
CHECKSUM DEVIATION                     00.00000%
DEVIATION FROM SCYLLA                  00.15000%
DEVIATION FROM PRIOR                   00.37500%
END RESULTS
SIMULATION SUCCESSFUL
```

Magnusen's brow furrowed.

"Is everything all right?" Neidelman asked.

"Yes." The engineer sighed. "No. Well, I don't know. The computer seems to be acting flaky."

"Tell me about it," Neidelman said quietly.

"It's running a little sluggishly, especially when the emergency interrupts were tested. And look at those deviation numbers. The island network itself shows everything normal. But there's a deviation from the simulation that we ran on the *Cerberus* system. And there's even more of a deviation from the run we did last night."

"But it's within tolerances?"

Magnusen nodded. "It might be some anomaly in the checksum algorithms."

"That's a polite way of saying it's a bug." Neidelman turned to Streeter. "Where's Wopner?"

"Asleep on the *Cerberus*."

"Wake him up." Neidelman turned to Hatch and nodded toward the door. They walked out into the hazy sunlight.

There's something I'd like to show you," the Captain said. Without waiting for an answer, he set off at his usual terrific stride, his long legs sweeping through the grass, leaving a backwash of pipe smoke and confidence. Twice he was stopped by Thalassa employees, and he appeared to be directing several operations at once with cool precision. Hatch scrambled to keep up, barely having time to glance at all the changes around him. They were following a roped path, certified safe by the Thalassa surveyors. Here and there, short aluminum bridges spanned old pits and rotten areas of ground.

"Nice morning for a stroll," Hatch panted.

Neidelman smiled. "How do you like your office?"

"Everything's shipshape and Bristol fashion, thanks. I could service an entire village from it."

"In a sense, you're going to have to," came the reply.

The path climbed the island's incline toward the central hump of land, where most of the old shafts were clustered. Several aluminum platforms and small derricks had been placed over the muddy maws of shafts. Here, the main trail forked into several roped paths that wound around the ancient works. Nodding to a lone surveyor, Neidelman chose one of the central paths. A minute later, Hatch found himself standing at the edge of a gaping hole. Except for the presence of two engineers on the far side, taking measurements with an instrument Hatch didn't recognize, it seemed identical to a dozen other pits in the vicinity. Grass and bushes hung over the lip and sagged down into darkness, almost obscuring the edge of a rotting beam. Gingerly, Hatch leaned forward. Only blackness showed below. A flexible, metal-jointed hose of enormous circumference rose from the invisible depths, snaked across the muddy ground, and wound its way toward the distant western shore.

"It's a pit, all right," Hatch said. "Too bad I didn't bring along a picnic basket and a book of verses."

Neidelman smiled, removed a folded computer printout from his pocket, and handed it to Hatch. It consisted of a long column of dates, with numbers beside them. One of the pairs was highlighted in yellow: *1690±40*.

"The carbon 14 tests were completed at the *Cerberus*'s lab early this morning," Neidelman said. "Those are the results." He tapped his finger on the highlighted date.

Hatch took another look, then handed back the paper. "So what's it mean?"

"This is it," Neidelman said quietly.

There was a momentary silence. "The Water Pit?" Hatch heard the disbelief in his own voice.

Neidelman nodded. "The original. The wood used for the cribbing of this shaft was cut around 1690. All the other shafts date between 1800 and 1930. There can be no question. This is the Water Pit designed by Macallan and built by Ockham's crew." He pointed to another, smaller hole about thirty yards away. "And unless I'm mistaken, that's the

Boston Shaft, dug 150 years later. You can tell because of its gradual incline, after the initial drop."

"But you found the real Water Pit so quickly!" said Hatch, amazed. "Why didn't anyone else think of carbon dating?"

"The last person to dig on the island was your grandfather in the late forties. Carbon dating wasn't invented until the next decade. Just one of the many technological advantages we'll be bringing to bear in the coming days." He waved his hand over the Pit. "We'll begin construction of Orthanc this afternoon. Its components are already down at the supplies dock, waiting for reassembly."

Hatch frowned. "Orthanc?"

Neidelman laughed. "It's something we created for a salvage job in Corfu last year. A glass-floored observation post built atop a large derrick. Somebody on last year's team was a Tolkien fanatic, and the nickname stuck. It's fitted with winches and remote sensing gear. We'll be able to look right down the throat of the beast, literally and electronically."

"And what's this hose for?" Hatch asked, nodding toward the pit.

"This morning's dye test. That hose is connected to a series of pumps on the west shore." Neidelman glanced at his watch. "In an hour or so, when the tide reaches the flood, we'll start pumping 10,000 gallons of seawater per minute through this hose into the Water Pit. Once a good flow is established, we'll drop a special, high-intensity dye. With the tide ebbing, the pumps will help push the dye down into Macallan's hidden flood tunnel, and back out to the ocean. Since we don't know which side of the island the dye will emerge on, we'll use both the *Naiad* and the *Grampus*, spotting on opposite sides of the island. All we have to do is keep an eye out for the place where the dye appears offshore, send divers to the spot, and seal the tunnel with explosives. With the seawater blocked, we can pump out the water and drain all the works. Macallan's pit will be defanged. By this time on Friday, you and I will be able to climb down in there with nothing more than a slicker and a pair of Wellingtons. Then we can make the final excavation of the treasure at our leisure."

Hatch opened his mouth, then shut it again with a shake of his head.

"What?" Neidelman said, an amused smile on his face, his pale eyes glittering gold in the rising sun.

"I don't know. Things are moving so fast, that's all."

Neidelman drew a deep breath and looked around at the workings spread across the island. "You said it yourself," he replied after a moment. "We don't have much time."

They stood for a moment in silence.

"We'd better get back," Neidelman said at last. "I've asked the *Naiad* to come pick you up. You'll be able to watch the dye test from its deck." The two men turned and headed back toward Base Camp.

"You've assembled a good crew," Hatch said, glancing down at the figures below them on the supply dock, moving in ordered precision.

"Yes," Neidelman murmured. "Eccentric, difficult at times, but all good people. I don't surround myself with yes-men—it's too dangerous in this business."

"That fellow Wopner is certainly a strange one. Reminds me of an obnoxious thirteen-year-old. Or some surgeons I've known. Is he really as good as he thinks he is?"

Neidelman smiled. "Remember that scandal in 1992, when every retiree in a certain Brooklyn zip code got two extra zeros added to the end of their social security checks?"

"Vaguely."

"That was Kerry. Did three years in Allenwood as a result. But he's kind of sensitive about it, so avoid any jailbird jokes."

Hatch whistled. "Jesus."

"And he's as good a cryptanalyst as he is a hacker. If it

wasn't for those on-line role-playing games he refuses to abandon, he'd be a perfect worker. Don't let his personality throw you. He's a good man."

They were approaching Base Camp, and as if on cue Hatch could hear Wopner's querulous voice floating out of Island One. "You woke me up because you had a *feeling*? I ran that program a hundred times on Scylla and it was perfect. *Perfect*. A simple program for simple people. All it does is run those stupid pumps."

Magnusen's answer was lost in the rumble of the *Naiad*'s engine as it slid into the slip at the end of the dock. Hatch ran to get his medical kit, then jumped aboard the powerful twin-engine outboard. Beyond lay its sister, the *Grampus*, waiting to pick up Neidelman and assume its position on the far side of the island.

Hatch was sorry to see Streeter at the helm of the *Naiad*, expressionless and severe as a granite bust. He nodded and flashed what he hoped was a friendly smile, getting a curt nod in return. Hatch wondered briefly if he had made an enemy, then dismissed the thought. Streeter seemed like a professional; that was what counted. If he was still sore about what happened during the emergency, it was his problem.

Forward, in the half-cabin, two divers were checking their gear. The dye would not stay on the surface for long, and they'd have to act quickly to find the underwater flood tunnel. The geologist, Rankin, was standing beside Streeter. On seeing Hatch he grinned and strode over, crushing Hatch's hand in a great hairy paw.

"Hey, Dr. Hatch!" he said, white teeth flashing through an enormous beard, his long brown hair plaited behind. "Man, this is one fascinating island you've got."

Hatch had already heard several variants of this remark from other Thalassa employees. "Well, I guess that's why we're all here," he answered with a smile.

"No, no. I mean *geologically*."

"Really? I always thought it was like the others, just a big granite rock in the ocean."

Rankin dug into a pocket of his rain vest and pulled out what looked like a handful of granola. "Hell, no." He munched. "Granite? It's biotite schist, highly metamorphosed, checked, and faulted to an incredible degree. And with a drumlin on top. Wild, man, just wild."

"Drumlin?"

"A really weird kind of glacial hill, pointed at one side and tapered at the other. No one knows how they form, but if I didn't know better I'd say—"

"Divers, get ready," came Neidelman's voice over the radio. "All stations, check in, by the numbers."

"Monitoring station, roger," squawked the voice of Magnusen.

"Computer station, roger," said Wopner, sounding bored and annoyed even over the radio.

"Spotter alpha, roger."

"Spotter beta, roger."

"Spotter gamma, roger."

"*Naiad*, roger," Streeter spoke into the radio.

"*Grampus* affirms," came Neidelman's voice. "Proceed to position."

As the *Naiad* picked up speed beneath him, Hatch checked his watch: 8:20. The tide would turn shortly. As he stowed his medical kit, the two divers came out of the cabin, laughing at some private joke. One was a man, tall and slender, with a black mustache. He wore a wetsuit of thin neoprene so tight it left no anatomical feature to the imagination.

The other, a woman, turned and saw Hatch. A playful smile appeared on her lips. "Ah! You are the mysterious doctor?"

"I didn't know I was mysterious," said Hatch.

"But this is the dreaded Island of Dr. Hatch, *non*?" she

said pointing, with a peal of laughter. "I hope you will not be hurt if I avoid your services."

"I hope you avoid them too," said Hatch, trying to think of something less inane to say. Drops of water glistened on her olive skin, and her hazel eyes sparkled with little flecks of gold. She couldn't be more than twenty-five, Hatch decided. Her accent was exotic—French, with a touch of the islands thrown in.

"I am Isobel Bonterre," she said, pulling off her neoprene glove and holding out her hand. Hatch took it. It was cool and wet.

"What a hot hand you have!" she cried.

"The pleasure is mine," Hatch replied belatedly.

"And you are the brilliant Harvard doctor that Gerard has been talking about," she said, gazing into his face. "He likes you very much, you know."

Hatch found himself blushing. "Glad to hear it." He had never really thought about whether Neidelman liked him, but he found himself unaccountably pleased to hear it. He caught, just out of the corner of his eye, a glance of hatred from Streeter.

"I am glad you are aboard. It saves me the trouble of tracking you down."

Hatch frowned his lack of understanding.

"I will be locating the old pirate encampment, excavating it." She gave him a shrewd look. "You own this island, *non*? Where would you camp, if you had to spend three months on it?"

Hatch thought for a moment. "Originally, the island was heavily wooded in spruce and oak. I imagine they would have cut a clearing on the leeward side of the island. On the shore, near where their boats were moored."

"The lee shore? But would that not mean they could be seen from the mainland on clear days?"

"Well, I suppose so, yes. This coast was already settled in 1696, though sparsely."

"And they would need to keep watch on the windward shore, *n'est-ce pas*? For any shipping that might chance on them."

"Yes, that's right," Hatch said, secretly nettled. *If she knows all the answers, then why is she asking me?* "The main shipping route between Halifax and Boston went right past here, across the Gulf of Maine." He paused. "But if this coast was settled, how would they have hidden nine ships?"

"I too thought of that question. There is a very deep harbor two miles up the coast, shielded by an island."

"Black Harbor," said Hatch.

"Exactement."

"That makes sense," Hatch replied. "Black Harbor wasn't settled until the mid seventeen hundreds. The work crew and Macallan could have lived on the island, while the ships sheltered unseen in the harbor."

"The windward side, then!" Bonterre said. "You've been most helpful. Now I must get ready." Any lingering annoyance Hatch felt melted away under the archaeologist's dazzling smile. She balled up her hair and slid the hood over it, then donned her mask. The other diver sidled over to adjust her tanks, introducing himself as Sergio Scopatti.

Bonterre glanced up and down the man's suit appraisingly, as if seeing it for the first time. *"Grande merde du noir,"* she muttered fervently. "I did not know Speedo made wetsuits."

"Italians make everything fashionable," Scopatti laughed. "And *molto svelta.*"

"How's my video working?" Bonterre called over her shoulder to Streeter, tapping a small camera mounted on her mask.

Streeter ran his hand down a bank of switches and a video

screen popped to life on the control console, showing the jiggling, grinning face of Scopatti.

"Look somewhere else," said Scopatti to Bonterre, "or you'll break your camera."

"I shall look at the doctor then," said Bonterre, and Hatch saw his own face appear on the screen.

"That wouldn't just break the camera, it would implode the lens," Hatch said, wondering why this woman kept him at a loss for words.

"Next time, *I* get the comm set," said Scopatti, in a joking whine.

"Never," said Bonterre. "I am the famous archaeologist. You are just cheap hired Italian labor."

Scopatti grinned, not at all put out.

Neidelman's voice broke in: "Five minutes to the turn of the tide. Is the *Naiad* in position?"

Streeter acknowledged.

"Mr. Wopner, is the program running properly?"

"No problemo, Captain," came the nasal voice over the channel. "Running fine now. Now that I'm here, I mean."

"Understood. Dr. Magnusen?"

"The pumps are primed and ready to go, Captain. The crew reports that the dye bomb is suspended over the Water Pit, and the remote's in place."

"Excellent. Dr. Magnusen, you'll drop the bomb on my signal."

The people on the *Naiad* fell silent. A pair of guillemots whirred past, flying just above the surface of the water. On the far side of the island, Hatch could make out the *Grampus*, riding the even swell just beyond the ledges. The air of excitement, of something about to happen, increased.

"Mean high tide," came Neidelman's quiet voice. "Start the pumps."

The throb of the pumps came rumbling across the water.

As if in response, the island groaned and coughed with the reversal of the tide. Hatch shuddered involuntarily; if there was one thing that still gave him a shiver of horror, it was that sound.

"Pumps at ten," came Magnusen's voice.

"Keep it steady. Mr. Wopner?"

"Charybdis responding normally, Captain. All systems within normal tolerances."

"Very well," said Neidelman. "Let's proceed. *Naiad*, are you ready?"

"Affirmative," said Streeter into the mike.

"Hold steady and keep an eye out for the spot where the dye appears. Spotters ready?"

There was another chorus of *ayes*. Looking toward the island, Hatch could see several teams ranged along the bluffs with binoculars.

"First one who spots the dye gets a bonus. All right, release the dye bomb."

There was a momentary silence, then a faint *crump* sounded from the vicinity of the Water Pit.

"Dye released," said Magnusen.

All hands peered across the gently undulating surface of the ocean. The water had a dark, almost black, color, but there was no wind and only the faintest chop, making conditions ideal. Despite the growing rip current, Streeter kept the boat stationary with an expert handling of the throttles. A minute passed, and another, the only sound the throb of the pumps pouring sea-water into the Water Pit, driving the dye down into the heart of the island and out to sea. Bonterre and Scopatti waited in the stern, silent and alert.

"*Dye at twenty-two degrees,*" came the urgent voice of one of the spotters on the island. "*One hundred forty feet off-shore.*"

"*Naiad*, that's your quadrant," said Neidelman. "The

Grampus will come over to assist. Well done!" A small cheer erupted over the frequency.

That's the spot I saw the whirlpool, Hatch thought.

Streeter swung the boat around, gunning the engine, and in a moment Hatch could see a light spot on the ocean about three hundred yards away. Both Bonterre and Sergio had their masks and regulators in place and were already at the gunwales, bolt guns in their hands and buoys at their belts, ready to go over the side.

"*Dye at 297 degrees, one hundred feet offshore,*" came the voice of another spotter, cutting through the cheering.

"What?" came Neidelman's voice. "You mean to say that dye is appearing in *another* place?"

"Affirmative, Captain."

There was a moment of shocked silence. "Looks like we've got two flood tunnels to seal," said Neidelman. "The *Grampus* will mark the second. Let's go."

The *Naiad* was closing in on the swirl of yellow dye breaking the surface just inside the reefs. Streeter cut the throttle and sent the boat in a circling idle as the divers went over the side. Hatch turned eagerly to the screens, shoulder-to-shoulder with Rankin. At first the video image consisted only of clouds of yellow dye. Then the picture cleared. A large, rough crack appeared at the murky bottom of the reef, dye jetting out of it like smoke.

"*Le voilà!*" came Bonterre's excited voice over the comm channel. The image jiggled wildly as she swam toward the crack, shot a small explosive bolt into the rock nearby, and attached an inflatable buoy. It bobbed upward and Hatch looked over the rail in time to see it surface, a small solar cell and antenna bobbing at its top. "Marked!" said Bonterre. "Preparing to set charges."

"Look at that," breathed Rankin, swiveling his gaze from the video to the sonar and back again. "A radiating fault pattern. All they had to do was tunnel along existing fractures in the rock. Still, incredibly advanced for seventeenth-century construction—"

"Dye at five degrees, ninety feet offshore," came another call.

"Are you certain?" Disbelief mixed with uncertainty in Neidelman's voice. "Okay, we've got a third tunnel. *Naiad,* it's yours. Spotters, for God's sake keep your scopes trained in case the dye spreads before we can get to it."

"More dye! Three hundred thirty-two degrees, seventy feet offshore."

And then the first voice again: *"Dye appearing at eighty-five degrees, I repeat, eighty-five degrees, forty feet offshore."*

"We'll take the one at 332," said Neidelman, a strange tone creeping into his voice. "Just how many tunnels did this bloody architect build? Streeter, that makes two for you to deal with. Get your divers up as soon as possible. Just mark the exits for now and we'll set the plastique later. We've only got five minutes before that dye dissipates."

In another moment Bonterre and Scopatti were up and in the boat, and without a word Streeter spun the wheel and took off at a roar. Now Hatch could see another cloud of yellow dye boiling to the surface. The boat circled as Bonterre and Scopatti went over the side. Soon another buoy had popped up; the divers emerged, and the *Naiad* moved to the spot where the third cloud of dye was appearing. Again Bonterre and Scopatti went over the side, and Hatch turned his attention to the video screen.

Scopatti swam ahead, his form visible on Bonterre's headset, a ghostly figure among the billowing clouds of dye. They were already deeper than at any point on the first two dives. Suddenly, the jagged rocks at the bottom of the reef became visible, along with a square opening, much larger than the others, through which the last tendrils of dye were now drifting.

"What's this?" Hatch heard Bonterre say in a voice of disbelief. "Sergio, *attends*!"

Suddenly Wopner's voice crackled over the radio. "Got a problem, Captain."

"What is it?" Neidelman responded.

"Dunno. I'm getting error messages, but the system reports normal function."

"Switch to the redundant system."

"I'm doing that, but . . . Wait, now the hub's getting . . . Oh, shit."

"What?" came Neidelman's sharp voice.

At the same time Hatch heard the sound of the pumps on the island faltering.

"System crash," said Wopner.

There was a sudden, sharp, garbled noise from Bonterre. Hatch glanced toward the video screen and saw it had gone dead. *No*, he corrected himself: not dead, but *black*. And then snow began to creep into the blackness until the signal was lost in a howling storm of electronic distortion.

"What the hell?" Streeter said, frantically punching the comm button. "Bonterre, can you hear me? We've lost your feed. *Bonterre!*"

Scopatti broke the surface ten feet from the boat and tore the regulator from his mouth. "Bonterre's been sucked into the tunnel!" he gasped.

"What was that?" Neidelman cried over the radio.

"He said, Bonterre's been sucked—" Streeter began.

"Goddammit, go back after her!" Neidelman barked, his electronic voice rasping across the water.

"It's murder down there!" Scopatti yelled. "There's a massive backcurrent, and—"

"Streeter, give him a lifeline!" Neidelman called. "And

Magnusen, bypass that computer control, get the pumps started manually. Losing them must have created some kind of backflow."

"Yes, sir," said Magnusen. "The team will have to reprime them by hand. I'll need at least five minutes, minimum."

"Run," came Neidelman's voice, hard but suddenly calm. "And do it in three."

"Yes, sir."

"And Wopner, get the system on-line."

"Captain," Wopner began, "the diagnostics are telling me that everything's—"

"Stop talking," snapped Neidelman. "Start fixing."

Scopatti clipped a lifeline around his belt and disappeared again over the side.

"I'm clearing this area," Hatch said to Streeter as he began to spread towels over the deck to receive his potential patient.

Streeter played the lifeline out, helped by Rankin. There was a sudden tug, then steady tension.

"Streeter?" came Neidelman's voice.

"Scopatti's in the backflow," said Streeter. "I can feel him on the line."

Hatch stared at the snow on the screen with a macabre sense of déjà vu. It was as if she had disappeared, vanished, just as suddenly as . . .

He took a deep breath and looked away. There was nothing he could do until they got her to the surface. Nothing.

Suddenly there was a noise from the island as the pumps roared into life.

"Good work," came Neidelman's voice from the comm set.

"Line's gone slack," said Streeter.

There was a tense silence. Hatch could see the last bits of dye boiling off as the flow came back out the tunnel. And suddenly the video screen went black again, and then he heard gasping over the audio line. The black on the screen grew lighter until, with a flood of relief, he saw a green square of light growing across the screen: the exit to the flood tunnel.

"Merde," came Bonterre's voice as she was ejected from the opening, the view from the camera tumbling wildly.

Moments later, there was a swirl at the surface. Hatch and Rankin rushed to the side of the boat and lifted Bonterre aboard. Scopatti followed, stripping off her tanks and hood as Hatch laid her down on the towels.

Opening her mouth, Hatch checked the airway: all clear. He unzipped her wetsuit at the chest and placed a stethoscope. She was breathing well, no sound of water in the lungs, and her heartbeat was fast and strong. He noticed a gash in the suit along her stomach, skin and a ribbon of blood swelling along its edge.

"Incroyable," Bonterre coughed, trying to sit up, waving a chip of something gray.

"Keep still," Hatch said sharply.

"Cement!" she cried, clutching the chip. "Three-hundred-year-old cement! There was a row of stones set into the reef—"

Hatch felt quickly around the base of her skull, looking for evidence of a concussion or spinal injury. There were no swellings, cuts, dislocations.

"Ça suffit!" she said, turning her head. "What are you, a *phrénologiste?*"

"Streeter, report!" Neidelman barked over the radio.

"They're aboard, sir," Streeter said. "Bonterre seems to be fine."

"I *am* fine, except for this meddlesome doctor!" she cried, struggling.

"Just a moment while I look at your stomach," Hatch said, gently restraining her.

"Those stones, they looked like the foundation to some- thing," she continued, lying back. "Sergio, did you see that? What could it be?"

With a single movement, Hatch unzipped the wetsuit down to her navel.

"Hey!" cried Bonterre.

Ignoring the outcry, Hatch quickly explored the cut. There was a nasty scrape below her ribs, but it seemed superficial along its entire length.

"It is just a scratch," protested Bonterre, craning her neck to see what Hatch was doing.

He snatched his hand from her belly as a distinctly un- professional stirring coursed through his loins. "Perhaps you're right," he said a little more sarcastically than he in- tended, fishing in his bag for a topical antibiotic ointment. "Next time let me play in the water, and you can be the doc- tor. Meanwhile, I'm going to apply some of this anyway, in case of infection. You had a close call." He rubbed ointment into the scrape.

"That tickles," said Bonterre.

Scopatti had stripped off his suit to the waist, and stood with his arms crossed, his tanned physique gleaming in the sun, grinning fondly. Rankin stood next to him, hirsute and massive, watching Bonterre with a distinct gleam in his eyes. *Everyone,* thought Malin, *is in love with this woman.*

"I ended up in a big underwater cavern," she was saying. "For a moment I couldn't find the walls, and I thought that was the end. *Fin.*"

"A cavern?" Neidelman asked doubtfully over the open channel.

"*Mais oui.* A big cavern. But my radio was dead. Why would that be?"

"The tunnel must have blocked the transmission," Neidel- man said.

"But why the backcurrent?" Bonterre said. "The tide was going out."

There was a brief silence. "I don't have an answer to that," Neidelman's voice came at last. "Perhaps once we've drained the Pit and its tunnels, we'll learn why. I'll be waiting for a full report. Meanwhile, why don't you rest? *Grampus* out."

Streeter turned. "Markers set. Returning to base."

The boat rumbled to life and planed across the water, riding the gentle swells. Hatch stowed his gear, listening to the chatter on the radio bands. Neidelman, on the *Grampus*, was talking to Island One.

"I'm telling you, we've got a cybergeist," came the voice of Wopner. "I just did a ROM dump on Charybdis, and ran it against Scylla. Everything's messed up nine ways to Sunday. But that's burned-in code, Captain. The goddamn system's cursed. Not even a hacker could rewrite ROM—"

"Don't start talking about curses," said Neidelman sharply.

As they approached the dock, Bonterre peeled off her wetsuit, packed it into a deck locker, wrung out her hair, and turned toward Hatch. "Well, Doctor, my nightmare came true. I did need your services, after all."

"It was nothing," said Hatch, blushing and furiously aware of it.

"Oh, but it was very nice."

16

The stone ruins of Fort Blacklock stood in a meadow looking down on the entrance to Stormhaven harbor. The circular fort was surrounded by a large meadow dotted with white pines, which fell away to farmers' fields and a "sugarbush," a thick stand of sugar maples. Across the meadow from the old fort a large yellow-and-white pavilion had been erected, decorated with ribbons and pennants that fluttered merrily in the breeze. A banner over the pavilion proclaimed in hand-painted letters: 71ST ANNUAL STORMHAVEN LOBSTER BAKE!!!

Hatch headed apprehensively up the gentle slope of the grassy hill. The lobster bake was the first real opportunity for him to meet the town at large, and he wasn't at all sure what kind of reception to expect. But there was little doubt in his mind about what kind of reception the expedition itself would receive.

Although Thalassa had been in Stormhaven little more than a week, the company's impact had been considerable. Crew members had taken most of the available rental houses and spare rooms, sometimes paying premium prices. They had filled the tiny bed-and-breakfast. The two restaurants in town, Anchors Away and The Landing, were packed every night. The gas station at the wharf had been forced to triple its deliveries, and business at the Superette—though Bud would never admit to it—was up at least fifty percent. The town was in such a fine mood about the Ragged Island treasure hunt that the mayor had hastily made Thalassa the collective guest of honor at the lobster bake. And Neidelman's quietly picking up half the tab—at Hatch's suggestion—had simply been icing on the cake.

As he approached the pavilion, Hatch could make out the table of honor, already occupied by prominent town citizens and Thalassa officials. A small podium and microphone had been placed behind it. Beyond, townspeople and expedition members were milling around, drinking lemonade or beer, and lining up to get their lobsters.

As he ducked inside, he heard a familiar nasal shout. Kerry Wopner was carrying a paper plate groaning under the weight of twin lobsters, potato salad, and corn on the cob. A huge draft beer was balanced in his other hand. The cryptanalyst walked gingerly along, arms straight ahead, trying to keep the food and beer from dripping on his trademark Hawaiian shirt, Bermuda shorts, high white socks, and black sneakers.

"How do you eat these things?" Wopner cried, buttonholing a confused lobsterman.

"What's that?" the lobsterman said, inclining his head as if he hadn't heard properly.

"We didn't have lobsters where I grew up."

"No lobsters?" the man said, as if considering this.

"Yeah. In Brooklyn. It's part of America. You should visit the country some time. Anyway, I never learned how to eat one." Wopner's loud drawl echoed up and down the pavilion. "I mean, how do you open the shells?"

With a stolid face, the lobsterman replied. "You sit on 'em real hard."

There was a guffaw of laughter from nearby townspeople.

"Very funny," said Wopner.

"Well, now," the lobsterman said in a gentler tone. "You need crackers."

"I got crackers," Wopner replied eagerly, waving the plate heaped with oyster crackers under the man's nose. There was another round of laughter from the locals.

"Crackers to crack the shells, see?" the lobsterman said. "Or you can use a hammer." He held up a boat hammer, covered with lobster juice, tomalley, and bits of pink shell.

"Eat with a dirty hammer?" Wopner cried. "Hepatitis city, here we come."

Hatch moved in. "I'll give him a hand," he said to the lobsterman, who went off shaking his head. Hatch ushered Wopner to one of the tables, sat him down, and gave him a quick lesson in lobster consumption: how to crack open the shells, what to eat, what not to eat. Then he went off to get some food himself, stopping along the way to fill a pint cup at an enormous keg. The beer, from a small brewery in Camden, was cold and malty; he gulped it down, feeling the tightness in his chest unraveling, and refilled the cup before getting in line.

The lobsters and corn had been steamed in piles of seaweed heaped over burning oak, sending clouds of fragrant smoke spiraling into the blue sky. Three cooks were busily at work behind the mounds of seaweed, checking the fires, dumping bright red lobsters onto paper plates.

"Dr. Hatch!" came a voice. Hatch turned to see Doris Bowditch, another splendid muumuu billowing behind her like a purple parachute. Her husband stood to one side, small, razor-burned, and silent. "How did you find the house?"

"Wonderful," said Hatch with genuine warmth. "Thanks for tuning the piano."

"You're certainly welcome. No problems with the power or the water, I expect? Good. You know, I wondered if you'd had a chance to think about that nice couple from Manchester—"

"Yes," said Hatch quickly, ready now. "I won't be selling."

"Oh," said Doris, her face falling. "They were *so* counting on—"

"Yes, but Doris, it's the house I *grew up in*," Hatch said gently but firmly.

The woman gave a start, as if remembering the circumstances of Hatch's childhood and departure from the town. "Of course," she said, with an attempt at a smile, laying her hand on his arm. "I understand. It's hard to give up the family home. We'll say no more about it." She gave his arm a squeeze. "For now."

Hatch reached the front of the line, and turned his attention to the enormous, steaming piles of seaweed. The nearest cook flipped over one of the piles, exposing a row of red lobsters, some ears of corn, and a scattering of eggs. He picked up an egg with a mitted hand, chopped it in half with a knife, and peered inside to see if it was hard. That, Hatch remembered, was how they judged when the lobsters were cooked.

"Perfecto!" the cook said. The voice was distantly familiar, and Hatch suddenly recognized his old high-school classmate Donny Truitt. He braced himself.

"Why, if it ain't Mally Hatch!" said Truitt, recognizing him. "I was wondering when I'd run into you. Damn it to hell, how are you?"

"Donny," Hatch cried, grasping his hand. "I'm not bad. You?"

"The same. Four kids. Looking for a new job since Martin's Marine went under."

"Four kids?" Hatch whistled. "You've been busy."

"Busier than you think. Divorced twice, too. What the hell. You hitched?"

"Not yet," Hatch said.

Donny smirked. "Seen Claire yet?"

"No." Hatch felt a sudden swell of irritation.

As Donny slipped a lobster onto his plate, Hatch looked at his old classmate. He'd grown paunchy, a little slow. But otherwise, they'd picked up right where they left off, twenty-five years before. The talkative kid with few brains but a big heart had obviously grown up into the adult equivalent.

Donny gave Hatch a suggestive leer.

"Come on, Donny," Hatch said. "Claire and I were just friends."

"Oh, yeah. Friends. I didn't think *friends* were caught kissing in Squeaker's Glen. It *was* just kissing, Mal . . . wasn't it?"

"That was a long time ago. I don't remember every detail of my every romance."

"Nothing like first love, though, eh, Mal?" Donny chuckled, one goggle eye winking below the mop of carrot-colored hair. "She's around here somewhere. Anyway, you'll have to look elsewhere, 'cause she ended up—"

Suddenly Hatch had heard enough about Claire. "I'm holding up the line," he interrupted.

"You sure are. I'll see you later." Donny waved his fork with another grin, expertly flipping open more layers of seaweed to expose another row of gleaming red lobsters.

So Donny needs a job, Hatch thought as he headed back toward the table of honor. *Wouldn't hurt for Thalassa to hire a few locals.*

He found a seat at the table between Bill Banns, the editor of the paper, and Bud Rowell. Captain Neidelman was two seats down, next to Mayor Jasper Fitzgerald and the local Congregational minister, Woody Clay. On the far side of Clay sat Lyle Streeter.

Hatch looked at the two locals curiously. Jasper Fitzgerald's father had run the local funeral home, and no doubt the son had inherited it. Fitzgerald was in his early fifties, a florid man with handlebar mustaches, alligator-clip suspenders, and a baritone voice that carried like a contrabassoon.

Hatch's eyes traveled to Woody Clay. *He's obviously an outsider,* he thought. Clay was, in almost every way, the opposite of Fitzgerald. He had the spare frame of an ascetic, coupled with the hollow, spiritual face of a saint just in from the desert. But there was also a crabbed, narrow intensity to his gaze. Hatch could see he was ill at ease being part of the table of honor; he was one of those people who spoke to you in a low voice, as if he didn't want anyone else to overhear, evident from his low-pitched conversation with Streeter. Hatch wondered what the minister was saying that was making the team leader look so uncomfortable.

"Seen the paper, Malin?" Bill Banns interrupted Hatch's thoughts with his characteristic lazy drawl. As a young man, Banns had seen *The Front Page* at the local cinema. Ever since, his views of what a newsman should look like had never altered. His sleeves were always rolled, even on the coldest day, and he'd worn a green visor so long that today his forehead seemed lonely without it.

"No, I haven't," Hatch replied. "I didn't know it was out."

"Just this morning," Banns answered. "Yup, think you'll like it. Wrote the lead article myself. With your help, of course." He touched a finger to his nose, as if to say, *you keep me in the pipeline, and I'll keep the good words flow-*

ing. Hatch made a mental note to stop by the Superette that evening for a copy.

Various instruments for lobster dissection lay on the table: hammers, crackers, and wooden mallets, all slick with lobster gore. Two great bowls in the center were heaped with broken shells and split carapaces. Everyone was pounding, cracking, and eating. Glancing around the pavilion, Hatch could see that Wopner had somehow ended up at the table with the workers from the local Lobsterman's Co-op. He could just catch Wopner's abrasive voice drifting on the wind. "Did you know," the cryptanalyst was saying, "that, biologically speaking, lobsters are basically insects? When you really get down to it, they're big red underwater cockroaches. . . ."

Hatch turned away and took another generous pull on his beer. This was turning out to be bearable, after all; perhaps more than bearable. He was sure that everyone in town knew his story, word for word. Yet—perhaps out of politeness, perhaps out of pure rural bashfulness—not a word had been said. For that, he was grateful.

He looked across the crowd, scanning for familiar faces. He saw Christopher St. John, sandwiched at a table between two overweight locals, apparently contemplating how to dismantle his lobster while making the least degree of mess. Hatch's eyes roved farther, and he picked out Kai Estenson, proprietor of the hardware store, and Tyra Thompson, commandant of the Free Library, not looking a day older than when she used to shoo him and Johnny out of the building for telling jokes and giggling too loudly. *Guess it's true what they say about vinegar being a preservative,* he thought. Then, in a flash of recognition, he saw the white head and stooped shoulders of Dr. Horn, his old biology teacher, standing on the outskirts of the pavilion as if not deigning to soil his hands with lobster ruin. Dr. Horn, who'd graded him more toughly than any graduate school professor ever did; who told him he'd seen roadkill that was better dissected than the frogs Hatch worked on. The intimidating, yet fiercely supportive Dr. Horn, who more than any other person had fired Hatch's interest in science and medicine. Hatch was surprised and relieved to see him still among the living.

Looking away, Hatch turned toward Bud, who was sucking lobster meat out of a leg. "Tell me about Woody Clay," Hatch said.

Bud tossed the leg into the nearest bowl. "Reverend Clay? He's the minister. Used to be a hippie, I hear."

"Where'd he come from?" asked Hatch.

"Somewhere down around Boston. Came up here twenty years ago to do some preaching, decided to stay. They say he gave away a big inheritance when he took the cloth."

Bud sliced open the tail with an expert hand and extracted it in one piece. There was a hesitant note in his voice that puzzled Hatch.

"Why'd he stay?" Hatch asked.

"Oh, liked the place, prob'ly. You know how it goes." Bud fell silent as he polished off the tail.

Hatch glanced over at Clay, who was no longer talking to Streeter. As he examined the intense face curiously, the man suddenly looked up and met his gaze. Hatch looked away awkwardly, turning back toward Bud Rowell, only to find that the grocer had gone off in search of more lobster. Out of the corner of his eye he could see the minister rise from the table and approach.

"Malin Hatch?" the man said, extending his hand. "I'm Reverend Clay."

"Nice to meet you, Reverend." Hatch stood up and took the cold, tentative hand.

Clay hesitated a moment, then gestured at the empty chair. "May I?"

"If Bud doesn't mind, I don't," Hatch said.

The minister awkwardly eased his angular frame into the small chair, his bony knees sticking up almost to the level of the table, and turned a pair of large, intense eyes on Hatch.

"I've seen all the activity out at Ragged Island," he began in a low voice. "I've heard it, too. Banging and clanging, by night as well as by day."

"Guess we're a little like the post office," Hatch said, trying to sound lighthearted, uncertain of where this was heading. "We never sleep."

If Clay was amused, he didn't show it. "This operation must be costing somebody a good deal," he said, raising his eyebrows to make it a question.

"We've got investors," Hatch said.

"Investors," Clay repeated. "That's when somebody gives you ten dollars and hopes you'll give back twenty."

"You could put it that way."

Clay nodded. "My father loved money, too. Not that it made him a happier man, or prolonged his life by even an hour. When he died, I inherited his stocks and bonds. The accountant called it a portfolio. When I got to looking into it, I found tobacco companies, mining companies tearing open whole mountains, timber companies that were clear-cutting virgin forests."

As he spoke, his eyes never strayed from Hatch's. "I see," Hatch said at last.

"Here my father had given money to these people, hoping they'd give back twice as much. And that's just what had happened. They'd given back two, three, or four times more. And now all these immoral gains were mine."

Hatch nodded.

Clay lowered his head and his voice. "May I ask how much wealth, exactly, you and your investors hope to gain from all this?"

Something in the way the minister pronounced *wealth*

made Hatch more wary. But to refuse to answer the question would be a mistake. "Let's just say it's well into seven figures," he replied.

Clay nodded slowly. "I'm a direct man," he began. "And I'm not good at small talk. I never learned how to say things gracefully, so I just say them the best way I can. I don't like this treasure hunt."

"I'm sorry to hear that," Hatch replied.

Clay blinked back at him intently. "I don't like all these people coming into our town and throwing their money around."

From the beginning, Hatch had steeled himself against the possibility of such a response. Now that he was hearing it at last, he felt strangely relaxed. "I'm not sure that the other townspeople share your disdain of money," he said evenly. "Many of these people have been poor all their lives. They didn't have the luxury of choosing poverty, as you did."

Clay's face tightened, and Hatch could see he'd hit a nerve. "Money isn't the panacea people think it is," the minister continued. "You know that as well as I. These people have their dignity. Money will ruin this town. It'll spoil the lobstering, spoil the tranquility, spoil everything. And the poorest people won't see any of that money, anyway. They'll be pushed out by development. By *progress*."

Hatch did not reply. On one level, he understood what Clay was saying. It would be a tragedy if Stormhaven turned into another overdeveloped, overpriced summer playground like Boothbay Harbor, down the coast. But that didn't seem likely, whether or not Thalassa succeeded.

"There's not much I can say," Hatch said. "The operation will be over in a matter of weeks."

"How long it takes isn't the point," Clay said, a strident note entering his voice. "The point is the motivation behind it. This treasure hunt is about greed—pure, naked greed. Already, a man lost his legs. No good will come of this. That island is a bad place, cursed, if you care to call it that. I'm not superstitious, but God has a way of punishing those with impure motives."

Hatch's feeling of calm suddenly dissolved in a flood of anger. *Our town? Impure motives?* "If you'd grown up in this town, you'd know why I'm doing this," he snapped. "Don't presume to know what my motives are."

"I don't presume anything," Clay said, his lanky body stiffening like a spring. "I *know*. I may not have grown up in this town, but I at least know what's in its best interests. Everyone here's been seduced by this treasure hunt, by the promise of easy money. But not me, by the Lord God, not me. I'm going to protect this town. Protect it from you, and from itself."

"Reverend Clay, I think you should read your Bible before you start throwing around accusations like that: *Judge not, that ye be not judged.*"

Hatch realized he was shouting, voice shaking with anger. The surrounding tables had fallen silent, the people staring down at their plates. Abruptly he rose, strode past the silent, white-faced Clay, and made for the dark ruins of the fort across the meadow.

17

The fort was dark and chill with damp. Swallows flitted about the interior of the granite tower, whipping back and forth like bullets in the sunlight that angled sharply through the ancient gunports.

Hatch entered through the stone archway and paused, breathing heavily, trying to recover his composure. Despite himself, he'd allowed the minister to provoke him. Half the town had seen it, and the half that hadn't would soon know about it.

He took a seat on an outcropping of the stone foundation. No doubt Clay had been talking to others. Hatch doubted most people would listen, except perhaps the lobstermen. They could be a superstitious lot, and talk about curses might weigh heavily. And then that remark about the dig ruining the lobstering . . . Hatch just hoped it was going to be a good season.

Slowly he calmed down, letting the peace of the fort wash away his anger, listening to the faint clamor of the festival across the meadow. He really had to control himself better. The man was an obnoxious prig, but he wasn't worth flying off the handle over.

It was a tranquil, womblike space, and Hatch felt he could stay there, enjoying the coolness, for hours. But he knew he should be returning to the festival, putting up a nonchalant front, smoothing things over. In any case, he needed to be back before the inevitable speeches began. He stood up and turned to go, and saw with surprise a stooped figure waiting in the shadows of the archway. It stepped forward into a shaft of light.

"Professor Horn!" Hatch cried.

The man's canny old face crinkled with delight. "I wondered when you'd notice me," he said, advancing with his cane. He shook Hatch's hand warmly. "That was quite a little scene back there."

Hatch shook his head. "I lost my temper, like an idiot. What is it about that man that gets my goat?"

"No mystery there. Clay is awkward, socially inept, morally rigid. But beneath that bitter exterior there beats a heart as big and generous as the ocean. As violent and unknowable, too, I'll bet. He's a complex man, Malin; don't underestimate him." The professor grasped Hatch's shoulder. "Enough about the reverend. By God, Malin, you're looking well. I'm prodigiously proud of you. Harvard Medical School, research position at Mount Auburn. You were always a smart boy. Too bad it didn't always equate to being a good student."

"I owe a lot of it to you," Hatch said. He remembered afternoons in the professor's huge Victorian house in the back meadows—poring over his collections of rocks, beetles, and butterflies—in those last years before leaving Stormhaven.

"Nonsense. I still have your bird nest collection, by the way. Never knew where to send it after you left."

Hatch felt a twinge of guilt. It had never occurred to him that the august professor would have wanted to hear from him. "I'm surprised you didn't throw that junk away."

"Actually, it was a remarkably good collection." He shifted his hand to Hatch's arm and held it in a bony clasp. "See me out the fort and across the meadow, would you? I'm a little shaky on my wheels these days."

"I would have gotten in touch . . ." Hatch's voice trailed away.

"Not a word, not even a forwarding address," the professor said acidly. "Then I read about you in the *Globe* last year."

Hatch turned away, feeling shame burning his face.

The professor gave a gruff snort. "No matter. According to the actuarial tables I should be dead. I'll be eighty-nine next Thursday, and damn you if you don't bring me a present."

They emerged into the sunlight of the meadow. Voices raised in laughter drifted toward them on the breeze.

"You must have heard why I came back," Hatch said tentatively.

"Who hasn't?" was the tart reply. The professor offered nothing further, and they walked on in silence for a moment.

"So?" Hatch said at last.

The old man looked at him inquiringly.

"So drop the other shoe," Hatch continued. "What do you think of this treasure hunt?"

The professor walked on for a minute, then stopped and turned toward Malin, lowering his arm as he did so. "Remember, *you* asked," he said.

Hatch nodded.

"I think you're a goddamned fool."

There was a moment of stunned surprise. He'd been prepared for Clay, but not for this. "What makes you say that?"

"You, of all the people on this earth, should know better. Whatever's down there, you won't get it out."

"Look, Dr. Horn, we've got technology those old treasure hunters never even dreamed of. Hardbody sonar, proton magnetometers, a photoreconnaissance satellite downlink. We've got twenty million dollars in funding, and we even have the private journal of the man who designed the Pit." Hatch's voice had risen. He suddenly realized that it was very important for him to have this man's good opinion.

Dr. Horn shook his head. "Malin, for almost a century I've seen them come and go. Everyone had the latest equipment. Everyone had gobs of money. Everyone had some crucial piece of information, some brilliant insight. It was always going to be different. And they all ended up the same. Bankruptcy, misery, even death." He glanced at Hatch. "Have you found any treasure yet?"

"Well, not yet," Hatch said. "There's been one small problem. We knew that the Pit must have an underground flood tunnel leading to the sea, that's why it's always filled with water. We used dye to locate the flood tunnel's exit on the sea floor. Only, it seems there's not one flood tunnel, but five, and—"

"I see," Dr. Horn interrupted. "Just one small problem. I've heard that before, too. Maybe you'll solve your problem. Only then there will be another problem, and another, until you're all bankrupt. Or dead. Or both."

"But this *will* be different," Hatch cried. "You can't tell me it's impossible to raise the treasure. What man created, man can defeat."

The professor suddenly gripped Hatch's arm again. He had alarmingly strong hands, corded like ancient tree roots, sinewy and dry. "I knew your grandfather, Malin. He was a lot like you: young, smart as hell, promising career ahead of him, terrific enthusiasm for life. What you just said is exactly what he said to me, word for word, fifty years ago." He lowered his voice to a fierce whisper. "Look at the legacy he left your family. You asked my opinion. So here it is in a nutshell. Go back to Boston before history repeats itself."

He turned brusquely and hobbled off, his cane flicking irritably through the grass, until he had disappeared over the brow of the hill.

18

The next morning, a little bleary-eyed from the beer of the previous day, Hatch closeted himself in the medical hut, laying out instruments and taking inventory. There had been a number of injuries over the last several days, but nothing more serious than a few scrapes and a cracked rib. As he moved through his shelves, checking against a printed master list, he could hear the monotonous hiss of surf from the nearby reefs. The sun struggled wanly through the metal-sided window, attenuated by the omnipresent curtain of mist.

Finishing the inventory, Hatch hung his clipboard beside the shelves and glanced out the window. He could see the tall, slope-shouldered form of Christopher St. John, walking gingerly over the rough ground of Base Camp. The Englishman dodged a heavy cable and a length of PVC pipe, then ducked into Wopner's quarters, his unruly gray hair barely clearing the door frame. Hatch stood for a moment, then picked up the two black binders and exited the medical office, following the historian. Maybe there was some progress to report on the code.

Wopner's Base Camp office was, if anything, even more messy than his stateroom on the *Cerberus*. Small to begin with, banks of monitoring and servo control equipment made it claustrophobic. Wopner occupied the office's lone chair, crammed into a far corner by the relay racks that surrounded him. Cold air was blasting from two ducts overhead, and a massive air conditioner grumbled on the far side of the wall.

Despite the air-conditioning, the room was stuffy with hot electronics, and as Hatch walked in St. John was looking for a place to hang his jacket. His search unsuccessful, he laid it carefully on a nearby console.

"Jeez," said Wopner, "you lay your hairy old tweed there and it's gonna short-circuit the whole works."

Frowning, St. John picked it up again. "Kerry, do you have a minute?" he said. "We really need to discuss this problem with the code."

"Do I look like I have a minute?" came the response. Wopner leaned away from his terminal with a glare. "I've just now finished an all-island diagnostic. The whole ball of wax, right down to the microcode. Took an hour, even at maximum bandwidth. Everything checks out: pumps, compressors, servos, you name it. No problems or discrepancies of any kind."

"That's great," Hatch broke in.

Wopner looked at him incredulously. "Grow a brain, willya? Great? It's frigging terrible!"

"I don't understand."

"We had a system crash, remember? The goddamn pumps went south on us. Afterward, I compared the island computer system with Scylla over on the *Cerberus*, and guess what? The ROM chips on Charybdis, here, had been altered.

Altered!" He angrily smacked one of the CPUs upside its cabinet.

"And?"

"And now I run the diagnostics again, and everything's fine. Not only that, but the entire grid shows no deviations of any kind." Wopner leaned forward. "No deviations. Don't you get it? That's a *physical and computational* impossibility."

St. John was glancing at the equipment around him, hands tucked behind his back. "Ghost in the machine, Kerry?" he ventured.

Wopner ignored this.

"I don't know much about computers," St. John continued, his plummy accent filling the air, "but I do know one term: GIGO. Garbage in, garbage out."

"Bite me. It's not the programming."

"Ah. I see. Couldn't *possibly* be human error. As I recall, all it took was one incorrect FORTRAN equation to send Mariner 1 off on some outer space scavenger hunt, never to be heard from again."

"The point is, things are working now," Hatch said. "So why not move on?"

"Sure, and have it happen again. I want to know *why* all this shit failed at once."

"You can't do anything about it now," St. John said. "Meanwhile, we're falling behind schedule on the cryptanalysis. Nothing's worked. I've done some more research, and I think we've been far too quick to dismiss—"

"Shit on a *stick*!" Wopner snapped, wheeling toward him. "You're not going to start mumbling about polyalphabetics again, are you, old *thing*? Look, I'm going to modify the algorithm of my brute-force attack, give it fifty percent system priority, really get things moving. Why don't you retire to your library? Come back at the end of the day with some useful ideas."

St. John looked briefly at Wopner. Then he shrugged into his tweed and ducked back out into the gauzy morning light. Hatch followed him to his own office.

"Thanks," Hatch said, passing the two folders to St. John.

"He's right, you know," the historian said, taking a seat at his tidy desk and wearily pulling the old typewriter toward him. "It's just that I've tried everything else. I've based my attacks on all the encryption methods known during Macallan's time. I've approached it as an arithmetic problem, as an astronomic or astrologic system, as a foreign language code. Nothing."

"What are polyalphabetics?" Hatch asked.

St. John sighed. "A polyalphabetic cipher. It's quite simple, really. You see, most codes in Macallan's day were simple, monophonic substitutions. You had the regular alphabet, then you had a cipher alphabet, all higgledy-piggledy. To encode something, you simply looked up which cipher letter matched the next regular letter in your document. Maybe the code for *s* was *y*, and the code for *e* was *z*. So, when you coded the word 'see,' you'd get 'yzz.' That's how the cryptograms in your local newspaper work."

"Seems clear enough."

"Yes. But it's not a very secure system. So what if you had several *different* cipher alphabets to work with? Let's say instead of just one, you had ten. And, as you encrypted your document letter by letter, you'd move through all ten cipher alphabets, and then start over again with the first. That's a polyalphabetic cipher. Now, 'see' wouldn't just be 'yzz.' Each letter would be coded from a different cipher table."

"Sounds difficult to crack."

"Yes, they are very difficult. But Kerry's point is that polyalphabetics weren't used in Macallan's day. Oh, people knew about them. But they were considered too time-consuming, too prone to error." St. John sighed again. "But in this case, the biggest problem is one of concealment. If Macallan used a polyalphabetic cipher, how could he have safely hidden all the code alphabet tables he would have needed? Just one chance look at those by Red Ned Ockham would give the whole game away. And as bright as he was, he couldn't have memorized them."

"If you think there's the chance it's a polyalphabetic code, why don't you try cracking it on your own?"

The corners of St. John's lips lifted in what might have been a smile. "If I had two months, I'd be happy to give it a try. But I don't. Besides, I have no idea how long a key he was using, if any, or how liberally he'd strewn his nulls."

"Nulls?"

"*Nihil importantes*. Letters that don't stand for anything, but are tossed in to confuse the codebreaker."

A boat horn sounded outside, deep and mysterious, and Hatch checked his watch. "It's ten," he said. "I'd better go. They'll be sealing the flood tunnels and draining the Water Pit in a few minutes. Good luck with Kerry."

19

Leaving Base Camp, Hatch began jogging up the path toward Orthanc, eager to see the new structure that had materialized over the Water Pit in just forty-eight hours. Even before he reached the crest of the island, he could make out the glassed-in observation tower, a narrow deck running around its outer edge. As he drew closer, he could see the massive supports that suspended the derrick almost forty feet above the sandy ground. Winches and cables dangled from the underside of the tower, reaching down into the darkness of the Pit. *My God,* Hatch thought. *They must be able to see this thing from the mainland.*

With this, his thoughts drifted back to the lobster festival and to what Clay and his old teacher had said. He knew that Professor Horn would keep his opinions to himself. Clay, though, was another matter. So far, public sentiment toward Thalassa seemed overwhelmingly favorable; he'd have to be careful to keep it that way. Even before the festival had come to a close, he'd spoken to Neidelman about giving Donny

Truitt a job. The Captain had promptly added him to the excavation crew that would start digging at the bottom of the Water Pit as soon as it was drained.

Hatch approached the derrick and climbed the external ladder. The view from the observation deck was magnificent. The ever-present mist was breaking into tatters under the hot summer sun, and he could just make out the dark purple stripe of the mainland. The sun glinted off the ocean, turning it the color of beaten metal, and the surf broke over the windward reefs, surrounding them with spume and a line of drifting wrack. A phrase from Rupert Brooke surfaced unbidden in his mind:

> *The little dulling edge of foam*
> *That browns and dwindles as the wave goes home.*

He raised his head at the sound of voices. On the far side of the observation deck he could see Isobel Bonterre, her wetsuit shining damply in the sun. She was leaning over the railing, twisting the excess water out of her hair and talking animatedly to Neidelman.

As Hatch strolled over, she turned to him with a grin. "Well, well! The man who saved my life!"

"How's your wound?" Hatch replied.

"*De rien, monsieur le docteur.* I was out diving this morning at six, no doubt while you were still snoring the loud snores. And you will not believe what I have discovered!"

Hatch glanced at Neidelman, who was nodding and puffing on his pipe, clearly pleased.

"That stone foundation I found on the seabed the other day?" she continued. "It runs along the inside wall of the reefs, all around the southern end of the island. I traced the remains this morning. There is only one explanation for it: the foundation to an ancient cofferdam."

"An ancient cofferdam? Built around the end of the island? But why?" Even as Hatch asked the question, he realized the answer. "Jesus," he exhaled.

Bonterre grinned. "The pirates built a semicircular dam all along the southern reefs. They sunk wooden pilings, arcing out from the shore into the shallow water, then coming back to land again, like a stockade fence in the sea. I found tracings of pitch and oakum, which they probably used to make the pilings watertight. Then they pumped out the seawater, exposed the sea floor around the beach, and excavated the five flood tunnels. When they were done, they simply destroyed the cofferdam and let the water back in. *Et voilà,* the traps were set!"

"Yes," Neidelman added. "Almost obvious, when you think of it. How else could they build underwater flood tunnels without the benefit of scuba gear? Macallan was an engineer as well as an architect. He advised on the construction of Old Battersea Bridge, so he knew about shallow-water construction. He undoubtedly planned all of this, down to the last detail."

"A cofferdam around the entire end of the island?" Hatch said. "Sounds like a huge task."

"Huge, yes. But remember, he had over a thousand enthusiastic laborers to do it. And they had enormous chain pumps from the bilges of their ships." There was another blast from a boat horn, and Neidelman checked his watch. "Fifteen minutes until we blow the explosives and seal those five flood tunnels. The mist is clearing nicely; we should have a fine view. Come on inside."

The Captain ushered them inside Orthanc. Beneath the windows that lined the walls of the tower, Hatch could see banks of equipment and horizontally mounted monitors. Magnusen and Rankin, the geologist, stood at stations in opposite corners of the tower, while a couple of technicians

Hatch didn't recognize were busy wiring and testing components. Against one wall, a series of screens showed closed-circuit video feeds from around the island: the Command Center, the mouth of the Pit, the interior of Orthanc itself.

The most remarkable feature of the tower was a massive glass plate that occupied the center of the floor. Hatch stepped forward and gazed down into the maw of the Water Pit.

"Watch this," Neidelman said, flicking a switch on a nearby console.

A powerful mercury arc lamp snapped on, its beam stabbing down into the darkness. Below, the Pit was drowned in seawater. Bits of seaweed floated in the water and brine shrimp, attracted by the light, jerked and played just below the surface. A few feet into the murky water, he could make out stumps of old timbers, heavy with barnacles, their ragged lengths disappearing into the depths. The fat, metal-jointed pump hose ran along the ground and over the side of the Pit, joining half a dozen other, narrower cables and feeder lines.

"The throat of the beast," Neidelman said with grim satisfaction. He swept his hand over the consoles ranged beneath the windows. "We've equipped the tower with the latest remote-sensing equipment, including L-band and X-band synthetic-aperture downward-pointing radar. All with dedicated links to the Base Camp computer."

He checked his watch again. "Dr. Magnusen, is the comm station in order?"

"Yes, Captain," the engineer said, brushing her short hair back. "All five marker buoys are transmitting clearly, ready for your arming signal."

"Is Wopner in Island One?"

"I beeped him about five minutes ago. He should be there shortly, if he isn't already."

Neidelman strode toward a bank of controls and snapped the radio to life. "*Naiad* and *Grampus*, this is Orthanc. Do you read?"

The boats acknowledged.

"Take your stations. We blow the charges in ten minutes."

Hatch moved to the window. The mist had retreated to a distant haze, and he could see the two launches power away from the pier and take up positions offshore. Ringing the inside of the reef, along the southern end of the island, he could make out the five electronic buoys that marked the flood tunnel exits. Each flood tunnel, he knew, had now been mined with several pounds of Semtex. The buoy antennas winked in the light, ready to receive the detonation signals.

"Island One, report," Neidelman spoke into the radio.

"Wopner here."

"Are the monitoring systems on-line?"

"Yes, everything's hunky-dory." Wopner sounded dejected.

"Good. Advise me of any changes."

"Captain, why am I here?" the voice complained. "The tower's fully networked, and you're gonna be running the pumps manually. Anything you need to do, you can do there. I should be working on that damn code."

"I don't want any more surprises," Neidelman replied. "We'll set off the charges, seal the flood tunnels, then pump the water out of the Pit. You should be curled up with that journal again in no time."

There was a flurry of activity below, and Hatch could see Streeter directing a team into position around the pump hose. Bonterre came back in from the deck, her hair streaming behind her. "How long until the fireworks start?" she asked.

"Five minutes," said Neidelman.

"How exciting! I love a big explosion." She looked at Hatch with a wink.

"Dr. Magnusen," Neidelman said. "A final check, if you please."

"Certainly, Captain." There was a brief silence. "Everything's green. Comm signals are good. Pumps primed and idling."

Rankin gestured Hatch over and pointed toward a screen. "Check it out."

The screen showed a cross section of the Pit, marked in ten-foot intervals down to one hundred feet. A blue column sat inside the cross section, level with the surface.

"We were able to snake a miniature depth meter into the Pit," he said excitedly. "Streeter sent a dive team down earlier, but they couldn't get farther than thirty feet because of all the debris clogging the works. You wouldn't believe how much junk has collected down there." He nodded at the screen. "With this, we'll be able to monitor the water level drop from here."

"All stations, listen up," Neidelman said. "We'll blow in series."

A silence fell in the observation tower.

"Arming one through five," Magnusen said quietly, her stubby fingers moving across a console.

"Ten seconds," Neidelman murmured. The atmosphere deepened.

"Fire one."

Hatch looked seaward. For a pregnant moment, all seemed still. Then an enormous geyser ripped out of the ocean, shot from within by orange light. A second later, the shock wave shivered the windows of the observation deck. The sound rumbled across the water, and thirty seconds later a faint answering rumble echoed back from the mainland.

The geyser ascended in a strange kind of slow motion, followed by a haze of pulverized rock, mud, and seaweed. As it began falling back in a dirty plume, steep-walled waves spread out across the ocean, beating against the chop. *Naiad*, the nearer of the two boats, rocked crazily in the sudden swell.

"Fire two," Neidelman said, and a second explosion ripped the underwater reef a hundred yards from the first. One by one, he detonated the underwater explosives, until it seemed to Hatch that the entire southern coast of Ragged Island had been caught in a lashing waterstorm. *Too bad it's not Sunday,* he thought. *We'd have done Clay a favor, waking all those people asleep at his sermon.*

There was a brief pause while the water settled and dive teams examined the results. After receiving word that all five tunnel entrances were sealed, Neidelman turned to Magnusen. "Set the outflow valves on the pumps," he said. "Maintain a 20,000 GPM rate of flow out of the pit. Streeter, have your team stand by."

Radio in hand, he turned toward the group assembled in the tower.

"Let's drain the Water Pit," he said.

There was a roar on the southern shore as the pump engines came to life. Almost simultaneously, Hatch heard a great, reluctant throbbing from the Pit as water was sucked up from its depths. Looking down, he could see the thick hose stiffening as the water began its journey out of the Pit, across the island, and back to the ocean. Rankin and Bonterre were glued to the depth display, while Magnusen was monitoring the pump subsystem. The tower began to vibrate slightly.

A few minutes passed.

"Water level down five feet," Magnusen said.

Neidelman leaned toward Hatch. "Tidal displacement

here is eight feet," he said. "Water never drops lower than eight feet in the Pit, even at the lowest low tide. Once we reach ten feet, we'll know we've won."

There was an endless, tense moment. Then Magnusen lifted her face from a dial.

"Water level down ten feet," she said matter-of-factly.

The team looked at each other. Then, suddenly, Neidelman broke into a broad grin.

In an instant, Orthanc's observation tower became a place of happy bedlam. Bonterre whistled loudly and jumped into the arms of a surprised Rankin. The technicians slapped each other's backs enthusiastically. Even Magnusen's lips twisted into what might have been a smile before she returned her gaze to the monitor. Amid the clapping and cheering, someone produced a bottle of Veuve Cliquot and some plastic champagne glasses.

"We did it, by God," Neidelman said, shaking hands around the room. "We're draining the Water Pit!" He reached for the champagne, tore off the foil, and popped the cork.

"This place got its name for a reason," he said, pouring glasses. Hatch thought he could detect an emotional tremor in the Captain's voice. "For two hundred years, the enemy has been the water. Until the Water Pit could be drained, there could be no recovery of the treasure. But my friends, as of tomorrow, this place will need a different name. My thanks and congratulations to you all." He raised his glass. Faint cheers resounded across the island.

"Water level down fifteen feet," Magnusen said.

Holding his champagne in one hand, Hatch walked toward the center of the room and looked down into the glass. It was unsettling, looking into the mouth of the Pit. Streeter's team was standing beside the enormous hose, monitoring the flow. As the water was pumped out at a rate of 20,000

GPM—one swimming pool's worth of water every two minutes—Hatch thought he could actually see the surface level dropping. It crept down the seaweed-covered beams, exposing, millimeter by millimeter, the barnacle- and kelp-encrusted walls. Perversely, he found himself struggling with a strange feeling of regret. It seemed anticlimactic, almost unfair, that they should accomplish in less than two weeks what two hundred years of pain, suffering, and death had been unable to achieve.

Neidelman was at the radio. "This is the Captain speaking." His voice echoed across the island and out over the dark water. "I am hereby exercising my right as acting commander of this venture. All nonessential personnel may have the afternoon off."

Another cheer went up, general across the island. Hatch glanced over at Magnusen, wondering what she was studying so intently.

"Captain?" Rankin said, staring at his own screen once again. Seeing his expression, Bonterre moved toward him, pressing her own face close to the monitor.

"Captain?" Rankin said in a louder tone.

Neidelman, in the midst of pouring more champagne, turned toward the geologist.

Rankin gestured toward the screen. "The water's no longer dropping."

There was a silence as all eyes turned to the glass floor.

A faint but continuous hissing began to rise from the Pit. The dark surface of the water swirled as bubbles came streaming out of the black depths.

Neidelman stepped away from the glass window. "Increase the pump rate to thirty," he said in a quiet voice.

"Yes, sir," Magnusen said. The roar from the southern end of the island grew stronger.

Without a word, Hatch joined Rankin and Bonterre at the

geologist's screen. The blue band of water had dropped mid-way between the ten- and the twenty-foot marks. As they watched, the band wavered on the screen, then began creeping slowly, inexorably upward.

"The water's back to fifteen feet," Magnusen said.

"How can that be?" Hatch asked. "The flood tunnels have all been sealed. No water can get into the Pit."

Neidelman spoke into the radio. "Streeter, what's redline on those pumps?"

"Forty thousand is the rating, sir," came the response.

"I didn't ask what they were rated to. I asked where the redline was."

"Fifty thousand. But Captain—"

He turned to Magnusen. "Do it."

Outside, the roar of the pump engines became almost deafening, and the tower shook violently from their effort. Nobody spoke as all eyes were locked on the monitors. As Hatch watched, the blue line steadied once again, and wavered, almost seeming to drop a bit. He exhaled gradually, realizing he had been holding his breath.

"Grande merde du noir," Bonterre whispered. In disbelief, Hatch saw the level in the Pit begin to rise again.

"We're back at ten feet," Magnusen said implacably.

"Give me sixty on the pumps," Neidelman said.

"Sir!" the voice of Streeter crackled over the radio. "We can't push the—"

"Do it!" Neidelman barked at Magnusen, his voice hard, his lips compressed into narrow white lines. The engineer resolutely turned the dials.

Once again, Hatch found himself drawn to the observation port. Below, he could see Streeter's team, bolting additional metal straps around the pump hose, which was twitching and thrashing like a live thing. Hatch tensed, aware that if the hose burst, the water pressure at sixty thousand gallons per minute could cut a person in two.

The roar of the pumps had become a howl, a bansheelike cry that seemed to fill his head with its pressure. He could feel the island shuddering under his feet. Small bits of dirt shook free from the mouth of the Pit and dropped into the dark roiling water below. The green line wavered, but did not sink.

"Captain!" Streeter cried again. "The forward seal is beginning to fail!"

Neidelman stood motionless, staring into the Pit as if transfixed.

"Captain!" the voice of Streeter cried over the radio, struggling above the noise. "If the hose blows, it could take out Orthanc!"

As Hatch opened his mouth to speak, Neidelman turned abruptly toward Magnusen. "Kill the pumps," he said.

In the descending silence that followed, Hatch could hear the groans and whispers of the Water Pit beneath them.

"Water level returning to normal, sir," Magnusen said without turning from her console.

"This is bullshit, man," Rankin muttered, snapping through sonar readings. "We sealed all five tunnels. This is going to be one hell of a problem."

Neidelman half turned his head at this, and Hatch could see the chiseled profile, the hard glitter in the eyes. "It's not a problem," he said in a low, strange voice. "We'll simply do what Macallan did. We'll cofferdam the shore."

20

At quarter to ten that evening, Hatch emerged from the boarding hatch of the *Cerberus* and walked across the gangway to his own boat. At the end of the working day, he'd motored over to the big ship to inspect the CBC machine he'd be using if blood work was needed for any of the expedition members. While on board, he'd struck up a conversation with Thalassa's quartermaster, and in short order had been invited to stay for dinner in the ship's galley and to meet the half-dozen occupants. At last, full of vegetable lasagna and espresso, he'd said his farewells to the easygoing crewmen and lab technicians and headed back through the white corridors toward the exit hatch. Along the way, he'd passed the door to Wopner's stateroom. For a moment, he'd considered checking in with the programmer, but decided the unpleasant reception he was sure to get outweighed the benefits of a status report.

Now, back on the *Plain Jane*, he powered up the engine, cast off the lines, and pointed the boat into the warm night.

The distant lights of the mainland were strung out across the dark, and a nearer cluster on Ragged Island glowed softly through the mantle of mist. Venus hung low over the western horizon, reflected in the water as a wavering thread of white. The motor ran a little roughly, but eased as Hatch moved the throttle forward. A glowing trail of phosphorescence sprang from the boat's stern: sparks swirling from a green fire. Hatch sighed contentedly, looking forward to the placid journey ahead despite the lateness of the hour.

Suddenly the roughness returned. Quickly, Hatch cut the motor and let the boat drift. *Feels like water in the fuel line,* he thought. With a sigh, he went forward for a flashlight and some tools, then returned to the cockpit and pulled up the deckpads, exposing the engine beneath. He licked the beam about, searching for the fuel-water separator. Locating it, he reached in and unscrewed the small bowl. Sure enough, it was full of dark liquid. Emptying it over the side, he bent forward again to replace it.

Then he stopped. In the silence left by the killing of his engine, Hatch could make out a sound, coming toward him out of the nocturnal stillness. He paused and listened, uncomprehending for a moment. Then he recognized it: a woman's voice, low and melodious, singing an enchanting aria. He stood up and turned involuntarily in the direction of the voice. It floated across the dark waves, bewitchingly out of place, ravishing in its note of sweet suffering.

Hatch waited, listening as if transfixed. As he looked across the expanse of water, he saw it was coming from the dark form of the *Griffin*, its running lights extinguished. A single point of red glowed out from Neidelman's vessel: through his binoculars he could see it was the Captain, smoking his pipe on the forward deck.

Hatch closed the deckpads, then tried the engine again. It sprang to life on the second crank, running sweet and clear.

Hatch eased the throttle forward and, on an impulse, moved slowly toward the *Griffin.*

"Evening," said the Captain as he approached, the quiet voice unnaturally clear in the night air.

"And to you too," said Hatch, putting the *Plain Jane* into neutral. "I'd bet my eyeteeth that's Mozart, but I don't know the opera. *The Marriage of Figaro*, perhaps?"

The Captain shook his head. "It's 'Zeffiretti Lusinghieri.' "

"Ah. From *Idomeneo.*"

"Yes. Sylvia McNair sings it beautifully, doesn't she? Are you a fan of opera?"

"My mother was. Every Saturday afternoon, the radio would fill our house with trios and *tutti*s. I've only learned to appreciate it these last five years or so."

There was a moment of silence. "Care to come aboard?" Neidelman asked suddenly.

Hatch tied the *Plain Jane* to the rail, killed the engine, and hopped over, the Captain giving him a hand up. There was a glow from the pipe, and Neidelman's face was briefly illuminated with a reddish aura, accentuating the hollows of his cheeks and eyes. A wink of precious metal shone from the pilothouse as the curl of gold reflected the moonlight.

They stood at the rail, silent, listening to the final dying notes of the aria. When it ended and the recitative began, Neidelman breathed deeply, then rapped out his dottle on the side of the boat. "Why haven't you ever asked me to quit smoking?" he asked. "Every doctor I've ever known has tried to get me to quit, except you."

Hatch considered this. "It seems to me I'd be wasting my breath."

Neidelman gave a soft laugh. "You know me well enough, then. Shall we go below for a glass of port?"

Hatch shot a surprised glance at the Captain. Just that night, in the galley of the *Cerberus*, he'd heard that nobody was ever invited below on the *Griffin*; that nobody, in fact, even knew what it looked like. The Captain, although personable and friendly with his crew, always kept his distance.

"Good thing I didn't start lecturing you on your vices, isn't it?" Hatch said. "Thanks, I'd love a glass of port."

He followed Neidelman into the pilothouse, then down the steps and under the low door. Another narrow half-flight of metal stairs, another door, and Hatch found himself in a large, low-ceilinged room. He looked around in wonder. The paneling was a rich, lustrous mahogany, carved in Georgian style and inlaid with mother-of-pearl. Delicate Tiffany stained glass was set into each porthole, and leather banquettes were placed against the walls. At the far end, a small fire glowed, filling the cabin with warmth and the faint, fragrant smell of birch. Glass-fronted library cabinets flanked either side of the mantelpiece; Hatch could see bound calfskin and the gleam of gold stamping. He moved forward to examine the titles: Hakluyt's *Voyages*, an early copy of Newton's *Principia*. Here and there, priceless illuminated manuscripts and other incunabula were arranged face outward; Hatch recognized a fine copy of *Les Très Riches Heures du Duc de Berry*. There was also a small shelf devoted to original editions of early pirate texts: Lionel Wafer's *Batchelor's Delight*, Alexander Esquemelion's *Bucaniers of America*, and *A General History of the Robberies and Murders of the most notorious Pyrates*, by Charles Johnson. The library alone must have cost a small fortune. Hatch wondered if Neidelman had furnished the boat with earnings from prior salvages.

Beside one of the cabinets was a small seascape in a gilt frame. Hatch moved in for a closer look. Then he drew in his breath sharply.

"My God," he said. "This is a Turner, isn't it?"

Neidelman nodded. "It's a study for his painting, *Squall Off Beachy Head, 1874.*"

"That's the one in the Tate?" Hatch said. "When I was in London a few years back, I tried sketching it several times."

"Are you a painter?" Neidelman asked.

"I'm a dabbler. Watercolors, mostly." Hatch stepped back, glancing around again. The other pictures that hung on the walls were not paintings, but precise copperplate engravings of botanical specimens: heavy flowers, odd grasses, exotic plants.

Neidelman approached a small baize-covered dry sink, laid with cut-glass ship's decanters and small glasses. Pulling two tumblers from their felt-covered moorings, he poured a few fingers of port in each. "Those engravings," he said, following Hatch's gaze, "are by Sir Joseph Banks, the botanist who accompanied Captain Cook on his first voyage around the world. They're plant specimens he collected in Botany Bay, shortly after they discovered Australia. It was the fantastic variety of plant specimens, you know, that caused Banks to give the bay its name."

"They're beautiful," murmured Hatch, accepting a glass.

"They're probably the finest copperplate engravings ever made. What a fortunate man he was: a botanist, given the gift of a brand-new continent."

"Are you interested in botany?" Hatch asked.

"I'm interested in brand-new continents," Neidelman said, staring into the fire. "But I was born a little too late. All those have been snapped up." He smiled quickly, covering what seemed like a wistful gleam in his eyes.

"But in the Water Pit you have a mystery worthy of attention."

"Yes," Neidelman replied. "Perhaps the only one left. That's why I suppose setbacks such as today's shouldn't dismay me. Great mysteries don't yield up their secrets easily."

There was a long silence as Hatch sipped his port. Most people, he knew, found silence in a conversation to be uncomfortable. But Neidelman seemed to welcome it.

"I meant to ask you," the Captain said at last. "What did you think of our reception in town yesterday?"

"By and large, everyone seems happy with our presence here. We're certainly a boon to local business."

"Yes," Neidelman replied. "But what do you mean, 'by and large'?"

"Well, not everyone's a merchant." Hatch decided there was no point in being evasive. "We seem to have aroused the moral opposition of the local minister."

Neidelman gave a wry smile. "The minister disapproves, does he? After two thousand years of murder, inquisition, and intolerance, it's a wonder any Christian minister still feels he holds the moral high ground."

Hatch shifted a little uncomfortably; this was a voluble Neidelman, quite unlike the cold figure that just a few hours before had ordered the pumps run at a critically dangerous level.

"They told Columbus his ship would fall off the earth. And they forced Galileo to publicly repudiate his greatest discovery." Neidelman fished his pipe out of his pocket and went through the elaborate ritual of lighting it. "My father was a Lutheran minister himself," he said more quietly, shaking out the match. "I had quite enough to last me a lifetime."

"You don't believe in God?" Hatch asked.

Neidelman gazed at Hatch in silence. Then he lowered his head. "To be honest, I've often wished I did. Religion played such a large role in my childhood that being without it now myself sometimes feels like a void. But I'm the kind of person who cannot believe in the absence of proof. It isn't something I have any control over. I must have *proof.*" He sipped his port. "Why? Do you have any religious beliefs?"

Hatch turned toward him. "Well, yes, I do."

Neidelman waited, smoking.

"But I don't care to discuss them."

A smile spread over Neidelman's face. "Excellent. Can I give you a dividend?"

Hatch handed over his glass. "That wasn't the only opposing voice I heard in town," he continued. "I have an old friend, a teacher of natural history, who thinks we're going to fail."

"And you?" Neidelman asked coolly, busy with the port, not looking at him.

"I wouldn't be in it if I thought we'd fail. But I'd be lying if I said today's setback didn't give me pause."

"Malin," Neidelman said almost gently as he returned the glass, "I can't blame you for that. I confess to feeling a moment of something like despair when the pumps failed us. But there's not the slightest doubt in my mind that we'll succeed. I see now where we've gone wrong."

"I suppose there are even more than five flood tunnels," Hatch said. "Or maybe some hydraulic trick was played on us."

"Undoubtedly. But that's not what I mean. You see, we've been focusing all our attention on the Water Pit. But I've realized the Water Pit is *not* our adversary."

Hatch raised his eyebrows inquiringly, and the Captain turned toward him, pipe clenched in one fist, eyes glittering brightly. "It's not the Pit. It's the man. Macallan, the designer. He's been one step ahead of us all the way. He's *anticipated* our moves, and those who came before us."

Placing his glass on a felt-topped table, he walked over to the wall and swung open a wood panel, revealing a small safe. He punched several buttons on the adjoining keypad, and the safe door swung open. He reached inside, removed something, then turned and laid it on the table in front of Hatch. It was a quarto volume, bound in leather: Macallan's book, *On Sacred Structures*. The captain opened it with great care, caressing it with long fingers. There in the margins, next to the printed blocks of text, appeared a neat little hand in a pale brown wash that looked almost like watercolor: line after line of monotonous characters, broken only by the occasional small, deft mechanical drawing of various joints, arches, braces, and cribbing.

Neidelman tapped the page. "If the Pit is Macallan's armor, then this is the soft joint where we can slip in the knife. Very soon now, we'll have the second half of the code deciphered. And with it, the key to the treasure."

"How can you be so sure this journal contains the secret to the Pit?" Hatch asked.

"Because nothing else makes sense. Why else would he have kept a secret journal, not only in code, but written in an invisible ink? Remember, Red Ned Ockham needed Macallan to create an impregnable fortress for his treasure. A fortress that would not only resist looters, but would physically endanger them by drowning, or crushing, or whatever. But you don't create a bomb without knowing how to disarm it first. So Macallan would have had to create a secret way for Ockham *himself* to remove his treasure when he chose: a hidden tunnel perhaps, or a way to defuse the traps. It stands to reason Macallan would keep a record of it." He leveled his gaze at his guest. "But this journal holds more than just the key to the Pit. It gives us a window into the man's mind. And it is the *man* we must defeat." He spoke in the same low, strangely forceful tone that Hatch remembered from earlier in the day.

Hatch bent over the book, inhaling the aroma of mildew, leather, dust, and dry rot. "One thing surprises me," he said.

"And that's the thought of an architect, kidnapped and forced to work for pirates on some godforsaken island, having the presence of mind to keep a secret journal."

Neidelman nodded slowly. "It's not the act of a faint-hearted man. Perhaps he wanted to leave a record, for posterity, of his most ingenious structure. I suppose it's hard to say what motivated him, exactly. After all, the man was a bit of a cipher himself. There's a gap of three years in the historical record, following his leaving Cambridge, during which he seems to have disappeared. And his personal life as a whole remains a mystery. Take a look at this dedication." He carefully turned to the title page of the book, then slid it toward Hatch:

With Gratefulle admiration
For shewing the Way
The Author respectfully dedicates this humble Work
To Eta Onis

"We've searched high and low, but haven't been able to determine the identity of this Eta Onis," Neidelman went on. "Was she Macallan's teacher? Confidante? Mistress?" He carefully closed the book. "It's the same with the rest of his life."

"I'm embarrassed to say that, until you came along, I'd never even heard of the man," Hatch said.

"Most people haven't. But in his day he was a brilliant visionary, a true Renaissance man. He was born in 1657, the illegitimate but favored son of an earl. Like Milton, he claimed to have read every book then published in English, Latin, and Greek. He read law at Cambridge and was being groomed for a bishopric, but then apparently had some kind of secret conversion to Catholicism. He turned his attention to the arts, natural philosophy, and mathematics. And he was an extraordinary athlete, supposedly able to fling a coin so that it rang out against the vault of his largest cathedral."

Neidelman stood up, returned to the safe, and placed the volume within it. "And an interest in hydraulics seems to extend through all his work. In this book, he describes an ingenious aqueduct and siphon system he designed to supply water to Houndsbury Cathedral. He also sketched out a hydraulic system for locks on the Severn canal. It was never built—it seemed a crazy idea at the time—but Magnusen did some modeling and believes it would have worked."

"Did Ockham seek him out deliberately?"

Neidelman smiled. "Tempting to think so, isn't it? But highly doubtful. It was probably one of those fateful coincidences of history."

Hatch nodded toward the safe. "And how did you happen to come across that volume? Was that also a coincidence?"

Neidelman's smile widened. "No, not exactly. When I first started looking into the Ragged Island treasure, I did some research into Ockham. You know that when his command ship was found floating derelict, all hands dead, it was towed into Plymouth and its contents sold at public auction. We managed to dig up the auctioneer's list at the London Public Records Office, and on it were the contents of a captain's chest full of books. Ockham was an educated man, and I assumed this must be his personal library. One volume, *On Sacred Structures*, caught my eye; it stood out among the maps, French pornography, and naval works that made up the rest of the library. It took three years, on and off, but we finally managed to track that volume down in a heap of rotting books in the undercroft of a half-ruined kirk in Glenfarkille, Scotland."

He stood closer to the fire and spoke in a voice that was low, almost dreamlike. "I'll never forget opening that book for the first time and realizing that the ugly soiling in the margins was a 'white' ink, only then becoming perceivable through the ravages of time and rot. At that moment, I knew—I *knew*—that the Water Pit and its treasure were going to be mine."

He fell silent, his pipe dead, the glowing coals of the fire weaving a mazy light through the darkening room.

21

Kerry Wopner walked jauntily up the cobbled street, whistling the theme from *Star Wars*. Every now and then, he would stop long enough to snort derisively at the shopfronts he passed. Useless, all of them. Like that Coast to Coast hardware store, there, sporting dusty tools and yard implements old enough to be preindustrial. He knew full well there wasn't a decent software store within three hundred miles. As for bagels, he'd have to cross at least two state lines before he found anyone who even knew what the damn word meant.

He stopped abruptly in front of a crisp white Victorian structure. This had to be it, even if it did look more like an old house than a post office. The large American flag that hung from the porch, and the STORMHAVEN, ME 04564 sign sunk into the front lawn, were dead giveaways. Opening the screen door, Wopner realized that it *was* a house: The post office itself took up the front parlor, while a strong smell of cooking indicated that domesticity was hidden farther within.

He looked around the small room, shaking his head at the ancient bank of PO boxes and decade-old Wanted posters, until his eyes fell on a large wooden counter marked ROSA POUNDCOOK, POSTMISTRESS. On the far side of the counter sat the woman herself, gray head bent over a cross-stitch panel of a four-masted schooner. Wopner realized with surprise that there was no line; that, in fact, he was the only patron in the place.

" 'Scuse me," he said, approaching the counter. "This is the post office, right?"

"Yes, indeed," said Rosa, tightening one last stitch and carefully laying the panel on the arm of her rocker before raising her eyes. When she saw Wopner, she gave a start. "Oh, my," she said, a hand moving involuntarily to her chin as if to reassure herself that Wopner's straggly goatee wasn't catching.

"That's good, because I'm expecting an important package by courier, see?" Wopner squinted at her from across the counter. "The pony express delivers to these parts, doesn't it?"

"Oh!" Rosa Poundcook repeated, rising from her rocker and knocking the cross-stitch frame askew. "Do you have a name, I mean, may I have your name, please?"

Wopner let out a short nasal laugh. "It's Wopner. Kerry Wopner."

"Wopner?" She began searching through a small wooden cardfile filled with yellow slips. "W-h-o-p-p—"

"No, no, no. *Wop*ner. No *h*. One *p*," came the annoyed response.

"I see," said Rosa, her composure recovering as she found the slip. "Just a moment." Taking one last, wondering look at the programmer, she disappeared through a door in the back.

Wopner lounged against the counter, whistling again, as the screen door creaked open in protest. Glancing over, he saw a tall, skinny man shut the door carefully behind him. The man turned around, and Wopner was immediately reminded of Abraham Lincoln: gaunt, hollow-eyed, loose-limbed. He wore a clerical collar under a simple black suit, and held a small sheaf of letters in one hand. Wopner looked away quickly, but it was too late; eye contact had been made, and he saw with alarm that the man was already walking over to him. Wopner had never met a priest before, let alone spoken to one, and he had no intention of starting now. He hurriedly reached for a nearby stack of postal publications and began to read intently about the new line of Amish quilt stamps.

"Hello," he heard the man say. Turning reluctantly, Wopner found the priest standing directly behind him, one hand outstretched, a narrow smile creasing his pinched face.

"Yeah, hey," he said, giving the hand a limp shake and quickly returning to his publication.

"I'm Woody Clay," the man said.

"Okay," Wopner said, not looking at him.

"And you must be one of the Thalassa crew," said Clay, stepping up to the counter beside Wopner.

"Right, sure am." Wopner flipped over the brochure as a diversionary tactic while he slid a foot farther away from the stranger.

"Mind if I ask you a question?"

"No, shoot," said Wopner as he read. He'd never known there were so many different kinds of blankets in the whole world.

"Do you really expect to recover a fortune in gold?"

Wopner looked up from the brochure. "Well, I plan to do a pretty good imitation of it." The man didn't smile. "Sure, I expect to. Why not?"

"Why not? Shouldn't the question be *why*?"

Something in the man's tone disconcerted Wopner. "Whaddya mean, why? It's two billion dollars."

"Two billion dollars," the man repeated, momentarily surprised. Then he nodded, as if in affirmation of something he'd suspected. "So it's just for the money. There's no other reason."

Wopner laughed. "*Just* for the money? You need a better reason? Let's be realistic. I mean, you're not talking to Mother Teresa here, for Chrissakes." Suddenly he remembered the clerical collar. "Oh, sorry," he said, abashed, "I didn't mean, you being a priest and all, it's just—"

The man gave a clipped smile. "It's all right, I've heard it before. And I'm not a priest. I'm a Congregational minister."

"I see," said Wopner. "That's some kind of sect, right?"

"Is the money *really* that important to you?" Clay gazed at Wopner steadily. "Under the circumstances, I mean?"

Wopner returned the look. "What circumstances?" He glanced nervously into the bowels of the post office. What the hell was taking that fat lady so long, anyway? She'd have had time to *walk* to frigging Brooklyn by now.

The man leaned forward. "So what do you do for Thalassa?"

"I run the computers."

"Ah. That must be interesting."

Wopner shrugged. "Yeah. When they work."

As he listened, the man's face became a picture of concern. "And everything's running smoothly? No complaints?"

Wopner frowned. "No," he said guardedly.

Clay nodded. "Good."

Wopner put the brochure back on the counter. "Why are you asking, anyway?" he said with feigned nonchalance.

"No reason," the minister replied. "Nothing important, anyway. Except . . ." he paused.

Wopner craned his neck forward slightly.

"In the past, that island—well, it created difficulties for anyone who set foot on it. Boilers exploded. Machines failed without any reason. People got hurt. People got *killed*."

Wopner stepped back with a snort. "You're talking about the Ragged Island curse," he said. "The curse stone, and all that stuff? It's a load of bullpoop, if you'll excuse my French."

Clay's eyebrows shot up. "Is it, now? Well, there are people who've been here a lot longer than you who don't think so. And as for the stone, it's locked in the basement of my church right now, where it's been for the last one hundred years."

"Really?" Wopner asked, mouth open.

Clay nodded.

There was a silence.

The minister leaned closer and lowered his voice conspiratorially. "Ever wonder why there's no lobster buoys around that island?"

"You mean those things floating on the water everywhere?"

"That's right."

"I never noticed there weren't any."

"Next time you go out there, take a look." Clay dropped his voice even further. "There's a good reason for that."

"Yeah?"

"It happened about a hundred years ago. As I heard it, there was a lobsterman, name of Hiram Colcord. He used to drop his pots around Ragged Island. Everybody warned him not to, but the lobstering was fine and he said he didn't give a fig for any curse. One summer day—not unlike this one— he disappeared into that mist to set his traps. Around sundown his boat came drifting back out on the tide. Only this time he wasn't on it. There were lobster traps piled up, and a barrel full of live lobsters. But no Colcord. They found his

lunch, half-eaten on the galley board, and a half-drunk bottle of beer, left as if he'd just stood up and walked away."

"He fell overboard and got his butt drowned. So what?"

"No," Clay continued. "Because that evening his brother
went out to the island to see if Hiram had been stranded
somehow. He never came back, either. The next day, *his* boat
drifted out of the mists."

Wopner swallowed. "So they *both* fell out and drowned."

"Two weeks later," Clay said, "their bodies washed up on
Breed's Point. One of the locals who saw what had happened
went mad with fright. And none of the rest would say what
they had seen. Not ever."

"Come on," said Wopner, nervously.

"People said it wasn't just the Pit that guarded the treasure
now. Understand? You know that terrible sound the island
makes, every time the tide changes? They say—"

There was a bustling noise from the rear of the house.
"Sorry I took so long," panted Rosa as she emerged, a package tucked under one plump arm. "It was under that load of
bird feeders for the Coast to Coast, and with Eustace down
at the pound this morning, you know, I had to shift everything myself."

"Hey, no problem, thanks." Wopner grabbed the package
gratefully and headed quickly for the door.

"Excuse me, mister!" the postmistress said.

Wopner stopped short. Then, unwillingly, he looked
around, the package clasped to his chest.

The woman was holding out the yellow sheet. "You have
to sign for it."

Wordlessly, Wopner stepped forward and scrawled a hasty
signature. Then, turning away again, he moved quickly out
of the parlor, letting the screen door slam behind him.

Once outside, he took a deep breath. "The hell with this,"
he muttered. Priest or no priest, he wasn't going back to the

boat until he'd made sure they hadn't screwed up his order again. He wrestled with the small box, tugging at the tab, first gingerly, then enthusiastically. The seam of the box gave way suddenly and a dozen role-playing figurines spilled out, wizards and sorcerers clattering across the cobbles at his feet. Fluttering after them came a pack of gamer's witching cards: pentagrams, spells, reverse prayers, devil's circles. With a cry and a curse, Wopner stooped to pick them up.

Clay stepped outside, once again shutting the door carefully behind him. He stepped off the porch and into the street, took one long look at the plastic figurines and the cards, then hurried up the lane without another word.

22

The following day was cool and damp, but by the end of the afternoon the drizzle had lifted and low clouds were scudding across a freshening sky. *Tomorrow will be crisp and windy,* Hatch thought as he strode up the narrow, yellow-taped path behind Orthanc. This daily hike to the top of the island had become a closing ritual for him. Reaching the height of land, he walked around the edge of the southern bluffs until he had a good view of Streeter's crew, wrapping up the day's work on the offshore cofferdam.

As usual, Neidelman had come up with a simple, but elegant, plan. While the cargo vessel was dispatched to Portland for cement and building materials, Bonterre had mapped out the exact lie of the ancient pirate cofferdam, taking samples for later archaeological analysis. Next, divers had poured an underwater concrete footing directly atop the remains of the old foundation. This had been followed by the sinking of steel I-beams into the footing. Hatch stared at the enormous beams, rising vertically out of the water at ten-foot intervals, forming a narrow arc around the southern end of the island. From his vantage point, he could see Streeter in the cab of the floating crane, positioned near the barge and just outside the row of steel beams. A massive section of reinforced concrete dangled from the crane's sling. As Hatch watched, Streeter maneuvered the rectangle of concrete into the slot formed by two of the I-beams, then slid it home. Once it was securely in place, two divers unhooked the slings. Then, Streeter deftly swung the crane around toward the barge, where more sections of concrete were waiting.

There was a flash of red hair: Hatch could see that one of the deckhands on the barge was Donny Truitt. Neidelman had found work for him despite the delay in draining the Pit, and Hatch was pleased that Donny seemed to be working efficiently.

There was a roar from the floating crane as Streeter swung it back toward the semicircle of beams, slotting a new piece of concrete into place beside the other.

When the cofferdam was finished, Hatch knew, it would completely enclose the southern end of the island and the flood tunnel exits. Then, the Water Pit and all its connected underwater works could be pumped dry, with the dam holding back the sea—just as the pirates' cofferdam had done 300 years before.

A whistle sounded, signaling quitting time; the crew on the barge began throwing tie-downs over the stacked sections of cofferdam, while the waiting tugboat came in out of the offshore mist to tow the crane toward the dock. Hatch took a final look around, and turned back down the trail toward Base Camp. He stopped in at his office, collected his bag and locked the door, then headed toward the dock. He'd have a simple dinner at home, he decided, then head into town and look up Bill Banns. The next issue of the *Stormhaven Gazette* was due out shortly, and Hatch wanted to make sure the old man had plenty of appropriate copy for the front page.

The mooring at the safest section of the reef had been enlarged and Hatch given a berth. As he started the engine of the *Plain Jane* and prepared to cast off, he heard a nearby voice cry, "Ahoy, the frigate!" Looking up, he saw Bonterre coming down the dock toward him, dressed in bib overalls and wearing a red bandanna around her neck. Mud was splashed generously across her clothes, hands, and face. She stopped at the foot of the dock, then stuck out her thumb like a hitchhiker, impishly raising one pant leg to expose a foot or so of tan calf.

"Need a lift?" Hatch asked.

"How did you guess?" Bonterre replied, tossing her bag into the boat and jumping in. "I am already sick of your ugly old island."

Hatch cast off and heeled the boat around, easing it past the reefs and through the inlet. "Your tummy healing up?"

"There is a nasty scab on my otherwise beautiful stomach."

"Don't worry, it's nothing permanent." Hatch took another look at her dirty coveralls. "Making mud pies?"

Bonterre frowned. "Mud . . . pies?"

"You know. Playing in the mud."

She snorted a laugh. "Of course! It is what archaeologists do best."

"So I see." They were approaching the thin circle of mist, and Hatch throttled down until they were clear. "I didn't see you out among the divers."

Bonterre snorted again. "I am an archaeologist first, a diver second. I've done the important work, gridding out the old cofferdam. Sergio and his friends can do the labor of the beasts."

"I'll tell him you said that." Hatch brought the boat through Old Hump Channel and swung it around Hermit Island. Stormhaven harbor came into view, a shining strip of white and green against the dark blue of the ocean. Leaning against the fantail, Bonterre shook out her hair, a glossy cascade of black.

"So what is there to do in this one-horse town?" she said, nodding toward the mainland.

"Not much."

"No disco dancing until three? *Merde,* what is a single woman to do?"

"I admit, it's a difficult problem," Hatch replied, resisting the impulse to return her flirtations. *Don't forget, this woman is trouble.*

She looked at him, a tiny smile curling the corners of her lips. "Well, I could have dinner with the doctor."

"Doctor?" Hatch said, with mock surprise. "Why, I suppose Dr. Frazier would be delighted. For sixty, he's still pretty spry."

"You bad boy! I meant *this* doctor." She poked him playfully in the chest.

Hatch looked at her. *Why not?* he thought. *What kind of trouble could I get into over dinner?* "There are only two restaurants in town, you know. Both seafood places, naturally. Although one does a reasonable steak."

"Steak? That is for me. I am a strict carnivore. Vegetables are for pigs and monkeys. As for fish—" She made an elaborate gesture of retching over the side.

"I thought you grew up in the Caribbean."

"Yes, and my father was a fisherman, and that is all we ate, forever and ever. Except at Christmas, when we had *chèvre.*"

"Goat?" Hatch asked.

"Yes. I love goat. Cooked for eight hours in a hole on the beach, washed down with homemade *Ponlac* beer."

"Delectable," said Hatch, laughing. "You're staying in town, right?"

"Yes. Everything was booked up, so I placed a notice in the post office. The lady behind the counter saw it and offered me a room."

"You mean, upstairs? At the Poundcooks?"

"Naturellement."

"The postmistress and her husband. They're a nice quiet couple."

"Yes. Sometimes I think they might be dead, it's so quiet downstairs."

Wait and see what happens if you try to bring home a man, thought Hatch. *Or even if you stay out after eleven.*

They reached the harbor, and Hatch eased the boat up to its mooring. "I must change out of these dirty clothes," Bonterre said, leaping into the dinghy, "and of course you must put on something better than that boring old blazer."

"But I like this jacket," Hatch protested.

"You American men do not know how to dress at all. What you need is a good suit of Italian linen."

"I hate linen," Hatch said. "It's always wrinkled."

"That is the point!" Bonterre laughed. "What size are you? Forty-two long?"

"How did you know?"

"I am good at measuring a man."

23

Hatch picked her up outside the post office, and they walked down the steep cobbled streets toward The Landing. It was a beautiful, cool evening; the clouds had blown away, and a vast bowl of stars hung over the harbor. In the clear evening light, with the little yellow lights of the town twinkling in windows and above doorways, Stormhaven seemed to Hatch like a place from a remote and friendlier past.

"This is truly a charming place," Bonterre said as she took his arm. "Saint Pierre, where I grew up on Martinique, is also beautiful, but *alors,* such a difference! It is all lights and colors. Not like here, where everything is black and white. And there is much to do there, very good nightclubs for wild times."

"I don't like nightclubs," said Hatch.

"How boring," said Bonterre, good-naturedly.

They arrived at the restaurant, and the waiter, recognizing Hatch, seated them immediately. It was a cozy place: two rambling rooms and a bar, decorated with nets, wooden lob-

ster pots, and glass floats. Taking a seat, Hatch looked
around. Fully a third of the patrons were Thalassa employees.

"Que de monde!" Bonterre whispered. "One cannot get
away from company people. I cannot wait for Gerard to send
them all home."

"It's like that in a small town. The only way you can get
away is to go out on the water. And even then, there's always
someone in the town looking at you with a telescope."

"No sex on deck, then," said Bonterre.

"No," said Hatch. "We New Englanders always have sex
below." He watched her break into a delighted smile, and he
wondered what kind of havoc she'd wreak among the male
crew in the days to come. "So what was it you did today that
made you so dirty?"

"What is this obsession with dirt?" she frowned. "Mud is
the archaeologist's friend." She leaned across the table. "As
it happens, I made a little discovery on your muddy old island."

"Tell me about it."

She took a sip from her water glass. "We discovered the
pirate encampment."

Hatch looked at her. "You're kidding."

"Mais non! This morning, we set out to examine the
windward side of the island. You know that spot where a
large bluff stands off by itself, maybe ten meters down the
rocks?"

"Yes."

"Right there, where the bluff was eroding, there was a perfect soil profile. A vertical cut, very convenient to the archaeologist. I was able to locate a lens of charcoal."

Hatch frowned. "A what?"

"You know. A black lens of charcoal. The remains of an
ancient fire. So we ran a metal detector across the site and

right then began finding things. Grapeshot, a musket ball, and several horseshoe nails." She ticked the items on her fingers.

"Horseshoe nails?"

"Yes. They used horses for the heavy work."

"Where did they get them?"

"Are you so ignorant of naval history, *monsieur le docteur*? It was common to carry livestock on ships. Horses, goats, chickens, pigs."

Their dinners arrived—steamers and lobsters for Hatch, a bloody top sirloin for Bonterre. The archaeologist tucked into the food at an alarming rate, and Hatch watched her eat with amusement: juice dripping from her chin, a furrowed, intent look in her face.

"Anyway," she went on, spearing an extravagantly large morsel of steak with her fork, "after those discoveries, we dug a test trench just behind the bluffs. And what do you think? More charcoal, a circular tent depression, a few broken turkey and deer bones. Rankin has some fancy sensors he wants to drag over to the site, in case we miss any spots. But meanwhile, we have gridded the camp and will start excavation tomorrow. My little Christophe is becoming an excellent digger."

"St. John? Digging?"

"But of course. I made him get rid of those horrid shoes and jacket. Once he resigned himself to getting his hands dirty, he proved most able. Now he is my prime digger. He follows me everywhere and comes when I whistle." She laughed in a kindly way.

"Don't be too hard on the poor man."

"*Au contraire,* I am doing him good. He needs the fresh air and the exercise, or he will stay as white and fat as a grub. You wait. When I am through with him, he will be all wire and gristle, like *le petit homme.*"

"Who?"

"You know. The little man." The corners of Bonterre's mouth turned down impishly. "Streeter."

"Ah." The way Bonterre said it, Hatch could tell the nickname wasn't meant fondly. "What's his story, anyway?"

Bonterre shrugged. "One hears things. Hard to know what is the truth and what is not. He was under Neidelman in Vietnam. That is how you say it, *non*? Somebody told me that Neidelman once saved his life during combat. That story is one I believe. You see how devoted he is to the Captain? Like a dog to his master. He is the only one the Captain really trusts." She stared at Hatch. "Except for you, of course."

Hatch frowned. "Well, I suppose it's good the Captain cares about him. Somebody has to. I mean, the guy's not exactly Mr. Personality."

Bonterre raised her eyebrows. "*Certainement*. And I can see that the two of you got off on the other foot."

"The wrong foot," Hatch corrected.

"Whatever. But you are wrong when you say that Captain Neidelman cares about Streeter. There's only one thing he cares about." She gave the briefest of nods in the direction of Ragged Island. "He does not talk about it much, but only an *imbécile* would not see. Do you know that, as long as I have known him, he has had a small photograph of your island, sitting on his desk at Thalassa?"

"No, I didn't." Hatch's thoughts went back to the first trip out to the island with Neidelman. What was it the Captain had said? *I didn't want to see it unless we'd have the chance to dig it.*

Something seemed to have upset Bonterre. As Hatch opened his mouth to change the subject, he sensed something, someone—a presence across the room—and when he looked up there was Claire, coming around the corner. The intended remark died on his lips.

She was just as he'd imagined she would be: tall and willowy, with the same dash of freckles across the upturned nose. She saw him and stopped dead, her face wrinkling into that same funny frown of surprise he remembered.

"Hello, Claire," Hatch said, standing up awkwardly and trying to keep his voice neutral.

She stepped forward. "Hello," she said, shaking his hand, and at the touch of his skin against hers a pink flush formed on her cheeks. "I heard you were in town." She gave a self-deprecating laugh. "Of course, who hasn't. I mean, with all that—" and she made a vague gesture over her shoulder, as if to indicate the Water Pit.

"You look great," Hatch said. And she did: the years had made her slender and turned her dark blue eyes a penetrating gray. The mischievous smile once etched permanently on her lips had given way to a more serious, introspective look. She smoothed her pleated skirt unconsciously as she felt his eyes on her.

There was movement at the restaurant entrance, then the minister, Woody Clay, stepped in. He looked around the room until his eyes landed on Hatch. A spasm of displeasure moved quickly across his sallow face, and he came forward. *Not here,* Hatch thought, bracing himself for another lecture about greed and the ethics of treasure hunting. Sure enough, the minister stopped at their table, glancing from Hatch to Bonterre and back. Hatch wondered if the man would actually have the gall to interrupt their dinner.

"Oh," said Claire, looking at the minister and touching her long blond hair. "Woody, this is Malin Hatch."

"We've met," Clay nodded.

With relief, Hatch realized it wasn't likely that Clay would launch into another tirade with the two women looking on.

"This is Dr. Isobel Bonterre," he said, recovering his composure. "May I introduce Claire Northcutt and—"

"Reverend and Mrs. Woodruff Clay," said the minister crisply, extending his hand to Bonterre.

Hatch was stunned, his mind almost refusing to accept this fresh surprise.

Bonterre dabbed at her lips with a napkin and stood up with a languid motion, giving Claire and Woody each a hearty handshake, exposing a row of dazzling teeth. There was an awkward pause, and then Clay ushered his wife away with a curt nod to Hatch.

Bonterre glanced at the retreating figure of Claire, then back at Hatch. "Old friends?" she asked.

"What?" Hatch murmured. He was staring at Clay's left hand, possessively placed in the small of Claire's back.

An arch smile formed on Bonterre's face. "No, I can see I am wrong," she said, leaning over the table. "Old *lovers*. How awkward it is to meet again! And yet how sweet."

"You have a keen eye," mumbled Hatch, still too off balance from the encounter—and the revelation that followed—to make any kind of denial.

"But you and the husband, you are *not* old friends. In fact, it seemed to me that he does not like you at all. That tiresome frown, and those big black bags under his eyes. He looks like he had a *nuit blanche*."

"A what?"

"A *nuit blanche*. A—how do you say it?—a sleepless night. For one reason or another." She smiled wickedly.

Instead of replying, Hatch picked up his fork and tried to busy himself with his lobster.

"I can see you still carry her torch," Bonterre purred, with a cheerful smile. "Someday you must tell me of her. But first, let me hear about *you*. The Captain's mentioned your travels. So tell me all about your adventures in Suriname."

Almost two hours later, Hatch forced himself to his feet and followed Bonterre out of the restaurant. He had overindulged ridiculously, obscenely: two desserts, two pots of coffee, several brandies. Bonterre had matched him enthusiastically, order for order, yet she did not seem any worse for wear as she threw open her arms and breathed in the crisp night breeze.

"How refreshing this air is!" she cried. "I could almost learn to love a place like this."

"Just wait," Hatch replied. "Another two weeks, and you won't be able to leave. It gets in your blood."

"Another two weeks, and you will not be able to get out of my way fast enough, *monsieur le docteur.*" She looked at him appraisingly. "So what do we do now?"

Hatch hesitated a moment. He'd never thought about what might happen after dinner. He returned the gaze, warning bells once again sounding faintly in his head. Silhouetted in the yellow glow of the streetlamps, the archaeologist looked captivatingly beautiful, her tawny skin and almond eyes bewitchingly exotic in the small Maine village. *Careful,* the voice said.

"I think we say good night," he managed to say. "We've got a busy day tomorrow."

Immediately, her eyebrows creased in an exaggerated frown. *"C'est tout!"* she pouted. "You Yankees have had all the marrow sucked from your bones. I should have gone out with Sergio. He at least has the fire in the belly, even if his body odor could kill a goat." She squinted up at him. "So how exactly *do* you say good night in Stormhaven, Doctor Hatch?"

"Like this." Hatch stepped forward and gave her hand a shake.

"Ah." Bonterre nodded slowly, as if comprehending. "I see." Then, quickly, she took his face in her hands and pulled it toward her, letting her lips graze his. As her hands dropped away from his face caressingly, Hatch could feel the tip of her tongue flick teasingly against his for the briefest of moments.

"And that is how we say good night in Martinique," she murmured. Then she turned in the direction of the post office and, without glancing back, walked into the night.

24

The following afternoon, as Hatch came up the path from the dock after treating a diver's sprained wrist, he heard a crash resound from the direction of Wopner's hut. Hatch sprinted into Base Camp, fearing the worst. But instead of finding the programmer pinned beneath a large rack of equipment, he found him sitting back in his chair, a shattered CPU at his feet, eating an ice-cream sandwich, an irritated expression on his face.

"Is everything all right?"

Wopner chewed noisily. "No," he said.

"What happened?"

The programmer turned a pair of large, mournful eyes toward Hatch. "That computer impacted with my foot, is what happened."

Hatch looked around for a place to sit, remembered there was none, and leaned against the doorway. "Tell me about it."

Wopner shoved the last piece in his mouth and dropped the wrapper on the floor. "It's all messed up."

"What is?"

"Charybdis. The Ragged Island network." Wopner jerked a thumb in the direction of Island One.

"How so?"

"I've been running my brute-force program against that goddamn second code. Even with increased priority, the routines were sluggish. And I was getting error messages, strange data. So I tried running the same routines remotely over on Scylla, the *Cerberus* computer. It ran lickety-split, no errors." He gave a disgusted scoff.

"Any idea what the problem is?"

"Yeah. I got a good idea. I ran some low-level diagnostics. Some of the ROM microcode was rewritten. Just like when the pumps went haywire. Rewritten randomly, in bursts of a regular Fourier pattern."

"I'm not following you."

"Basically, it's *not possible.* Follow that? There's no known process that can rewrite ROM that way. And on top of that, in a regular, mathematical pattern?" Wopner stood up, opened the door to what looked like a refrigerated corpse locker, and slipped out another ice-cream sandwich. "And the same thing's happening to my hard disks and magneto-opticals. It only happens *here.* Not on the boat, not in Brooklyn. Just here."

"You can't tell me it's not possible. I mean, you saw it happen. You just don't know why yet."

"Oh, I know why. The frigging Ragged Island curse."

Hatch laughed, then saw Wopner was not smiling.

The programmer unwrapped the ice cream and took a massive bite. "Yeah, yeah, I know. Show me another reason, and I'll buy into it. But everyone who's come to this goddamn place has had things go wrong. Unexplainable things. When you get right down to it, we're no different from the rest. We just have newer toys."

Hatch had never heard Wopner talk like this. "What's gotten into you?" he asked.

"Nothing's gotten into me. That priest explained the whole thing. I ran into him at the post office yesterday."

So Clay's been talking to Thalassa employees, now, spreading his poison, Hatch thought, surprised at the strength of his anger. *The man's an irritant. Someone ought to squeeze him like a sebaceous cyst.*

His thoughts were interrupted when St. John appeared in the doorway. "There you are," he said to Hatch.

Hatch stared back. The historian was dressed in a bizarre combination of muddy Wellingtons, old tweed, and Maine oilcloth. His chest was heaving from exertion.

"What is it?" Hatch asked, rising instinctively, expecting to hear that there had been another accident.

"Why, nothing serious," said St. John, self-consciously smoothing down the front of his sou'wester. "Isobel sent me to bring you to our dig."

"Our dig?"

"Yes. You probably know I've been helping Isobel with the excavation of the pirate encampment." *Isobel this, Isobel that.* Hatch found himself mildly annoyed by the historian's familiar attitude toward Bonterre.

St. John turned to Wopner. "Did the program finish executing on the *Cerberus* computer?"

Wopner nodded. "No errors. No luck, either."

"Then, Kerry, there's no choice but to try—"

"I'm not going to rewrite the program for polyalphabetics!" Wopner said, giving the ruined CPU a childish kick. "It's too much work for nothing. We're running out of time as it is."

"Just a minute," Hatch said, trying to defuse the argument before it started. "St. John was telling me about polyalphabetic codes."

"Then he was wasting his breath," Wopner replied. "They didn't become popular until the end of the nineteenth century. People thought they were too error-prone, too slow. Besides, where would Macallan have hidden all his code tables? He couldn't have memorized the hundreds of letter sequences himself."

Hatch sighed. "I don't know much about codes, but I know a little about human nature. From what Captain Neidelman's been saying, this Macallan was a real visionary. We know he changed codes halfway through in order to protect his secret—"

"So it stands to reason he would have changed to a more difficult code," St. John interrupted.

"We know that, dummy," Wopner snapped. "What do you think we've been trying to crack for the last two weeks?"

"Hush up a minute," Hatch went on. "We also know that Macallan switched to a code containing all numbers."

"So?"

"So Macallan wasn't only a visionary, he was also a pragmatist. You've been approaching this second code as just a technical problem. But what if there's more to it than that? Could there be some pressing reason why Macallan used *only numbers* in the new code?"

There was a sudden silence in the hut as the cryptologist and the historian fell into thought.

"No," Wopner said after a moment.

"Yes!" St. John cried, snapping his fingers. "He used numbers *to conceal his code tables*!"

"What are you talking about?" Wopner grumbled.

"Look, Macallan was ahead of his time. He knew that polyalphabetics were the strongest codes around. But to use them, he needed several cipher alphabets, not just one. But he couldn't leave a lot of alphabet tables lying around where they might be discovered. So he used numbers! He was an architect and an engineer. He was *supposed* to have lots of numbers around. Mathematical tables, blueprints, hydraulic equations—any one of those could have done double duty, concealing a code table, and nobody would have been the wiser!"

St. John's voice had a clear, excited ring to it, and there was an eager flush on his face Hatch hadn't seen before. Wopner noticed it, too. He sat forward, the forgotten ice-cream sandwich melting into a brown-and-white pool on his desk.

"You might have something there, Chris old boy," he muttered. "I'm not saying you do, but you might." He pulled the keyboard toward him. "Tell you what. I'll reprogram the *Cerberus* computer to try a chosen-plaintext attack on the code. Now you boys let me be, okay? I'm busy."

Hatch accompanied St. John out of the hut and into the drizzle that cloaked Base Camp. It was one of those New England days when the moisture seemed to congeal out of the air itself.

"I should thank you," the historian said, pulling the sou'wester tighter around his plump face. "That was a good idea you had, you know. Besides, he'd never have listened to me. I was thinking about bringing the Captain into it."

"I don't know if I did anything, but you're welcome." Hatch paused. "Didn't you say that Isobel was looking for me?"

St. John nodded. "She said to say we've got a patient for you at the far end of the island."

Hatch started. "Patient? Why didn't you tell me first thing?"

"It's not urgent," said St. John with a knowing smile. "No, I wouldn't call it urgent, at all."

25

As they mounted the rise of land, Hatch glanced southward. The cofferdam had been completed, and Streeter's crew was now working on the massive pumps arrayed along the western shore, tuning them up after their recent ordeal and preparing them for use again the next day. Orthanc stood gray and indistinct, the illumination from the observation tower casting a greenish neon glow into the surrounding mists. Hatch could see the faint shadow of someone moving about inside.

They topped the crown of the island and descended toward the east, following a muddy path that wound its way through an especially dense area of old shafts. The excavation site itself was spread across a flat meadow lying behind a sharp bluff on the eastern shore. A portable storage shed was standing on a platform of concrete blocks at the far end of the meadow. In front of it, the heavy grass had been trampled flat, and a great checkerboard grid had been marked out in white string across an acre of ground. Several large tarps lay in a disorganized heap. Here and there, Hatch could see that some of the meter-square grids had already been opened, exposing rich, iron-stained earth that contrasted sharply with the wet grass. Bonterre and several diggers were crowded together on an earthen balk beside one of the squares, their slicker-clad backs glistening, while another excavator was cutting out the sod in an adjacent square. A few large orange markers had been posted beyond the gridsite. *It's a perfect spot for a pirate encampment,* Hatch thought. *Hidden from both the sea and the mainland.*

A hundred yards from the site, the ATV had been parked at a crazy angle on the rough ground, a large gray box trailer in tow. Several large pieces of equipment on three-wheeled carts were lined up behind. Rankin was kneeling beside one, preparing to winch it back into the trailer.

"Where'd these toys come from?" Hatch asked, nodding at the equipment.

Rankin grinned. "The *Cerberus,* man, where else? Tomographic detectors."

"Come again?"

The grin widened. "You know. Ground-penetrating sensors." He began pointing to the various carts. "You got your ground-penetrating radar. Good resolution of bodies and, say, mines up to a dozen feet or so, depending on the wavelength. Next to it is an infrared reflector, good in sand but with relatively low saturation. And there at the end is—"

"Okay, okay, I get the idea," Hatch laughed. "All for nonmetallic stuff, right?"

"You got it. Never thought I'd get a chance to use any of it on this gig. As it was, Isobel nearly had all the fun to herself." Rankin pointed at the orange markers. "You can see, I found a few scraps here and there, but she'd already struck the mother lode."

Hatch waved good-bye and trotted ahead to catch St. John. As they walked down to the site, Bonterre detached herself from the group and came over, slipping a hand pick into her belt and wiping her muddy hands on her rear. Her hair was tied back and her face and tawny arms were again smeared with dirt.

"I found Dr. Hatch," said St. John unnecessarily, a sheepish grin on his face.

"Thank you, *Christophe.*"

Hatch wondered at the sheepish grin. Surely St. John hadn't become the latest victim of Bonterre's charms? But nothing else, he realized, could possibly have pried the man away from his books to grub about in the mud and rain.

"Come," she said, grabbing Hatch's hand and pulling him toward the edge of the pit. "Move aside," she barked amiably at the workers, "the doctor is here. Clear up your loose."

"What's this?" Hatch asked in amazement, gazing down at a dirty brown skull rearing out of the dirt, along with what looked like two feet and a jumble of other ancient bones.

"Pirate grave," she said, triumphantly. "Jump in. But do not step on anything."

"So this is the patient." Hatch climbed down into the excavated square. He examined the skull for a moment with interest, then turned his attention to the other bones. "Or should I say, patients."

"*Pardon?*"

Hatch looked up. "Unless this pirate had two right feet, you've got two skeletons here."

"Two? That is *vachement bien!*" cried Bonterre, clapping her hands.

"Were they murdered?" Hatch asked.

"*Monsieur le docteur,* that is your department."

Hatch knelt and examined the bones more closely. A brass buckle lay on a nearby pelvis, and several brass buttons were scattered across what remained of a rib cage, along with an unraveling string of gold piping. He tapped the skull slightly, careful not to prize it from the surrounding matrix. It was turned to one side, mouth gaping open. There were no obvious pathologies: no musket ball holes, broken bones, cutlass marks, or other signs of violence. He couldn't really be sure what killed the pirate until the excavation was complete and the bones had been removed. On the other hand, it was clear that the original body had been buried in haste, even thrown into the grave: the arms lay askew, the head was turned and the legs bent. He wondered for a moment if the rest of the second skeleton lay beneath. Then his eyes were suddenly arrested by a golden gleam near one of the feet.

"What's this?" he asked. A compact mass of gold coins and a large, carved gemstone lay embedded in the earth near the lower tibia. Only a little of the soil had been brushed away, keeping the coins *in situ*.

A peal of laughter came from Bonterre. "I was wondering when you would see that. I believe the gentleman must have kept a pouch in his boot. Between *Christophe* and myself, we have identified them all. A gold mohur from India, two English guineas, a French louis d'or, and four Portuguese cruzados. All dating prior to 1694. The stone is an emerald, probably Inca from Peru, carved into the head of a jaguar. It must have given the pirate quite a blister!"

"So this is it at last," breathed Hatch. "The first of Edward Ockham's treasure."

"Yes," she replied more soberly. "Now it is fact."

As Hatch stared at the compact mass of gold—in itself a small numismatic fortune—a strange tingling began at the base of his spine. What had always seemed theoretical, even academic, was suddenly real. "Does the Captain know about this?" he asked.

"Not yet. Come, there is more to see."

But Hatch could not take his eyes off the fresh, thick gleam of metal. *What is it,* he thought, *that makes the sight so compelling?* There was something almost atavistic in the human response to gold.

Shaking the thought from his head, he climbed out of the excavated square. "Now you must see the pirate camp itself!" Bonterre said, slipping her arm into his elbow. "For it is stranger yet."

Hatch followed her toward another section of the dig, a few dozen yards off. It didn't look like much: the grass and topsoil had been cleared from an area perhaps a hundred yards square, leaving a brown, hardpacked dirt floor. He could see several blackened areas of charcoal, where fires had evidently been lit, and numerous circular depressions dug into the soil in no regular order. Countless tiny plastic flags had been stuck in the ground, each containing a number written in black marker.

"Those round areas were probably tent depressions," Bonterre said. "Where the workers who built the Water Pit lived. But look at all the artifacts that were left behind! Each flag marks a discovery, and we have been at work less than two days." She led Hatch to the far side of the storage shed, where a large tarp had been laid. She peeled it back, and Hatch looked down in astonishment. Dozens of artifacts had been laid out in neat rows, each numbered and tagged.

"Two flintlock pistols," she said, pointing. "Three daggers, two boarding axes, a cutlass, and a blunderbuss. A cask of grapeshot, and several bags of musket balls. A dozen pieces of eight, several items of silver dinner plate, a backstaff and a dozen ten-inch ship spikes."

She looked up. "Never have I found so much, so quickly. And then there's this." She picked up a gold coin and handed it to Hatch. "I do not care how rich you are, you do not lose a doubloon like this."

Hatch hefted the coin. It was a massive Spanish doubloon, cold and wonderfully heavy. The gold gleamed as brilliantly as if the coin had been minted a week ago, the heavy Cross of Jerusalem stamped off-center, embracing the lion and castle that symbolized León and Castile. The inscription PHILIPPVS+IV+DEI+GRAT ran around the rim. The gold warmed in his palm as his heart quickened despite himself.

"Now here is another mystery," said Bonterre. "In the seventeenth century, sailors never buried people with their clothes on. Because on board ship, *tu sais,* clothes were extremely valuable. But if you did bury them clothed, you would at least search them, *non*? That packet of gold in the boot was worth a fortune to anyone, even a pirate. And then, why did they leave all these other things behind? Pistols, cutlasses, cannon, spikes—these were the heart's blood of a pirate. And a backstaff, the very means of finding your way home? None would leave such things behind willingly."

At that moment St. John appeared. "Some more bones are appearing, Isobel," he said, touching her elbow lightly.

"More? In a different grid? *Christophe,* how exciting!"

Hatch followed them back to the site. The workers had cleared the second grid down to bone, and were now feverishly working on a third. As Hatch looked down at the new excavation, his excitement gave way to unease. Three more skulls were exposed in the second grid, along with a careless riot of other bones. Turning, he watched the workers in the third grid brush the damp dirt away with bristled brushes. He saw the cranium of one skull appear; and then another. They continued to work, the virgin soil yielding up brown: a long bone, then the talus and calcaneus of a heel, pointing skyward as if the corpse had been placed in the earth facedown.

"Teeth gripping the ground soil," Hatch murmured.

"What?" St. John started.

"Nothing. A line from the *Iliad.*"

No one buried their dead facedown, at least not respectfully. *A mass grave,* Hatch thought. *The bodies thrown in willy-nilly.* It reminded him of something he had once been called to examine in Central America, peasant victims of a military death squad.

Even Bonterre had fallen silent, her high spirits fading fast. "What could have happened here?" she asked, looking around.

"I don't know," Hatch said, a strange, cold feeling in the pit of his stomach.

"There do not appear to be signs of violence on the bones."

"Violence sometimes leaves only subtle traces," Hatch replied. "Or they might have died of disease or starvation. A forensic examination would help." He looked back over the grisly sight. Masses of brown bones were now coming to light, the skeletons stacked three deep in places, sprawled across each other, their tattered bits of rotten leather darkening in the light rain.

"Could you do such an examination?" Bonterre asked.

Hatch stood at the edge of the grave, not answering for a moment. It was nearing the close of day and the light was fading. In the rain, mist, and growing twilight, against the mournful sound of the distant surf, everything seemed to turn gray and lifeless, as if the vitality itself was being sucked out of the landscape.

"Yes," he said after a moment.

There was another long silence.

"What could have happened here?" Bonterre repeated to herself, in a whisper.

26

At dawn the next morning, the senior crew gathered in the pilothouse of the *Griffin*. The atmosphere was far different than the subdued, demoralized atmosphere Hatch remembered after Ken Field's accident. Today there was electricity in the air, a kind of pregnant expectation. At one end of the table, Bonterre was talking to Streeter about transporting the excavation findings to the storage facility, while the team leader listened silently. At the other end, a remarkably disheveled and unkempt-looking Wopner was whispering animatedly to St. John, punctuating his sentences with wild hand gestures. As usual, Neidelman was not to be seen, remaining in his private quarters until all had assembled. Hatch helped himself to a cup of hot coffee and a massive, greasy donut, then settled into a chair next to Rankin.

The door to the cabin opened and Neidelman emerged. As he came up the steps, Hatch could tell instantly that the Captain's mood matched that of the rest of the pilothouse. He motioned Hatch to the door of the cabin.

"I want you to have this, Malin," he said in a low tone, pressing something heavy into Hatch's hand. With surprise, Hatch recognized the massive gold doubloon Bonterre had uncovered the day before. He looked at the Captain, mutely questioning.

"It's not much," Neidelman said with a slight smile. "The smallest fraction of your eventual share. But it's the first fruit of our labors. I wanted you to have it as a token of our thanks. For making such a difficult choice."

Hatch mumbled his thanks as he slipped the coin into his pocket, feeling unaccountably awkward as he walked back up the steps and took a seat at the table. Somehow, he felt an aversion to taking the doubloon off the island, as if it would be bad luck to do so before the rest of the treasure had been found. *Am I growing superstitious, too?* he wondered half-seriously, making a mental note to lock the coin up in the medical hut.

Neidelman strode to the head of the table and contemplated his crew, emanating a remarkable nervous energy. Neidelman looked impeccable: showered, shaved, dressed in pressed khakis, the skin tight and clean across his bones. His gray eyes looked almost white in the warm light of the cabin.

"I believe there's a lot to report this morning," he said, glancing around the table. "Dr. Magnusen, let's start with you."

"The pumps are primed and ready, Captain," the engineer replied. "We've set up additional sensors in some secondary shafts, as well as inside the cofferdam to monitor water depth during draining."

Neidelman nodded, his sharp, eager eyes moving down the table. "Mr. Streeter?"

"The cofferdam's complete. All tests for stability and structural integrity are positive. The grappling hook's in place, and the excavating team is standing by on the *Cerberus*, awaiting instructions."

"Excellent." Neidelman looked toward the historian and the programmer. "Gentlemen, I believe you have news of a rather different nature."

"Indeed we have," St. John began. "As—"

"Let me handle this, Chris baby," Wopner said. "We've cracked the second code."

There was an audible intake of breath around the table. Hatch sat forward, his grip on the armrests tightening involuntarily.

"What does it say?" Bonterre blurted out.

Wopner held up his hands. "I said we'd *cracked* it. I didn't say we'd *deciphered* it. We've found some repeating letter sequences, we've set up an electronic contact sheet, and we've deciphered enough words that match the first half of the journal to know we're on track."

"That is all?" Bonterre slumped back in her chair.

"Whaddya mean, that's all?" Wopner looked incredulous. "That's the whole ball of wax! We know what kind of code it is: a polyalphabetic, using somewhere between five and fifteen cipher alphabets. Once we know the exact number, it's just a question of letting the computer do its thing. Using 'probable word' analysis, we should know that in a matter of hours."

"A polyalphabetic cipher," Hatch repeated. "That was Christopher's theory all along, wasn't it?" This elicited a grateful look from St. John and a dark glare from Wopner.

Neidelman nodded. "And the programs for the ladder array?"

"I've tested the simulation on the *Cerberus* computer," Wopner said, flinging back a lock of limp hair. "Smooth as butter. Of course, the thing isn't in the Pit yet," he added significantly.

"Very well." Neidelman stood and moved to the arc of window, then turned to face the group. "I don't think there's much I need add. Everything is ready. At ten hundred hours, we will start the pumps and begin draining the Water Pit. Mr. Streeter, I want you to keep a close watch on the cofferdam. Alert us at the first sign of any problem. Keep *Naiad* and *Grampus* nearby, just in case. Mr. Wopner, you'll be monitoring the situation from Island One, running final tests on the ladder array. Dr. Magnusen will direct the overall pumping process from Orthanc."

He stepped toward the table. "If all goes according to plan, the Pit will be drained by noon tomorrow. The structure will be monitored closely while it stabilizes. During that afternoon, our crews will remove the largest obstructions from the Pit and insert the ladder array. And the following morning, we'll make our first descent."

His voice dropped, and his eyes moved from person to person. "I don't need to remind you that, even free of water, the Pit will remain a highly dangerous place. In fact, removing the water places a much greater load on its wooden members. Until we've braced it with titanium struts, there could still be cave-ins or collapses. A small team will be inserted to make initial observations and place piezoelectric stress sensors on the critical wooden beams. Once the sensors are in place, Kerry here will calibrate them remotely from Island One. If there is any sudden increase in stress—signaling a possible collapse—these sensors will give us an early warning. The sensors will be remotely linked with the network via RF, so we'll have instantaneous response. Once they're in place, we can insert teams to begin a formal mapping process."

Neidelman placed his hands on the table. "I've thought carefully about the composition of this first team, but in the end there's really no question about who has to go. There will be three people: Dr. Bonterre, Dr. Hatch, and myself.

Dr. Bonterre's expertise in archaeology, soil analysis, and pirate construction will be vital in this first look at the Pit. Dr. Hatch must accompany us in case any unforeseen medical emergencies arise. And as for the third position on the team, I'm claiming Captain's privilege." A glint sparkled briefly in his eyes.

"I know that most, if not all of you, are anxious to see what awaits us. I fully understand. And let me assure you that, in the days to come, every one of you will get the chance to become familiar—no doubt all too familiar—with Macallan's creation."

He straightened up. "Any questions?"

The pilothouse was still.

The Captain nodded. "In that case, let's take care of business."

The following afternoon, Hatch left the island in fine high spirits. The pumps had been chugging in tandem all the previous day and on into the night, sucking millions of gallons of brown seawater out of the Pit, piping it across the island, and dumping it back into the ocean. Finally, after thirty hours, the uptake hoses had struck silt at the bottom of the Water Pit, one hundred forty feet down.

Hatch had waited tensely in his medical office, but by five he'd received word that high tide had come and gone without any apparent seepage of seawater into the Pit. There had been an anxious watch as the massive timbering groaned, creaked, and settled under its heavier burden. Seismographic sensors registered some small cave-ins, but they were in adjoining side tunnels and pits, not the main shaft. After a few hours the major settling seemed to cease. The cofferdam had held. Now, a crew was at work with a magnetized grappling hook, clearing out debris that had fallen into the Water Pit over the centuries and snagged on various crossbeams and timbers.

After mooring his boat in Stormhaven, Hatch stopped by the Co-op to pick up a salmon fillet. Then, on impulse, he drove the eight miles down the coast to Southport. Driving along Route 1A, the old coastal highway, he could see a line of sullen lightning flicker jaggedly across forty degrees of sea horizon, pale yellow against the blues and pinks of the evening. A massive thunderhead had reared up beyond Monhegan Island far to the south, rising to thirty thousand feet, its steel-colored interior glinting with internal electricity: a typical summer storm, promising a heavy rain and perhaps a few bolts, but without the virulence to blow up a dangerous sea.

Southport's grocery, though poorly stocked by Cambridge standards, carried a number of things not found in Bud's Superette. As he got out of his Jaguar, Hatch made a quick scan of the street: it wouldn't do for anyone to recognize him and report the treasonous act to Bud. He smiled to himself, thinking how alien this small-town logic would seem to a Bostonian.

Arriving home, Hatch made a pot of coffee and poached the salmon with lemon, dill, and asparagus, then whipped up a sauce of curried horseradish mayonnaise. Most of the dining room table was covered with a large green canvas, and he cleared a space at the far end and sat down with his dinner and the *Stormhaven Gazette*. He was partly pleased, and partly disappointed, to see that the Ragged Island dig had been relegated to second page. Pride of place on the front page went to the Lobster Bake, and to the moose that had wandered into the storage lot behind Kai Estenson's hardware store, run amok, and been tranquilized by game officials. The article on the dig mentioned "excellent progress, despite a few unanticipated setbacks," and went on to say that the man wounded in the prior week's accident was resting comfortably at home. As Hatch had requested, his own name did not appear.

Finishing his dinner, he dumped the dishes in the sink, then returned to the dining room and the large green canvas. Sipping a fresh cup of coffee, he pulled the canvas away, exposing a smaller canvas and, on it, two of the skeletons that had been uncovered the day before. He had chosen what he thought were the most complete and representative specimens from the staggeringly large burial group and brought the remains back to his house, where he could examine them in peace.

The bones were clean and hard and stained a light brown by the iron-rich soil of the island. In the dry air of the house, they emitted a faint odor of old earth. Hatch stood back, arms akimbo, and contemplated the skeletons and the pathetic collections of buttons, buckles, and hobnails that had been found with them. One had been wearing a ring—a gold ring set with an inferior cabochon garnet, valuable more for historical reasons than anything else. Hatch picked it up from among the neat array of items. He tried it on his little finger, found that it fit, and left it there, somehow pleased at this connection with the long-dead pirate.

Summer twilight lay across the meadow beyond the open windows, and frogs in the millpond at the bottom of the fields had begun their evening vespers. Hatch pulled out a small notebook, writing "Pirate A" on the left side of a page and "Pirate B" on the right. Then he scratched these out, replacing them with "Blackbeard" and "Captain Kidd." Somehow, it made them more human. Underneath each heading he began jotting his first impressions.

First, Hatch sexed the skeletons carefully: he knew there were more female pirates plying the seas in the 1700s than most people realized. Both were male. They were also nearly toothless, a characteristic shared with the other skeletons in the mass grave. Hatch picked up a loose mandible, examining it with a magnifying glass. Along the mandibular process there was scarring due to lesions of the gums, and places where the bone had been thinned and apparently eaten away. The few remaining teeth showed a striking pathology: a separation of the odontoblast layer from the dentin. Hatch laid the jawbone down, wondering whether this was due to disease, starvation, or simply poor hygiene.

He cradled the skull of the pirate he'd labeled Blackbeard and examined it, Yorick style. Blackbeard's one remaining upper incisor was distinctly shoveled: That implied either East Asian or Amerindian stock. He replaced the skull and continued his examination. The other pirate, Kidd, had broken his leg in the past: The ends of the bone around the fracture were abraded and calcified, and the break had not knitted together well. Probably walked around with a limp and in severe pain. In life, Kidd would not have been a good-tempered pirate. The man also had an old wound in the clavicle; there was a deep score in the bone, surrounded by spurs. *Cutlass blow?* Hatch wondered.

Both men appeared to be under forty. If Blackbeard was Asiatic, Captain Kidd was probably Caucasian. Hatch made a mental note to ask St. John if he knew anything about the racial makeup of Ockham's crew.

Hatch walked around the table, musing, then picked up a femur. It seemed light and insubstantial. He bent it and, to his surprise, felt it snap like a dry twig between his fingers. He peered at the ends. Clearly a case of osteoporosis—thinning of the bone—rather than simple graveyard decay. Looking more closely now, he examined the bones of the other skeleton and found the same symptoms.

The pirates were too young for this to be gerontological in origin. Again, it could be either poor diet or disease. But what disease? He ran through the symptoms of several possibilities, his diagnostic mind working, and then suddenly broke into a broad smile.

He turned to his working bookshelf and plucked off the well-thumbed copy of Harrison's *Principles of Internal Medicine.* He flipped through the index until he found what he was looking for, then turned quickly to the page. Scurvy, it read: Scorbutus (Vitamin C Deficiency). Yes, there were the symptoms: loss of teeth, osteoporosis, cessation of the healing process, even the reopening of old wounds.

He shut the book and slipped it back on the shelf. Mystery solved. Hatch knew that scurvy was now rare in most of the world. Even the poorest Third World areas he had practiced in produced fresh fruits and vegetables, and in all his career he had never seen a case. Until now. He stepped back from the table, feeling uncommonly pleased with himself.

The doorbell rang. *Damn,* he thought, hastily pulling the canvas cover over the skeletons before stepping into the living room. One of the prices of living in a small town was that nobody thought to telephone before dropping by. It wouldn't do, he thought, to be seen with his dining room table laid with ancient skeletons instead of the family silver.

Stepping up to the front and glancing out the window, Hatch was surprised to see the stooped form of Professor Orville Horn. The old man was leaning on his cane, wisps of white hair standing from his head as if charged up with a Van de Graaf generator.

"Ah, the abominable Doctor Hatch!" the professor said as the door opened. "I was just passing by and saw the lights burning in this old mausoleum of yours." His small bright eyes roved restlessly as he spoke. "I thought perhaps you'd been down in the dungeon, cutting up bodies. Some young girls are missing from the village, you know, and the townsfolk are restless." His gaze landed on the large canvas lump on the dining room table. "Hullo! What's this?"

"Pirate skeletons," said Hatch with a grin. "You wanted a present, right? Well, happy birthday."

The professor's eyes went incandescent with delight as he stepped unbidden into the living room. "Marvelous!" he cried. "My suspicions were well-founded, I see. Where did you get them?"

"Thalassa's archaeologist uncovered the site of the pirate encampment on Ragged Island a couple of days ago," Hatch replied, leading the old man into the dining room. "They found a mass grave. I thought I'd bring a couple back and try to determine cause of death."

The professor's shaggy brows raised at this information. Hatch pulled back the canvas cover and his guest leaned forward with interest, peering closely, poking an occasional bone with his cane.

"I believe I've figured out what killed them," said Hatch.

The professor held up his hand. "Hush. Let me try my hand."

Hatch smiled, remembering the professor's love of scientific challenges. It was a game they had played on many an afternoon, the professor giving Hatch a bizarre specimen or scientific conundrum to puzzle over.

Dr. Horn picked up Blackbeard's skull, turned it over, looking at the teeth. "East Asian," he said, putting it down.

"Very good."

"Not terribly surprising," replied the professor. "Pirates were the first equal opportunity employers. I imagine this one was Burmese or Bornean. Might have been a Lascar."

"I'm impressed," Hatch said.

"How soon they forget." The professor moved around the skeletons, his beady eyes glittering, like a cat circling a mouse. He picked up the bone Hatch had broken. "Osteoporosis," he said, raising an eye in Hatch's direction.

Hatch smiled and said nothing.

Dr. Horn picked up a mandible. "Evidently these pirates did not believe in flossing twice a day." He examined the teeth, stroked his face with a long, thoughtful finger, and straightened up. "All indications point to scurvy."

Hatch could feel his face fall. "You figured that out a lot faster than I did."

"Scurvy was endemic on sailing ships in past centuries. Common knowledge, I'm afraid."

"Maybe it was rather obvious," said Hatch, a little crestfallen.

The professor gave him a pointed look, but said nothing.

"Come on, have a seat in the parlor," Hatch said. "Let me get you a cup of coffee."

When he returned with a tray of cups and saucers a few minutes later, the professor had taken a seat in an easy chair and was idly flipping through one of the old mysteries Hatch's mother had so adored. She'd kept about thirty on the shelf—just enough, she'd said, so that by the time she'd finished the last, she would have forgotten the first, and could start over again. Seeing this man out of his own childhood, sitting in his front parlor and reading his mother's book, gave Hatch a sudden stab of bittersweet nostalgia so intense that he banged the tray harder than he intended onto the small table. The professor accepted a cup, and they sat for a moment drinking in silence.

"Malin," the old man said, clearing his throat. "I owe you an apology."

"Please," Hatch replied. "Don't even mention it. I appreciated your candor."

"To hell with my candor. I spoke hastily the other day. I still think Stormhaven would be better off without that goddamned treasure island, but that's neither here nor there. I have no right to judge your motives. You do what you have to do."

"Thanks."

"As atonement, I've brought along a little something for show-and-tell this evening," he said, the old familiar gleam in his eye. He removed a box from his pocket and opened it to reveal a strange, double-lobed shell, a complicated pattern of dots and striations set into its surface. "What is it? You've got five minutes."

"Siamese sea urchin," Hatch said, handing the shell back. "Nice specimen, too."

"Damn. Well, if you refuse to be stumped, at least make yourself useful by explaining the circumstances surrounding *that*." The professor jerked a thumb in the direction of the dining room. "I want all details, no matter how trivial. Any oversights will be dealt with most harshly."

Stretching out his legs and crossing his feet on the braided carpet, Hatch related how Bonterre found the encampment; the initial excavations; the discovery of the mass grave; the gold; the astonishing array of artifacts; the dense tangle of bodies. The professor listened, nodding vigorously, eyebrows alternately rising and falling at each fresh piece of information.

"What surprises me most," Hatch concluded, "is the sheer body count. The teams had identified eighty individuals by the end of this afternoon, and the site isn't fully excavated yet."

"Indeed." The professor fell into silence, his gaze resting vaguely in the middle distance. Then he roused himself, put down his cup, brushed the lapels of his jacket with a curiously delicate gesture, and stood up. "Scurvy," he repeated, almost to himself, and followed with a snort of derision. "Walk me to the door, will you? I've taken up enough of your time for one evening."

At the door the professor paused, and turned. He gave Hatch a steady look, his eyes dancing with veiled interest. "Tell me, Malin, what are the dominant flora of Ragged Island? I've never been there."

"Well," said Hatch, "it's a typical outer island, no trees to speak of, covered with sawgrass, chokecherries, burdock, and tea roses."

"Ah. Chokecherry pie—delicious. And have you ever experienced the pleasure of rose hip tea?"

"Of course," said Malin. "My mother drank lots of rose hip tea—for her health, she said. Hated the stuff myself."

Professor Horn coughed into his hand, a gesture that Hatch remembered as one of disapproval. "What?" he asked defensively.

"Chokecherries and rose hips," the professor said, "were a staple part of the diet along this coast in centuries past. Both are very good for you, extremely high in vitamin C."

There was a silence. "Oh," said Hatch. "I see what you're getting at."

"Seventeenth-century sailors may not have known what caused scurvy, but they *did* know that almost any fresh berries, fruits, roots, or vegetables cured it." The professor looked searchingly at Hatch. "And there's another problem with our hasty diagnosis."

"What's that?"

"It's the *way* those bodies were buried." The old man rapped his cane on the floor for emphasis. "Malin, scurvy doesn't make you toss fourscore people into a common grave and skedaddle in such a hurry that you leave gold and emeralds behind."

There was a distant flash, then a roll of thunder far to the south. "But what would?" Hatch asked.

Dr. Horn's only answer was an affectionate pat on the shoulder. Then he turned, limped down the steps, and hobbled away, the faint tapping of his cane sounding long after his form had disappeared into the warm enveloping darkness of Ocean Lane.

28

Early the next morning, Hatch entered Island One to find the small command-and-control center jammed with an unusually large gathering. Bonterre, Kerry Wopner, and St. John were all talking at once. Only Magnusen and Captain Neidelman were silent: Magnusen quietly running diagnostics, and Neidelman standing in the center, lighting his pipe, calm as the eye of a hurricane.

"Are you nuts or something?" Wopner was saying. "I should be back on the *Cerberus*, decrypting that journal, not frigging spelunking. I'm a programmer, not a sewer worker."

"There's no other choice," Neidelman said, taking his pipe from his mouth and looking at Wopner. "You saw the numbers."

"Yeah, yeah. What did you expect? Nothing works right on this damn island."

"Did I miss something?" Hatch said, coming forward.

"Ah. Good morning, Malin," Neidelman said, giving him

a brief smile. "Nothing major. We've had a few problems with the electronics on the ladder array."

"A few," Wopner scoffed.

"The upshot is that we'll have to take Kerry along with us this morning on our exploration of the Pit."

"The hell with that!" Wopner said petulantly. "I keep telling you, the last domino has fallen. That code is mine, believe you me. Scylla'll have the bad boy fully deciphered in a couple of hours."

"If the last domino has fallen, then Christopher here can do the monitoring," Neidelman said, a little more sharply.

"That's correct," St. John replied, his chest swelling slightly. "It's just a question of taking the output and making some character substitutions."

Wopner looked from one to the other, his lower lip projecting in an exaggerated pout.

"It's a simple matter of where you're most needed," Neidelman said. "And you're most needed on our team." He turned to Hatch. "It's imperative that we get these piezo-electric sensors in place throughout the Pit. Once they're linked to the computer network, they'll serve as an early warning system in case of structural failure anywhere underground. But so far, Kerry's been unsuccessful at calibrating the sensors remotely from Island One." He glanced at Wopner. "With the network acting flaky, that means he's going to have to come along with us and calibrate them manually, using a palmtop computer. Then he can download the information into the computer's registry. It's a nuisance, but there's nothing else for it."

"A nuisance?" Wopner said. "A major pain in the ass is more like it."

"Most of the crew would give half their shares to be along on the first penetration," St. John said.

"Penetrate this," Wopner muttered as he turned away. Bonterre giggled.

Neidelman turned to the historian. "Tell Dr. Hatch about the sentence you just deciphered from the second half of the journal."

St. John cleared his throat self-importantly. "It's not a sentence, really," he said. "More of a sentence fragment: *Ye who luste after the key to the,* some word or other, *Pitt shall find. . . .*"

Hatch looked at the Captain in amazement. "So there *is* a secret key to the Water Pit."

Neidelman smiled, rubbing his hands together with anticipation. "It's almost eight," he said. "Assemble your gear and let's get started."

Hatch returned to his office for his medical field kit, then met up with the group as they were trekking up the rise of the island toward Orthanc. "*Merde,* it's cold," Bonterre said, blowing on her hands and hugging herself. "What kind of a summer morning do you call this?"

"A summer morning in Maine," Hatch replied. "Enjoy it. The air will put hair on your chest."

"That is something I have little need of, *monsieur le docteur.*" She jogged ahead, trying to keep warm, and as Hatch followed he realized that he, too, was shivering slightly; whether from the cold or the anticipation of the coming descent he wasn't sure. The tattered edge of a front had at last begun to cast a long shadow across the island, swiftly followed by ranks of piling thunderheads.

As he reached the crest of the island, Hatch could see the tall form of Orthanc, bundles of multicolored cable streaming from its dark underbelly down into the maw of the Water Pit. Only it was no longer the Water Pit: Now it was drained, accessible, its innermost secrets waiting to be plumbed.

Hatch shivered again and moved forward. From this vantage point, he could see the gray crescent of the cofferdam, tracing an arc into the sea around the southern end of the island. It was a bizarre sight. On the far side of the cofferdam lay the dark blue expanse of ocean, disappearing into the perpetual veiling mist; on the closer side, the stony seabed lay exposed almost obscenely, scattered with pools of stagnant water. Here and there on the dry ocean floor, Hatch could see markers placed in rocky outcroppings: the flood tunnel entrances, tagged for later examination and analysis. On the beach beside the cofferdam there were several piles of rusted junk, waterlogged wood, and other debris grappled up from the depths of the Pit, cleared for their expedition.

Streeter and his crew were standing at the staging area beside the mouth of the Pit, pulling up some cables, dropping others. Approaching, Hatch saw what looked like the end of a massive ladder peering over the top of the Pit. The siderails of the ladder were made from thick gleaming tubes of metal, with two sets of rubber-covered rungs in between. Hatch knew it had taken the team much of the night to bolt the sections together and work them down, maneuvering past invisible obstacles and the remaining snarls of junk caught on the bracing timbers that crisscrossed the shaft.

"That's what I call a ladder on steroids," he said, whistling.

"It's more than a ladder," Neidelman replied. "It's a ladder array. Those tubular siderails are made from a titanium alloy. It'll serve as the backbone for the Pit's support structure. In time, we'll build a radiating web of titanium struts from the array, which will brace the walls and timbers and keep the Pit stable while we dig. And we'll attach a platform lift to the ladder, like an elevator."

He pointed toward the ladder struts. "Each tube is wired with fiber-optic, coax, and electrical cable, and every rung has a kick light. Eventually, every part of the structure will be computer controlled, from the servos to the monitoring cameras. But so far, friend Wopner has not been entirely successful in bringing the installation under remote control. Hence, his invitation to join us." He tapped the upper works with one foot. "Built to Thalassa specifications at a cost of nearly two hundred thousand dollars."

Wopner, overhearing, came over with a grin. "Hey, Captain," he said. "I know where you can pick up some really nice $600 toilet seats, too."

Neidelman smiled. "Glad to see your mood improving, Mr. Wopner. Let's get geared up."

He turned to the group. "Our most important task today is to attach these piezoelectric stress sensors into the cribbing and shoring beams of the Pit." He pulled one from his pack and handed it around. It was a small strip of metal, with a computer chip in its center, sealed in hard, clear plastic. At each end, sticking out at right angles, was a half-inch tack. "Just tap or press it into the wood. Mr. Wopner will calibrate and register it into his palmtop database."

While Neidelman talked, a technician approached Hatch and helped him shrug into a harness. Then the man handed him a helmet and showed him how to use the intercom and halogen headlamp. Next, he was handed a satchel containing a quantity of the piezoelectric sensors.

As he arranged his medical kit, Hatch saw Neidelman motioning him toward the railing. He stepped forward, and the Captain spoke into the mike attached to his helmet. "Magnusen, restore power to the array."

As Hatch watched, a string of lights snapped on along the ladder, illuminating in a brilliant yellow light the entire ghastly length of the Water Pit. The triple row of glowing struts descended into the earth like some pathway to hell.

For the first time, Hatch could see just what the Pit looked like. It was a ragged square, perhaps ten feet across, cribbed on all four sides with heavy logs, which were notched and mortised into massive vertical beams at each corner. Every ten feet, the shaft was crisscrossed by four smaller beams that met in the middle of the Pit, evidently bracing the sides and preventing them from collapsing inward. Hatch was struck by how overengineered the Pit seemed to be: It was as if Macallan had built it to last a millennium, instead of the few years it would take for Ockham to return and retrieve his treasure.

Staring down the descending rows of lights, Hatch finally realized, in his gut, just how deep the Pit was. The lights seemed to stretch toward a pinpoint of darkness, so far below that the rails of the ladder almost converged in the murky depths. The Pit was alive, rustling with the sounds of ticking, dripping, and creaking, along with indeterminate whispers and moans.

A distant rumble of thunder rolled over the island, and a sudden wind pressed down the sawgrass around the Pit. Then a hard rain followed, drowning bracken and machine alike. Hatch stood where he was, partly sheltered by the massive bulk of Orthanc. Within a matter of minutes, he thought, they would simply mount the ladder and climb to the bottom. Once again, the perverse feeling returned that everything was too easy—until he felt the Pit exhale the cold odor of the mudflat: a powerful smell of saltwater mingled with suppuration and decay, the outgassing of dead fish, and rotting seaweed. A sudden thought rushed into his mind: *Somewhere in that warren of tunnels is Johnny's body.* It was a discovery he both wanted and dreaded with all his soul.

A technician handed Neidelman a small gas-monitoring meter, and he slipped it around his neck. "Remember, we're not going down for a leisurely stroll," Neidelman said, glancing at the team. "The only time you are to be unclipped from the array is when it becomes necessary to place a sensor. We'll set them, calibrate them, and get out quickly. But while we're at it, I want everyone to make as many observations as possible: the condition of the cribbing, the size and number of the tunnels, anything that seems pertinent. The bottom itself is still deep in mud, so we'll be concentrating on the walls and the mouths of the side tunnels." He paused, adjusting his helmet. "Okay. Clip on your lifelines and let's go."

The lifelines were snapped onto their harnesses. Neidelman moved among them, double-checking the karabiners and testing each line.

"I feel like a frigging telephone repairman," Wopner complained. Hatch glanced over at the programmer, who, in addition to his satchel of piezoelectric sensors, had two palmtop computers dangling from his belt.

"Why, Kerry," said Bonterre teasingly. "For the first time, you look like a *man*."

By now, much of the crew still on the island had gathered behind the staging area. A cheer went up. Hatch looked around at the elated faces: this was the critical moment they—and he—had been waiting for. Bonterre was grinning widely. Even Wopner seemed affected by the growing excitement: he arranged his equipment and tugged on his harness with a self-important air.

Neidelman took a last look around, waving at the assembled group. Then he stepped to the rim of the staging area, buckled his line to the ladder array, and began to descend.

29

Hatch was the last to set foot on the ladder. The others were already stretched out for twenty feet below him. The lights on their helmets played through the murk as they descended hand over hand. A sense of vertigo passed over him, and he looked up, grabbing at the rung. The ladder was rock solid, he knew; even if he fell, the lifeline would keep him from tumbling far.

As they went deeper, a curious hush fell over the team and among the Orthanc crew, monitoring the mission over the live channel. The incessant sounds of the settling Pit, the soft creakings and tickings, filled the air like the whispered teeming of invisible sea creatures. Hatch passed the first cluster of terminal hubs, electrical outlets, and cable jacks that had been set into the ladder at fifteen-foot intervals.

"Everyone all right?" came Neidelman's low voice over the intercom. Positive responses came back, one by one.

"Dr. Magnusen?" Neidelman asked.

"Instruments normal," came the voice from inside Orthanc. "All boards are green."

"Dr. Rankin?"

"Scopes inactive, Captain. No sign of any seismic disturbances or magnetic anomalies."

"Mr. Streeter?"

"All systems on the array are nominal," the laconic voice replied.

"Very well," Neidelman said. "We'll continue descending to the fifty-foot platform, placing sensors as necessary, then stop for a breather. Be careful not to catch your lifelines on any beams. Dr. Bonterre, Dr. Hatch, Mr. Wopner, keep your eyes open. If you see anything strange, I want to know."

"You kidding?" came Wopner's voice. "The whole place is strange."

As he followed the group, Hatch felt almost as if he was sinking into a deep pool of brackish water. The air was clammy and cold, redolent of decay. Each exhalation condensed into a cloud of vapor that hung in the supersaturated air, refusing to dissipate. He looked about, the light on his helmet swiveling with his head. They were now in the tidal zone of the Pit, where the water had formerly risen and fallen twice a day. He was surprised to see the same bands of life he'd observed countless times among rocks and tidal pools at the sea edge: first barnacles, then seaweed, then mussels and limpets; followed by a band of starfish; next, sea cucumbers, periwinkles, sea urchins, and anemones. As he continued to descend, he passed strata of coral and seaweed. Hundreds of whelks still clung pitifully to the walls and beams, hoping in vain for a return of the tide. Now and then a whelk would at last lose its grip and fall into the echoing vastness.

Though an immense amount of flotsam and jetsam had already been removed from the drained Pit, an obstacle course of ancient junk remained. The ladder array had been deftly threaded through rotting beams, tangles of metal, and discarded pieces of drilling apparatus. The team stopped as Neidelman tapped a sensor into a small opening on one side of the Pit. As they waited for Wopner to calibrate the sensor, Hatch found his spirits beginning to flag in the mephitic atmosphere. He wondered if the rest of the team shared the feeling, or if he was simply laboring under the additional knowledge that, somewhere in this cold, dripping labyrinth, lay his brother's body.

"Man, it *stinks* down here," said Wopner, bending over his handheld computer.

"Air readings normal," came the voice of Neidelman. "We'll be installing a ventilation system over the next few days."

As they descended once again, the original cribbing in the shaft became more clearly defined as thick layers of seaweed gave way to long hanging strings of kelp. A muffled rumble came from above: thunder. Hatch glanced up and saw the mouth of the Pit etched against the sky, the dark bulk of Orthanc rising in a greenish glow. Farther above, lowering clouds had turned the heavens iron gray. A flicker of lightning flashed a momentary, ghastly illumination into the Pit.

Suddenly, the group below him stopped. Glancing down, Hatch could see Neidelman playing his beam into two ragged openings on either side of the shaft, tunnels that led off into darkness.

"What do you think?" asked Neidelman, tapping in another sensor.

"It is not original," said Bonterre, bending carefully into the second opening to affix a sensor and take a closer look. "Look at the cribbing: it is small and ripsawed, not adzed. Perhaps from the Parkhurst expedition of the 1830s, *non*?"

She straightened, then gazed up at Hatch, the lance of her headlamp illuminating his legs. "I can see up your dress." She smirked.

"Maybe we should switch places," Hatch replied.

They worked their way down the ladder, placing stress sensors into the beams and cribbing as they went, until they reached the narrow platform at the fifty-foot level. In the reflected light of his helmet, Hatch could see the Captain's face was pale with excitement. His skin was covered with a sheen of sweat despite the chilly air.

There came another flash of lightning and a distant sound of thunder. The rivulets of water seemed to be trickling faster now, and Hatch guessed it must be raining heavily up top. He looked upward, but the opening was now almost completely obscured by the crisscrossing beams they had passed, the drops of water flying down past his lamp. He wondered if the swell had increased, and hoped the cofferdam would hold it; he had a momentary image of the sea bursting through the cofferdam and roaring back into the Pit, drowning them instantly.

"I'm freezing," complained Wopner. "Why didn't you warn me to bring an electric blanket? And it stinks even worse than before."

"Slightly elevated levels of methane and carbon dioxide," Neidelman said, looking at his monitor. "Nothing to get worried about."

"He is right, though," said Bonterre, adjusting a canteen on her belt. "It *is* chilly."

"Forty-eight degrees," said Neidelman tersely. "Any other observations?"

There was a silence.

"Let's continue, then. We're likely to start finding more shafts and side tunnels beyond this point. We'll alternate placing the sensors. Since Mr. Wopner must calibrate each of them manually, he's going to fall behind. We'll wait for him at the hundred-foot platform."

At this depth, the crisscrossing support beams had accumulated an incredible variety of trash. Old cables, chains, gears, hoses, even rotting leather gloves were tangled in the crossbeams. They began to come across additional openings cut into the cribbed walls, where tunnels branched off or secondary shafts intersected the main pit. Neidelman took the first one, placing sensors back twenty feet; Bonterre took the next. Then it was his own turn.

Carefully, Hatch played out some line from his harness, stepping back from the ladder into the cross-shaft. He felt his foot sink into yielding ooze. The tunnel was narrow and low, stretching off at a sharp upward angle. It had been crudely hacked out of the glacial till, nothing as elegant as the Water Pit shaft, obviously of a later date. Stooping, he went twenty feet up the tunnel, then fished a piezoelectric sensor from his satchel and drove it into the calcified earth. He returned to the central Pit, placing a small fluorescent flag at the mouth of the shaft to alert Wopner.

As he stepped back onto the array, Hatch heard a loud, agonizing complaint from a nearby timber, followed by a flurry of creakings that whispered quickly up and down the shaft. He froze, gripping the ladder tightly, holding his breath.

"Just the Pit settling," came the voice of Neidelman. He had already set his sensor and moved farther down the ladder to the next cross-shaft. As he spoke, there came another screech—sharp and strangely human—echoing from a side tunnel.

"What the hell was that?" Wopner said, behind them now, his voice a little too loud in the confined space.

"More of the same," said Neidelman. "The protest of old wood."

There was another shriek, followed by a low gibbering.

"That's no goddamn wood," said Wopner. "That sounds alive."

Hatch looked up. The programmer had frozen in the act of calibrating one of the sensors: His palmtop computer was held in one outstretched hand, and the index finger of his other was resting on it, looking ridiculously as if he was pointing into his own palm.

"Get that light out of my eyes, willya?" Wopner said. "The faster I can get these suckers calibrated, the faster I can get out of this shithole."

"You just want to get back to the ship before *Christophe* steals your glory," said Bonterre good-humoredly. She had emerged from her side shaft and was now descending the ladder.

As they approached the hundred-foot platform, another sight came into view. Until now, the horizontal tunnels opening into the side of the shaft had been crude and ragged, poorly shored, some partially caved in. But here, they could see a tunnel opening that had obviously been carefully formed.

Bonterre shone her light at the square opening. "This is definitely part of the original Pit," she said.

"What's its purpose?" asked Neidelman, pulling a sensor out of his satchel.

Bonterre leaned into the tunnel. "I cannot say for sure. But you can see how Macallan used the natural fissures in the rock for his construction."

"Mr. Wopner?" Neidelman said, glancing up the shaft.

There was a brief silence. Then Hatch heard Wopner respond: "Yes?" It was a quiet, unusually subdued voice. Glancing up, he saw the young man leaning on the ladder perhaps twenty feet above him, beside a flag Hatch had placed, calibrating the sensor. Wet hair was plastered down the sides of his face, and the programmer was shivering.

"Kerry?" Hatch asked. "Are you all right?"

"I'm *fine.*"

Neidelman glanced first at Bonterre, then at Hatch, his eyes strangely eager. "It'll take him some time to calibrate all the sensors we've placed so far," he said. "Why don't we take a closer look at this side tunnel?"

The Captain stepped across the gap into the shaft, then helped the others across. They found themselves in a long, narrow tunnel, perhaps five feet high and three feet across, shored with massive timbers similar to those in the Water Pit itself. Neidelman took a small knife from his pocket and stuck it into one of the timbers. "Soft for a half inch, and then solid," he said, replacing the knife. "Looks safe."

They moved forward cautiously, stooping in the low tunnel. Neidelman stopped frequently to test the solidity of the beams. The tunnel ran straight ahead for fifty yards. Suddenly, the Captain stopped and gave a low whistle.

Glancing ahead, Hatch could see a curious stone chamber, perhaps fifteen feet in diameter. It appeared to have eight sides, each side ending in arches that rose to a groined ceiling. In the center of the floor was an iron grating, puffy with rust, covering an unguessably deep hole. They stood in the entrance to this chamber, each breath adding more mist to the gathering miasma. The quality of the air had grown sharply worse, and Hatch found himself becoming slightly lightheaded. Faint noises came from below the central grate: the whisperings of water, perhaps, or the settling of earth.

Bonterre was flashing her light along the ceiling. *"Mon dieu,"* she breathed, "a classic example of the English Baroque style. A little crude, perhaps, but unmistakable."

Neidelman gazed at the ceiling. "Yes," he said, "you can actually see the hand of Sir William here. Look at that tierceron and lierne work: remarkable."

"Remarkable to think it's been here all this time, a hundred feet beneath the earth," Hatch said. "But what was it for?"

"If I had to guess," Bonterre said, "I would say the room served some kind of hydraulic function, yes?" She blew a long cloud of mist toward the center of the room. They all watched as it glided toward the grate, then was suddenly sucked down into the depths.

"We'll figure it out when we've mapped all this," said Neidelman. "For now, let's set two sensors, here and here." He tapped the sensors into joints between the stones on opposite sides of the room, then rose and glanced at his gas meter. "Carbon dioxide levels are getting a little high," he said. "I think perhaps we ought to cut this visit short."

They returned to the central shaft to find that Wopner had almost caught up with them. "There are two sensors in a room at the end of this tunnel," Neidelman said to him, placing a second flag in the shaft's mouth.

Above, Wopner mumbled something unintelligible, his back to them as he worked with his palmtop computer. Hatch found that if he stayed in one place too long, his breath collected into a cloud of fog around his head, making it difficult to see.

"Dr. Magnusen," Neidelman spoke into his radio. "Status, please."

"Dr. Rankin is getting a few seismic anomalies on the monitors, Captain, but nothing serious. It could well be the weather." As if in response, a low *crump* of thunder echoed faintly down the shaft.

"Understood." Neidelman turned to Bonterre and Hatch. "Let's get to the bottom and tag the rest of the shafts."

Once again, they began their descent. As Hatch moved past the hundred-foot platform toward the base of the Water Pit, he found his arms and legs beginning to shake from weariness and cold.

"Take a look at this," Neidelman said, swiveling his light around. "Another well-constructed tunnel, directly below the first. No doubt this is part of the original workings, as well." Bonterre placed a sensor into the nearby joist, and they began moving again.

Suddenly, there was a sharp intake of breath beneath Hatch, and he heard Bonterre mutter a fervent curse. He looked down, and his heart leaped immediately into his mouth.

Below him, tangled in a massive snarl of junk, lay a partially skeletonized corpse, draped in chains and rusting iron, the eyeless sockets of its skull flickering crazily in the light of Bonterre's headlamp. Ribbons of clothing hung from its shoulders and hips, and its jaw hung open as if laughing at some hilarious joke. Hatch felt a curious feeling of displacement, a detached sensation, even as part of his brain realized that the skeleton was far too big to be that of his brother. Looking away and trembling violently, he leaned against the ladder, fighting to get his breath and heartbeat under control, concentrating on the rush of air into, and out of, his lungs.

"Malin!" came the urgent voice of Bonterre. *"Malin!* This skeleton is very old. *Comprends?* Two hundred years old, at least."

Hatch waited another long moment, breathing, until he was sure he could answer. "I understand," he said. Slowly, he unlocked his arm from the titanium rung. Then, equally slowly, he lowered first one foot, then the other, until he was level with Bonterre and Neidelman.

The Captain played his light over the skeleton, fascinated, oblivious to Hatch's reaction. "Look at the design of this shirt," he said. "Homespun, raglan seams, a common garment among early nineteenth-century fishermen. I believe we've found the body of Simon Rutter, the Pit's original victim." They stared at the skeleton until a distant rumble of thunder broke the spell.

The Captain wordlessly aimed his headlamp beneath his feet. Following the beam with his own, Hatch could now make out their final destination: the bottom of the Water Pit itself. A huge snarl of broken crosspieces, rusting iron, hoses, gears, rods, and all manner of machinery poked up out of a pool of mud and silt perhaps twenty feet beneath them. Directly above the snarl, Hatch could see several large shaftways converge onto the main Pit, damp seaweed and kelp dangling like steaming beards from their mouths. Neidelman moved his light around the wildly tangled ruin. Then he turned back to Bonterre and Hatch, his slender form haloed in the chill mist of his own breath.

"Perhaps fifty feet beneath that wreckage," he said in a low voice, "lies a two-billion-dollar treasure." Though his eyes moved between them restlessly, they appeared to be focusing on something far beyond. Then he began to laugh, a low, soft, curious laugh. "Fifty feet," he repeated. "And all we have to do now is *dig*."

Suddenly, the radio crackled. "Captain, this is Streeter." To Hatch, listening in his headpiece, the dry voice had a note of urgency in it. "We've got a problem here."

"What?" the Captain said, his voice hard, the dreamlike quality suddenly gone.

There was a pause, then Streeter came on again. "Captain, we—just a minute, please—we recommend that you abort your mission and return to the surface at once."

"Why?" Neidelman asked. "Is there some problem with the equipment?"

"No, nothing like that." Streeter seemed uncertain how to proceed. "Let me patch St. John in to you, he'll explain."

Neidelman flashed a quick, questioning look at Bonterre, who shrugged in return.

The clipped tones of the historian came across the radio. "Captain Neidelman, it's Christopher St. John. I'm on the

Cerberus. Scylla has just cracked several portions of the journal."

"Excellent," the Captain said. "But what's the emergency?"

"It's what Macallan wrote in this second part. Let me read it to you."

As Hatch stood on the ladder array—waiting in clammy darkness at the heart of the Water Pit—the voice of the Englishman reading Macallan's journal seemed to be coming from a different world entirely:

> *I have not been easy this se'ennight past. I feel it a certainty that Ockham has plans to dispatch me, as he hath so easily dispatched many others, once my usefulness in this vile enterprise has come to an ende. And so, by dint of the harrowing of my soule in the small hours, I have decided upon a course of action. It is this foul treasure, as much as the pirate Ockham, that is evil, and hath caused our miserie upon this forsaken island; and the death of so many in its taking. It is the treasure of the devil himself, and as such shall I treate it . . .*

St. John paused and there was the rustling of a computer printout.

"You want us to abort the mission over *this*?" The exasperation of Neidelman's voice was plain.

"Captain, there's more. Here it is:

> *Now that the Treasure Pitt hath been constructed, I know my time draweth to a close. My soule is at rest. Under my direction the pirate Ockham and his bande, unbeknownst, have cre-*

ated a permanent Tombe for these unholie gains, got by such suffering and grief. This hoard shall not be repossessed by mortal means. It is thus that I have labored, by various stratagems and conceits, to place this treasure in such wise that not Ockham, nor any other man, shall ever retrieve it. The Pitt is unconquerable, invincible. Ockham believes that he holds the key, and he shall Die for that belief. I tell ye now, ye who decipher these lines, heed my warning: to descend the Pitt means grave danger to lyfe and limbe; to seize the treasure means certayne Death. Ye who luste after the key to the Treasure Pitt shall find instead the key to the next world, and your carcase shall rot close to the Hell where your soule hath gone."

St. John's voice stopped, and the group remained silent. Hatch looked at Neidelman: a slight tremor had taken hold of his jaw, and his eyes were narrow.

"So you see," St. John began again. "It appears the key to the Water Pit is that there is no key. It must have been Macallan's ultimate revenge against the pirate who kidnapped him: to bury his treasure in such a way that it could never be retrieved. Not by Ockham. Not by anyone."

"The point is," Streeter's voice broke in, "it's not safe for anyone to remain in the Pit until we've deciphered the rest of the code and analyzed this further. It sounds like Macallan has some kind of trap in store for anyone who—"

"Nonsense," interrupted Neidelman. "The danger he's talking about is the booby trap that killed Simon Rutter two hundred years ago and flooded the Pit."

There was another long silence. Hatch looked at Bonterre,

then at Neidelman. The Captain's face remained stony, his lips compressed and set.

"Captain?" Streeter's voice came again. "St. John doesn't quite read it that way—"

"This is moot," the Captain snapped. "We're almost done here, just another couple of sensors to set and calibrate, and then we'll come up."

"I think St. John has a point," Hatch said. "We should cut this short, at least until we figure out what Macallan was talking about."

"I agree," said Bonterre.

Neidelman's glance flitted between them. "Absolutely not," he said brusquely. He closed his satchel, then looked upward. "Mr. Wopner?"

The programmer was not on the ladder, and there was no response on the intercom. "He must be down the passage, calibrating the sensors we placed inside the vault," Bonterre said.

"Then let's call him back. Christ, he probably switched off his transmitter." The Captain began to ascend the ladder, brushing past them as he climbed. The ladder trembled slightly under his weight.

Just a moment, Hatch thought. *That isn't right.* The ladder array had never trembled before.

Then it came again: a slight shudder, barely perceptible beneath his fingertips and under his instep. He looked questioningly at Bonterre, and in her glance he could see that she felt it, too.

"Dr. Magnusen, report!" Neidelman spoke sharply. "What's going on?"

"All normal, Captain."

"Rankin?" Neidelman asked into his radio.

"The scopes show a seismic event, but it's threshold, way below the danger level. Is there a problem?"

"We're feeling a—" the Captain began. Suddenly, a violent shudder twisted the ladder, shaking Hatch's hold. One of his feet skidded from the rung and he grabbed desperately to maintain his purchase. Out of the corner of his eye he saw Bonterre clinging tightly to the array. There was another jolt, then another. Above him, Hatch could hear a distant crumbling sound, like earth collapsing, and a low, barely audible rumble.

"What the hell's happening?" the Captain shouted.

"Sir!" came Magnusen's voice. "We're picking up ground displacement somewhere in your vicinity."

"Okay, you win. Let's find Wopner and get the hell out."

They scrambled up the ladder to the hundred-foot platform, the entrance to the vaulted tunnel opening above them, a yawning mouth of rotting wood and earth. Neidelman peered inside, lancing his beam into the dampness. "Wopner? Get a move on. We're aborting the mission."

As Hatch listened, only silence and a faint, chill wind emanated from the tunnel.

Neidelman continued looking into the tunnel for a moment. Then he glanced first at Bonterre, then at Hatch, his eyes narrowing.

Suddenly, as if galvanized by the same thought, all three unfastened their karabiners and scrambled toward the mouth of the shaft, stepping inside and running down the tunnel. Hatch didn't remember the low passage being this dark, somehow, or this claustrophobic. The very air felt different.

Then the tunnel opened into a small stone chamber. The two piezoelectric sensors lay on opposite walls of the chamber. Beside one was Wopner's palmtop computer, its RF antenna bent at a crazy angle. Tendrils of mist drifted in the chamber, lanced by their headlamps.

"Wopner?" Neidelman called, swinging his light around. "Where the hell did he go?"

Hatch stepped past Neidelman and saw something that sent a chill through his vitals. One of the massive groined stones of the ceiling had swung down against the chamber wall. Hatch could see a gap in the ceiling, like a missing tooth, from which damp brown earth dribbled. At floor level, where the base of the fallen ceiling stone pressed against the wall, he could make out something black and white. Moving closer, Hatch realized that it was the canvas-and-rubber toe of Wopner's sneaker, peeping out between the slabs. In a moment he was beside it, shining his light between the two faces of stone.

"Oh, my God," Neidelman said behind him.

Hatch could see Wopner, pressed tightly between the two granite faces, one arm pinned to his side, the other canted upward at a crazy angle. His helmeted head was turned to the side, gazing out at Hatch. His eyes were wide and full of tears.

Wopner's mouth worked silently as Hatch stared. *Please . . .*

"Kerry, try to stay calm," Hatch said, running his beam of light up and down the narrow crack while fumbling with his intercom. *My God, it's amazing he's still alive.* "Streeter!" he called into the intercom. "We have a man trapped between two slabs of rock. Get some hydraulic jacks down here. I want oxygen, blood, and saline."

He turned back to Wopner. "Kerry, we're going to jack these slabs apart and get you out very, very soon. Right now, I need to know where you hurt."

Again the mouth worked. "I don't know." The response came as a high-pitched exhalation. "I feel . . . all broken up inside." The voice was oddly slurred, and Hatch realized that the programmer was barely able to move his jaw to speak. Hatch stepped away from the wall face and tore open his medical kit, pulling out a hypo and sucking up two ccs of morphine. He wormed his hand between the rough slabs of stone and sank the needle into Wopner's shoulder. There was no flinching, no reaction, nothing.

"How is he?" Neidelman said, hovering behind him, the air clouding from his breath.

"Get back, for Chrissakes!" Hatch said. "He needs air." Now he found himself panting, drawing more and more air into his own lungs, feeling increasingly short of breath.

"Be careful!" Bonterre said from behind him. "There may be more than one trap."

A trap? It had not occurred to Hatch that this was a trap. But then, how else could that huge ceiling stone swing down so neatly . . . He tried to reach Wopner's hand to take his pulse, but it was bent too far out of reach.

"Jacks, oxygen, and plasma on their way," came Streeter's voice over the intercom.

"Good. Have a collapsible stretcher lowered to the hundred-foot platform, with inflatable splints and a cervical collar—"

"Water . . ." Wopner breathed.

Bonterre stepped up and handed Hatch a canteen. He reached into the crack, angling a thin stream of water from the canteen down the side of Wopner's helmet. As the tongue fluttered out to catch the water, Hatch could see that it was blue-black, droplets of blood glistening along its length. *Jesus, where the hell are those jacks . . .*

"Help me, please!" Wopner rattled, and coughed quietly. A few flecks of blood appeared on his chin.

Punctured lung, thought Hatch. "Hold on, Kerry, just a couple of minutes," he said as soothingly as he could, and then turned away and stabbed savagely at his intercom. "Streeter," he hissed, "the jacks, goddamnit, where are the jacks?" He felt a wave of dizziness, and gulped more air.

"Air quality is moving into the red zone," Neidelman said quietly.

"Lowering now," said Streeter amid a burst of static.

Hatch turned to Neidelman and saw he had already gone to retrieve them. "Can you feel your arms and legs?" he asked Wopner.

"I don't know." There was a pause while the programmer gasped for breath. "I can feel one leg. It feels like the bone has come out."

Hatch angled his light down, but was unable to see anything but a twist of trouser in the narrow space, the denim sodden to a dark crimson color. "Kerry, I'm looking at your left hand. Try to move your fingers."

The hand, strangely bluish and plump-looking, remained motionless for a long moment. Then the index and middle fingers twitched slightly. Relief coursed through Hatch. *CNS function is still there. If we can get this rock off him in the next few minutes, we've got a chance.* He shook his head, trying to clear it.

There was another tremor underfoot and a rain of dirt, and Wopner squealed: a high-pitched, inhuman sound.

"*Mon dieu*, what was that?" Bonterre said, quickly glancing up at the ceiling.

"I think you'd better leave," said Hatch quietly.

"Absolutely not."

"Kerry?" Hatch peered anxiously into the crack once again. "Kerry, can you answer me?"

Wopner stared out at him, a low, hoarse moan escaping his lips. His breath was now wheezing and gurgling.

Outside the tunnel, Hatch could hear the thud and clatter of machinery as Neidelman pulled in the cable that had been dropped from the surface. He sucked air desperately as a strange buzzing began sounding faintly in his head.

"Can't breathe," Wopner managed to say, his eyes pale and glassy.

"Kerry? You're doing great. Just hold on." Kerry gasped

and coughed again. A trickle of blood ran down from his lips to dangle from his chin.

The sound of running footsteps, then Neidelman reappeared. He slung two hydraulic jacks to the ground, followed by a portable oxygen cylinder. Hatch grabbed the mask and began screwing the nozzle onto the regulator. Then he spun the dial on the top of the cylinder and heard the reassuring hiss of oxygen.

Neidelman and Bonterre worked feverishly behind him, tearing off the plastic coverings, unfastening the jacks from the rods, screwing the pieces together. There was another shudder, and Hatch could feel the tall shaft of rock shift under his hand, inching inexorably toward the wall.

"Hurry!" he cried, head swimming. Dialing the flow to maximum, he snaked the oxygen mask into the narrow gap between the rocks. "Kerry," he said, "I'm going to place this mask over your face." He gasped, trying to find the air to keep talking. "I want you to take slow, shallow breaths. Okay? In just a few seconds we're going to jack this rock off you."

He placed the oxygen mask over Kerry's face, trying to slip it beneath the programmer's misshapen helmet. He had to mold the mask with his fingers to make it narrow enough to fit around the programmer's mashed nose and mouth; only now did he realize just how tightly the young man was wedged. The moist, panicked eyes looked at him imploringly.

Neidelman and Bonterre said nothing, working with intense concentration, fitting the pieces of jack together.

Craning to get a glimpse into the thinning space, Hatch could see Wopner's face, narrowed alarmingly, his jaw locked open by the pressure. Blood flowed from his cheeks where the edge of the helmet cut into his flesh. He could no longer speak, or even scream. His left hand twitched spasmodically, caressing the rock face with purple fingertips. A slight sound of escaping air came from his mouth and nostrils. Hatch knew that the pressure of the rock made breathing almost impossible.

"Here it is," Neidelman hissed, handing the jack to Hatch. Hatch tried to jam it in the narrowing crack.

"It's too wide!" he gasped, tossing it back. "Crank it down!"

He turned back to Wopner. "Now Kerry, I want you to breathe along with me. I'll count them with you, okay? One . . . two . . ."

With a violent trembling underfoot and a harsh grating sound, the slab lunged closer; Hatch felt his own hand and wrist suddenly squeezed between the tightening rocks. Wopner gave a violent shudder, then a wet gasp. As Hatch watched in horror, the beam of his light angling into the narrow space with pitiless clarity, he saw the programmer's eyes, bulging from his head, turn first pink, then red, then black. There was a splitting sound, and the helmet burst along its seams. Sweat on the crushed cheeks and nose grew tinged with pink as the slab inched still closer. A jet of blood came rushing from one ear, and more blood burst from the tips of Wopner's fingertips. His jaw buckled, sagging sideways, the tongue protruding into the oxygen mask.

"The rock's still slipping!" Hatch screamed. "Get me something, *anything*, to—"

But even as he spoke, he felt the programmer's head come apart under his hand. The oxygen mask began to burble as its airway grew clogged by a rush of fluids. There was a strange vibration between his fingers and to his horror he realized it was Wopner's tongue, twitching spastically as the nerves that fired the muscles burned out.

"No!" Hatch cried in despair. "Please God, *no!*"

Black spots appeared before his eyes as he staggered

against the rock, unable to catch his breath in the thick air, fighting to pull his own hand free from the increasing pressure.

"Dr. Hatch, step away!" Neidelman warned.

"Malin!" screamed Bonterre.

"Hey, Mal!" Hatch heard his brother, Johnny, whisper out of the rushing darkness. *Hey, Mal! Over here!*

Then the darkness closed upon him and he knew no more.

30

By midnight the ocean had taken on the kind of oily, slow-motion swell that often came after a summer blow. Hatch stood up from his desk and went to the Quonset hut window, moving carefully through the darkened office. He stared past the unlit huts of Base Camp, looking for lights that would indicate the coroner was finally on his way. Lines of spindrift lay in ghostly threads across the dark water. The rough weather seemed to have temporarily blown the fog from the island, and the mainland was visible on the horizon, an uncertain strand of phosphorescence under the star-strewn sky.

He sighed and turned from the window, unconsciously massaging a bandaged hand. He'd sat alone in his office as the evening turned to night, unwilling to move, unwilling even to turn on the lights. Somehow, the darkness made it easier to avoid the irregular shape that lay on the gurney, under a white sheet. It made it easier for him to push back all the thoughts and quiet whispers that kept intruding onto the edges of his consciousness.

There came a soft knock and the turn of a door handle. Moonlight framed the spare outline of Captain Neidelman, standing in the doorway. He slipped into the hut and disappeared into the dark shape of a chair. There was a scratching noise, and the room briefly flared yellow as a pipe was lit; the faint sounds of drawing smoke reached Hatch's ears a moment before the scent of Turkish latakia.

"No sign of the coroner, then?" Neidelman asked.

Hatch's silence was answer enough. They had wanted to bring Wopner to the mainland, but the coroner, a fussy, suspicious man who had come down all the way from Machiasport, insisted on moving the body as little as possible.

The Captain smoked in silence for several minutes, the only evidence of his presence the intermittent glow from the pipe bowl. Then he laid the pipe aside and cleared his throat.

"Malin?" he asked softly.

"Yes," Hatch replied, his own voice sounding husky and foreign in his ears.

"This has been a devastating tragedy. For all of us. I was very fond of Kerry."

"Yes," said Hatch again.

"I remember," the Captain went on, "leading a team working deepwater salvage off Sable Island. The graveyard of the Atlantic. We had six divers in a barometric pressure chamber, decompressing after a hundred-meter dive to a Nazi sub loaded with gold. Something went wrong, the seal of the chamber failed." Hatch heard him shifting in his chair. "You can imagine what happened. Massive embolisms. Blows apart your brain, then stops your heart."

Hatch said nothing.

"One of those young divers was my son."

Hatch looked at the dark figure. "I'm very sorry," he said. "I had no idea . . ." He stopped. *I had no idea you were a fa-*

ther. Or a husband. In fact, he really knew next to nothing about Neidelman's personal life.

"Jeff was our only child. The death was very hard on both of us, and my wife, Adelaide—well, she couldn't quite forgive me."

Hatch fell silent again, remembering the stark outline of his own mother's face that November afternoon they learned of his father's death. She had picked up a china candlestick from the mantelpiece, polished it absently with her apron, replaced it, then picked it up and polished it again, over and over, her face as gray as the empty sky. He wondered what Kerry Wopner's mother was doing at that moment.

"God, I'm tired." Neidelman shifted again in his chair, more briskly this time, as if to force himself awake. "These things happen in this business," he said. "They're unavoidable."

"Unavoidable," Hatch repeated.

"I'm not trying to excuse it. Kerry was aware of the risks, and he made that choice. Just as we all did."

Despite himself, Hatch found his eyes straying involuntarily to the misshapen form under the sheet. Dark stains had seeped through the material, ragged black holes in the moonlight. He wondered if Wopner really had made the choice.

"The point is"—the Captain lowered his voice—*"we must not let this defeat us."*

With an effort, Hatch pulled his eyes away. He sighed deeply. "I suppose I feel the same way. We've come this far. Kerry's death would be even more pointless if we abandoned the project completely. We'll take the time we need to review our safety procedures. Then we can—"

Neidelman sat forward in his chair. "The time we need? You misunderstand me, Malin. We must move forward *tomorrow.*"

Hatch frowned. "How can we, in the wake of all this? For one thing, morale is rock-bottom. Just this afternoon I heard a couple of workers outside my window, saying the whole venture's cursed, that nobody will ever recover the treasure."

"But that's exactly why we *must* press on," the Captain continued, his voice now urgent. "Stop the malingering, make them lose themselves in their work. It's not surprising people are rattled. What would you expect after such a tragedy? Talk of curses and supernatural folderol is a seductive, undermining force. And that's really what I'm here to discuss."

He moved his chair closer. "All these equipment troubles we've been having. Everything works just fine until it's installed on the island, then inexplicable problems crop up. It's caused us delays and cost overruns. Not to mention the loss of morale." He picked up his pipe. "Have you thought about a possible cause?"

"Not really. I don't know much about computers. Kerry didn't understand it. He kept saying there was some kind of malevolent force at work."

Neidelman made a faint sound of derision. "Yes, even him. Funny that a computer expert should be so superstitious." He turned, and even in the dark Malin could feel his stare. "Well, I *have* been giving it a lot of thought, and I've come to a conclusion. And it's not some kind of curse."

"What, then?"

The Captain's face glowed briefly as he relit his pipe. "Sabotage."

"Sabotage?" Hatch said incredulously. "But who? And why?"

"I don't know. Yet. But it's obviously someone in our inner circle, someone with complete access to the computer system and the equipment. That gives us Rankin, Magnusen,

St. John, Bonterre. Perhaps even Wopner, hoisted on his own petard."

Hatch was secretly surprised that Neidelman could talk so calculatingly about Wopner with the programmer's broken body lying only six feet away. "What about Streeter?" he asked.

The Captain shook his head. "Streeter and I have been together since Vietnam. He was petty officer on my gunboat. I know you and he don't see eye-to-eye, and I know he's a bit of an odd duck, but there's no chance he could be the saboteur. None. Everything he has is invested in this venture. But it goes deeper than that. I once saved his life. When you've been at war, side by side in combat with a man, there can never be a lie between you."

"Very well," Hatch replied. "But I can't think of a reason why anyone would want to sabotage the dig."

"I can think of several," said Neidelman. "Here's one. Industrial espionage. Thalassa isn't the only treasure hunting company in the world, remember. If we fail or go bankrupt, it would open the door to someone else."

"Not without my cooperation."

"They don't know that." Neidelman paused. "And even if they did, minds can always be changed."

"I don't know," Hatch said. "It's hard for me to believe that . . ." His voice trailed off as he remembered running into Magnusen the day before, in the holding area where artifacts were catalogued. She had been examining the gold doubloon found by Bonterre. At the time, he'd been surprised: the engineer, normally so controlled and devoid of personality, had been staring intently at the coin, a look of raw, naked desire on her face. She'd put it down quickly when he entered, with a furtive, almost guilty movement.

"Remember," the Captain was saying, "there's a two-billion-dollar fortune to be won here. Plenty of people in this world would shoot a liquor store clerk for twenty dollars. How many more would commit any crime, including murder, for two billion?"

The question hung in the air. Neidelman stood up and paced restlessly in front of the window, drawing heavily on his pipe. "Now that the Pit's been drained, we can reduce our workforce by half. I've already sent the sea barge and the floating crane back to Portland. That should make the job of security easier. But let us be clear about one thing. A saboteur may well be at work. He or she may have tampered with the computers, in effect forcing Kerry to join our team this morning. But it was *Macallan* who murdered Kerry Wopner." He turned suddenly from the window. "Just as he murdered your brother. The man has reached across three centuries to strike at us. By God, Malin, we can't let him defeat us now. We will break his Pit and take his gold. *And* the sword."

Hatch sat in the dark, a host of conflicting feelings welling up in him. He had never quite looked at the Pit in those terms. But it was true: Macallan had, in a way, murdered his innocent brother and the almost equally innocent computer programmer. The Water Pit was, at base, a cruel, cold-blooded engine of death.

"I don't know about any saboteur," he said, speaking slowly. "But I think you're right about Macallan. Look at what he said in his last journal entry. He's designed that Pit to kill anyone who tries to plunder it. That's all the more reason to take a breather, study the journal, rethink our approach. We've been moving too fast, way too fast."

"Malin, that's exactly the *wrong* approach." Neidelman's voice was suddenly loud in the small office. "Don't you realize that would play right into the saboteur's hands? We have to move ahead with all possible speed, map out the interior of the Pit, get the support structures in place. Besides, every day we delay means more complications, more hindrances. It's only a matter of time before the press gets wind of this. And Thalassa is already paying Lloyd's $300,000 a week in insurance. This accident is going to double our premiums. We're over budget, and our investors aren't happy. Malin, we're *so* close. How can you suggest we slow down now?"

"Actually," said Hatch steadily, "I was suggesting we knock off for the season and resume in the spring."

There was a hiss as Neidelman sucked in his breath. "My God, what are you saying? We'd have to take down the cofferdam, reflood the whole works, disassemble Orthanc and Island One—you can't be serious."

"Look," said Hatch. "All along, we've assumed that there was some key to the treasure chamber. Now we learn that there isn't. In fact, it's just the opposite. We've been here three weeks already. August is almost over. Every day we stay increases the chance of a storm bearing down on us."

Neidelman made a dismissive gesture. "We're not building with Tinkertoys here. We can ride out any storm that comes along. Even a hurricane, if it comes to that."

"I'm not talking about hurricanes or sou'westers. Those kinds of storms give three or four days' warning, plenty of time to evacuate the island. I'm talking about a Nor'easter. They can swoop down on this coast with less than twenty-four hours' notice. If that happened, we'd be lucky just to get the boats into port."

Neidelman frowned. "I know what a Nor'easter is."

"Then you'll know it can bring crosswinds and a steep-walled sea even more dangerous than the swell of a hurricane. I don't care how heavily it's been reinforced—your cofferdam would be battered down like a child's toy."

Neidelman's jaw was raised at a truculent angle; it was clear to Hatch that none of his arguments was making any headway. "Look," Hatch continued, in as reasonable a tone as he could muster. "We've had a setback. But it isn't a showstopper. The appendix may be inflamed, but it hasn't burst. All I'm saying is that we take the time to really study the Pit, examine Macallan's other structures, try to understand how his mind worked. Forging blindly ahead is simply too dangerous."

"I tell you we may have a saboteur among us, that we can't afford to slow down, and you talk to *me* of blindness?" Neidelman said harshly. "This is exactly the kind of pusillanimous attitude Macallan counted on. Take your time, don't do anything risky, piss your money away until nothing's left. No, Malin. Research is all very fine, but"—the Captain suddenly lowered his voice, but the determination in it was startling— "now's the time to go for the man's *jugular*."

Hatch had never been called pusillanimous before—had never even heard the word used, outside of books—and he didn't like it much. He could feel the old hot anger rising within him, but he mastered it with an effort. *Fly off the handle now, and you'll wreck everything,* he thought. *Maybe the Captain's right. Maybe Wopner's death has me rattled. After all, we've come this far. And we're close now, very close.* In the tense silence, he could make out the faint whine of an outboard coming over the water.

"That must be the coroner's launch," Neidelman said. He had turned back toward the window, and Hatch could no longer see his face. "I think I'll leave this business in your hands." He stepped away and headed toward the door.

"Captain Neidelman?" Hatch asked.

The Captain stopped and turned back, hand on the knob. Although Hatch could not make out his face in the dark, he could feel the extraordinary force of the Captain's gaze, directed inquiringly toward him.

"That sub full of Nazi gold," Hatch went on. "What did you do? After your son died, I mean?"

"We continued the operation, of course," Neidelman answered crisply. "It's what he would have wanted."

Then he was gone, the only mark of his visit the faint smell of pipe smoke, lingering in the night air.

31

Bud Rowell was not a particularly churchgoing man. He'd become even less of one in the years following Woody Clay's arrival; the minister had a severe, fire-and-brimstone manner rarely found in the Congregational church. Frequently, the man would lace his sermons with calls for his parishioners to take up a spiritual life rather more exacting than Bud cared for. But in Stormhaven, the ability to gossip fluently was required of a shopkeeper. And as a professional gossip, Rowell hated to miss anything important. Word had gone round that Reverend Clay had prepared a special sermon—a sermon that would include a very interesting surprise.

Rowell arrived ten minutes before the service to find the little church already wall-to-wall with townspeople. He worked his way toward the back rows, searching for a seat behind a pillar, from which he could escape unnoticed. Unsuccessful in this, he settled his bulk near the end of a pew, his joints complaining at the hardness of the wooden seat.

He gazed slowly around the congregation, nodding at the various Superette patrons who caught his eye. He saw Mayor Jasper Fitzgerald up near the front, gladhanding the head of the city council. Bill Banns, the editor of the paper, was a few rows back, his green visor as firmly on his head as if it had been planted there. And Claire Clay was in her usual position of second-row center. She'd become the perfect minister's wife, right down to the sad smile and lonely eyes. There were also a couple of strangers scattered about that he assumed were Thalassa employees. This was unusual; nobody from the excavation had shown up in church before. Maybe the bad business that had taken place out there shook them up a bit.

Then his eyes fell on an unfamiliar object, sitting on a small table next to the pulpit and covered with a crisp linen sheet. This was decidedly odd. Ministers in Stormhaven didn't make a practice of using stage props, any more than they made a practice of yelling or shaking their fists or thumping Bibles.

The church was standing room only by the time Mrs. Fanning arranged herself primly on the pipe organ bench and struck up the opening chords to "A Mighty Fortress Is Our God." After the weekly notices and the prayers of the people, Clay strode forward, his black robe loose on his gaunt frame. He moved into position behind the pulpit and looked around at the congregation, a humorless, fiercely determined expression on his face.

"Some people," he began, "might think that a minister's job is to comfort people. Make them feel good. I am not here today to make anyone feel good. It is not my mission, or my calling, to blind with consoling platitudes, or soothing half-truths. I'm a plain-speaking man, and what I'm going to say will make some people uncomfortable. *Thou hast showed thy people hard things.*"

He looked about again, then bowed his head and said a short prayer. After a moment of silence, he turned to his Bible and opened it to the text of his sermon.

"And the fifth angel sounded," he began in a strong, vibrant voice,

> "... And I saw a star fall from heaven unto the earth: and to him was given the key of the bottomless pit. And he opened the bottomless pit; and there arose a smoke out of the pit, as the smoke of a great furnace. And they had a king over them, which is the angel of the bottomless pit, whose name in the Hebrew tongue is Abaddon. The beast that ascendeth out of the bottomless pit shall make war against them, and shall overcome them, and kill them. And their dead bodies shall lie in the streets. But the rest of the men repented not of the works of their hands, that they should not worship idols of gold, and silver."

Clay raised his head and slowly closed the book. "Revelation, chapter nine," he said, and let an uncomfortable silence grow.

Then he began more quietly. "A few weeks ago, a large company came here to begin yet another doomed effort to recover the Ragged Island treasure. You have all heard the dynamite, the engines running night and day, the sirens, and the helicopters. You have seen the island lit up in the dark like an oil platform. Some of you are working for the company, have rented rooms to its employees, or benefited financially from the treasure hunt." His eyes roved the room, stopping momentarily on Bud. The grocer shifted in his seat and glanced toward the door.

"Those of you who are environmentally concerned might

be wondering what effect all the pumping, the muddy water, the gas and oil, the explosions, and the unceasing activity is having on the ecology of the bay. And those fishermen and lobstermen among you might wonder if all this has anything to do with the lobster catch being off twenty percent recently, and the mackerel run down almost as much."

The minister paused. Bud knew that the catch had been steadily dropping over the last two decades, dig or no dig. But this did not stop the considerable number of fishermen in the room from shifting restlessly in their seats.

"But my concern today is not simply with the noise, the pollution, the ruination of the catch, or the despoliation of the bay. These worldly matters are the proper domain of the mayor, if he would only take them up." Clay let a pointed glance fall upon the mayor. Bud watched as Fitzgerald smiled uncomfortably, a hand flying up to smooth one of his magnificent mustaches.

"My concern is the *spiritual* effect of this treasure hunt." Clay stepped back from the pulpit. "The Bible is very clear on this matter. Love of gold is the root of all evil. And only the poor go to heaven. There's no ambiguity, no arguing over interpretation. That's a hard thing to hear, but there it is. And when a wealthy man wanted to follow Jesus, He said give away all your riches first. But the man couldn't do it. Remember Lazarus, the beggar who died at the rich man's gates and went to the bosom of Abraham? The rich man who lived behind the gates went to hell, and begged for a drop of water to cool his parched tongue. But he did not receive it. Jesus couldn't have said it more clearly: *It is easier for a camel to go through the eye of a needle, than for a rich man to enter the kingdom of God.*"

He paused to look around. "Maybe this always seemed like someone else's problem to you. After all, most people in this town are not rich by any standard. But this treasure hunt has changed everything. Have you, any of you, stopped to think what will happen to our town if they succeed? Let me give you an idea. Stormhaven will become the biggest tourist attraction since Disneyland. It will make Bar Harbor and Freeport look like ghost towns. If you think the fishing is bad now, wait until you see the hundreds of tourist boats that will ply these waters, the hotels and the summer cottages that will spring up along the shore. The traffic. Think about the countless venture capitalists and gold seekers who will come, digging here, digging there, onshore and off, plundering and littering, until the land is destroyed and the fishing beds obliterated. Sure, some in this room will make money. But will your fate be any different than that of the rich man in the parable of Lazarus? And the poorest among you—those who make their living from the sea—will be out of luck. There will be only two choices: public assistance or a one-way bus ticket to Boston." At this mention of the two most despised things in Stormhaven—welfare and Boston—there was an unhappy murmur.

Suddenly Clay leaned back, gripping the pulpit. *"They will unleash the beast whose name is Abaddon.* Abaddon, king of the Pit. Abaddon, which in Hebrew means the Destroyer."

He scanned the rows sternly. "Let me show you something." Stepping away from the pulpit, he reached for the linen-covered shape on the small table. Bud leaned forward as an expectant hush filled the room.

Clay paused a moment, then plucked the sheet away. Beneath was a flat, black stone, perhaps twelve by eighteen inches, its edges badly worn and chipped. It was propped against an old box of dark wood. Carved into the face of the stone were three faint lines of letters, crudely highlighted in yellow chalk.

Clay stepped up to the pulpit and in a loud, trembling voice repeated the inscription:

> *"First will ye Lie*
> *Curst shall ye Crye*
> *Worst must ye Die*

"It's no coincidence this stone was found when the Pit was first discovered, and that its removal triggered the Water Pit's first death. The prophecy on this evil stone has held true ever since. All of you who would seek idols of gold and silver—whether it be directly, by digging, or indirectly, by profiting from the diggers—should remember the progression it describes. *First will ye Lie:* The greed for riches will pervert your nobler instincts."

He drew himself up. "At the lobster festival, Malin Hatch himself told me the treasure was worth a couple of million dollars. Not an inconsiderable sum, even for a man from Boston. But I later learned the real estimate was closer to two billion. Two *billion*. Why would Dr. Hatch deceive me like that? I can tell you only this: The idols of gold are a seductive force. *First will ye Lie*."

His voice dropped. "Then there's the next line: *Curst shall ye Crye*. The gold brings with it the curse of sorrow. If you doubt that, talk to the man who lost his legs. And what is the last line of the curse? *Worst must ye Die*."

His hollow eyes parsed the audience. "Today, many of you want to lift the stone, so to speak, to get the gold idol underneath. The same thing Simon Rutter wanted, two hundred years ago. Well, remember what happened to Rutter."

He returned to the pulpit. "The other day, a man was killed in the Pit. I spoke to that man not one week ago. He offered no excuses for his own lust for gold. In fact, he was brazen about it. 'I'm no Mother Teresa,' he told me. Now, that man has died. Died in the *worst* way, the very life crushed out of him by a great stone. *Worst must ye Die.* 'Verily, I tell you, he hath his reward.'"

Clay paused to draw breath. Bud glanced across the congregation. The fishermen and lobstermen were murmuring among themselves. Claire was looking away from the minister, down at her hands.

Clay began again. "What about all the others who have died, or been crippled, or bankrupted, by this accursed hoard? This treasure hunt is evil incarnate. And all who profit from it, directly or indirectly, must expect to be held accountable. You see, in the final reckoning, it will not matter whether or not treasure is found. The mere *search* is a sin, abhorrent to God. And the more Stormhaven follows that path of sin, the more penance we can expect to pay. Penance in ruined livelihood. Penance in ruined fishing. Penance in ruined *lives.*"

He cleared his throat. "Over the years, there's been a great deal of talk about a curse on Ragged Island and the Water Pit. Now, a lot of people will dismiss such talk. They'll tell you that only ignorant, uneducated folk believe that kind of superstition." He pointed toward the stone. "Tell that to Simon Rutter. Tell that to Ezekiel Harris. *Tell that to John Hatch.*"

Clay's voice fell almost to a whisper. "There have been some strange doings on the island. Doings they're not telling you about. Equipment is malfunctioning mysteriously. Unexplained events are throwing things off schedule. And just a few days ago, they uncovered a mass grave on the island. A grave hastily filled with the bones of pirates. Eighty, perhaps one hundred people. There were no marks of violence. Nobody knows how they died. *The beast that ascendeth out of the bottomless pit shall make war against them. And their dead bodies shall lie in the streets.*

"How did these men die?" Clay suddenly thundered. "It was the hand of God. Because do you know what else was found with the dead?"

The room fell so silent that Bud could hear the brushing of a twig against a nearby window.

"Gold," Clay said in a harsh whisper.

32

As site doctor for the Ragged Island venture, Hatch was required to handle the red tape relating to Wopner's death. So, bringing in a registered nurse from downcoast to watch the medical hut, he locked up the big house on Ocean Lane and drove to Machiasport, where a formal inquest was held. The following morning, he left for Bangor. By the time he finished filling out the reams of archaic paperwork and returned home to Stormhaven, three working days had passed.

Heading to the island that same afternoon, he soon felt more confident he'd made the right decision in not challenging Neidelman's decision to press on. Though the Captain had been driving the crews hard over the last several days, the effort—and the exhaustive new precautions the teams had been taking since Wopner's death—seemed to have dispelled much of the gloom. Still, the pace was taking its toll: Hatch found himself attending to almost half a dozen minor injuries during the course of the afternoon. And in addition to the injuries, the nurse had referred three cases of illness among the crew to him: a fairly high count, considering that the total personnel on the island had now dropped to half the original number. One complained of apathy and nausea, while another had developed a bacterial infection Hatch had read about but never seen. Yet another had a simple, nonspecific viral infection: not serious, but the man was running a pretty good fever. *At least Neidelman can't accuse him of malingering,* Hatch thought as he drew blood for later testing on the *Cerberus*.

Early the next morning, he wandered up the trail to the mouth of the Water Pit. The pace was obviously frantic—even Bonterre, emerging from the Pit with a handheld laser for measuring distances, barely had time for more than a nod and a smile. But a remarkable amount of work had been accomplished. The ladder array was now fully braced from top to bottom, and a small lift had been attached to one side for quick transport into the depths. A technician told him that the soundings and measurements of the Pit's interior were now almost complete. Neidelman was nowhere to be found, but the technician said the Captain had gone practically without sleep for the last three days, closeted in Orthanc, directing the gridding-out of the Pit.

Hatch found himself speculating on what the Captain would do next. It wasn't surprising, his throwing himself into his work in the wake of Wopner's death. But now the obvious tasks were almost done: the ladder array was complete, and the Pit would soon be fully mapped. Nothing remained except to descend the Pit and dig—with extreme caution—for the gold.

Hatch stood silently for a minute, thinking about the gold and what he would do with his share. A billion dollars was a stupendous amount of money. Perhaps it was unnecessary to put the entire sum into the Johnny Hatch Foundation. It would be hard even to *give* away such a sum. Besides, it would be nice to have a new boat for his berth in Lynn. And he found himself recalling a beautiful, secluded house on Brattle Street, close to the hospital, that was for sale. He also shouldn't forget that someday he would have children. Was it right to deprive them of a generous inheritance? The more he thought about it, the more it made sense to keep back a few million, perhaps as much as five, for personal use. Maybe even ten, as a cushion. Nobody would object to that.

He stared down into the Pit a moment longer, wondering if his old friend Donny Truitt was on one of the teams working somewhere in the dark spaces beneath his feet. Then he turned and headed back down the path.

Entering Island One, he found Magnusen in front of the computer, her fingers moving rapidly over a keyboard, mouth set in a disapproving line. The ice-cream sandwich wrappers and discarded circuit boards were gone, and the crowded racks of computer equipment, along with their fat looping cables and multicolored ribbons, had been placed in severe order. All traces of Wopner had vanished. Looking around, Hatch had the illogical feeling that the rapid cleanup was, in some strange way, a slight against the programmer's memory. As usual, Magnusen continued her work, completely ignoring Hatch.

He looked around another minute. "Excuse me!" he barked at last, feeling unaccountably gratified at the slight jump she gave. "I wanted to pick up a plaintext transcript of the journal," he explained as Magnusen stopped typing and turned to look at him with her curiously empty face.

"Of course," she said evenly. Then she sat, waiting expectantly.

"Well?"

"Where is it?" she replied.

This made no sense. "Where is what?" Hatch asked.

For a moment, Hatch was certain a look of triumph flitted over the engineer's face before the mask descended once again. "You mean you don't have the Captain's permission?"

His look of surprise was answer enough. "New rules," she went on. "Only one hardcopy of the decrypted journal is to be kept in Stores, not to be signed out without written authorization from the Captain."

Momentarily, Hatch found himself left without a response. "Dr. Magnusen," he said as calmly as possible, "that rule can't apply to me."

"The Captain didn't mention any exceptions."

Without a word, Hatch stepped over to the telephone. Accessing the island's phone network, he dialed the number for Orthanc and asked for the Captain.

"Malin!" came the strong voice of Neidelman. "I've been meaning to drop by to find out how everything went on the mainland."

"Captain, I'm here in Island One with Dr. Magnusen. What's this about me needing authorization to access the Macallan journal?"

"It's just a security formality," came the reply. "A way to keep the plaintext accounted for. You and I talked about the need for that. Don't take it personally."

"I'm afraid I do take it personally."

"Malin, even *I* am signing out the journal text. It's to protect your interests as much as Thalassa's. Now, if you'd put Sandra on, I'll explain to her that you have permission."

Hatch handed the phone to Magnusen, who listened for a long moment without comment or change of expression. Wordlessly she hung up the phone, then reached into a drawer and filled out a small yellow-colored chit.

"Hand this to the duty guard over in Stores," she said. "You'll need to put your name, signature, date, and time in the book."

Hatch placed the chit in his pocket, wondering at Neidelman's choice of guardian. Wasn't Magnusen on the Captain's shortlist of saboteur suspects?

But in any case, in the cold light of day the whole idea of a saboteur seemed very far-fetched. Everyone on the island was being extremely well paid. Some stood to gain millions. Would some saboteur jeopardize a sure fortune over a larger, but very uncertain one? It made no sense.

The door swung open again and the tall, stooped form of St. John entered the command center. "Good morning," he said with a nod.

Hatch nodded back, surprised at the change that had come over the historian since Wopner's death. The plump white cheeks and the cheerful, smug look had given way to slack skin and bags beneath reddened eyes. The requisite tweed jacket was unusually rumpled.

St. John turned to Magnusen. "Is it ready yet?"

"Just about," she said. "We're waiting for one more set of readings. Your friend Wopner made rather a mess of the system, and it's taken time to straighten everything out."

A look of displeasure, even pain, crossed St. John's face.

Magnusen nodded at the screen. "I'm correlating the mapping team's data with the latest satellite images."

Hatch's eyes traveled to the large monitor in front of Magnusen. It was covered with an impossible tangle of interconnected lines, in various lengths and colors. A message appeared along the bottom of the screen:

Restricted video feed commencing 11:23 EDT on Telstar 704
Transponder 8Z (KU Band) Downlink frequency 14,044 MHZ
Receiving and Integrating

The complex tangle on the screen refreshed itself. For a moment, St. John stared at the screen wordlessly. "I'd like to work with it for a while," he said at last.

Magnusen nodded.

"Alone, if you don't mind."

Magnusen stood up. "The three-button mouse operates the three axes. Or you can—"

"I'm aware of how the program works."

Magnusen left, closing the door to Island One behind her without another word. St. John sighed and settled into the now-vacant chair. Hatch turned to leave.

"I didn't mean for you to go," St. John said. "Just her. What a dreadful woman." He shook his head. "Have you seen this yet? It's remarkable, really."

"No," Hatch said, "What is it?"

"The Water Pit and all its workings. Or rather, what's been mapped so far."

Hatch leaned closer. What looked like a nonsensical jumble of multicolored lines was, he realized, a three-dimensional wireframe outline of the Pit, with depth gradations along one edge. St. John pressed a key and the whole complex began to move, the Pit and its retinue of side shafts and tunnels rotating slowly in the ghostly blackness of the computer screen.

"My God," Hatch breathed. "I had no idea it was so complex."

"The mapping teams have been downloading their measurements into the computer twice a day. My job is to examine the Pit's architecture for any historical parallels. If I can find similarities to other constructions of the time, even other works of Macallan's, it may help us figure out what booby traps remain and how they can be defused. But I'm having a difficult time. It's hard not to get swept away by the complexity. And despite what I said a minute ago, I have only the faintest conception of how this contraption works. But I'd rather swing from a gibbet than ask that woman for help."

He struck a few keys. "Let's see if we can clear away everything but the original works." Most of the colored lines disappeared, leaving only red. Now the diagram made more sense to Hatch: He could clearly see the big central shaft plunging into the earth. At the hundred-foot level, a tunnel led to a large room: the vault where Wopner was killed. Deeper, near the bottom of the Pit, six smaller tunnels angled away like the fingers of a hand; directly above, a large tunnel climbed sharply to the surface. There was another narrow tunnel angling away from the bottom, plus a small array of side workings.

St. John pointed to the lower set. "Those are the six flood tunnels?"

"Six?"

"Yes. The five we found, plus one devilish tunnel that didn't expel any dye during the test. Magnusen said something about a clever hydrological backflow system. I didn't understand half of it, to be honest." He frowned. "Hmm. That tunnel right above with the gentle slope is the Boston Shaft, which was built much later. It shouldn't be displayed as part of the original works." A few more keystrokes, and the offending tunnel disappeared from the screen.

St. John glanced quickly at Hatch, then looked back at the screen again. "Now, this tunnel, the one that angles toward the shore—" He swallowed. "It isn't part of the central Pit, and it won't be fully explored for some time yet. At first, I thought it was the original back door to the Pit. But it seems to come to a waterproofed dead end about halfway to the shore. Perhaps it's somehow linked to the booby trap that your brother . . ." His voice trailed off awkwardly.

"I understand," Hatch managed to say, his own voice

sounding dry and unnaturally thin to his ears. He took a deep breath. "They're making every effort to explore it, correct?"

"Of course." St. John stared at the computer screen. "You know, until three days ago I admired Macallan enormously. Now I feel very differently. His design was brilliant, and I can't blame him for wanting his revenge on the pirate who abducted him. But he knew perfectly well this Pit could just as easily kill the innocent as the guilty."

He began rotating the structure again. "Of course, the historian in me would say Macallan had every reason to believe Ockham would live long enough to come back and spring the trap himself. But the Pit was designed to live on and on, guarding the treasure long after Ockham died trying to get it out."

He punched another key, and the diagram lit up with a forest of green lines. "Here you can see all the bracing and cribbing in the main Pit. Four hundred thousand board feet of heart-of-oak. Enough to build two frigates. The structure was engineered to last hundreds of years. Why do you suppose Macallan had to build his engine of death so strong? Now, if you rotate it this way—" He poked another button, then another and another. "Damn," he muttered as the structure began to whirl quickly around the screen.

"Hey, you're going to burn out the video RAM if you twirl that thing any faster!" Rankin, the geologist, stood in the doorway, his bearlike form blotting out the hazy morning light. His blond beard was parted in a lopsided smile.

"Step away from that before you break it," he joked, closing the door and coming toward the screen. Taking St. John's seat, he tapped a couple of keys and the image obediently stopped spinning, standing still on the screen as if at attention. "Anything yet?" he asked the historian.

St. John shook his head. "It's hard to see any obvious patterns. I can see parallels here and there to some of Macallan's hydraulic structures, but that's about it."

"Let's turn it around the Z-axis at five revolutions per minute. See if it inspires us." Rankin hit a few keys and the structure on the screen began rotating again. He settled back in his chair, threw his arms behind his head, and glanced at Hatch. "It's pretty amazing, man. Seems your old architect may have had some help with his digging, in a manner of speaking."

"What kind of help, exactly?"

Rankin winked. "From Mother Nature. The latest tomographic readings show that much of the original Pit was already in place when the pirates arrived. In natural form, I mean. A huge vertical crack in the bedrock. That might even have been the reason Ockham chose this island."

"I'm not sure I understand."

"There's a huge amount of faulting and displacement in the metamorphic rock underlying the island."

"Now I'm *sure* I don't understand," Hatch said.

"I'm talking about an intersection of fault planes right under the island. Planes that got pulled apart somehow."

"So there were underground cavities all along?"

Rankin nodded. "Lots. Open cracks and fractures running every which way. Our friend Macallan merely widened and added as needed. But the question I'm still struggling with is, why are they here, under this island only? Normally, you'd see that kind of displacement on a wider scale. But here it seems restricted to Ragged Island."

Their talk was interrupted as Neidelman stepped into the hut. He looked at each of them in turn, a smile flicking across his face, then vanishing again. "Well, Malin, did Sandra give you the permission chit?"

"She did, thanks," Hatch replied.

Neidelman turned toward Rankin. "Don't stop on my account."

"I was just helping St. John here with the 3-D model," Rankin said.

Hatch looked from one to the other. The easygoing geologist suddenly seemed formal, on edge. *Has something happened between these two?* he wondered. Then he realized it was something in the way Neidelman was looking at them. He, too, felt an almost irresistible urge to stammer out excuses, explanations for what they were doing.

"I see," Neidelman said. "In that case, I have good news for you. The final set of measurements has been entered into the network."

"Great," Rankin said, and tapped a few more keys. "Got it. I'm integrating now."

As Hatch watched the screen, he saw small line segments being added to the diagram with blinding speed. In a second or two, the download was complete. The image looked much the same, though even more densely woven than before.

St. John, looking over the geologist's shoulder, sighed deeply. Rankin hit a few keys and the model began spinning slowly on its vertical axis once again.

"Take out all but the very earliest structures," St. John said.

Rankin tapped a few keys and countless tiny lines disappeared from the image on the screen. Now, Hatch could see just a depiction of the central Pit itself.

"So the water traps were added toward the end," Neidelman said. "Nothing we didn't already know."

"See any design elements common to Macallan's other structures?" Rankin asked. "Or anything that might be a trap?"

St. John shook his head. "Remove everything but the wooden beams, please." Some more tapping and a strangely skeletal image appeared against the blackness of the screen.

The historian sucked in his breath with a sudden hiss.

"What is it?" Neidelman asked quickly.

There was a pause. Then St. John shook his head. "I don't know." He pointed to two places on the screen where several lines intersected. "There's something familiar about those joints, but I'm not sure what."

They stood a moment, a silent semicircle, gazing at the screen.

"Perhaps this is a pointless exercise," St. John went on. "I mean, what kind of parallels can we really hope to find to Macallan's other structures? What buildings are ten feet across and a hundred forty plus feet tall?"

"The leaning tower of Pisa?" Hatch suggested.

"Just a minute!" St. John interrupted sharply. He peered more closely at the screen. "Look at the symmetrical lines on the left, there, and there. And look at those curved areas, one below the other. If I didn't know better, I'd say they were transverse arches." He turned toward Neidelman. "Did you know the Pit narrowed at the halfway point?"

The Captain nodded. "From twelve feet across to about nine at the seventy-foot level."

The historian began to trace points of contact across the wireframe model with his finger. "Yes," he whispered. "That would be the end of an upside-down column. And that would be the base of an interior buttress. And this arch, here, would concentrate mass distribution at one point. The opposite of a normal arch."

"Would you mind telling us what you're talking about?" Neidelman said. His voice was calm, but Hatch could see sharp interest kindling in his eyes.

St. John took a step away from the monitor, his face full of wonder. "It makes perfect sense. Deep and narrow like that . . . and Macallan was a religious architect, after all . . ." His voice trailed off.

"What, man?" Neidelman hissed.

St. John turned his large calf eyes to Rankin. "Rotate the Y-axis 180 degrees."

Rankin obliged, and the diagram on the screen rotated into an upside-down position. Now the outline of the Water Pit stood upright, frozen on the screen, a glowing red skeleton of lines.

Suddenly there was a sharp intake of breath from the Captain.

"My God," he breathed. "It's a cathedral."

The historian nodded, a triumphant smile on his face. "Macallan designed what he knew best. The Water Pit is nothing but a spire. A bloody upside-down cathedral spire."

33

The attic was more or less as Hatch remembered it: cluttered to overflowing with the kind of flotsam and jetsam families collect over decades of accumulated life. The dormer windows let in a feeble stream of afternoon light, which was quickly drowned in the gloomy stacks of dark furniture, old wardrobes and bedsteads, hat racks and boxes, and stacks of chairs. As Hatch stepped off the last step onto the worn boards, the heat, dust, and smell of mothballs brought back a single memory with razor sharpness: playing hide and seek under the eaves with his brother, rain drumming loudly on the roof.

He took a deep breath, then moved forward cautiously, fearful of upsetting something or making a loud noise. Somehow, this storehouse of memories was now a holy place, and he almost felt like a trespasser, violating its sanctuary.

With the surveying of the original Pit now completed by the mapping teams, and an insurance adjuster due on the island in the afternoon, Neidelman had little choice but to call a half-day halt to activity. Malin took the opportunity to head home for a bite of lunch and perhaps a bit of research. He remembered a large picture book, *The Great Cathedrals of Europe,* that had once been his great-aunt's. With any luck, he'd find it among the boxes of books that his mother had carefully stowed away in the attic. He wanted a private chance to understand, a little better, exactly what this discovery of St. John's meant.

He made his way through the clutter, barking one shin on a scuffed bumper-pool table and almost upsetting a hoary old Victrola, precariously balanced on a box full of 78s. He carefully replaced the Victrola, then glanced at the old records, scratched and worn to mere whispers of their original tunes: "Puttin' On the Ritz," "The Varsity Drag," "Let's Misbehave," Bing Crosby and the Andrews Sisters riffing to "Is You Is Or Is You Ain't My Baby." He remembered how his father insisted on playing the ancient thing on summer evenings, the raucous old show tunes and dance numbers floating incongruously over the yard and down toward the pebbled shore.

In the dim light of the attic, he could make out the great carved maple headboard of the family bed, leaning against a far corner. It had been presented by his great-grandfather to his great-grandmother on their wedding day. *Interesting present,* he thought to himself.

Sure enough: beside the headboard was an ancient wardrobe. And behind the wardrobe he could make out the boxes of books, as neatly stacked as when he and Johnny had put them there, under orders from his mother.

Hatch stepped up to the wardrobe and tried to force it aside. It moved an inch, perhaps a little more. He stepped back, contemplating the hideous, solid, topheavy piece of Victoriana, an artifact from his grandfather's day. He heaved at it with his shoulders and it moved a few inches, wobbling unsteadily. Considering how much the wood must have dried over the years, it was still damned heavy. Maybe some stuff remained inside. He sighed and wiped his brow.

The wardrobe's upper doors were unlocked, and they swung open to reveal a musty, vacant interior. Hatch tried the drawers at the bottom and found them empty as well. All except for the bottom drawer: stuffed in the back, torn and faded, was an old T-shirt with an iron-on Led Zeppelin logo. Claire had bought this for him, he remembered, on a high-school outing to Bar Harbor. He turned the shirt over in his hands for a moment, remembering the day she'd given it to him. Now it was just a two-decade-old rag. He put it aside. She'd found her happiness now—or lost it, depending on whom you asked.

One more try. He grabbed the wardrobe and wrestled with it, rocking it back and forth. Suddenly it shifted under his grasp, tilting forward dangerously, and he leaped out of the way as the thing went plummeting to the floor with a terrific crash. He scrambled to his feet as an enormous cloud of dust billowed up.

Then he bent down curiously, waving away the dust with an impatient hand.

The wooden backing of the wardrobe had broken apart in two places, revealing a narrow recess. Inside, he could make out the faint lines of newspaper clippings and pages covered with loopy, narrow handwriting, their edges thin and brittle against the old mahogany.

34

The long point of ochre-colored land called Burnt Head lay south of town, jutting out into the sea like a giant's gnarled finger. On the far side of this promontory, the cliff tumbled wooded and wild down to the bay known as Squeaker's Cove. Countless millions of mussel shells, rubbing against each other in the brittle surf, had given the deserted spot its name. The wooded paths and hollows that lay in the shadow of the lighthouse had become known as Squeaker's Glen. The name had a double meaning for students at Stormhaven High School; the glen also functioned as the local lovers' lane, and virginity had been lost there on more than one occasion.

Twenty-odd years before, Malin Hatch had himself been one of those fumbling virgins. Now he found himself strolling the wooded paths again, uncertain what impulse had brought him to this spot. He had recognized the handwriting on the sheets hidden in the wardrobe as his grandfather's. Unable to bring himself to read them right away, he'd left the house intent on strolling down along the waterfront. But his feet had taken him back of the town, skirting the meadows around Fort Blacklock, and angling at last toward the lighthouse and Squeaker's Cove.

He veered off onto a rutted path, a thin pencil line of black dropping through the thick growth. After several yards, the path opened into a small glade. On three sides, the rocky escarpment of Burnt Head rose steeply, covered in moss and creepers. On the fourth side, dense foliage blocked any view of the water, though the strange whispering of the mussel shells in the surf betrayed the nearness of the coast. Dim bars of light striped diagonally through the tree cover, highlighting ragged patches of grass. Despite himself, Hatch smiled as Emily Dickinson came unbidden to mind. " 'There's a certain Slant of light,' " he murmured,

> *Winter Afternoons—*
> *Which oppresses, like the Heft*
> *Of Cathedral Tunes—*

He looked around the secluded glade as the memories came charging back. Of one May afternoon in particular, full of nervous roving hands and short, tentative gasps. The newness of it, the exotic sense of venturing into adult territory, had been intoxicating. He shook the memory away, surprised at how the thought of something that had happened so long ago could still be so arousing. That had been six months before his mother packed them off to Boston. Claire, more than anyone, had accepted his moods; accepted all the baggage that had come with being Malin Hatch, the boy who'd lost the better part of his family.

I can't believe the place is still here, he thought to himself. His eyes caught a crumpled beer can peeping from beneath a rock; still here, and still apparently used for the same purposes.

He sat down on the fragrant grass. A beautiful late summer afternoon, and he had the glen all to himself.

No, not quite to himself. Hatch became aware of a rustling on the path behind him. He turned suddenly, and to his surprise saw Claire step out into the glade.

She stopped dead as she saw him, then flushed deeply. She was wearing a summery, low-cut print dress, and her long golden hair was gathered in a French braid that reached down her freckled back. She hesitated a moment, then stepped forward resolutely.

"Hello again," Hatch said, jumping to his feet. "Nice day to bump into you." He tried to make his tone light and easy. He wondered if he should shake her hand or kiss her cheek, and in the period of hesitation realized the time for doing either had already passed.

She smiled briefly and nodded.

"How was your dinner?" he asked. The question sounded inane even as it left his lips.

"Fine."

There was an awkward pause.

"I'm sorry," she said. "I must be intruding on your privacy." She turned to go.

"Wait!" he cried, louder than he'd intended. "I mean, you don't have to go. I was just out wandering. Besides, I'd like to catch up."

Claire looked around a little nervously. "You know how small towns are. If anyone were to find us here, they'd think—"

"Nobody's going to find us," he said. "This is Squeaker's Glen, remember?" He sat down again and patted the ground next to him.

She came forward and smoothed her dress with the self-conscious gesture he remembered.

"Funny we should meet here, of all places," he said.

She nodded. "I remember the time you put oak leaves over your ears and stood on that stone over there, quoting the whole of 'Lycidas.' "

Hatch was tempted to mention a few other things he remembered. "And now that I'm an old bonecutter, I throw medical metaphors in with the obscure poetry."

"What's it been, twenty-five years?" she asked.

"Just about." He paused for an awkward moment. "So what have you been doing all this time?"

"You know. Graduated from high school, planned to go to Orono and attend U Maine, but met Woody instead. Got married. No kids." She shrugged and took a seat on a nearby rock, hugging her knees. "That's about it."

"No kids?" Hatch asked. Even in high school, Claire had talked of her desire for children.

"No," she said matter-of-factly. "Low sperm count."

There was a silence. And then Hatch—to his own horror, and for some reason he couldn't begin to understand—felt an irresistible wave of mirth sweep over him at the incongruous turn the stumbling conversation had taken. He snorted involuntarily, then burst out laughing and continued laughing until his chest hurt and tears started. Dimly, he realized that Claire was laughing as hard as he was.

"Oh, Lord," she said, wiping her eyes at last, "what a relief it is to just laugh. Especially over this. Malin, you can't imagine what a terribly forbidden subject this is at home. Low sperm count." And they broke once again into choking peals of laughter.

As the laughter fell away, it seemed as if the years and the awkwardness fell with it. Hatch regaled her with stories of medical school, gruesome pranks they played in human anatomy class, and his adventures in Suriname and Sierra Leone, while she told him the various fates of their common friends. Almost all of them had moved to Bangor, Portland, or Manchester.

At last, she fell silent. "I have a confession, Malin," she said. "This meeting wasn't a complete accident."

Hatch nodded.

"You see, I saw you walking past Fort Blacklock, and . . . well, I took a wild guess where you were headed."

"Not so wild, it turns out."

She looked at him. "I wanted to apologize. I mean, I don't share Woody's feelings about what you're doing here. I know you're not in it for the money, and I wanted you to hear that from me. I hope you succeed."

"No need to apologize." He paused. "Tell me how you ended up marrying him."

She sighed and averted her eyes. "Must I?"

"You must."

"Oh, Malin, I was so . . . I don't know. You left, and you never wrote. No, no," she went on quickly, "I'm not blaming you. I know I stopped going out with you before then."

"That's right. For Richard Moe, star quarterback. How is old Dick?"

"I don't know. I broke up with him three weeks after you left Stormhaven. I never cared for him much, anyway. I was mad at you, more than anything else. There was this part of you I could never reach, this hard place you kept from me. You had left Stormhaven long before you really left, if you know what I mean. It got to me after a while." She shrugged. "I kept hoping you'd come after me. But then one day, you and your mother were gone."

"Yup. Off to Boston. I guess I was a pretty gloomy kid."

"After you left, it was all the same old guys in Stormhaven. God, they were so boring. I was all set to go to college. And then this young minister came. He'd been to Woodstock, been tear-gassed at the '68 Chicago convention. He seemed so fiery and sincere. He'd inherited millions, you know—margarine—and he gave it all to the poor, every penny. Malin, I wish you'd known him then. He was so different. Full of passion for the big causes, a man who really believed he could change the world. He was so intense. I couldn't believe that he could have any interest in *me*. And you know, he never talked God to me. He just tried to live by His example. I still remember how he couldn't bear the thought of being the reason I didn't get my degree. He insisted I go to the Community College. He's the only man I've ever met who would never tell a lie, no matter how much the truth might hurt."

"So what happened?"

Claire sighed and dropped her chin onto her knees. "I'm not sure, exactly. Over the years, he seemed to shrink somehow. Small towns can be deadly, Malin, especially for someone like Woody. You know how it is. Stormhaven is its own little world. Nobody cared about politics here, nobody cared about nuclear proliferation, about starving children in Biafra. I begged Woody to leave, but he's so stubborn. He'd come here to change this little town, and he wasn't going to leave until he did. Oh, people tolerated him, and looked on all his causes and fund-raisers with a kind of amusement. Nobody even got mad about his liberal politics. They just ignored it. That was the worst for him—being politely ignored. He became more and more—" She paused, thinking. "I don't know how to say it, exactly. Rigid and moralistic. Even at home. He never learned to lighten up. And having no sense of humor made it harder."

"Well, Maine humor can take some getting used to," Hatch said as charitably as he could.

"No, Malin, I mean it literally. Woody never laughs. He

never finds anything funny. He just doesn't get it. I don't know if it's something in his background, or his genes, or what. We don't talk about it. Maybe that's one reason he's so ardent, so unmoving in the things he believes in." She hesitated. "And now he has something to believe in, all right. With this crusade against your treasure hunt, it's like he has a new cause. Something he thinks Stormhaven *will* care about."

"What is it about the dig, anyway?" Hatch asked. "Or is it the dig? Does he know about us?"

She turned to look at him. "Of course he knows about us. A long time ago, he demanded honesty, so I told him everything. Wasn't all that much to tell." She gave a short laugh.

Serves me right for asking, Hatch thought. "Well, he'd better start looking for another cause. We're almost done."

"Really? How can you be sure?"

"The crew historian made a discovery this morning. He learned that Macallan, the guy who built the Water Pit, designed it as a kind of cathedral spire."

Claire frowned. "A spire? There's no spire on the island."

"No, no, I mean an *upside-down* spire. It sounded crazy to me, too. But when you think about it, it makes a lot of sense. He was explaining it to me." It felt good to talk. And Hatch somehow knew that he could trust Claire to keep a confidence. "See, Red Ned Ockham wanted this Macallan to build something that would keep his treasure safe until he came back to retrieve it."

"Retrieve it how?"

"Through a secret back door. But Macallan had other ideas. In revenge for being kidnapped, he designed the Pit so that *nobody,* not even Red Ned, could get at the treasure. He made sure that if Red Ned ever tried, he'd be killed. Of course, Red Ned died before he could return to claim his hoard, and the Pit has resisted attack ever since. But we're using technologies Macallan never dreamed of. And now that the Pit is drained of water, we've been able to figure out exactly what he built. Macallan *designed* churches. And you know how churches have a complex internal and external buttressing to keep them from falling down, right? Well, Macallan just inverted the whole scheme, and used it as the supports for his Pit during its construction. Then he secretly removed the most important supports as the Pit was filled in. None of the pirates would have guessed anything was wrong. When Ockham returned, he'd have rebuilt his coffer-dam, sealed his flood tunnels and pumped out the Pit, if necessary. But when he tried to actually retrieve the treasure, the whole Pit would have collapsed on him. That was Macallan's trap. But, by re-creating the cathedral braces, we can stabilize the Pit, extract the treasure without fear."

"That's incredible," she said.

"Yes, it is."

"Then why aren't you more excited?"

Hatch paused. "Is it that obvious?" he laughed quietly. "Despite everything that's happened, I guess there are times when I still feel a little ambivalent about the whole project. Gold, or the lure of gold, does strange things to people. I'm no exception. I keep telling myself this is all about finding out what happened to Johnny. I'd planned to put my share into a foundation in his memory. But every now and then I catch myself thinking about what I could do with all that money."

"That's only natural, Malin."

"Maybe. But that doesn't make me feel any better about it. Your Reverend gave all his away, remember?" He sighed. "Maybe he's a little bit right about me, after all. Anyway, he doesn't seem to have caused much damage with his opposition."

"You're wrong about that." Claire looked at him. "You know about the sermon last Sunday?"

"I heard something about it."

"He read a passage out of Revelation. It had a huge effect on the fishermen. And did you hear he brought out the Curse Stone?"

Hatch frowned. "No."

"He said the treasure was worth two billion. That you'd lied, telling him it was worth much less. Did you lie to him, Malin?"

"I—" Hatch stopped, uncertain of whether to feel more angry at Clay or at himself. "I guess I got defensive, the way he cornered me at the lobster festival like that. So, yes, I lowballed the number. I didn't want to arm him with more information than necessary."

"Well, he's armed now. The haul is down this year, and in the minds of the fishermen he's linked that to the dig. He really was able to split the town over this one. He's finally found the issue he's been looking for these twenty years."

"Claire, the haul is down *every* year. They've been overfishing and overlobstering for half a century."

"You know that, and I know that. But now they've got something to blame it on. Malin, they're planning some kind of protest."

Hatch looked at her.

"I don't know the details. But I've never seen Woody so charged up, not since we were first married. It's all come together over the last day or two. He's gotten the fishermen and lobstermen together, and they're planning something big."

"Can you find out more?"

Claire fell silent, looking at the ground. "I've told you this much," she said after a moment. "Don't ask me to spy on my husband."

"I'm sorry," Hatch said. "I didn't mean that. You know that's the last thing I'd want."

Suddenly, Claire hid her face in her hands. "You don't understand," she cried. "Oh, Malin, if only I *could* . . ." Her shoulders sagged as she began to sob.

Gently, Malin pulled her head to his shoulder. "I'm sorry," she murmured. "I'm acting like such a child."

"Shhh," Malin whispered quietly, patting her shoulders. As her sobs died away, he smelled the fresh apple scent of her hair, felt the moistness of her breath through his shirt. Her cheek was smooth against his and as she mumbled something indistinct he felt the hot trickle of a tear touch his lips. His tongue came forward to it. As she turned toward him he pulled his head back just enough to let his lips graze hers. He kissed her lightly, feeling the smooth line of her lips, sensing the looseness in her jaw. He kissed her again, tentatively, then a little harder. And then, suddenly, their mouths were locked together and her hands were tangled in his hair. The strange noise of the surf, the warmth of the glade, seemed to recede into nothingness. The world was instantly bounded by themselves. His heart raced as he slid his tongue into her mouth and she sucked on it. Her hands were clutching his shoulder blades now, digging into his shirt. Dimly, he was aware that, as kids, they had never kissed with this kind of abandon. *Or was it just that we didn't know how?* He leaned toward her hungrily, one hand gently teasing the fine hairs of her neck while the other slid almost involuntarily down the curve of her blouse, to her waist, to her loosening knees. A moan escaped her lips as her legs parted. He felt the narrow line of sweat that creased the inside of her knee. The apple-heavy air became tinged with a scent of musk.

Suddenly she pulled away from him. "No, Malin," she

said huskily, clambering to her feet and brushing at her dress.

"Claire—" he began, reaching out one hand. But she had already turned away.

He watched her stumble back up the path, disappearing almost immediately into the green fastness of the glen. His heart was pounding, and an uncomfortable mixture of lust, guilt, and adrenaline coursed through his veins. An affair with the minister's wife: Stormhaven would never tolerate it. He'd just done one of the stupidest things he had ever managed to do in his life. It was a mistake, a foolish lapse of judgment—yet as he rose to his feet and moved slowly down a different path, he found his hot imagination turning to what would have happened if she had not pulled herself away.

Early the next morning, Hatch jogged up the short path toward Base Camp and opened the door to St. John's office. To his surprise, the historian was already there, his aged typewriter pushed to one side, a half dozen books open before him.

"I didn't think I'd find you here so early," Hatch said. "I was planning to leave you a note asking you to stop by the medical hut."

The Englishman sat back, rubbing weary eyes with plump fingers. "Actually, I wanted a word with you anyway. I've made an interesting discovery."

"So have I." Wordlessly, Hatch held out a large sheaf of yellowed pages, stuffed into several folders. Making space on his cluttered desk, St. John spread the folders in front of him. Gradually, the tired look on his face fell away. In the act of picking up an old sheet of parchment, he looked up.

"Where did you get these?" he asked.

"They were hidden in an old armoire in my attic. They're

records from my grandfather's own research. I recognize his handwriting on some of the sheets. He became obsessed with the treasure, you know, and it ruined him. My father burned most of the records after my grandfather's death, but I guess he missed these."

St. John turned back to the parchment. "Extraordinary," he murmured. "Some of these even escaped our researchers at the *Archivos de los Indios* in Seville."

"My Spanish is a little rusty, so I wasn't able to translate everything. But this was the thing I found most interesting." Hatch pointed to a folder marked *Archivos de la Ciudad de Cádiz.* Inside was a dark, blurry photograph of an original manuscript, much soiled by handling.

"Let's see," St. John began. *"Records from the Court of Cádiz, 1661 to 1700. Octavo 16.* Hmm. *Throughout the reign of the Holy Roman Emperor Carolus II*—in other words Charles II—*we were sorely troubled by pirates. In 1690 alone, the Royal Plate Fleet*—or the silver fleet, although the Flota de Plata also carried a great deal of gold . . ."*

"Go on."

". . . Was seized and plundered by the heathen pirate, Edward Ockham, at a cost to the crown of ninety million reales. He became our greatest plague, a pestilence sent by the very devil himself. At length, upon much debate, privy counselors allowed us to wield St. Michael's Sword, our greatest, most secret, and most terrible treasure. In nomine patre, may God have mercy on our souls for doing so."

St. John put the folder down, his brow furrowed in interest. "What does this mean, *our greatest, most secret, and most terrible treasure?*"

"No idea. Maybe they thought the sword had magical properties. That it would scare away Ockham. Some kind of Spanish Excalibur."

"Unlikely. The world was poised at the Age of Enlightenment, remember, and Spain was one of the most civilized countries in Europe. Surely the emperor's privy counselors would not have believed a medieval superstition, let alone hung a matter of state on it."

"Unless the sword was truly cursed," Hatch murmured facetiously, widening his eyes dramatically.

St. John did not smile. "Have you shown these to Captain Neidelman yet?"

"No. Actually, I was thinking of e-mailing the transcriptions to an old friend who lives in Cádiz. Marquesa Hermione Concha de Hohenzollern."

"Marquesa?" St. John asked.

Hatch smiled. "You wouldn't know it to look at her. But she loves to bore you with her long and distinguished pedigree. I met her when I was involved with *Médecins sans Frontières*. She's very eccentric, almost eighty but a topnotch researcher, reads every European language and many dialects and archaic forms."

"Perhaps you're right to look outside for assistance," St. John said. "The Captain's so involved with the Water Pit I doubt he'd spare the time to look at this. You know, he came to me yesterday after the insurance adjustor left, asking me to compare the depth and width of the Pit to various cathedral spires. Then he wanted to sketch out more bracing that could act as the internal support system of a cathedral, recreating the stresses and loads of Macallan's original spire. Essentially, defuse the Pit."

"So I understand. Sounds like a hell of a job."

"The actual construction won't be very involved," St. John said. "It was the background research that was so complex." He spread his hands at the flurry of books. "It took me the rest of the day and all night just to sketch things out."

"You'd better rack out for a while, then. I'm headed down

to Stores to pick up Macallan's second journal. Thanks for your help with the translation." Hatch gathered the folders and turned to go.

"Just a moment!" St. John said.

As Hatch looked back, the Englishman stood up and came around the desk. "I mentioned I'd made a discovery."

"That's right, you did."

"It has to do with Macallan." St. John played with his tie knot self-consciously. "Well, indirectly with Macallan. Take a look at this." He took a sheet of paper from his desk and held it out. Hatch examined the single line of letters it contained:

ETAONISHRDLCUGMWFPYBKVJXZQ

"Looks like gibberish," Hatch said.

"Look more closely at the first seven letters."

Hatch spelled them out loud. "E, T, A, O . . . hey, wait a minute. Eta Onis! That's who Macallan dedicated his book on architecture to." He paused, looking at the sheet.

"It's the frequency table of the English language," St. John explained. "The order that letters are most likely to be used in sentences. Cryptanalysts use it to decrypt coded messages."

Hatch whistled. "When did you notice this?"

St. John grew even more self-conscious. "The day after Kerry died, actually. I didn't say anything about it to anyone. I felt so stupid. To think it had been staring me in the face all this time. But the more I thought about it, the more it seemed to explain. I realized Macallan had been much more than just an architect. If he knew about the frequency table, it means he was probably involved with London's intelligence community, or at the very least some secret society. So I did some wider background checking. And I stumbled across some bits of information too intriguing to be coincidental. I'm now sure that, during those missing years of Macallan's life, he worked for the Black Chamber."

"The what?"

"It's fascinating, really. You see—" St. John stopped suddenly and looked over his shoulder. Hatch realized, with a sympathetic pang, that St. John had been looking in the direction of Wopner's room, anticipating a caustic remark about what the dusty old antiquarian found fascinating.

"Come on," Hatch said. "You can explain as I walk down to Stores."

"The Black Chamber," St. John continued as they stepped out into the morning mist, "was a secret department of the English post office. Their duty was to intercept sealed communications, transcribe the contents, then reseal them with forged seals. If the transcribed documents were in code, they were sent to something called the deciphering branch. The plaintext was eventually sent on to the king or certain high ministers, depending on the communication."

"That much cloak-and-dagger stuff went on in Stuart England?"

"It wasn't just England. All European countries had similar set-ups. It was actually a popular place for highly intelligent, well-placed young aristocrats to work. If they made good cryptanalysts, they were rewarded with high pay and positions at court."

Hatch shook his head. "I had no idea."

"Not only that. Reading between the lines of some of the old court records, I believe Macallan was most likely a double agent, working for Spain because of his Irish sympathies. But he was found out. I think the real reason he left the country was to save his life. Perhaps he was being sent to America not only to construct a cathedral for New Spain, but for other, clandestine, reasons."

"And Ockham put a stop to those plans."

"Yes. But in Macallan, he got much more than he ever bargained for."

Hatch nodded. "That would explain why Macallan was so adept at using codes and secret inks in his journal."

"And why his second code was so devilish. Not many people would have the presence of mind to plan a double cross as elaborate as the Water Pit." St. John fell silent a moment. "I mentioned this to Neidelman when we spoke yesterday afternoon."

"And?"

"He told me it was interesting, and that we should look into it at some point, but that the priority was stabilizing the Pit and retrieving the gold." A pale smile moved quickly across his features. "That's why there's little reason to show him those documents you uncovered. He's simply too involved with the dig to think of anything that isn't directly related."

They arrived at the storage shed. Since the initial finds at the pirate encampment, the shed had been beefed up from its original ramshackle appearance. Now, bars had been placed at the two small windows, and a Thalassa guard sat inside the entrance, logging everything that went in and out.

"Sorry about this," St. John said with a grimace as Hatch requisitioned Macallan's decrypted journal and showed Neidelman's note to the guard. "I'd be happy just to print you off a copy, but Streeter came by the other day and had all the cryptological material downloaded onto disks. All of it, including the log. Then everything was erased from the servers, and the backups wiped. If I knew more about computers, I might have—"

He was interrupted by a shout from the dim interior of the shed. A moment later Bonterre emerged, a clipboard in one hand and a curious circular object in the other. "My two fa-vorite of men!" she said with a wide smile.

St. John, suddenly embarrassed, fell abruptly silent.

"How are things down at Pirateville?" Hatch asked.

"The work is almost done," Bonterre replied. "This morn-ing we finish the last grid. But, as with lovemaking, the best comes at the end. Look at what one of my diggers unearthed yesterday." She held up the object in her hand, grin widen-ing.

Hatch could see it was intricately worked, seemingly made of bronze, with numbers etched finely into the outer edge. Two pointed lengths of metal ran out from its center like the hands of a clock. "What is it?" he asked.

"An astrolabe. Used to determine latitude from the alti-tude of the sun. Worth ten times its weight in gold to any mariner in Red Ned's day. Yet it too was left behind." Bon-terre ran her thumb caressingly along its surface. "The more I find, the more I am confused."

Suddenly, a loud cry sounded nearby.

"What was that?" St. John said, starting.

"Sounded like a howl of pain," Hatch said.

Bonterre pointed. "I think it came from the hut of the *géologiste.*"

The three sprinted the short distance to Rankin's office. To Hatch's surprise, the blond bear of a man was not col-lapsed in agony, but was instead sitting in his chair, looking from a computer monitor to a lengthy printout, then back to the screen again.

"What's up?" Hatch cried.

Without looking at them, Rankin held out a palm, com-manding silence. He checked the printout again, his lips moving as if counting something. Then he set it down. "Checks out both ways," he said. "Can't be a glitch this time."

"Has the man turned *fou*?" Bonterre asked.

Rankin turned toward them. "It's right," he said excitedly. "It's got to be. Neidelman's been ragging me to get data on what was buried at the bottom of the Pit. When the thing was finally drained, I thought maybe all the weird readings would vanish. But they didn't. No matter what I tried, I kept getting different readings every run. Until now. Take a look."

He held up the printout, an unintelligible series of black blobs and lines along with one fuzzy dark rectangle.

"What is it?" Hatch asked. "A Motherwell print?"

"No, man. It's an iron chamber, perhaps ten feet on a side and fifty feet below the cleared part of the Pit. Doesn't seem to have been broached by water. And I've just managed to narrow down its contents. Among other things, there's a mass of perhaps fifteen, maybe twenty tons of dense, non-ferrous metal. Specific gravity just over nineteen."

"Wait a minute," Hatch said. "There's only one metal with that specific gravity."

Rankin's grin widened. "Yup. And it ain't lead."

There was a brief, electrifying silence. Then Bonterre shrieked with glee and bounded into Hatch's arms. Rankin bellowed again and pounded St. John's back. The foursome tumbled out of the hut, shouting and cheering.

As more people heard the commotion and came running, word of Rankin's discovery quickly spread. Immediately, a spontaneous celebration erupted among the dozen or so Thalassa employees still working on the island. The oppressive aftermath of the Wopner tragedy, the continuous setbacks, and brutally hard work were forgotten in a frantic, almost hysterical, jubilation. Scopatti capered around, removing his boat shoes and tossing them into the air, clutching his diving knife between his teeth. Bonterre ran into Stores and emerged with the old cutlass excavated from the pirate encampment. She ripped off a strip of denim from the base of her shorts and tied it around her head as an eyepatch. Then she pulled her pockets inside out and tore a long gash in her blouse, exposing a dangerously large swath of breast in the process. Brandishing the cutlass, she swaggered around, leering horribly, the image of a dissolute pirate.

Hatch was almost surprised to find himself shouting with the rest, hugging technicians he barely knew, cavorting over proof—at last—of all that gold lying beneath them. Yet he realized this was a kind of release everyone desperately needed. *It's not about the gold,* he thought to himself. *It's about not letting this damned island defeat us.*

The cheering faltered as Captain Neidelman strode quickly into Base Camp. He looked around, his tired eyes cold and gray.

"What the hell is going on here?" he said in a voice tight with suppressed rage.

"Captain!" Rankin said. "There's gold, fifty feet below the bottom of the shaft. At least fifteen tons!"

"Of course there is," the Captain snapped. "Did you all think we were digging for our health?" He looked around in the sudden hush. "This isn't a nursery school field trip. We're doing serious business here, and you are all to treat it as such." He glanced in the direction of the historian. "Dr. St. John, have you finished your analysis?"

St. John nodded.

"Then let's get it loaded into the *Cerberus* computer. The rest of you should remember that we're on a critically tight schedule. Now get back to work."

He turned and strode down the hill toward the boat dock, St. John at his heels, scurrying to keep up.

36

The following day was Saturday, but there was little rest on Ragged Island. Hatch, uncharacteristically oversleeping, dashed out the door of 5 Ocean Lane and hurried down the front walk, stopping only to grab Friday's neglected mail from the box before heading for the pier.

Heading out through Old Hump Channel, he frowned at the lead-gray sky. There was talk on the radio of an atmospheric disturbance forming over the Grand Banks. And it was already August 28, just days away from his self-imposed deadline; from now on, the weather could only get worse.

The accumulated equipment failures and computer problems had put work seriously behind schedule, and the recent rash of illnesses and accidents among the crew only added to the delays: when Hatch showed up at the medical office around quarter to ten, two people were already waiting to see him. One had developed an unusual bacterial infection of the teeth; it would take blood work to determine exactly what kind. The other, alarmingly, had come down with viral pneumonia.

As Hatch arranged transportation to a mainland hospital for the second patient and prepared blood work on the first for testing on the *Cerberus,* a third showed up; a ventilation pump operator who had lacerated his shin on a servo motor. It wasn't until almost noon that Hatch had time to boot up his computer, access the Internet, and e-mail his friend the marquesa in Cádiz. Sketching out the background in two or three brief paragraphs, he attached transcripts of a few of his grandfather's most obscure documents, asking her to search for any additional material on St. Michael's Sword she could find.

He signed off, then turned to the small packet he'd grabbed from his mailbox that morning: the September issue of *JAMA*; a flyer advertising a spaghetti dinner at the firehouse; the latest issue of the *Gazette*; a small cream-colored envelope, without name or stamp.

He opened the envelope and recognized the handwriting instantly.

> Dear Malin,
>
> I don't quite know how to say these things to you, and sometimes I'm not so good at expressing myself, so I will just write them as plainly as I can.
>
> I've decided to leave Clay. It's something I can't avoid any longer. I don't want to stay here, growing more bitter and resentful. That would be wrong for both of us. I'll tell him after the protest ends. Maybe then it will be a little easier for him to take. No matter what, it's going to hurt him terribly. But I know it's the right thing to do.
>
> I also know that you and I are not for each other. I have some wonderful memories, and I hope you do, too. But this thing we almost started

is a way of clinging to that past. It will end up hurting us both.

What almost happened at Squeaker's Glen—what I almost allowed to happen—scared me. But it also clarified a lot of vague ideas, feelings, that had been knocking around in my head. So I thank you for that.

I guess I owe you an explanation of what I plan to do. I'm going to New York. I called an old friend from the Community College who runs a small architectural firm down there. She offered me a secretarial job and promised to train me in drafting. It's a new start in a city I've always longed to see.

Please do not answer this letter or try to change my mind. Let's not spoil the past by something stupid we might do in the present.

Love,

Claire

The interisland telephone rang. Moving slowly, as if in a dream, Hatch picked up the receiver.

"It's Streeter," came the brusque voice.

"What?" said Hatch, still in shock.

"The Captain wants to see you in Orthanc. Right away."

"Tell him I'll—" Hatch began. But Streeter had hung up and there was nothing, not even a dial tone, on the line.

37

Hatch stepped over the last series of ramps and bridges to the base of Orthanc. The newly installed ventilation housing rose up above the Pit: three massive ducts that sucked foul air out of the depths and ejected it skyward, where it condensed into great plumes of fog. Light from the Pit itself spilled into the surrounding fog.

Stepping forward, Hatch grasped the ladder, then climbed to the observation railing that circled Orthanc's control tower.

Neidelman was nowhere to be seen. In fact, the tower was empty of anyone except Magnusen, scanning the sensor arrays that monitored the loads on the timbers in the Pit. The sensors were banked in rows of green lights. Any increase in strain on one of the timbers, the slightest shifting of a brace, and the appropriate light would turn red to the shrill sound of an alarm. As the bracing and buttressing had continued, the alarms had steadily decreased in frequency. Even the bugs that perpetually plagued the island's computer systems had, in this case, seemingly been ironed out. The complex placement of sensors that had its beginning in Wopner's last hours was now complete.

Hatch moved to the center of the room and gazed through the glass porthole into the Pit below. There were numerous side tunnels and shafts that were still extremely dangerous, but they had been marked with yellow tape and were off limits to all but the remote mapping teams.

A gust of wind blew the plumes of fog away from the Pit's mouth, and the view cleared. The ladder array plunged downward, three gleaming rails from which numerous platforms branched. Radiating out from the array was an extraordinary pattern of titanium struts. The visual effect was breathtaking: the polished struts, struck by countless lights, threw sprays of light around the mossy shaft, reflecting and re-reflecting the welter of titanium, stretching down into infinity.

There was a complex pattern to the struts. That morning, Neidelman's crew had been hard at work replacing the missing members of Macallan's original bracing with additional titanium members, following St. John's specifications. Other struts had been added, based on the results of a computer model run on the *Cerberus* computer. They might be ready to begin digging the final fifty feet to the treasure chamber by the end of the day.

As he stared into the brilliant depths, still struggling with the reality of Claire's letter, Hatch noticed movement: it was Neidelman, ascending in the mechanical lift. Bonterre stood beside him, hugging herself as if chilled. The sodium-vapor lights of the Pit turned the Captain's sandy hair to gold.

Hatch wondered why the Captain wanted to meet him there. *Maybe he's got a canker sore,* he thought bitterly. Actually, he wouldn't be surprised if it did turn out to be health-related. He'd never seen a man work so hard, or go so long without sleep, as had Neidelman during these last days.

The Captain swung up to the staging platform, then climbed the ladder into Orthanc, his muddy boots marking the metal floor. He faced Hatch wordlessly. Bonterre stepped up onto the deck, then entered the chamber behind the Captain. Hatch glanced at her, then tensed suddenly, alarmed by the expression on her face. Both were strangely silent.

Neidelman turned to Magnusen. "Sandra, may we have some privacy for a moment?"

The engineer stood up, walked out onto the observation deck, and shut the door behind her. Neidelman drew a deep breath, his tired gray eyes on Hatch.

"You'd better steady yourself," he said quietly.

Bonterre said nothing, looking at Hatch.

"Malin, we found your brother."

Hatch felt a sudden sense of dislocation, almost as if he was pulling away from the world around him, into a remote and shrouded distance.

"Where?" he managed.

"In a deep cavity, below the vaulted tunnel. Under the grate."

"You're sure?" Hatch whispered. "No chance of mistake?"

"It is the skeleton of a child," Bonterre said. "Twelve years old, perhaps thirteen, blue dungaree shorts, baseball cap—"

"Yes," Hatch whispered, sitting down suddenly as a wave of dizziness passed over him, leaving his knees weak and his head light. "Yes."

The tower was silent for the space of a minute.

"I need to see for myself," Hatch said at last.

"We know you do," Bonterre said, gently helping him to his feet. "Come."

"There's a tight drop down a vertical passage," said Neidelman. "The final cavity's not fully braced. There's a certain danger."

Hatch waved his hand.

Shrugging into a slicker, stepping onto the small electric lift, descending the ladder array—the next minutes passed in a gray blur. His limbs ached, and as he gripped the lift railing his own hands looked gray and lifeless in the stark light of the Pit. Neidelman and Bonterre crowded in at either side, while members of the bracing crews looked on from a distance as they went past.

Reaching the hundred-foot level, Neidelman stopped the lift. Stepping off the metal plate, they crossed a walkway to the mouth of the tunnel. Hatch hesitated.

"It's the only way," said Neidelman.

Hatch stepped into the tunnel, past a large air-filtration unit. Within, the ceiling was now braced by a series of metal plates, held up by a row of titanium screw jacks. A few more nightmare steps and Hatch found himself back in the octagonal stone chamber where Wopner had died. The great rock lay against the wall, seemingly undisturbed, a chilling memorial to the programmer and the engine of death that destroyed him. A twin set of jacks still braced the rock at the place where the body had been removed. A large stain coated the inside of the rock and the wall, rust-colored in the bright lights. Hatch looked away.

"It's what you wanted, isn't it?" Neidelman said in a curious tone.

With a tremendous effort, Hatch willed his feet forward, past the stone, past the rust-colored stain, to the well in the center of the room. The iron grating had been removed and a rope ladder led down into darkness.

"Our remote mapping teams only started working the secondary tunnels yesterday," Neidelman said. "When they returned to this vault, they examined the grating and calculated the shaft beneath it intersected the shore tunnel. The one you discovered as a boy. So they sent someone down to investigate. He broke through what seems to have once been some kind of watertight seal." He stepped forward. "I'll go first."

The Captain disappeared down the ladder. Hatch waited, his mind empty of everything but the chill breath from the well before him. Silently, Bonterre took his hand in hers.

A few minutes later, Neidelman called up. Hatch stepped forward, bent down, and gripped the rails of the narrow ladder.

The well was only four feet in diameter. Hatch climbed down, following the smooth-walled shaft as it curved around a large rock. He stepped off the bottom rung, sank his foot into foul-smelling ooze, and looked around, almost drowning in dread.

He was in a small chamber, cut into the hard glacial till. It had the look of a cramped dungeon, massive rock walls on all sides. But then he noticed that one of the walls did not reach the floor. In fact, what he thought was a wall was a massive piece of dressed stone, hewn square.

Neidelman angled his light beneath the stone. There was a dim flash of white.

The pulse pounding at his temples, Hatch took a step forward, then bent down. He unhooked his flashlight from the harness and snapped it on.

Jammed beneath the stone was a skeleton. The Red Sox cap still hung on the skull, clumps of brown hair peeking out from beneath. A rotten shirt clung to the rib cage. Below was a pair of ragged dungaree shorts, still attached by a belt. One bony knee peered out from the denim. A red, high-top Keds sneaker covered the right foot, while the left was still trapped behind the rear of the stone, ground into a rubbery mass.

The distant part of Hatch could see that the legs and arms were massively fractured, the ribs sprung from the breast-plate, the skull crushed. Johnny—for this could only be Johnny—had fallen victim to one of Macallan's traps, similar to that which killed Wopner. But without the helmet to slow the movement of the rock, death had been much quicker. At least, Hatch could always hope so.

He reached out, gently touching the brim of the cap. It was Johnny's favorite, signed by Jim Lonborg. Their father had bought it for him on that trip down to Boston, the day the Red Sox won the pennant. His fingers moved down to caress a lock of hair, then traced the curve of the mandible, past the chin to the crushed rib cage, along the arm bones to the skeletonized hand. He noticed every detail as if in a dream: distant, yet with that peculiar intensification that sometimes occurs in dream, every detail etched into his brain with jewellike clarity.

Hatch remained motionless, cradling the cold, birdlike bones in his own hand, in the sepulchral silence of the hole.

38

Hatch swung the *Plain Jane*'s dinghy past Cranberry Neck and into the broad, slow reach of the Passabec River. He glanced over his shoulder as he angled the boat closer to shore: Burnt Head lay three miles behind, a reddish-colored smudge against the southern horizon. The late summer morning air held a chill that was pregnant with the promise of winter.

He kept the little engine running hard, concentrating on thinking about nothing.

As the river narrowed and became less tidal, the water grew calm and green. Now he was passing what as a boy he'd called Millionaire's Row: a series of grand nineteenth-century "cottages" adorned with turrets, gables, and mansard roofs. A small child, dressed in the fantastically anachronistic outfit of pinafore and yellow umbrella, waved to him from a porch swing as he went by.

Inland, the landscape softened. Rocky shores gave way to low pebbled beaches, and spruce trees were replaced by mossy oaks and stands of birches. He passed a ruined pier, then a fishing shack on stilts. Not much farther now. Around another bend, and there it was: the shingle beach he remembered so well, its massive, improbable banks of oyster shells heaped twenty feet high. It was deserted, as he knew it would be. Most local residents of Stormhaven and Black Harbor had little interest in prehistoric Indian encampments, or the shell heaps they'd left behind. Most, but not all: this was the place Professor Horn had taken him and his brother one warm cloudless afternoon, the day before Johnny died.

Hatch pulled the dinghy up onto the beach, then retrieved his battered paintbox and collapsible chair from the bow. He looked around a moment, deciding on a spot beneath a lone birch tree. It was out of the glare of the sun, and his paints wouldn't dry up in the heat. He placed the paintbox and chair in the shade of the tree, then went back to the dinghy for the fold-up easel and portfolio.

As he set up, he found himself looking around, choosing theme and viewpoint, arranging landscape elements. Sitting down, he gazed out at the scene through a viewing frame, squinting to better understand the distribution of color and mass. The light gray of the shell heaps in the foreground made a perfect contrast to the distant purple bulk of Mount Lovell. No need for a quick pencil sketch here; he could go straight to the watercolor.

Opening the portfolio, he carefully removed a large sheet of 240-pound, cold-pressed paper. He taped it to the easel, then ran his fingertips appreciatively over the pure linen rag. An expensive indulgence, but worth every penny: the paper had a tooth that would hold the paint and make detail work easier, even with the kind of wet-on-wet style he favored.

He unrolled the cardboard from around each of the brushes, then examined his selection: a square-end, a couple of sable rounds, a goat-hair mop, and an old quarter-inch flat for dry-brushing clouds into the background. Next, he half-filled a palette well with water. Reaching into the paintbox and removing a tube of cerulean blue, he squeezed the paint into the well and stirred, momentarily annoyed that his injured hand wasn't healing as quickly as it should. He dampened the paper with a cotton ball, then glanced out at the landscape for a long moment. Finally, fetching a deep breath, he dipped a brush in the well and laid a flat blue wash over the top two-thirds of the sheet.

As the brush ran along the paper in thick, broad strokes, Hatch felt something coiled tight within him begin to come loose. It was healing work, painting this landscape; cleansing work. And it felt right, somehow, returning to this place. In the years after Johnny's death, he'd never been able to come back to the Indian shell heaps. And yet, returning to Stormhaven a quarter century later—and especially now, after the discovery of his brother's body—Hatch sensed himself turning a corner. There was pain, but there was also an end to pain. His brother's bones had been found. Perhaps—if he could decide on a fitting memorial—they would be removed from the earth where they had lain for so long. Perhaps there would also be time to understand the fiendish mechanism that caused his death. But even that was less important now. He could close the chapter and move on.

He returned to the painting. Time to lay down a foreground. The stony pebbles of the beach were an almost perfect match for his yellow ochre. And he could mix the ochre with the tube of Payne's gray to catch the color of the shell heaps.

As he reached for another brush, he heard the sound of an inboard coming upriver. Looking up, he saw a familiar figure scanning the riverbanks, the tanned skin dark under a large-brimmed straw hat. Bonterre caught sight of him, smiled and waved, then nosed the Thalassa launch gently toward the shore and killed the motor.

"Isobel!" he said.

She anchored the boat on the beach, then came toward him, removing the hat and shaking her long hair back. "I have been spying on you from the post office. They have a nice old telescope there. I watched you take your little boat into this river, and I got curious."

So that's how she's going to play it, he thought: business as usual, no dewy-eyed empathy, no treacly references to what happened the day before. He felt vastly relieved.

She jerked her thumb downriver. "Impressive houses back there."

"A group of wealthy New York families used to come up to Black Harbor in the summertime," Hatch replied. "Built all those houses. FDR used to spend his summers at Campobello Island, ten miles north of here."

Bonterre frowned. "FDR?"

"President Roosevelt."

She nodded. "Ah. You Americans, so fond of abbreviating your leaders. JFK. LBJ." Her eyes widened. "But look at you! Painting! *Monsieur le docteur,* I never expected such artistic depth."

"You'd better reserve judgment until you see the finished product," he replied, dabbing in the shingle beach with short brush strokes. "I became interested in med school. Helped me relax. I found I enjoyed watercolors most. Especially for landscapes like this."

"And what a landscape!" Bonterre said, pointing at the shell heaps. "*Mon dieu,* they are enormous!"

"Yes. The oyster shells at the bottom supposedly date back three thousand years, and the ones at the top are early seventeenth century, when the Indians were driven out." Hatch gestured upriver. "There are several prehistoric Indian encampments along the river. And there's an interesting Micmac site on Rackitash Island."

Bonterre moved away, scrambling up the oyster-covered bank to the bottom of the nearest heap. "But why did they leave their shells in just this place?" she called back.

"Nobody knows. It must've been a lot of trouble. I remember reading that there may have been some kind of religious reasons."

Bonterre broke into laughter. "Ah. *Religious* reasons. That is what we archaeologists always say when we do not understand something."

Hatch chose another brush. "Tell me, Isobel," he said. "To what do I owe this visit? Surely you have better ways to spend your Sundays than following old bachelor doctors around."

Bonterre grinned mischievously. "I wanted to find out why you had not asked me for a second date."

"I figured you thought I was a weak reed. Remember what you said about us northerners having had the marrow sucked from our bones?"

"That is true enough. But I would not call you a weak reed, if I understand the term. Perhaps a kitchen match would be a better analogy, *non*? All you really need is the right woman to ignite you." She carelessly picked up an oyster shell and sent it spinning into the water. "The real problem will be making sure you do not flare out too quickly."

Hatch turned back to his painting. In this kind of sparring, Bonterre would always be the victor.

Bonterre approached him again. "Besides, I was afraid you were seeing that other woman."

Hatch looked up.

"Yes, what is her name: the minister's wife. Your old, *old* friend."

"That's all she is," Hatch said, more sharply than he intended. "A friend." Bonterre scrutinized him curiously, and he sighed. "She's made that very clear to me."

Bonterre arched her brows. "You are disappointed."

Hatch lowered his brush. "To tell you the truth, I don't know what I expected when I came home. But she's made it clear that our relationship belongs to the past, not the present. Wrote me a letter, in fact. That part hurt. But you know what? She's absolutely right."

Bonterre looked at him, a smile slowly forming.

"What are you grinning at?" Hatch said. "The doctor and his romance problems? You must have had your share of peccadilloes."

Bonterre laughed out loud, refusing to be baited. "I am grinning with relief, *monsieur.* But you have obviously misunderstood me all along." She slid an index finger along the back of his wrist. "I like to play the game, *comprends*? But only for the right man will I allow myself to be caught. My mother raised a good Catholic."

Hatch stared at her for a minute in surprise. Then he lifted the paintbrush again. "I'd have guessed you'd be closeted with Neidelman today, poring over charts and diagrams."

At this change of subject, a cloud passed over her face. "No," she said, good humor suddenly gone. "The Captain no longer has the patience for careful archaeology. He wants to rush, rush, *vitement,* and to hell with everything else. He is down in the Pit now, preparing to excavate the bottom of the shaft. No screening for artifacts, no stratigraphic analysis. I cannot bear it."

Hatch looked at her in surprise. "He's working today?" Working on Sunday, with the medical office unmanned, was a breach of regulations.

Bonterre nodded. "Since the discovery of the spire, he has been a man possessed. I do not think he has slept in a week, he is so busy. But do you know, despite all his eagerness, it still took him two days to ask my dear digger for help? I told him again and again that Christophe, with his knowledge of architecture, was the very man he needed to reconstruct the supports. But he did not seem to listen." She shook her head. "I never understood him. But now, I think, I understand him less."

For a moment, Hatch considered telling her about Neidelman's worries of a traitor, then decided against it. He thought of mentioning the documents he'd found, but once again decided it could wait. It could all wait. Let Neidelman dig his damned fool ass off on a Sunday if he wanted to. It was Hatch's day off, and what he wanted to do was finish his painting.

"Time for me to add Mount Lovell," he said, nodding at the dark shape in the distance. As Bonterre watched, he dipped a brush in the Payne's gray, mixing it with a touch of cobalt blue, then laid down a heavy line, dragging it above the spot on the paper where the land met the sky. Then, taking the board off the easel, he turned the painting upside down, waiting until the fresh paint had flowed into the horizon. Then he righted the board and placed it back on the easel.

"*Mon dieu!* Where did you learn that?"

"There's a trick in every trade," Hatch said, cleaning the bristles and replacing the tubes into the paintbox. He stood up. "It needs to dry a bit. Why don't we have a climb?"

They scrambled up the side of the tallest shell heap, oysters crunching beneath their feet. From the top, Hatch looked past their boats toward the river. Birds rustled in the spreading oaks. The air was warm and clear: if there was a storm gathering, it certainly wasn't evident. Upriver, there was no sign of human habitation, just the blue twists of water and the tops of trees, broken here and there by meadows, stretching as far as the eyes could see.

"*Magnifique,*" said Bonterre. "What a magical place."

"I used to come here with Johnny," Hatch said. "An old high school teacher of mine would bring us here, every now and then on Saturday afternoons. We were here the day before Johnny died."

"Tell me about him," Bonterre said simply.

Silently, Hatch took a seat, the oysters rustling and whispering under his weight. "Well, he was very bossy. There weren't that many kids in Stormhaven, so we did lots of things together. We were best friends, I guess—at least, when he wasn't busy beating me up."

Bonterre laughed.

"He loved everything to do with science—even more than me. He had incredible collections of butterflies, rocks, and fossils. He knew the names of all the constellations. He even built his own telescope."

Hatch leaned back on his elbows and looked through the trees. "Johnny would have done something amazing with his life. I think one of the reasons I worked so hard, got through Harvard Medical School, was to make up for what happened."

"What did you have to make up for?" Bonterre asked gently.

"It was my idea to go to Ragged Island that day," Hatch replied.

Bonterre repeated none of the usual platitudes, and again Hatch found himself feeling grateful. He fetched a deep breath, then another, letting them out slowly. It seemed that, with every breath, he was exhaling the pent-up poisons of many years.

"After Johnny disappeared in the tunnel," he went on, "it took me a while to find my way out. I don't remember how long. The fact is, I don't remember much of anything. I've tried, but there's a stretch of time that remains a complete blank. We were crawling down the shaft, and Johnny lit another match. . . . After that, the first thing I remember clearly is arriving at my parents' dock. They were just getting home from lunch or something, and they raced out to Ragged Island, along with half the town. I'll never forget my father's face when he reappeared at the entrance to the tunnel. He was covered with Johnny's blood. He was yelling out, pounding on the beams, crying."

He paused a minute, replaying the scene in his mind.

"They couldn't find the body. They searched, dug holes in the walls and ceiling. The Coast Guard came out, and a mining engineer with listening equipment. They floated out a backhoe, but the ground was too unstable and they couldn't get into position."

Bonterre remained silent, listening.

"They spent all that night, and the next day, and the next. Then, when it became clear Johnny couldn't possibly be alive, people began to drop away. The medical team said the amount of blood in the tunnel meant Johnny must be dead, but Dad kept looking. He refused to leave. After a week people pretty much gave up, even Mom, but Dad stayed out there. The tragedy did something to his mind. He wandered around, climbed down into the shafts, dug holes with a pick and shovel, yelling until he was so hoarse he couldn't speak. He wouldn't leave the island. God, weeks went by. Mom begged him to leave, but he wouldn't. Then one day she came out with food and he wasn't there. There was another search, and this time they found a body. Dad was floating in one of the shafts. Drowned. Nobody said anything to us. But talk turned to suicide."

Hatch continued staring at the pattern of leaves against the blue sky. He had never told anyone this much of the story before, and he could never have imagined what a vast relief it was simply to talk: the lifting of a burden that had been with him so long he'd forgotten it was there.

"We stayed in Stormhaven for another six years. I think Mom hoped it would go away, somehow. But it never did. A little town like this never forgets. Everyone was so . . . *nice*. But the talk never stopped. I didn't hear much of it, but I knew it was there, all the same. It went on and on. There was something about the body never being found that really preyed on people's minds. And, you know, some of the fishermen's families believed in the curse. Later, I learned that some parents wouldn't let their kids play with me. Finally, when I was sixteen, my mother couldn't stand it any longer. She took me to Boston for the summer. We were only supposed to stay a few months, but then September came, and I had to start school, and a year went by, then another. And then I went off to college. And I never came back. Until now."

A great blue heron glided down the length of the river, then settled on a dead branch, waiting.

"And then?"

"Medical school, the Peace Corps, *Médecins sans Frontières,* Mount Auburn Hospital. And then one day your Captain walked into my office. There you have it." Hatch paused. "You know, after the Pit was drained and they located the spot where the shore tunnel angled in, I kept quiet. I didn't insist they explore it right away. You'd have thought I would have been all over the Captain about it. But the fact was, now that we were this close, I was scared. I wasn't sure I wanted to know what really happened."

"So you're sorry you signed the Captain's agreement?" Bonterre asked.

"Actually, he signed my agreement." Hatch fell silent a moment. "But no, I'm not sorry. If I was, yesterday changed all that."

"And in a week or two, you can retire as one of the richest men in America."

Hatch laughed. "Isobel," he said, "I've decided to put the money into a foundation in my brother's name."

"All of it?"

"Yes." He hesitated. "Well, I'm still thinking about that."

Bonterre settled back on the shells, squinting at him skeptically. "I am a good judge of character, *monsieur le docteur*. You may put most of the money into this foundation. But I will be skinned alive if you do not keep a tidy little sum back for yourself. You would not be human otherwise. And I am sure I would not like you so much if you were not human."

Automatically, Hatch opened his mouth to protest. Then he relaxed again.

"Either way, you are a saint," said Bonterre. "I have more venal things planned for my share. Like buying a very fast car—and of course, I will send a large sum to my family in Martinique." She looked over at him, and he was surprised to see that she seemed to be seeking his approval.

"That's fine," he said. "For you, it's a professional thing. For me, it was personal."

"You and Gerard Neidelman both," Bonterre replied. "You may have exorcised your demons, but I think he is still summoning his, *n'est-ce pas*? The Ragged Island treasure has always held a special spell for him. But all this obsession with Macallan, *c'est incroyable*! Everything is now like a personal affront, a direct challenge. I do not think he will be happy until he wrangs that old architect's neck."

"Wrings," Hatch corrected lazily.

"Whatever." Bonterre shifted, searching for a more comfortable position. "A plague on both their houses."

They fell silent, lying on their backs in the late morning sun. A squirrel edged out on a branch above their heads, gathering acorns, chattering softly. Hatch closed his eyes. Vaguely, he realized that he'd have to tell Bill Banns at the paper about the discovery of Johnny's body. Bonterre was saying something, but he was growing too drowsy to listen. And then he drifted off into a peaceful, dreamless sleep.

39

It was the following afternoon that Hatch heard from the marquesa.

The small icon of a closed airmail envelope had appeared in the lower right corner of his laptop, indicating new e-mail. But when he'd tried to access it, Hatch found his Internet connection kept dropping. Deciding to take a short break, he trotted down to the pier and motored the *Plain Jane* away from her berth. Clear of the island and its perpetual fog bank, he connected the laptop's modem to his cell phone and retrieved the marquesa's message without difficulty. *What is it with computers and this island?* he thought.

Firing up the diesels again, he swung the *Plain Jane* back toward Ragged Island. The prow of the boat cut through the glassy swell, startling a cormorant, who disappeared into the water. It reappeared several dozen yards farther off, paddling furiously.

A weather report crackled on the marine radio: The disturbance over the Grand Banks had developed into a strong low-pressure system, currently headed toward the coast of northern Maine. If the storm kept to its present course, a small craft advisory would go into effect at noon the next day. *A classic Nor'easter,* thought Hatch grimly.

He could see an unusual number of lobster boats spread along the horizon, pulling their traps. Perhaps it was in preparation for the storm. Or perhaps there was another reason. Though he had not seen Claire since Squeaker's Cove, Bill Banns had called Sunday evening to let him know that Clay had scheduled the protest for the last day of August.

Back in his office, he drained the dregs of his coffee and turned to his laptop, eager to read the marquesa's message. In typical fashion, the wicked old lady began by talking about her latest young conquest.

> *He is terribly shy, but so sweet and eager to please that I find myself just doting upon him. His hair lies across his forehead in small brown ringlets that turn black from sweat when he has been exerting himself. And there is much to be said for enthusiasm, is there not?*

She went on to discuss past lovers and husbands, and to more specific details of her anatomical preferences in men. The marquesa always approached electronic mail as if it were a medium for gossipy confessions. If the woman held true to form, her message would turn next to her chronic shortage of ready money, and to a family ancestry that dated back through the Holy Roman emperors to Aleric the Visigoth himself. This time, however, she proceeded with uncharacteristic speed to the information she had unearthed in the archives of Cádiz Cathedral. Reading, then rereading her message, Hatch felt a chill course through him.

There was a knock on the door. "Come in," Hatch said as

he sent the marquesa's message to the nearby printer. He glanced up at the workman who stood in the doorway, then froze.

"My God," he breathed, pushing back from his desk. "What the hell happened to you?"

40

Fifty minutes later, Hatch was quickly climbing the path toward the Water Pit. The rays of the lowering sun blazed over the water, turning the island's fogbank into a fiery swirl.

Orthanc was empty save for Magnusen and a technician operating the winch. There was a grinding noise, and a massive bucket emerged from the Water Pit, hooked to a thick steel cable. As Hatch watched through the glass porthole, a crew at the edge of the Pit swung the bucket off to one side and tilted it into one of the abandoned tunnels. There was a loud sucking sound, and countless gallons of mud and dirt poured out in a rush. The crew righted the now-empty bucket and swung it back toward the mouth of the Water Pit, where it once again descended out of sight.

"Where's Gerard?" Hatch asked.

Magnusen was monitoring a wireframe grid of the base of the Water Pit. She turned to look at him for a moment, then returned to her screen. "With the digging team," she replied.

On the wall near the winch technician was a bank of six

red phones, hardwired to various points on the island network. Hatch picked up the phone labeled WATER PIT, FORWARD TEAM.

He heard three quick beeps. In a moment, Neidelman's voice came over the channel. "Yes?" Hatch could hear loud hammering in the background.

"I need to speak with you," Hatch said.

"Is it important?" Neidelman asked, irritation in his voice.

"Yes, it's important. I have some new information about St. Michael's Sword."

There was a pause during which the hammering grew louder. "If you must," Neidelman replied at last. "You'll have to come down here. We're in the midst of setting some braces."

Hatch returned the phone to its cradle, buckled on a safety helmet and harness, then stepped outside and climbed down the tower to the staging platform. In the gathering dusk, the Pit looked even more brilliant, projecting a shaft of white light into the mists above. One of the crew members at the Pit's mouth helped him onto the electric lift. He pressed a button on the housing and the small platform lurched and descended.

He passed through the gleaming web of titanium struts and cables, marveling despite himself at the complexity. The lift descended past a team checking a set of braces at the forty-foot level. Another ninety seconds and the bottom of the Water Pit became visible. Here, activity was more pronounced. The muck and mire had been removed, and a battery of lights erected. A smaller shaft now extended down from the base of the Pit, braced on all sides. Several small instruments and measuring devices—belonging to Magnusen, or maybe Rankin—dangled from slender wires. The winch cable descended into one corner, and in the opposite corner a titanium ladder had been fitted. Stepping off the lift, Hatch went down the ladder into a roar of sound: shovels, hammers, the rush of air-filtration units.

Thirty feet below, he reached the actual floor of the excavation. Here, under the gaze of a lone closed-circuit camera, workmen were digging out the sodden earth and dumping it into the large bucket. Others were using suction hoses to vacuum up the mud and water. Neidelman stood in one corner, a construction helmet on his head, directing the placement of the supports. Streeter hovered nearby, a set of blueprints in his hand.

Malin came toward them, and the Captain nodded. "I'm surprised you haven't been down here to see this before," he said. "Now that the Pit is stabilized, we've been able to proceed with the final digging at full speed."

There was a pause in which Hatch made no answer.

Neidelman turned his pale eyes toward him. "You know how pressed for time we are," he said. "I hope this is important."

A great change had taken place in the man in the week since Wopner's death. Gone was the look of calm certainty, the equanimity that had surrounded him like a mantle from the very first day he'd sat in Hatch's office and looked out over the Charles River. Now, there was a look Hatch found hard to describe: a haggard, almost wild, determination.

"It's important," said Hatch. "But private."

Neidelman looked at him a moment longer. Then he glanced at his watch. "Listen up!" he said to the men. "Shift ends in seven minutes. Knock off, get topside, and tell the next team to come down for an early start."

The workers laid aside their tools and began climbing the ladder toward the lift. Streeter remained where he was, silent. The large suction hoses fell silent, and the half-filled bucket rose toward the surface, bobbing on its heavy steel cable. Streeter remained, standing silently to one side. Neidelman turned back to Hatch. "You've got five minutes, maybe ten."

"A couple of days ago," Hatch began, "I came across a stash of my grandfather's papers, documents he'd gathered about the Water Pit and Ockham's treasure. They were hidden in the attic of the family house; that's why my father never destroyed them. Some mentioned St. Michael's Sword. They hinted that the sword was some kind of terrible weapon the Spanish government planned to use against Red Ned Ockham. There were other disturbing references, too. So I contacted a researcher I know in Cádiz and asked her to do some more digging into the sword's history."

Neidelman looked toward the muddy ground at their feet, his lips pursed. "That could be considered proprietary information. I'm surprised you took such a step without consulting me."

"She found this." Hatch reached into his jacket and handed Neidelman a piece of paper.

The Captain looked at it briefly. "It's in old Spanish," he said with a frown.

"Below is my friend's translation."

Neidelman handed it back. "Summarize it for me," he said curtly.

"It's fragmentary. But it describes the original discovery of St. Michael's Sword, and what happened afterwards."

Neidelman raised his eyebrows. "Indeed?"

"During the Black Plague, a wealthy Spanish merchant set out from Cádiz with his family on a barque. They crossed the Mediterranean and put ashore along an unpopulated stretch of the Barbary Coast. There they found the remains of an ancient Roman settlement. They settled down to ride out the plague. Some friendly Berber tribesmen warned them not to go near a ruined temple that lay on a hill some distance away, saying it was cursed. The warnings were repeated several times. After a while, when the plague started to abate, the merchant decided to explore the temple. Maybe he felt the Berbers had hidden something of value, and he didn't want to depart without taking a look. It seems that among the ruins he found a slab of marble behind an altar. Underneath was an ancient metal box that had been sealed shut, with an inscription in Latin. In effect, the inscription stated that the box contained a sword, which was the deadliest of weapons. Even to look upon it meant death. He had the box carried down to the ship, but the Berbers refused to help him open it. In fact, they drove him from the shore."

Neidelman listened, still looking at the ground.

"A few weeks later, on Michaelmas—St. Michael's Day— the merchant's ship was found drifting in the Mediterranean. The yard-arms were covered with vultures. All hands were dead. The box was shut, but the lead seal had been broken. It was brought to a monastery at Cádiz. The monks read the Latin inscription, along with the merchant's own log. They decided the sword was—and I quote from my friend's translation—*a fragment vomited up from Hell itself.* They sealed the box again and placed it in the catacombs under the cathedral. The document ends by saying that the monks who handled the box soon fell ill and died."

Neidelman looked up at Hatch. "Is this supposed to have some kind of bearing on our current effort?"

"Yes," said Hatch steadily. "Very much so."

"Enlighten me, then."

"Wherever St. Michael's Sword has been, people have died. First, the merchant's family. Then the monks. And when Ockham snaps it up, eighty of his crew die right here on the island. Six months later, Ockham's ship is found drifting just like the merchant ship, with all hands dead."

"Interesting story," Neidelman said. "But I don't think it's

worth stopping work for me to listen to. This is the twenti-
eth century. It has no bearing on us."

"That's where you're wrong. Haven't you noticed the recent rash of illnesses among the crew?"

Neidelman shrugged. "Sickness always occurs in a group
of this size. Especially when people are becoming tired and
the work is dangerous."

"This isn't malingering we're talking about. I've done the
blood work. In almost every case, the white cell counts are
extremely low. And just this afternoon, one of your digging
team came into my office with the most unusual skin disor-
der I've ever seen. He had ugly rashes and swelling across
his arms, thighs, and groin."

"What is it?" Neidelman asked.

"I don't know yet. I've checked my medical references,
and I haven't been able to make a specific diagnosis yet. If I
didn't know better, I'd say they were buboes."

Neidelman looked at Hatch with a raised eyebrow. "Black
death? Bubonic plague, in twentieth-century Maine?"

"As I said, I haven't been able to diagnose it yet."

Neidelman frowned. "Then what are you rabbiting on
about?"

Hatch took a breath, controlling his temper. "Gerard, I
don't know exactly what St. Michael's Sword is. But it's obviously very dangerous. It's left a trail of death wherever it's
gone. I wonder if we were right, assuming that the Spanish
meant to wield the sword against Ockham. Perhaps he was
meant to capture it."

"Ah," Neidelman nodded, an edge of sarcasm distorting
his voice. "Perhaps the sword is cursed after all?" Streeter,
standing to one side, sniffed derisively.

"You know I don't believe in curses any more than you
do," Hatch snapped. "That doesn't mean there isn't some un-

derlying physical *cause* to the legend. Like an epidemic. This sword has all the characteristics of a Typhoid Mary."

"And that would explain why several of our sick crew have bacterial infections, while another has viral pneumonia, and yet another a weird infection of the teeth. Just what kind of epidemic might this be, Doctor?"

Hatch looked at the lean face. "I know the diversity of diseases is puzzling. The point is, the sword *is* dangerous. We've got to figure out *how* and *why* before we plunge ahead and retrieve it."

Neidelman nodded, smiling distantly. "I see. You can't figure out why the crew is sick. You're not even sure what some of them are sick *of*. But the sword is somehow responsible for everything."

"It isn't just the illnesses," Hatch countered. "You must know that a big Nor'easter is brewing. If it keeps heading our way, it'll make last week's storm look like a spring shower. It would be crazy to continue."

"Crazy to continue," Neidelman repeated. "And just how do you propose to stop the dig?"

Hatch paused for a moment as this sunk in. "By appealing to your good sense," he said, as calmly as he could.

There was a tense silence. "No," said Neidelman, with a heavy tone of finality. "The dig continues."

"Then your stubbornness leaves me no choice. I'm going to have to shut down the dig myself for the season, effective immediately."

"How, exactly?"

"By invoking clause nineteen of our contract."

Nobody spoke.

"My clause, remember?" Hatch went on. "Giving me the right to stop the dig if I felt conditions had become too dangerous."

Slowly, Neidelman fished his pipe out of a pocket and

loaded it with tobacco. "Funny," he said in a quiet, dead voice, turning to Streeter. "Very funny, isn't it, Mr. Streeter? Now that we're only thirty hours from the treasure chamber, Dr. Hatch here wants to shut the whole operation down."

"In thirty hours," Hatch said, "the storm may be right on top of us—"

"Somehow," the Captain interrupted, "I'm not at all convinced it's the sword, or the storm, that you're really worried about. And these papers of yours are medieval mumbo jumbo, if they're real at all. I don't see why you . . ." He paused. Then something dawned in his eyes. "But yes. Of course I see why. You have another motive, don't you?"

"What are you talking about?"

"If we pull out now, Thalassa will lose its entire investment. You know very well that our investors have already faced ten percent overrun calls. They're not going to cough up another twenty million for next year's dig. But that's exactly what you're counting on, isn't it?"

"Don't lay your paranoid fantasies on me," Hatch said angrily.

"Oh, but they're not fantasy, are they?" Neidelman lowered his voice further. "Now that you've gotten the information you need out of Thalassa, now that we've practically opened the front door for you, you'd love nothing more than to see us fail. Then, next year, you could come in, finish the job, and get *all* the treasure. And most importantly, you'd get St. Michael's Sword." His eyes glittered with suspicion. "It all makes sense. It explains why, for example, you were so insistent on that clause nineteen. It explains the computer problems, the endless delays. Why everything worked on the *Cerberus* but went haywire on the island. You had it all figured out from the beginning." He shook his head bitterly. "And to think I trusted you. To think I came to *you* when I suspected we had a saboteur among us."

"I'm not trying to cheat you out of your treasure. I don't give a shit about your treasure. My only interest is in the safety of the crew."

"The safety of the crew," Neidelman repeated derisively. He fished a box of matches from his pocket, removed one, and scratched it into life. But instead of lighting his pipe, he suddenly thrust it close to Hatch's face. Hatch backed off slightly.

"I want you to understand something," Neidelman continued, flicking out the match. "In thirty hours, the treasure will be mine. Now that I know what your game is, Hatch, I'm simply not going to play. Any effort to stop me will be met with force. Do I make myself clear?"

Hatch looked carefully at Neidelman, trying to read what was going on behind the cold expression. "Force?" he repeated. "Is that a threat?"

There was a long silence. "That would be a reasonable interpretation," said Neidelman, dropping his voice even lower.

Hatch drew himself up. "When the sun rises tomorrow," he said, "if you're not gone from this island, you will be evicted. And I give you my personal guarantee that if anyone is killed or hurt, you will be charged with negligent homicide."

Neidelman turned. "Mr. Streeter?"

Streeter stepped forward.

"Escort Dr. Hatch to the dock."

Streeter's narrow features creased into a smile.

"You have no right to do this," Hatch said. "This is my island."

Streeter stepped forward and grasped Hatch's arm.

Taking a step to the side, Hatch balled his right hand into a fist and shot his knuckles into the man's solar plexus. It was not a hard blow, but it was placed with anatomical exactness. Streeter dropped to his knees, mouth gaping, the wind knocked out of him.

"Touch me again," Hatch said to the gasping figure, "and you'll be carrying your balls around in a cup."

Streeter struggled to his feet, violence in his eyes.

"Mr. Streeter, I don't think force will be necessary," said Neidelman sharply, as the team leader moved forward menacingly. "Dr. Hatch will return to his boat peaceably. He realizes there is absolutely nothing he can do here to stop us, now that we've smoked out his plan. And I think he realizes how foolish it would be to try."

He turned back to Hatch. "I'm a fair man. You took your best shot, and you failed. Your presence is no longer required on Ragged Island. If you leave, and allow me to finish as we agreed, you'll still get your share of the treasure. But if you try to stop me . . ." Silently, he swept his hands back and placed them on his hips, pulling his slicker aside in the process. Hatch could clearly see the handgun snugged into his belt.

"Well, what do you know," Hatch said. "The Captain's strapped."

"Get going," said Streeter, stepping forward.

"I can find my own way." Hatch backed up to the far wall, and then—without taking his eyes off the Captain—he climbed out of the excavation to the base of the array, where the lift was already depositing the first diggers of the next shift.

41

The rising sun tore free of a distant bar of cloud and cast a brilliant trail across the ocean, illuminating a crowd of boats packing Stormhaven's small harbor from channel entrance to piers.

Chugging slowly through a gap in the center of the crowd was a small dragger, Woody Clay standing at its wheel. The boat veered and almost brushed the peppercan buoy at the head of the channel before steadying and resuming its outward course; Clay was an indifferent sailor.

Reaching the harbor entrance, he turned the boat and cut the motor. Raising a battered megaphone, he shouted instructions to the surrounding crowd, his voice full of such conviction that even the ancient, buzzing amplification could not distort it. He was answered by a series of coughs and roars as numerous engines came to life. The boats at the front of the harbor cast off their moorings, pulled through the channel, and throttled up. They were followed by more, then still more, until the bay filled with long spreading wakes of the fleet as it headed in the direction of Ragged Island.

Three hours later and six miles to the southeast, the light struggled down through the mist into the vast, damp labyrinth of braces and cribbing that made up the Water Pit. It threw a dim, spectral illumination over the complex workings that filled the Pit's mouth.

At the lowest depths of the Pit, 180 feet down, neither day nor night had any relevance. Gerard Neidelman stood beside a small staging platform, watching the crew dig feverishly beneath him. It was a few minutes short of noon. Faintly, above the grumble of the air ducts and the clank of the winch chain, Neidelman could just make out a clamor of air horns and boat cannon on the surface.

He listened for a moment. Then he reached for his portable telephone.

"Streeter?"

"Here, Captain," came the voice from Orthanc, 200 feet above, faint and gravelly through a wash of static.

"Let's have your report."

"About two dozen boats in all, Captain. They've formed a ring around the *Cerberus*, trying to set up a blockade. Guess they think that's where everyone is." There was a further crackle of static that might have been a laugh. "Only Rogerson's on board to hear them. I sent the rest of the research team ashore last night."

"Any signs of sabotage or interference?"

"No, Captain, they're pretty tame. A lot of noise, but nothing to worry about."

"Anything else?"

"Magnusen's picking up a sensor anomaly at the sixty-four foot level. It's probably nothing, the secondary grid shows nothing unusual."

"I'll take a look." Neidelman thought for a moment. "Mr. Streeter, I'd like you to meet me there."

"Aye, aye."

Neidelman climbed up the ladder from the dig site to the base of the electric lift, his movements lithe and fluid despite his lack of sleep. He took the lift up to the sixty-foot level, then moved out onto the platform and climbed carefully down the spars to the errant sensor. He verified the sensor was operational and returned to the platform just as Streeter completed the descent down the far side of the array.

"Any problems?" Streeter asked.

"Not with the sensor," Neidelman reached over and switched off Streeter's comm link to Orthanc. "But I've been thinking about Hatch."

There was a squeal of gears, then a mechanical groan from below, as the powerful winch pulled another load of dirt and mud up from the dig site. The two men watched as the large iron bucket rose from the depths, condensation gleaming under the harsh lights.

"Only eight more feet to the treasure chamber," Neidelman murmured as he watched the bucket recede into the circle of light overhead. "Ninety-six inches."

He turned to Streeter. "I want all nonessential personnel off the island. Everyone. Say whatever you want, use that protest or the storm as excuses, if you like. We don't want a lot of extra bodies around rubbernecking during the actual extraction. When the shift changes at two, send the diggers home, too. This next shift should see the job finished. We'll winch the treasure up in the bucket, and I'll carry the sword myself. We need to get it out as soon as possible. Can Rogerson be trusted?"

"He'll do what I tell him, sir."

Neidelman nodded. "Bring the *Cerberus* and my command vessel close to the island, but keep them well clear of the reef. We'll use the launches and split the treasure between the two boats, as a precaution." He fell silent a moment, his eyes far away.

"I don't think we're through with him," he began again in a low voice, as if his thoughts had never left Hatch. "I've underestimated him all along and I may be underestimating him now. Once he gets home, he's going to start thinking. He'll realize it might take days, even weeks, to get a legal injunction against us. And possession is nine tenths of the law. He could cry clause nineteen until he's blue in the face. But by that point, everything would be academic."

He touched Streeter's lapel. "Who would have thought a billion dollars wouldn't be enough for the greedy bastard? He's going to think of a plan. I want you to find out what that plan is, and stop it. We're only hours away from Ockham's treasure, and, by God, I don't want any nasty surprises before we get to it." He gripped the lapel suddenly. "And for Chrissake, whatever you do, don't let Hatch set foot on this island again. He could do a lot of damage."

Streeter looked back impassively. "Any particular way you want him handled?"

Neidelman released the lapel and took a step back. "I've always found you to be a creative and resourceful seaman, Mr. Streeter. I leave the matter to your discretion."

Streeter's eyebrows rose momentarily in what might have been anticipation, or perhaps merely a muscle spasm.

"Aye, aye, sir," he said.

Neidelman leaned forward and switched the comm set back on. "Keep in touch, Mr. Streeter."

Then he was back on the lift and descending once again. Streeter turned back toward the ladder array. In a moment, he, too, was gone.

42

Hatch stood on the wide old porch of the house on Ocean Lane. What had been merely a weatherman's threat the day before was fast becoming reality. To the east, a heavy swell was coming in over the sea, creating a torn line of breakers on the reefs of Breed's Point. On the opposite side of the harbor, beyond the channel buoys, the surf flung itself again and again up the granite cliffs beyond Burnt Head Light, the boom of the rollers carrying across the bay in measured cadences. The sky was slung across with the ugly underbelly of a massive foul-weather front, the clouds churning and coiling as they raced across the water. Farther offshore, an evil patch of surf seethed about Old Hump. Hatch shook his head; if the swell was already smothering the bald rock, it was going to be a hell of a blow.

He gazed down toward the harbor, where a few vessels from the protest flotilla were already returning: smaller boats, and the million-dollar craft of the more cautious trawler captains.

Closer to home, movement caught his eye: he turned to see the familiar stubby form of a Federal Express van nosing into the lane, wildly out of place as it bumped down the old cobbles. It stopped in front of his house, and Hatch came down the steps to sign for the package.

He stepped back into the house, tearing open the box and eagerly removing the thick plastic packet inside. Professor Horn and Bonterre, standing beside one of the pirate skeletons, stopped talking when they saw the package.

"Straight from the Smithsonian's Phys Anthro lab," Hatch said as he broke the plastic seal. Pulling out the bulky computer printout within, he laid it on the table and began flipping pages. There was a heavy silence as they leaned over the results, disappointment palpable in the air. Finally Hatch sighed and flung himself into a nearby chair. The professor shuffled over, eased himself down opposite Hatch, rested his chin on his cane, and eyed Hatch meditatively.

"Not what you were looking for, I take it?" he asked.

"No," Hatch said, shaking his head. "Not at all."

The professor's brows contracted. "Malin, you were always too hasty to accept defeat."

Bonterre picked up the printout and began flipping through it. "I can not make foot or head of this medical jargon," she said. "What are all these horrible-sounding diseases?"

Hatch sighed. "A couple of days back, I sent off bone sections from these two skeletons to the Smithsonian. I also included a random sampling from a dozen of the skeletons you uncovered in the dig."

"Checking for disease," Professor Horn said.

"Yes. As more and more of our people began to get sick, I began to wonder about that mass pirate grave. I thought the skeletons might be useful in my examination. If a person dies of a disease, he usually dies with a large number of antibodies to that disease in his body."

"Or *her* body," said Bonterre. "Remember, there were three ladies in that grave."

"Large labs like the Smithsonian's can test old bone for small amounts of those antibodies, learn exactly what disease the person might have died from." Hatch paused. "Something about Ragged Island—then and now—makes people sick. The most likely candidate to me seemed the sword. I figured that, somehow, it was a carrier of disease. Everywhere it went, people died." He picked up the printout. "But according to these tests, no two pirates died of the same illness. Klebsiella, Bruniere's disease, Dentritic mycosis, Tahitian tick fever— they died of a whole suite of diseases, some of them extremely rare. And in almost half the cases, the cause is unknown."

He grabbed a sheaf of papers from an end table. "It's just as mystifying as the CBC results on the patients I've been seeing the last couple of days." He passed the top sheet to Professor Horn.

COMPLETE BLOOD COUNT

TEST NAME	RESULTS		UNITS
	ABNORMAL	NORMAL	
WBC	2.50		THOUS/CU.MM.
RBC		4.02	MIL/CU.MM.
HGB		14.4	GM/DL
HCT		41.2	PERCENT
MCV		81.2	FL
MCH		34.1	PG
MCHC		30	PERCENT
RDW		14.7	PERCENT
MPV		8	FL
PLATELET COUNT	75		THOUS/CU.MM.

DIFFERENTIAL

POLY	900	CU.MM.
LYMPH	600	CU.MM.
MONO	10	CU.MM.
EOS	.30	CU.MM.
BASO	.30	CU.MM.

"The blood work's always abnormal, but in different ways with each person. The only similarity is the low white blood cells. Look at this one. Two point five thousand cells per cubic millimeter. Five to ten thousand is normal. And the lymphocytes, monocytes, basophils, all way down. Jesus."

He dropped the sheet and walked away, sighing bitterly. "This was my last chance to stop Neidelman. If there was an obvious outbreak, or some kind of viral vector on the island, maybe I could have persuaded him or used my medical connections to quarantine the place. But there's no epidemiological pattern among the illnesses, past *or* present."

There was a long silence. "What about the legal route?" Bonterre asked.

"I spoke to my lawyer. He tells me it's a simple breach of contract. To stop Neidelman, I'd have to get an injunction." Hatch looked at his watch. "And we don't have weeks. At the rate they're digging, we've only got a few hours."

"Can't he be arrested for trespassing?" Bonterre asked.

"Technically, he's not trespassing. The contract gives him and Thalassa permission to be on the island."

"I can understand your concern," the professor said, "but not your conclusion. How could the sword itself be dangerous? Short of getting sliced open by its blade, I mean."

Hatch looked at him. "It's hard to explain. As a diagnostician, sometimes you develop a sixth sense. That's what I feel now. A sense, a *conviction*, that this sword is a carrier of some kind. We keep hearing about the Ragged Island curse.

Maybe this sword is something like that, only with a real-world explanation."

"Why have you discarded the idea of it being a real curse?"

Hatch looked at him in disbelief. "You're joking, right?"

"We live in a strange universe, Malin."

"Not *that* strange."

"All I'm asking is that you think the unthinkable. Look for the connection."

Hatch walked to the living room window. The wind was blowing back the leaves of the oak tree in the meadow. Drops of rain had begun to fall. More boats were crowding into the harbor; several smaller craft were at the ramp, waiting to be hauled out. The whitecaps flecked the bay as far as the eyes could see, and as the tide began to ebb a nasty cross-sea was developing.

He sighed and turned. "I can't see it. What could strepto-coccal pneumonia and, say, candidiasis, have in common?"

The professor pursed his lips. "Back in 1981 or '82, I remember reading a similar comment made by an epidemiologist at the National Institutes of Health."

"And what was that?"

"He asked what Kaposi's sarcoma and Pneumocystis carinii could possibly have in common."

Hatch turned sharply. "Look, this couldn't possibly be HIV." Then—before the professor had gathered himself for an acerbic reply—Hatch realized what the old man was getting at. "HIV kills by exhausting the human immune system," he went on. "Letting in a host of opportunistic diseases."

"Exactly. You have to filter out the pestilential noise, so to speak, and see what's left."

"So maybe we're looking for something that degrades the human immune system."

"I did not know we had so many sick on the island," Bonterre said. "None of my people are ill."

Hatch turned toward her. "None?"

Bonterre shook her head.

"There. You see?" Dr. Horn smiled and rapped his cane on the floor. "You asked for a common thread. Now you have several leads to follow."

He stood up and took Bonterre's hand. "It was very charming to meet you, *mademoiselle,* and I wish I could stay. But it's coming on to blow and I want to get home to my sherry, slippers, dog, and fire."

As the professor reached for his coat, there came the sound of heavy footsteps hurrying across the porch. The door was flung open in a gust of wind, and there was Donny Truitt, his slicker flapping open and rain running down his face in thick rivulets.

A flash of fire tore the sky, and the heavy boom of thunder echoed across the bay.

"Donny?" Hatch asked.

Truitt reached down to his damp shirt, tearing it open with both hands. Hatch heard the professor draw in a sharp breath.

"Grande merde du noir," Bonterre whispered.

Truitt's armpits were spotted with large, weeping lesions. Rainwater ran from them, tinged pinkish-green. Truitt's eyes were puffy, the bags beneath blue-black. There was another flash of lightning, and in the dying echo of thunder Truitt cried out. He took a staggering step forward, pulling the sou'wester from his head as he did so.

For a moment, all inside the house were paralyzed. Then Hatch and Bonterre caught Truitt's arm and eased him toward the living room sofa.

"Help me, Mal," Truitt gasped, grabbing his head with both hands. "I've never been sick a day in my life."

"I'll help," said Hatch. "But you need to lie down and let me examine your chest."

"Forget my damn chest," Donny gasped. "I'm talking about *this*!"

And as he jerked his head away from his hands with a convulsive movement, Hatch could see, with cold horror, that each hand now held a mat of thick, carrot-colored hair.

Clay stood at the stern rail of his single-diesel dragger, the megaphone upended in the fore cabin, drenched and useless, shorted out by the rain. He and the six remaining protestors had taken temporary shelter in the lee of the largest Thalassa ship—a ship they had originally tried to blockade.

Clay was wet to the bone, but a feeling of loss—of bitter, hollow loss—penetrated far deeper than the damp. The large ship, the *Cerberus,* was inexplicably vacant. Either that, or the people on board had orders not to show themselves: despite boat horns and shouts, not a single figure had come on deck. Perhaps it had been a mistake, he thought miserably, to target the largest ship. Perhaps they should have headed for the island itself and blockaded the piers. That, at least, was tenanted: about two hours before, a series of launches had left the island, loaded with passengers, angling directly away from the protest flotilla toward Stormhaven at high speed.

He looked toward the remnants of his protest flotilla. When they had left the harbor that morning, he'd felt empowered with the spirit: as full of conviction as he'd ever felt as a young man, maybe more. He had been certain that, finally, things would be different for him and the town. He could do something at last, make a difference to these good people. But as he gazed about at the six bedraggled boats heaving in the swell, he admitted to himself that the protest, like everything else he had tried to do in Stormhaven, seemed doomed to failure.

The head of the Lobsterman's Co-op, Lemuel Smith, threw out his fenders and brought his boat alongside Clay's. The two craft heaved and bumped against each other as the rain lashed the sea around them. Clay leaned over the gunwale. His hair was plastered to his angular skull, giving his already severe appearance a death's-head cast.

"It's time to head in, Reverend," the lobsterman shouted, grasping the side of his boat. "This is going to be one humdinger of a storm. Maybe when the mackerel run's over we can try again."

"By then it'll be too late," Clay cried over the wind and rain. "The damage will be done."

"We made our point," said the lobsterman.

"Lem, it's not about making a point," said Clay. "I'm cold and wet, just like you. But we have to make this sacrifice. We have to *stop* them."

The lobsterman shook his head. "We're not going to stop them in this weather, Reverend. Anyway, this little Nor'easter may do the job for us." Smith turned a weather eye upward and scanned the sky, then turned to the distant land, a mere ghost of blue vanishing into the driving rain. "I can't afford to lose my boat."

Clay fell silent. *I can't afford to lose my boat.* That was it in a nutshell. They didn't see that some things were more important than boats or money. And perhaps they never would see. He felt a strange tight sensation around his eyes and realized, vaguely, that he was crying. No matter; two more tears in an ocean. "I wouldn't want to be responsible for anybody losing his boat," he managed to say, turning away. "You go on back, Lem. I'm going to stay."

The lobsterman hesitated. "I'd sure feel better if you came in now. You can fight them another day, but you can't fight the ocean."

Clay waved his hand. "Maybe I'll land on the island, talk to Neidelman myself . . ." He stopped, hiding his face as he pretended to busy himself about the boat.

Smith gazed at him for a moment with creased, worried eyes. Clay wasn't much of a seaman. But telling a man what to do with his boat was an unforgivable offense. Besides, Smith could see something in the Reverend's face, a sudden uncaring recklessness, that told him anything he said would be useless.

He slapped the gunwale of Clay's boat. "I guess we'd better shove off, then. I'll be monitoring the ten point five channel, case you need help."

Clay hugged the lee of the *Cerberus,* engine idling, and stared as the remaining boats headed into the heaving sea, the sound of their diesels rising and falling on the wind. He pulled his slicker tighter and tried to hold himself steady against the deck. Twenty yards away, the curving white hull of the *Cerberus* rose up, rock solid in the water, the swell sliding noiselessly past.

Clay mechanically checked his boat. The bilge pumps were running smoothly, jetting fine streams of water over the side; the engine was purring nicely, and he still had plenty of diesel fuel. Now that it had come to this—now that he was alone, the Almighty his sole companion—he felt an odd sense of comfort. Perhaps it was a sin of presumption to expect so much from the people of Stormhaven. He couldn't rely on them, but he could rely on himself.

He would wait a little before heading toward Ragged Island. He had boat and time enough. All the time in the world.

He watched the remains of the fleet head back toward Stormhaven harbor, his arms braced hard upon the helm. Soon, they were nothing but distant, ghostly shapes against a sodden background of gray.

He did not see the Thalassa launch that pulled away from the island, pitching and yawing, the outboard cavitating with each plunge as it struggled toward the boarding hatch on the far side of the *Cerberus*.

44

Donny Truitt lay on the sofa, breathing more calmly now that the one-milligram IM dose of lorazepam had started to take effect. He stared at the ceiling, blinking patiently, while Hatch examined him. Bonterre and the professor had retreated to the kitchen, where they were talking in hushed tones.

"Donny, listen to me," Hatch said. "When did the symptoms begin to show?"

"About a week ago," Truitt replied miserably. "I didn't think anything of it. I started waking up nauseated. Lost my breakfast a couple of times. Then this rash thing appeared on my chest."

"What did it look like?"

"Red splotches at first. Then it got kind of bumpy. My neck started to hurt, too. On the sides, like. And I started noticing hair in my comb. First just a little, but now it's like I could pull it all out. But there's never been a touch of baldness in my family; we've always been buried with a full head of hair. Honest to God, Mally, I don't know how my wife'd take it if I went bald."

"Don't worry. It's not male pattern baldness. Once we figure out what's wrong and take care of it, it'll grow back."

"I sure as hell hope so," said Truitt. "I got off the midnight shift last night and went straight to bed, but I only felt worse in the morning. Never been to a doctor before. But I thought, hell, you're a friend, right? It wasn't like going to a clinic or something."

"Anything else I should know about?" Hatch asked.

Donny grew suddenly embarrassed. "Well, my—it kind of hurts around my hind end. There's sores back there, or something."

"Roll to one side," Hatch said. "I'll take a look."

A few minutes later, Hatch sat by himself in the dining room. He had called an ambulance from the hospital, but it would take at least another fifteen minutes to arrive. And then there would be the problem of getting Donny into it. A rural Mainer, Truitt had a horror of going to the doctor, and an even greater horror of the hospital.

Some of his symptoms were similar to what other crew members had complained of: apathy, nausea. But, as with the others, there were symptoms Donny presented that were maddeningly unique. Hatch reached for his battered copy of the Merck manual. A few minutes of study gave him a depressingly easy working diagnosis: Donny was suffering from chronic granulomatous disease. The widespread granular lesions of the skin, the suppurative lymph nodes, the all-too-obviously painful perianal abscesses made diagnosis almost unavoidable. *But CGD is usually inherited*, Hatch thought to himself. *An inability of the white blood cells to kill bacteria. Why would it be showing up only now?*

Putting the book down, he walked back into the living room.

"Donny," he said, "let me take another look at your scalp. I want to see if the hair is coming out in clean patches."

"Any cleaner, and I'd be Yul Brynner." Truitt touched his head with his hand, gingerly, and as he did so Hatch noticed an ugly cut he hadn't seen before.

"Lower your hand a moment." He rolled up Truitt's sleeve and examined the man's wrist. "What's this?"

"Nothing. Just a scratch I got in the Pit."

"It needs to be cleaned." Hatch reached for his bag, rummaged inside, irrigated the cut with saline solution and Betadine, then smeared on some topical antibacterial ointment. "How did this happen?"

"Got cut by a sharp edge of titanium, setting that fancy ladder thing into the Pit."

Hatch looked up, startled. "That was over a week ago. This wound looks fresh."

"Don't I know it. Damn thing keeps opening up. The missus puts liniment on it every night, I swear."

Hatch took a closer look at it. "Not infected," he said. Then: "How are your teeth?"

"Funny you should mention it. Just the other day, I noticed one of my buck teeth was a bit loose. Getting old, I guess."

Hair loss, tooth loss, cessation of the healing process. Just like the pirates. The pirates had other, unrelated diseases. But they all had those three things in common. As did some of the digging crew.

Hatch shook his head. They were all classic symptoms of scurvy. But all the other exotic symptoms made scurvy impossible. And yet something about it all was damnably familiar. *Like the professor said, forget the other diseases, subtract them all, and see what's left. Abnormal white blood cell count. Hair loss, tooth loss, cessation of the healing process, nausea, weakness, apathy . . .*

Suddenly, it became overwhelmingly clear.

Hatch stood up quickly.

"Oh, Jesus—" he began.

As the pieces flew into place he stood, thunderstruck, horrified at the implications.

"Excuse me a minute," he said to Truitt, pulling the blanket up and turning away. He looked at his watch: seven o'clock. Just a couple of hours until Neidelman reached the treasure chamber.

Hatch took a few deep breaths, waiting for a good ground of control to settle beneath his feet. Then he went to the phone and dialed the number for the island's automated cellular routing center.

It was down.

"Shit," he muttered to himself.

Reaching into his medical bag, he pulled out the emergency radio communicator. All Thalassa channels were awash in static.

He paused a minute, thinking quickly, trying to sort out his options. Just as quickly, he realized there was only one.

He stepped into the kitchen. The professor had spread out a dozen arrowheads on the kitchen table and was describing coastal Indian sites to Bonterre. She looked up excitedly, but her face fell when she saw Hatch.

"Isobel," he said in a low voice, "I have to go to the island. Will you make sure Donny gets on the ambulance and goes to the hospital?"

"Going to the island?" Bonterre cried. "Are you mad?"

"No time to explain," Hatch said on his way to the hall closet. Behind him, he could hear the rustle of chairs being pushed back as Bonterre and the professor rose to follow him. Opening the closet door, he pulled out two woolen sweaters and began shrugging into them.

"Malin—"

"Sorry, Isobel. I'll explain later."

"I will come with you."

"Forget it," Hatch said. "Too dangerous. Anyway, you have to stay here and see that Donny gets to the hospital."

"I ain't going to no hospital," rose the voice from the sofa.

"See what I mean?" Hatch pulled on his oilskin and stuffed a sou'wester into one pocket.

"No. I know the sea. It will take two to get across in this weather, and you know it." Bonterre began pulling clothes out of the closet: heavy sweaters, his father's old slicker.

"Sorry," Hatch said, tugging into a pair of boots.

He felt a hand laid on his arm. "The lady is right," the professor said. "I don't know what this is all about. But I do know you can't steer, navigate, and land a boat in this weather by yourself. I can get Donny on the ambulance and to the hospital."

"Did you hear me?" Donny called. "I ain't getting in no ambulance."

The professor turned and fixed him with a stern look. "One more word out of you and you'll be clapped on a stretcher and strapped down like a madman. One way or another, you *are* going."

There was a brief pause. "Yes, sir," Truitt answered.

The professor turned back and winked.

Hatch grabbed a flashlight and turned to look at Bonterre, her determined black eyes peering out from under an oversized yellow sou'wester.

"She's as capable as you are," the professor said. "More so, if I were being honest."

"Why do you need to do this?" Hatch asked quietly.

In answer, Bonterre slipped her hand around his elbow. "Because you are special, *monsieur le docteur*. You are special to *me*. I would never forgive myself if I stayed behind and something bad happened to you."

Hatch paused a moment to whisper Truitt's treatment instructions to the professor, then they raced out into the driving rain. In the last hour the storm had picked up dramatically, and above the howling wind and lashing trees Hatch could hear the boom of Atlantic rollers pounding the headland, so low and powerful it registered more in the gut than in the ear.

They dashed through streaming streets full of shuttered houses, lights gleaming in the premature dark. Within a minute Hatch was drenched despite the slicker. As they neared the wharf there was an immense flash of blue light, followed immediately by a thunderous crash. In the aftermath, Hatch could hear the pop of a transformer failing at the head of the harbor. Instantly, the town was plunged into blackness.

They made their way along the wharf, carefully stepping down the slick gangplank to the floating dock. All the dinghies had been lashed to the shaking structure. Pulling his knife from a pocket, Hatch cut the *Plain Jane*'s dinghy loose, and with Bonterre's help slid it into the water.

"It might swamp with two," said Hatch, stepping in. "I'll come back and pick you up."

"You had better," Bonterre said, comic in the oversized sweater and slicker.

Not bothering to start the dinghy's engine, Hatch ran the oars through the oarlocks and rowed out to the *Plain Jane*. The harbor waters were still relatively calm, but the wind had raised a steep chop. The dinghy was flung up and down, slapping the troughs with unwholesome shudders. As he rowed, his back to the sea, Hatch could see the outlines of the town, dim against the dark sky. He found his eyes drawn toward the narrow, tall structure of the rectory, a wooden finger of blackness. There was a flash of livid lightning, and in the brief glare Hatch saw, or thought he saw, Claire—

dressed in a yellow skirt, one hand on the open doorframe of the house, staring out to sea toward him—before darkness descended once again.

There was a thump as the dinghy nudged alongside his boat. Clipping it to a sternbolt, Hatch clambered aboard, primed the engine, then said a brief prayer and cranked the starter. The *Plain Jane* sprang to life. As he drew the anchor chain up through the hawsehole, Hatch was once again grateful to have secured such a weatherly craft.

He goosed the engine and made a passing swipe at the dock, pleased to see Bonterre leap aboard with a seaman's agility despite the bulky clothing. She strapped on the life jacket Hatch tossed her, then tucked her hair under the sou'wester. Hatch checked the binnacle and turned his gaze seaward, toward the two light buoys midchannel and the peppercan bell buoy at the mouth of the bay.

"When we hit the open ocean," he said, "I'm going to head diagonally into the sea at half throttle. It's going to buck like hell, so keep hold of something. Stay close by, in case I need your help with the wheel."

"You are foolish," said Bonterre, nerves turning her good humor testy. "Do you think storms are found only off Maine? What I want to know is what this insane trip is all about."

"I'll tell you," Hatch said, staring out to sea. "But you're not going to like it."

45

Clay peered through the screaming murk, gripping the wheel with aching arms. The boat struck each towering wave with a crashing shudder, water bursting over the bows, wind tearing foam from the crests. Every wave smothered the pilothouse windows in white as the dragger tipped and began its sickening descent into the trough. For a moment there would be sudden, windless silence; then the craft would lift with a sickening lurch and begin the cycle over again.

Ten minutes earlier, when he'd tried the forward searchlight, he learned the boat had blown some fuses and lost most of its electrical power. The backup batteries were dead, too—he hadn't checked them, as he knew he should. But he'd been busy with other things: Earlier, without warning, the *Cerberus* had raised anchor and gotten underway, ignoring his horn, the vast white bulk moving inexorably into the black, lashing sea. Alone, violently tossed, he had followed it for a time, fruitlessly hailing, until it disappeared into the furious darkness.

He looked around the cabin, trying to assess the situation. It had been a serious mistake to follow the *Cerberus,* he realized that now. If they had not heeded him before, they certainly would not stop to heed him now. Besides, out of the lee of Ragged Island, the ocean was literally boiling: the eastbound swell was beating against the outbound tide, creating a viciously steep cross-sea. The loran was dead, leaving him with the compass in the binnacle as his only navigational tool. He was trying to steer by the compass, using dead reckoning. But Clay knew he was no navigator, and with no light he could read the compass only by lightning flashes. There was a flashlight in his pocket, but Clay desperately needed both hands to steer.

Burnt Head Light was socked in, and the screaming wind and surf were so loud he'd practically have to run over the bell buoy to hear it. Clay wrapped both elbows around the wheel and leaned against it, trying desperately to think. The island was less than a half mile away. Clay knew even a superb mariner would have a difficult job bringing the boat in through the reefs to Thalassa's dock in this weather. But—even if his fierce determination to land on Ragged Island had wavered—it would have been more difficult still to cross the six miles of hell to Stormhaven.

Twice, he thought he heard the deep-throated sound of the *Cerberus*'s engines. But it made no sense: first it was heading east, later heading west, as if searching—or waiting—for something.

He checked the compass in a flash of lightning, holding the wheel with weakening arms, while the boat sagged into yet another trough. He made a slight correction to his course, heading now almost directly into the sea. The boat shuddered its way into another comber and a sheer wall of black-and-gray water rose off the bows, higher and higher, and he realized that the correction was in fact a mistake. As the wave toppled back down upon the pilothouse, the entire boat was jammed downward with a wrenching twist. The tremendous force of the water popped one of the windows from its frame and seawater slammed into Clay. He had just enough time to brace against the wheel and cling with all his might against the blast.

The boat shuddered, pressing lower and lower into the boiling sea, and just when he thought she would founder he again felt the grateful surge of buoyancy. The boat rose until the seas parted and rolled off the deck. As the boat crested and the lightning flashed, he had a brief glimpse of a heaving, storm-flecked ocean. Ahead lay a shadow of calmer water: the lee of Ragged Island.

Clay looked up into the black sky and a few words escaped his lips: *Oh Lord, if it be Thy will*—and then he was fighting the sea again, turning the boat diagonally and leaning against the wheel as another surge of water came crashing through the open window. He rode the swell down, the boat shuddering as it slid into calmer water.

Before Clay had time to draw a relieved breath, he realized that the water was calm only in comparison to the tempest that raged beyond. A heavy swell warped around the island from both sides, making a confused sea, but at least now he could turn directly toward the mooring. He pushed the throttle up a tick and listened to the responding rumble of the engine.

The increased speed seemed to give the boat a little more stability. It ploughed ahead, plunging, surging upward, then plunging again. With the window out and the searchlight dead, he had trouble navigating in those brief moments of vision at the top of the swells. He realized, dimly, that it might be wise to throttle back, just in case the—

There was a stunning crash as the boat bottomed itself against the reef. Clay was thrown violently forward into the wheel, breaking his nose; then he was tossed back against the far wall of the pilothouse. Surf, surging over the reef, slewed the boat sideways, then a second roller spun the boat full broadside. Clay fought his way back to the wheel, snorting blood and brine, trying to clear his head. Then a third wave slammed the boat over on its beam ends, and he was thrown free of the deck into a perfect chaos of water and wind.

46

Hatch swung the nose of the *Plain Jane* into the channel. Behind came a rattling symphony of lines slapping masts as the boats bobbed hysterically at their moorings. The wind was cold, the sky thick with water. He took a taste: as much salt as it was fresh. He'd seen seas like this before in his childhood. But he'd never been foolhardy enough to venture out in them.

He took one final look back at the shore, then turned to sea and throttled up. They passed the floating 5 MPH and NO WAKE signs, so thrashed by the sea that they hung sideways, as if admitting defeat.

Bonterre came up beside him, clinging to the instrument housing with both hands.

"Well?" she screamed in his ear.

"Isobel, I've been a damn fool," he shouted back. "I've seen those same basic symptoms a thousand times. It was staring me right in the face. Anyone who's ever undergone radiation treatment for cancer knows what it's all about."

"Radiation treatment?"

"Yes. What happens to those patients? They get nauseated. They lose their energy. Their hair. White cell counts go through the floor. Among all the weird ailments I've seen this last week, every one had those points in common."

Bonterre hesitated, eyes wide despite the blinding surf.

"St. Michael's Sword is *radioactive*. Think about it. Long-term exposure to radioactivity kills your bone marrow cells, basically stops cell division. It cripples the immune system, makes you an easy mark. That's why the Thalassa crew had all those exotic diseases that kept distracting me. But the lack of cell division also stops the healing process, causes hair loss. Look at how my own hand has been so slow to heal. Severe exposure leads to osteoporosis and loss of teeth. Symptoms similar to scurvy."

"And it might also explain the computer problems."

"What do you mean?"

"Stray radiation causes havoc with microelectronics." Bonterre squinted at him, rain and seawater streaming across her face. "But why go out in this murderous storm?"

"We know the sword is radioactive. But that's all we know about it. The thing's been shut up in a lead box, and yet it's still killed everyone who's come in contact with it over the last seven hundred years. God only knows what would happen if Neidelman took it out of the casket. We can't allow that to happen."

As the boat came out of the lee of Burnt Head, the sea slammed into the *Plain Jane*'s hull with brutal ferocity. Hatch shut up abruptly and spun the wheel, trying to take the heading sea at a diagonal. The air around the boat was filled with pulverized water and spindrift. He checked the binnacle, corrected course, and scanned the loran.

Bonterre gripped the rails with both hands, lowering her head against the driving rain. "But what *is* the sword, then?"

"God only knows. Whatever it is, it's hot as hell. I for one don't want to—"

He fell silent abruptly, staring ahead. A white line loomed out of the murk, towering over the top of the boat. For a moment, he wondered if it was a large ship.

"Jesus," he muttered, distantly surprised by the matter-of-fact tone in his own voice. "Look at that."

It was no ship. He realized, with horror, that it was the breaking top of a massive wave. "Help me hold the wheel!" he yelled.

Leaning forward, Bonterre clapped both hands on the wheel while he worked desperately at the throttle. The boat rose along the almost vertical face while Hatch gingerly increased the throttle, trying to keep the boat aligned. As the breaking top of the comber struck, there was an explosion of white and a tremendous hollow roar; he braced himself against the mass of water and held his breath.

The boat seemed suspended for a moment inside the wave; then it suddenly broke free and tipped over the crest with a violent corkscrew motion. He quickly eased up on the throttle and the boat sank into the following trough at a sickening speed. There was a moment of perverse, eerie calm as the boat was protected from the wind in the hollow between the waves. Then the next great face of green water, honeycombed with foam, rose up out of the dark before them.

"It'll get even worse beyond Wreck Island," he yelled.

Bonterre didn't bother to answer, clinging to the wheel as the boat lurched toward another crest with a jarring crash.

Glancing at the loran screen, Hatch saw the boat was being carried southeastward by a riptide at a good four knots. He corrected course to compensate, one hand on the throttle and the other on the wheel. Bonterre helped steady the helm through the dips.

"The professor was right," Hatch shouted. "I couldn't have done this without you."

The spray and wind had pulled Bonterre's long hair loose from her sou'wester, and it streamed behind her in a ravishing tangle of black. Her face was flushed, whether from fear or excitement he could not tell.

Another comber swept over the boat and he turned his eyes back to the fury.

"How will you convince Neidelman the sword is radioactive?" Bonterre hollered.

"When Thalassa set up my office, they included all kinds of crazy equipment. Including a radiologist's Radmeter. A high-tech Geiger counter. I never even turned the damn thing on." Hatch shook his head as they began to climb another wave. "If I had, it would have gone nuts. All those sick diggers, coming in covered with radioactive dirt. It doesn't matter how much Neidelman wants the sword. He won't be able to argue with that meter."

He could just barely hear, over the sound of the wind and his own shouting voice, the distant thudding of surf off the starboard side: Wreck Island. As they came out of the lee, the wind increased in intensity. Now, as if on cue, he could see a massive white line, far bigger than any previous wave, rising up above the *Plain Jane*. It loomed over their heads, water hissing along its crest. The boat fell into the silent trough and began to rise. His heart hammering in his chest, Hatch gave the boat a little more acceleration as he felt the swell begin to lift them once again.

"Hang on!" he yelled as the top of the wave reached them. Goosing the throttle, he pointed the boat straight into the roiling mass of water. The *Plain Jane* was thrown violently backward into a strange twilight world where both air and sea were made of water. Then, suddenly, they were through, the propeller whining helplessly as the prow fell down the foamy backside of the wave. As they slid into another glassy trough, Hatch saw a second white line materializing out of the gloom ahead, churning and shifting like a mad thing.

He struggled with the panic and despair that rose within him. That last hadn't been a freakish wave. It was going to be like this for the next three miles.

He began to feel an ominous sensation at each twist of the boat: a funny vibration, a tug at the wheel. The boat felt weighty and overballasted. He peered aft through the lashing wind. The bilge pumps had been running at full capacity since they left the harbor, but the old *Plain Jane* had no well meter. There was no way of knowing the depth of water in the hold without checking it himself.

"Isobel!" he roared, bracing his feet against the walls of the cabin and locking his hands around the wheel. "Go into the forward cabin and unscrew the metal hatch in the center of the floor. Tell me how much water's in the hold."

Bonterre shook the rain from her eyes and nodded her understanding. As Hatch watched, she crawled through the pilothouse and unlatched the cabin door. A moment later, she emerged again.

"It is one quarter full!" she shouted.

Hatch swore; they must have hit some piece of flotsam that stove in the hull, but he'd never felt the impact in the violent seas. He glanced again at the loran. Two and a half miles from the island. Too far out for them to turn around. Perhaps too far to make it.

"Take the wheel!" he yelled. "I'm going to check the dinghy!"

He crawled aft, hanging desperately to the gunwale railing with both hands.

The dinghy was still behind, bobbing like a cork at the end of its line. It was relatively dry, the *Plain Jane*'s bulk having kept most of the heavy seas out of it. But, dry or not, Hatch hoped to God they wouldn't have to use it.

The moment he relieved Bonterre at the helm, he could tell that the boat had grown distinctly heavier. It was taking longer to rise through the masses of water that pressed them down into the sea.

"You okay?" Bonterre called.

"So far," said Hatch. "You?"

"Scared."

The boat sank again into a trough, into that same eerie stillness, and Hatch tensed for the rise, hand on the throttle. But the rise did not come.

Hatch waited. And then it came, but more slowly. For a grateful moment, he thought perhaps the loran was off and they had already come into the lee of the island. Then he heard a strange rumble.

Towering far above his head was a smooth, Himalayan cliff face of water. A churning breaker topped its crown, growling and hissing like a living thing.

Craning her neck upward, Bonterre saw it as well. Neither said a word.

The boat rose and kept rising, ascending forever, while the water gradually filled the air with a waterfall's roar. There was a massive crash as the comber hit them straight on; the boat was flung backward and upward, the deck rising almost to vertical. Hatch clung desperately as he felt his feet slip from the deck beneath him. He could feel the water in the hold shift, twisting the boat sideways.

Then the wheel went abruptly slack. As the roaring water fell away, he realized the boat was swamped.

The *Plain Jane* came to rest on its side and began to sink rapidly, too full of water to right itself. Hatch looked rearward. The dinghy had also shipped a quantity of water, but was still afloat.

Bonterre followed Hatch's eyes and nodded. Clinging to the side, up to their waists in roiling water, they began working their way toward the stern. Hatch knew that a freakish wave was usually followed by a series of smaller ones. They had two minutes, maybe three, to get into the dinghy and free of the *Plain Jane* before she dragged them down with her.

Clinging to the railing, Hatch held his breath as the water surged over them, first once, then a second time. He felt his hand grasp the stern rail. Already, the eyebolt was too deep underwater to reach. Fumbling about in the chill sea, he located the painter. Letting go of the rail, he reeled in the rope, kicking frantically against the tug of the water until he felt himself bump the dinghy's bow. He scrambled in, falling heavily to the bottom, then rose and looked back for Bonterre.

She was clinging to the stern, the *Plain Jane* now almost under. He grabbed the painter and began pulling the dinghy in toward the eyebolt. Another great wave lifted him up, smothering him with briny foam. He leaned down and grasped Bonterre under the arms, pulling her into the dinghy. As the wave subsided, the *Plain Jane* turned bottom up and began to sink in a flurry of bubbles.

"We've got to cut loose!" Hatch shouted. He dug into his pocket for his knife and sawed desperately through the painter. The dinghy fell back into the swell as the *Plain Jane* turned its stern toward the inky sky and disappeared with a great sigh of air.

Without hesitation, Bonterre grabbed the bailer, working fast to lighten the dinghy's bottom. Moving aft, Hatch gave the outboard a tug, then another. There was a cough, a snort, then a tinny rasp above the scream of the ocean. Engine idling, Hatch quickly began working the second bailer. But it was no use: with the *Plain Jane* gone, the little dinghy was bearing the full brunt of the storm. More water was crashing over the side than could be bailed out.

"We need to be turned against the sea," said Bonterre. "You bail. I will manage the boat."

"But—"

"Do it!"

Crawling aft, Bonterre threw the little engine into forward and jammed the throttle open, swinging the boat broadside to the sea as she did so.

"For Chrissake, what are you doing?" Hatch howled.

"Bail!" she yelled in return. The boat sagged backward and upward, the water in its bottom flowing aft. Just as a great comber bore down, she gave the throttle a sudden twist, lifting it up and over. Immediately, she turned the boat again, surfing down the wave's backside, almost parallel to the sea.

This was in direct opposition to everything Hatch had ever learned about boats. In terror, he dropped the bailer and clung to the gunwale as they gathered speed.

"Keep bailing!" Bonterre reached back and pulled the stopcock in the stern. Water drained out as the boat picked up even more speed.

"You're going to kill us!" Hatch yelled.

"I have done this before!" Bonterre shouted. "I surfed the waves as a kid."

"Not waves like this!"

The dinghy skimmed down the middle of the trough, the propeller clearing the water with a nasty whine as they began to climb the leading side of the next wave. Sprawled in the bottom and clutching both gunwales, Hatch guessed their speed at twenty knots.

"Hold on!" Bonterre yelled. The little boat skidded sideways and skipped over the foaming crest. As Hatch watched in mingled horror and disbelief, the dinghy became airborne for a sickening moment before slamming down on the far side of the wave. It leveled out, shooting down the following edge.

"Can't you slow down?"

"It does not work if one slows down! The boat needs to be planing!"

Hatch peered over the bows. "But we're heading in the wrong direction!"

"Do not worry. In a few minutes I will come about."

Hatch sat up in the bow. He could see that Bonterre was staying as long as possible in the glassy troughs, where the wind and chop didn't reach, violating the cardinal rule that you never bring your boat broadside to a heavy sea. And yet the high speed of the boat kept it stable, allowing her to look for the best place to cross each wave.

As he watched, another wave crested before them. With a deliberate jerk, Bonterre jammed the engine handle around. The dinghy skipped over the top of the crest, reversing direction as it came hurtling down into the next trough.

"Sweet *Jesus*!" Hatch cried, scrabbling desperately at the bow seat.

The wind dropped a little as they came into the lee of the island. Here there was no regular swell, and it became far more difficult for the little boat to ride the confused sea.

"Turn back!" Hatch cried. "The riptide's going to sweep us past the island!"

Bonterre began to reply. Then she stopped.

"Lights!" she cried.

Emerging from the storm was the *Cerberus*, perhaps three hundred yards off, the powerful lights on its bridge and forward deck cutting through the dark. Now it was turning toward them, a saving vision in white, almost serene in the howling storm. Perhaps it had seen them, Hatch thought—

no, it *had* seen them. It must have picked up the *Plain Jane* on its scope and been coming to its rescue.

"Over here!" Bonterre yelled, waving her arms.

The *Cerberus* slowed, presenting its port side to the dinghy. They came to an uneasy rest as the great bulk of the ship cut them off from wind and waves.

"Open the boarding hatch!" Hatch yelled.

They bobbed for a moment, waiting, as the *Cerberus* remained silent and still.

"Vas-y, vas-y!" Bonterre cried impatiently. "We are freezing!"

Staring up at the white superstructure, Hatch heard the high whine of an electric motor. He glanced toward the boarding hatch, expecting to see it open. Yet it remained closed and motionless.

Twisted lightning seared the sky. Far above, Hatch thought he could see a single figure reflected against the light of the bridge instrumentation, looking down at them.

The whine continued. Then he noticed the harpoon gun on the forward deck, swiveling slowly in their direction.

Bonterre was staring at it also, puzzled. *"Grande merde du noire,"* she muttered.

"Turn the boat!" Hatch yelled.

Bonterre threw the throttle hard to starboard and the little craft spun around. Above, Hatch saw a peripheral glow, a blue flash. There was a sharp hissing noise, then a loud splash ahead of them. A thunderous *whump* followed, and a tower of water rose twenty feet off their port bow, its base lit an ugly orange.

"Explosive harpoon!" Hatch cried.

There was another flash and explosion, frighteningly close. The little dinghy pitched sharply, then heaved to one side. As they cleared the side of the *Cerberus,* wild water took them once again. There was an explosion ahead as another harpoon hit the water. Spray stung Hatch's face as they fell backward, nearly foundering.

Without a word, Bonterre spun the boat again, throttled up, and headed straight for the *Cerberus*. Hatch turned to yell out a warning, then realized what she was doing. At the last moment she turned the boat sideways, slamming hard against the huge vessel. They were under the pitch of the hull, too close for the harpoon gun.

"We'll make a dash by the stern!" Bonterre cried.

As Hatch leaned forward to bail, he saw a strange sight: a narrow line in the water, sputtering and snapping, heading toward them. Curious, he paused to watch. Then the line reached the bow in front of him, and with a tearing sound the nose of the dinghy vanished in a cloud of sawdust and wood smoke. Falling into the stern, glancing up, Hatch could see Streeter leaning over the ship's rail, an ugly weapon he recognized as a fléchette aimed directly at them.

Before Hatch could speak Bonterre had thrown the boat forward again. There was a sound like a demonic sewing machine as the fléchette in Streeter's hands tore apart the water where the dinghy had tossed just a moment before. Then they had cleared the stern and were back out in the storm, the boat bucking, water crashing over the ruined bows. With a roar, the *Cerberus* began to turn. Bonterre jammed the dinghy to port, almost overturning it as she headed in the direction of the Ragged Island piers.

But in the vicious ripping sea the small outboard was no match for the power and speed of the *Cerberus*. Looking through the heavy squall, Hatch could see the huge boat begin to gain. In another minute, they would be cut off from the inlet that led through the Ragged Island reefs to the pier beyond.

"Head for the reefs!" he yelled. "If you time the swell, you

5.ep77

might be able to ride right over. This boat hardly draws a foot!"

Bonterre jerked the boat to a new course. The *Cerberus* continued to bear down, coming inexorably at them through the storm.

"Make a feint, let him think we're going to turn at the reefs!" he shouted.

Bonterre brought them parallel to the reefs, just outside the breaking surf.

"He thinks he's got us!" Hatch said as the *Cerberus* turned again. There was another shattering explosion off the beam, and for a moment Hatch breathed salt water. Then they emerged from the spray. Glancing down, Hatch saw that half the port gunwale had been blown away by a harpoon.

"We'll only have a single chance!" he yelled. "Ride the next swell across!"

They bucked along the reef for an agonizingly long instant. Then he yelled: "Now!"

As Bonterre turned the ruined dinghy into the boiling hell of water that lay across the reef, there came another huge explosion. Hatch heard a strange crunching noise and felt himself hurtled violently into the air. Then everything around him was churning water and bits of planking, and the dying muffled roar of agitated bubbles. He felt himself being drawn down, and still down. There was only one brief moment of terror before it all began to seem very peaceful indeed.

47

Woody Clay lost his footing on a patch of seaweed, banged his shin, and came close to using the Lord's name in vain. The rocks along the shore were slippery and algae-covered. He decided it was safer to crawl.

Every limb of his body ached; his clothes were torn; the pain in his nose was worse than he could have ever imagined; and he was cold to the point of numbness. Yet he felt alive in a way that he had not in many, many years. He'd almost forgotten what it was like, this wild exhilaration of the spirit. The failed protest no longer had any significance. Indeed, it had not failed. He had been delivered onto this island. God worked in mysterious ways, but clearly He had brought Clay to Ragged Island for a reason. There was something he had to accomplish here, something of prime importance. Exactly what, he did not yet know. But he was confident that, at the right time, the mission would be revealed to him.

He scrambled beyond the high tide mark. Here the footing was better, and he stood up, coughing the last of the sea-water from his lungs. Every cough sent a hideous pain shooting through his ruined nose. But he did not mind the pain. What was it St. Lawrence had said, when the Romans were roasting him alive over a brazier of hot coals? "Turn me over, Lord. Cook me on the other side."

As a child, when other boys had been reading Hardy Boys mysteries and biographies of Babe Ruth and Ty Cobb, Clay's favorite book had been Foxe's *Book of Martyrs*. Even today, as a Congregational minister, he saw nothing wrong in quoting liberally from the lives of the Catholic saints, and even more liberally from their deaths. Those were people who had been blessed with visions, and with the courage to see them through, no matter what the cost. Clay was reasonably certain he had the courage. What he'd been lacking recently, he knew, was the vision.

Now he had to take shelter, get warm, and pray for the revelation of his purpose.

He scanned the shoreline, gray against a black sky, blasted and pelted by the fury of the storm. There were some large rocks off in the dimness to his right—the kind fishermen called Whalebacks. Beyond was the unnatural dry lagoon formed by Thalassa's cofferdam. Except the exposed seabed was not entirely dry. He noted, with a grunt of satisfaction, that the surf was battering the cofferdam relentlessly. Several of the stanchions were bent and one of the reinforced concrete slabs had warped. Every blow of the waves sent massive plumes of spray over the top of the wall.

Clay walked up the rocky shore and found shelter in the large earthen embankment, beneath some overhanging tree roots. But even here the rain was lashing down, and as soon as he stopped moving he began to shiver. Standing up again, he began walking along the base of the embankment, looking for some kind of windbreak. He saw nobody and heard nobody. Perhaps the island was tenantless, after all: the plunderers had evacuated in the face of the storm, scattered, like the moneylenders from the temple.

He came to the point of land. Around the edge of the bluff lay the seaward side of the island. Even from here, the sound of the pounding surf was intense. As he rounded the point, a strip of yellow police tape caught his eye, one end torn free and fluttering wildly in the wind. He moved forward. Beyond the tape lay a trio of braces, made out of some shiny metal, and behind them a dark, ragged opening led into the embankment. Maneuvering around the tape and the braces, Clay stepped into the opening, ducking his head under the low roof as he did so.

Inside, the sound of the surf dropped dramatically, and it was snug and dry. If it wasn't warm exactly, at least it wasn't chilly. He reached into one pocket and took out his little supply of emergency items: the flashlight, the plastic match case, the miniature first aid kit. He shone the flashlight around the walls and ceiling. It was some kind of small chamber, which narrowed to a tunnel at the far end.

It was very interesting, very gratifying. He had, in a way, been led to this tunnel. He had little doubt it connected somehow to the works that were said to honeycomb the center of the island. His shivering increased, and he decided that the first course of action should be to build a fire and dry out a bit.

He gathered some small driftwood that had washed into the cave, then unscrewed the circular plastic case and upended it. A dry wooden match fell out into his hand. He smiled with a certain suppressed feeling of triumph. He had carried this waterproof match case on every boat trip he'd ever taken since coming to Stormhaven. Claire had teased him about it, of course—being that it was Claire, kind-hearted teasing—but it had rankled nevertheless in that secret part of Clay's heart kept hidden from every living creature. And now, that match case was going to play its own part in his destiny.

In short order, a little fire was casting merry shadows on the wall of his cave. The storm howled past the tunnel entrance, leaving his nest practically untouched. The pain in his nose had subsided to a dull, steady throb.

Clay huddled closer, warming his hands. Soon—very soon, now—he knew the special task that had been set aside for him would at last be made clear.

48

Isobel Bonterre glanced wildly up and down the rocky shore, narrowing her eyes against the wind and lashing rain. Everywhere she looked, there were shapes in the sand, dark and indistinct, that could have been the body of Malin Hatch. But when she'd come close enough to investigate, they had all proved to be rocks.

She glanced out to sea. She could see Neidelman's boat, the *Griffin,* two anchors securing it close to the reef, doggedly riding out the howling gale. Farther out to sea, the elegant white bulk of the *Cerberus* was barely visible, lights ablaze, the crashing surf having lifted it off the reef onto which it had run aground. It had evidently lost steerage, and was now being carried out to sea on the strong tidal rip. It was also listing slightly, perhaps struggling with a flooded bulkhead or two. A few minutes before, she'd seen a small launch put over its side and struggle through the seas at a frantic pace, disappearing around the far end of the island, toward the Base Camp dock.

Whether it had been Streeter in the launch, or someone

else, she did not know. But she did know one thing: however advanced the research vessel, a person could not pilot and man the harpoon at the same time. And that meant that, whatever was happening here, it was not the work of a single madman. Streeter had help.

She shivered, drawing the waterlogged slicker closer around her. There was still no sign of Hatch. If he'd survived the destruction of the dinghy, chances were he'd have washed up along this stretch of beach. But he hadn't, she was now sure of that. The rest of the coastline was rock-bound, unprotected from the fury of the sea . . .

She stepped down hard on the terrible feeling that threatened to grip her heart. No matter what, she had to finish what they'd started.

She began heading toward Base Camp the long way, the careful way, skirting the black stretch of shoreline. The wind had increased its fury, whipping white spume off the crests of the waves and throwing it far inland. The roar of the surf on the reefs was so loud, so continuous, that Bonterre barely heard the cracks of thunder above the constant booming.

She slowly approached the cluster of huts. The communications tower was dark, the microwave horns hanging loose, swinging in the wind. One of the island generators had fallen silent, while the other was shaking and shuddering like a live thing on its steel platform, screaming in protest at the load. She crept up between the dead generator and the fuel tanks and scanned the camp. In its center, she could make out a series of small glowing rectangles: the windows of Island One.

She crept forward cautiously, keeping to the shadows that knitted the ground between the huts. Reaching Island One, she peered in the window. The command center was deserted.

She flitted across the rutted roadway to the window of the

medical hut. It, too, looked deserted. She tried the door, cursing when she found it locked, then crept to the rear of the structure. She reached down for a rock, raised it toward the small rear window, and rammed it through, knowing there was no chance of being heard over the storm. Reaching through the shards of glass, she unlocked the window from the inside and swung it open.

The room she slithered into was Hatch's emergency quarters. The narrow cot was unused, as pristine and rumple-free as the day it had been first installed. She moved quickly through the room, rummaging through drawers, looking for a gun, a knife, any kind of weapon. She found only a long, heavy flashlight. Snapping on the light and keeping its beam toward the ground, she moved through the doorway into the medical facility beyond. To one side was Hatch's private office, and to the other was a corridor leading to the waiting area. Along the far wall of the corridor was a door marked MEDICAL SUPPLIES. It was locked, as she knew it would be, but it seemed flimsy, constructed with a hollow core. Two well-placed kicks split it down the middle.

The small room was filled on three sides by glass-fronted cabinets, drugs above, equipment below. Bonterre had no idea what the Geiger counter would look like; she only knew that Hatch had called it a Radmeter. She broke the glass front of the nearest cabinet with the flashlight and rummaged through the lower drawers, spilling the contents to the floor. Nothing. Turning, she broke the glass of the second cabinet, pulling out the drawers, stopping briefly to slip something into her pocket. In the lowest drawer she found a small black nylon carrying case with a large Radmetrics logo sewn to its front. Inside was a strange-looking device with foldable handles and a leather strap. Its upper surface held a vacuum fluorescent display and a tiny keyboard. Extending from the front was a small boom similar to a condenser microphone.

She hunted for a power switch, found it, and snapped it on, praying the battery was charged. There was a low beep and a message appeared on the display:

RADMETRIC SYSTEMS INC.
RADIATION MONITORING AND POSITIONING SYSTEM
RUNNING RADMETRICS RELEASE 3.0.2(a) SOFTWARE
WELCOME, NEW USER
DO YOU NEED HELP? (Y/N)

"All that I can get," she muttered, hitting the *Y* key. A terse series of instructions scrolled slowly across the screen. She scanned them quickly, then shut the machine off, realizing it was a waste of time to try to master it. The batteries were working, but there was no way of knowing how much of a charge they held.

She zipped the machine back into its carrying case and returned to Hatch's quarters. Suddenly, she froze. A sound, sharp and foreign, had briefly separated itself from the dull howl of the storm: a sound like the report of a gun.

She slung the carrying case over her shoulder and headed for the broken window.

49

Hatch lay on the rocks, drowsy and comfortable, the sea washing around his chest. One part of his mind was mildly annoyed at having been plucked from the bosom of the sea. The other part, small but growing, was horrified at what the first part was thinking.

He was alive, that much he knew; alive, with all the pain and misery that came along with it. How long he had lain there he could only guess.

Now he gradually became aware of aches in his shoulders, knees, and shins. As he thought about them, the aches quickly grew into throbs. His hands and feet were stiff with cold, and his head felt waterlogged. The second part of his brain—the part that was saying all this was a good thing—was now telling him to get his sorry ass out of the water and up the rocky beach.

He wheezed in a breath full of seawater and was seized with a fit of coughing. The spasm brought him to his knees; his limbs collapsed and he fell again to the wet rocks. Struggling to a crawl, he managed to make the few feet out of reach of the water. There he rested on a large outcropping of granite, the rock cool and smooth beneath his cheek.

As his head cleared, memories began to return, one by one. He remembered Neidelman, and the sword, and why he'd returned to the island. He remembered the crossing, the *Plain Jane* capsizing, the dinghy, Streeter . . .

Streeter.

He sat up.

Isobel had been on the boat.

He tottered to his feet, fell back, then rose again, determined now. He'd fallen out the bow end of the dinghy, and the freakish riptide had pulled him to this rocky shore around the end of the island. Ahead, dark against the angry sky, he saw the low bluffs that guarded the pirate encampment. Bonterre would have landed nearer the beach. If she landed at all.

Suddenly, he could not bear the thought of her being dead.

He moved forward unsteadily, croaking Bonterre's name. After a moment he stopped to look about, realizing that, in his confusion, he was walking away from the beach toward the low bluffs. He staggered partway up the rise, then turned seaward. There was no sign of Bonterre, or of the dinghy's remains. Beyond the shore, the ocean was pounding the cofferdam relentlessly, every blow sending seawater shooting at high pressure through a web of cracks.

There was a brief flicker of light, fingering its way along the dark shore. He looked again, and it was gone: a flash of lightning, reflected off the rocks. He began to climb back down the bluff.

Suddenly the light was back again, closer this time, bobbing along the shoulder of the island. Then it swung upward, the powerful pale light of a halogen beam stabbing into the dark. It moved back and forth along the shore, then raked inland past him. Instinctively, Hatch began backing up the slope.

Then it was flaring in his eyes, blinding him. He dropped and turned, scrabbling up the bluff. The light licked the ground around him, searching. There was a glare, and he saw his shadow rise away up the hill in front of him. He'd been targeted.

The strange, stuttering sound he'd heard from the *Cerberus* came again, rattling over the roar of the surf and the howl of the wind: the clatter of giant knitting needles. To his right, small puffs of dirt and mud rose madly into the air in a jagged line. Streeter was behind him, in the dark, shooting at him with the fléchette.

Quickly, Hatch rolled to his left, angling desperately for the top of the bluff. There was another demonic clatter as the weapon tore into the spot where he'd lain a few seconds before, a hundred tungsten nails stitching ruin into the earth.

Half crawling, half rolling, Hatch crossed the top of the bluff and tumbled down the embankment on the far side, slipping on the wet grass. He righted himself and glanced around wildly. There was no tree cover, just a long exposed run across the meadow and up the rise of land toward Orthanc. Ahead, he could see the small equipment shed Bonterre used for fieldwork, and beside it a precise dark rectangle cut into the ground: the pirate grave.

His glance settled on the equipment shed. He could hide inside, or perhaps beneath. But that would be the first place Streeter looked.

Hatch hesitated another second. Then he sprinted down the meadow and leaped into the grave.

He staggered under the impact of the three-foot drop, then steadied himself. A tongue of lightning briefly illuminated the pit around him. Some of the pirate skeletons had been removed from the mass grave. But most remained *in situ*, covered with tarps. The excavation was scheduled to be filled in the following week; Bonterre, he knew, had removed only enough skeletons to get a unique cross section.

A shattering clap of thunder galvanized him into action. Quickly, he crawled beneath one of the tarps. There was something sharp and uncomfortable beneath him: he reached into the dirt and plucked out a large section of crushed cranium. Brushing it to one side, he lay still, waiting.

Beneath the tarp the dirt was damp but not muddy, and out of the rain and wind Hatch felt warmth begin to creep back into his frozen limbs.

There was the sound of a foot being pulled from sucking mud.

Hatch held his breath. He heard a sharp squeal of metal as the door to the equipment shed was torn open. Then, silence.

Footsteps again, farther, then closer. Heavy, regular breathing, perhaps ten feet away. Hatch heard the mechanical *snick* of a weapon being readied. And he knew that Streeter hadn't been fooled.

The fléchette barked, and suddenly the floor of the grave became alive, writhing with miniature clouds of dirt and sand and bone fragments. From the corner of his eye, Hatch could see the tarp rearing and bucking, lifted into the air by the impact of hundreds of tiny nails, the bones beneath collapsing into mud and powder. The frantic, deadly trails of needles came toward him, and Hatch realized he had a second, maybe two, to decide what, if any, options remained.

The weapon coughed, then fell silent. There was a clattering of metal. Taking a desperate chance, Hatch rose from the ground and jumped blindly from the grave in the direction of the sound, the tarp stretched wide before him. He slammed into Streeter, toppling him backward into the mud. The fléchette fell to the ground, a fresh ammo canister beside it, and the flashlight was knocked several feet into the grass. Streeter struggled wildly beneath the tarp, arms and legs flailing. Hatch brought his knee up into what he guessed to be Streeter's groin, and was rewarded by a gasp of pain.

"Bastard!" Hatch cried, smothering the figure with his own large body, battering and pounding through the tarp. "Runt *bastard*!"

There was a sudden blow to his chin and Hatch felt his teeth grind together. He staggered backward, head suddenly light; Streeter must have butted him with his head. Hatch fell heavily back onto the tarp but Streeter was wiry and strong for his size, and Hatch could feel him begin to twist free. Quickly, he leapt for the fresh canister and flung it far into the darkness. Then he moved toward the flashlight as Streeter jumped to his feet, tearing free of the muddy tarp. Streeter's hand reached toward his own belt and came away with a small automatic weapon. Making an instant decision, Hatch brought his foot down on the light.

Darkness clapped down as a shot rang out. Hatch ran blindly then, zigzagging through the meadow, heading for the central rise of land and the maze of trails beyond. A tongue of lightning illuminated Streeter, a hundred yards below; the man caught sight of him, turned, and approached at a dead run. Hatch dashed toward the main workings, moving first up one path, then another, relying on feel to keep within the borders of yellow tape. Behind, he could hear pounding tread and heavy breathing.

As he topped the rise he saw the glow of Orthanc, lancing through the mists. He started toward it, then shrank away again: even to go near the light, he realized, would give Streeter a clear shot.

Hatch thought quickly. He could head down to the Base Camp, try and lose Streeter in the cluster of buildings. But he could easily be trapped there. Besides, he had to shake Streeter soon.

He realized he wasn't going to do it on the surface of the island.

There was one tunnel, the Boston Shaft, that led down into the earth at a gentle angle. If he remembered correctly, it connected with the Water Pit at a great depth. Neidelman had pointed it out to him on the morning—just a few weeks before, was it possible?—when they'd first located the site of the original Pit.

There was no more time. He glanced up at the glow of Orthanc, oriented himself, then turned down another trail. There it was: a dark hole yawning behind safety tape, fringed with ragged weeds.

He slipped under the tape and stood at the edge of the Boston Shaft. It was very dark, and the wind blew the rain horizontally into his eyes. *Gentle angle?* In the blackness, the shaft looked like a vertical drop to him. He hesitated, peering downward. Then there was the sound of footsteps clattering over a metal walkway. He grabbed the slender trunk of a chokecherry bush, swung himself over the edge, and scrabbled on the slippery walls of the shaft, trying to find a purchase with his feet. But there was none; the roots came out with a tearing sound and Hatch felt himself falling through empty space.

A short, terrifying drop, and he hit muddy bottom with a jolt. He scrambled to his feet, shaken but unhurt. There was only the faintest square of sky visible above him, a blurred patch that was a lighter shade of black. But he saw, or thought he saw, a shape moving along its edge . . .

There was a deafening roar, accompanied by a brilliant flash of light. A second roar followed almost immediately, and something smacked into the muddy shaft inches from his head.

Hatch twisted out of the shaft and began running down the tunnel. He knew what Streeter was doing: using the muzzle flash from his first shot to aim a second.

The incline of the tunnel floor was steep, and Hatch found himself slipping. He began to lose his balance as he ran, and he fought to keep from plunging, out of control, into absolute darkness. After several terrifying seconds, the incline leveled out enough for him to gain a purchase and come to a stop.

He stood in the humid chill of the tunnel, listening, trying to control his gasping breath. To run blindly ahead was suicide. The tunnel could well be honeycombed with pits or shafts—

There was a wet thump behind him, followed by the sound of footsteps slapping against mud.

Hatch felt for the side of the tunnel. His hand closed over the slimy cribwork and he began descending again as quickly as he dared, trying to stay rational. Streeter would no doubt shoot again. He'd probably try another pair of shots. But Streeter's strategy could also be useful to Hatch: the light from the first shot might give him an idea of what lay ahead.

It was the second shot that would be deadly.

The first shot came almost in answer to his thought, echoing deafeningly within the narrow confines of the tunnel. As Hatch threw himself sideways into the mud, the second shot ripped into the cribbing directly behind him.

In the muzzle flash, he saw that the tunnel continued downward uninterrupted.

Pushing himself to his feet, he ran ahead blindly, arms outstretched, half stumbling, half sliding, as far as he dared and then farther. At last he stopped, felt for the wall again, and listened. Streeter would still be behind him, proceeding more cautiously. If Hatch could lose him somehow in the tunnel, maybe he could reach the point, deep beneath the ground, where the Boston Shaft intersected the Water Pit. Neidelman would be there. He couldn't possibly know what Streeter was up to; Streeter must have suffered a psychotic break, nothing else made sense. If he could just reach the main shaft . . .

Another shot came, much closer than he'd expected. He swung desperately away, the second barely missing him. Ahead, he saw that the tunnel branched, a narrow passage to his left ending in what appeared to be a gaping hole. There was a third shot, then a fourth, and something ripped through his ear with a tearing sting.

He'd been hit. Running now, he grabbed wildly at his face, feeling for the blood that trickled from his torn ear. He ducked down the narrow branch and went as far toward the hole as he dared. Then he flattened himself against the wall and waited in the close blackness, muscles tensed. At the next muzzle flash, he'd spring back, grab Streeter, and toss him down. It was even possible that Streeter, in his haste, might run right into the hole himself.

In the intense, listening dark he heard a faint pattering, barely louder than the pounding of his own heart. It was Streeter, feeling his way along the wall. Hatch waited. Now he could hear the faint rasp of breath. Streeter was being careful with his rounds. No doubt he had a limited supply. Perhaps he would be forced to . . .

Suddenly, there was the flash and roar of a shot. Hatch lunged, trying desperately to beat the second shot, and as he closed on Streeter there was an immense blow to his head. A stunning light filled his eyes, blotting out thought, blotting out everything.

50

Keeping as much as possible to the shelter of the rocks, Bonterre hiked inland from Base Camp to the narrow marked trail that mounted the rise of the island. She began ascending stealthily, pausing every few moments to listen. Away from the lights of the camp it was dark, so dark that at times she had to feel for the lines of yellow tape, broken and fluttering wildly in the gale. The muddy trail rose, then dipped again, following the contour of the island. She was soaked to the skin, rain running in thin rivulets from her chin, elbows, and hands.

The path climbed once again and she topped a rise. The skeletal structure of Orthanc lay several hundred yards ahead, a trio of lights winking atop its superstructure, the windows brilliant squares of light etched against the night. The ATV was there, its bulbous tires slick with rain. Two large, empty metal containers were in tow. Below the tower, the mouth of the Pit was dark. But a ghostly light shimmered up from below, as if from a great depth. She could hear the clank of machinery, the rumble of the air pumps, even over the howl of the storm.

Through the glass windows of Orthanc, she could make out a dark shape moving slowly.

She crept forward, keeping low, using the tall grass as cover. A hundred feet out she stopped again, hiding behind a clump of tea roses. Here the view was much better. The figure had its back to her, and she waited. As it moved into the light she saw the broad shoulders and long, dirty-blond hair of Rankin, the geologist. He appeared to be alone.

She hesitated, sheltering the Radmeter from the rain as best she could. It was possible that Rankin might know how to use it, or at least have a better idea. But that would mean taking him into her confidence.

Streeter had deliberately tried to kill them. Why? True, he'd hated Hatch from the beginning. But Bonterre couldn't believe that was enough provocation. Streeter didn't seem the type to act rashly.

Then again, Hatch was trying to shut down the dig.

Were others in on it?

Somehow, she could not imagine the open, hearty Rankin being party to first-degree murder. As for Neidelman . . . she couldn't allow her thoughts to turn that way.

There was a searing bolt of lightning overhead, and she shrank away from the thunderclap that followed. From the direction of Base Camp, there was a sharp crackle as the last generator failed. The lights atop Orthanc blinked out for a moment, and then the control tower was bathed in an orange glow as the emergency batteries came on.

Bonterre clutched the Radmeter closer. She could wait no longer. Right or wrong, she had to make a choice.

A faceful of mud brought Hatch back to the black reality of the tunnel. His head throbbed from Streeter's blow, and something was pressing relentlessly on his back. The cold steel of what Hatch knew must be a gun barrel was digging into his torn ear. He hadn't been shot, he realized groggily; he'd been knocked on the head.

"Listen up, Hatch," came Streeter's whisper. "We had a nice little chase, but the game's over now." The barrel ground into his ear. "And you're it. Understand?"

Hatch tried to nod as Streeter jerked his head back cruelly by the hair. "Yes or no?"

"Yes," Hatch croaked, choking mud.

"Don't twitch, don't jerk, don't even sneeze unless I tell you to, or I'll turn your brains into a pink mist."

"Yes," Hatch said again, trying to muster some energy. He felt stupid, cold, barely alive.

"Now we're going to get up, nice and smooth. Slip in the mud and you're dead."

The pressure on his back was released. Hatch rose to his knees, then his feet, slowly, carefully, fighting to quell the pounding in his head.

"Here's what we're going to do," came Streeter's voice. "We'll return to where the tunnel forked. Then we're going to head straight down the Boston Shaft. So start walking. Slow."

Hatch put one foot in front of the other as carefully as he could, trying not to stumble in the darkness. They reached the fork, then continued down the main shaft, following the wall.

It seemed to Hatch that he should be able to escape. It was pitch black, and all he had to do was break free somehow. But the combination of the gun barrel grinding into his hurt ear and the thickness in his mind made clear thinking impossible. He wondered, momentarily, why Streeter hadn't simply killed him.

As they moved forward cautiously, he began to wonder just how well Streeter knew the Boston Shaft. There were few horizontal tunnels on the island, and almost all of them were riddled with intersecting vertical shafts. "Any pits along here?" he asked at last.

There was a harsh laugh. "If there are, you'll be the first to know."

After what seemed an eternity of nightmare shuffling through the blackness, wondering if the next step would be into open space, Hatch saw a faint glow ahead. The tunnel took a gentle turn and he made out a ragged opening, framed in light. There was a faint hum of machinery. Streeter pushed him forward at a faster pace.

Hatch stopped at the point where the tunnel opened onto the main shaft of the Water Pit. Momentarily blinded after the long chase, it took him a moment to realize that only the banks of emergency lights running along the ladder array were still lit. Another sharp pain in his ear, and Streeter forced him forward onto the metal catwalk that connected the Boston Shaft to the array. Following behind, Streeter punched a keypad bolted to the side of the lift rail. There was a humming sound from below, and in a few moments the lift itself came into view, slowed, then locked into place beside the catwalk. Streeter prodded Hatch onto the platform, then took up position behind him.

As they descended toward the base of the shaft, Hatch realized the dank, rotten smell of the Water Pit was now mixed with something else: the stench of smoke and hot metal.

The ladder array ended at the base of the Pit. The walls were narrower here, the air thick despite the ventilation systems. In the center was the narrow shaft of freshly dug earth that led down to the treasure chamber itself. Streeter gestured for Hatch to climb down the ladder. Clinging to the rails, Hatch clambered past the complex tracery of titanium struts and braces. From below came the crack and fizzle of acetylene.

Then he was at the bottom of the shaft, at the very heart of the island, swaying on uncertain feet. Streeter dropped to the ground behind him. Hatch could see that the earth before him had been cleared away from the top of a massive, rusted plate of iron. As he stared, the last ember of hope died away. Gerard Neidelman was kneeling before the plate, angling an acetylene torch into a narrow cut about three feet square. A bolt had been welded to the top of the plate, and from it a cable was fixed to the large bucket. In the far corner of the shaft stood Magnusen, arms folded, staring at Hatch with a mixture of cold hatred and contempt.

There was an angry hiss as Neidelman cut the flame on the torch. Laying it aside, he stood up and raised his visor, staring expressionlessly at Hatch.

"You're a sorry sight," he said simply.

He turned to Streeter. "Where did you find him?"

"He and Bonterre were trying to come back to the island, Captain. I caught up with him in the Boston Tunnel."

"And Bonterre?"

"Their dinghy was crushed on the reef. There's a chance she survived drowning, too, but the odds are against it."

"I see. Pity she had to get involved in this. Still, you've done well."

Streeter flushed with the praise. "May I borrow your sidearm for a moment, Captain?"

Neidelman slid the pistol from his belt and handed it to Streeter, an inquiring expression on his face. Streeter pointed it at Hatch and gave his own gun to Neidelman. "Could you reload that for me, sir? I ran out of ammo."

He gave Hatch a crooked smile. "You missed your opportunity, Doctor. There won't be another."

Hatch turned to Neidelman. "Gerard, please. Hear me out."

The Captain slapped a fresh clip into the gun, then snugged it into his belt. "Hear you out? I've been hearing you out for weeks now, and it's getting rather tedious." He shrugged the visor from his head and handed it to Magnusen. "Sandra, take over the torch, please. The island's battery system will only last two hours, maybe three, and we can't waste any time."

"You *have* to listen," Hatch said. "St. Michael's Sword is radioactive. It'll be suicide to open that casket."

A weary look crossed Neidelman's face. "You never give up, do you. Wasn't a billion dollars enough?"

"Think," Hatch went on urgently. "Think past the treasure for a moment, think of what's been happening on this island. It explains everything. The problems with the computers, the system acting flaky. Stray radiation from the treasure chamber would cause the anomalies Wopner described. And the rash of illnesses we've had. Radiation suppresses the immune system, lowers the white blood count, allows opportunistic diseases to intrude. I'll bet that we'd find the worst cases among those who spent their time in this Pit, day after day, digging and setting braces."

The Captain stared at him, his gaze unreadable.

"Radiation poisoning causes hair loss, makes your teeth drop out. Just like those pirate skeletons. What else could be the cause of that mass grave? There were no signs of violence on the skeletons. Why else would the rest of the pirates have left in such a hurry? They were running from an invisible killer they didn't understand. And why do you suppose Ockham's ship was found derelict, the crew all dead? Because they'd received, over time, a fatal dose of radiation, leaking from the casket that held St. Michael's Sword."

Streeter dug the gun barrel cruelly into his ear, and Hatch tried vainly to twist free. "Don't you get it? God knows just how radioactive that sword is. It must be hot as hell. If you expose it, you'll kill not only yourself, but who knows how many others. You—"

"I've heard enough," Neidelman said. He looked at Hatch. "Funny. I never thought it would be you. When I was selling the idea of this dig to our backers, juggling numbers for risk analysis, you were the one stable factor in the equation. You hated the treasure. You'd never let anyone dig on your island. Hell, you'd never even been back to Stormhaven. If I could only secure your cooperation, I knew I'd never have to worry about greed." He shook his head. "It pains me to think how much I misjudged you."

There was a final hiss of steel, then Magnusen stood up. "Done, Captain," she said, removing the visor and reaching for the electrical box that controlled the winch. There was a whine as the cable went taut. With a thin metallic protest, the plate was lifted from the iron slab. Magnusen angled it to the far corner of the shaft floor, settled it to the earth, then unhooked the cable from the base of the large bucket.

Almost despite himself, Hatch found his eyes traveling toward the ragged square that had been cut into the iron plate. The dark opening to the treasure chamber exhaled the faint perfume of ambergris, frankincense, and sandalwood.

"Lower the light," the Captain said.

Her heavy body trembling with suppressed excitement, Magnusen plucked a basket lamp from the ladder and swung it down into the hole. Then Neidelman dropped to his hands and knees. Slowly, carefully, he peered inside.

There was a long silence, punctuated only by the dripping of water, the faint hiss of the forced air system, and the distant sound of thunder. At last the Captain rose to his feet. He staggered slightly, then caught himself. His face had become rigid, almost masklike, and his damp skin was white. Struggling with suppressed emotion, he mopped his face with a handkerchief and nodded to Magnusen.

Magnusen dropped quickly, pressing her face into the hole. Hatch could hear her involuntary gasp echo up, strangely hollow, from the chamber beneath. She remained at the opening in the floor, rigid, for several long minutes. Finally, she stood up and moved to one side.

Neidelman turned to Hatch. "Now it's your turn."

"My turn?"

"That's right. I'm not without feeling. These riches would have been half yours. And it's because of you we were able to dig here. For that I remain grateful, despite all the trouble you've caused. Surely you want to see what we've worked so hard for."

Hatch took a deep breath. "Captain, there's a Geiger counter in my office. I'm not asking you to believe without seeing—"

Neidelman slapped him across the jaw. It was not hard, but the pain that shot through Hatch's mouth and ear was so unbearable he sank to his knees. He was dimly aware that the

Captain's features had suddenly turned crimson, contorted into a look of intense anger.

Wordlessly, Neidelman gestured toward the iron plate. Streeter grabbed Hatch by the hair and twisted his head downward into the opening.

Hatch blinked once, then twice, as he struggled to comprehend. The light swung back and forth, sending shadows across the vault. The metal chamber was about ten feet square, the iron walls furred with rust but still intact. As he stared, Hatch forgot the pain in his head; forgot Streeter's hands twisting sadistically in his hair; forgot Neidelman; forgot everything.

As a boy, he had once seen a photograph of the antechamber to King Tutankhamen's tomb. Staring at the casks, boxes, chests, crates, and barrels that lined the walls of the chamber beneath him, the memory of that photo came rushing back.

He could see the treasure had once been carefully wrapped and stored by Ockham and his men. But time had taken its toll. The leather sacks had rotted and split, pouring out streams of gold and silver coins that mixed and mingled in small rivers. From the wormy, sprung staves of the casks spilled great uncut emeralds, rubies dark as pig's blood, sapphires winking in the flickering light, topazes, carved amethysts, pearls, and everywhere the scintillating rainbows of diamonds, cut and uncut, large and small. Against one wall lay bundles of elephant tusks, narwhal horns, and boar's ivory, yellowed and cracked. Against another were enormous bolts of a material that had clearly once been silk; now it had rotted into lumps of decaying black ash, shot through with masses of gold threads.

Along one wall rose a stack of small wooden crates. The sides of the topmost crates had fallen away and Hatch could see the butt ends of rough gold bars—hundreds, perhaps thousands of them—stacked back to back. Ranged along the fourth wall were crates and bags in odd shapes and sizes, some of which had tumbled over and broken open, revealing ecclesiastical treasures: gold crosses encrusted with pearls and gemstones, elaborately decorated gold chalices. Beside them, another bag had burst open, revealing a bundle of braided gold epaulettes taken from unfortunate sea captains.

Atop the center of this fantastic hoard was a long, lead coffin, trimmed and edged with gold, strapped with iron bands that anchored it to the vault's floor. A massive brass lock was attached to its top face, partly concealing the golden image of an unsheathed sword etched into its lid.

As Hatch stared, barely able to breathe, he heard a clink, then a rush, as a rotten sack burst and a stream of gold doubloons poured out, running in rivulets among the piled treasures.

Then he was jerked to his feet and the wondrous, nightmarish sight was gone.

"Get everything ready on the surface," Neidelman was saying. "Sandra will winch the treasure up in the bucket. Two trailers are attached to the ATV, correct? We should be able to get the bulk of the treasure out to the *Griffin* in half a dozen trips. That's all we can chance."

"And what do I do with him?" Streeter asked.

Neidelman simply nodded. A smile creased Streeter's features as he raised his gun toward Hatch's head.

"Not here," Neidelman murmured. The sudden rage had passed, and he was calm again, looking down toward the treasure chamber, his expression far away. "It must look like an accident. I wouldn't like to think of his rotten corpse drifting in on the tide with a bullet in its brainpan. Take him into a side tunnel, or . . ."

He paused.

"Put him with his brother," he said, his eyes drifting toward Streeter for the briefest of seconds before returning to the flickering hole at his feet. "And Mr. Streeter—"

Streeter paused in turning Hatch toward the ladder.

"You said there's a chance Isobel survived. Eliminate that chance, if you please."

52

As Bonterre clambered cautiously up to the observation post, ready to leap for the ground at a moment's notice, Rankin turned and saw her. His beard split into a huge grin, then fell almost comically as he got a better look.

"Isobel!" he cried, coming forward. "You're soaked. And what the hell—your face is all bloody!"

"Never mind," said Bonterre, stripping off her wet slicker and sweaters and wringing them out.

"What happened?"

Bonterre looked at him, wondering how much she should say. "Boat wreck," she replied after a moment.

"Jesus. Why didn't the—"

"I will explain later," she interrupted, shrugging back into the damp clothes. "Have you seen Malin?"

"Dr. Hatch?" Rankin asked. "Nope." A small beeping sounded on a far console and he hurried over to take a look. "Things have gotten pretty weird around here. The digging crew reached the iron plate over the treasure chamber around seven. Neidelman dismissed them, sent them home because of the storm. Then he called me up here to relieve Magnusen and monitor the major systems. Only most everything is down. The generators are off-line, and the backup batteries can't support the whole load. I've had to shut down all noncritical systems. Communications have been out since lightning trashed the uplink. They're on their own down there."

Bonterre walked toward the center of the structure and stared down through the glass porthole. The Water Pit was dark, a glowing ember of light deep at its core. The skeletal tracery of struts and braces that filled the Pit shone dimly in the reflected emergency lamps.

"So who's down there?" she asked.

"Just Neidelman and Magnusen, far as I know. Haven't seen anybody else on the monitors, anyway. And they went out when the generators failed." He jerked a thumb in the direction of the closed-circuit monitors, now awash in snow.

But Bonterre continued to stare down toward the faint light at the base of the Pit. "How about Streeter?"

"Haven't seen him since we had all that company in the lobster boats, earlier in the day."

Bonterre stepped away from the glass floor. "Has Neidelman broached the chamber?"

"Like I said, I lost the video feeds. All I got left are the instruments. At least the hardbody sonar is giving clearer signals now that all the dirt's been removed. I've been trying to get a cross section of . . ."

His voice died as Bonterre became aware of a faint vibration, a tremor at the edge of perceptibility. She glanced out the windows, sudden fear washing over her. But the battered cofferdam was still holding back the fury of the sea.

"What the hell?" breathed Rankin, staring at the sonar screen.

"Do you feel that?" Bonterre asked.

"Feel it? I can *see* it right here."

"What is it?"

"Damned if I know. Way too shallow to be an earthquake, and anyway it isn't throwing out the right P-waves." He tapped briefly on a keyboard. "There, it's stopped again. Some tunnel caving in somewhere, I'll bet."

"Look, Roger, I need your help." Bonterre set the sopping nylon bag onto an instrument panel and unzipped it. "Ever seen a machine such like this one?"

Rankin kept his eyes on the monitor. "What is it?"

"A Radmeter. It is for—"

"Wait a minute. A Radmeter?" Rankin looked over from the monitor. "Well, what the hell. Yeah, I know what it is. Those puppies aren't cheap. Where'd you get it?"

"You know how to work it?"

"More or less. Mining company I worked for used one for tracing strikes of pitchblende deposits. Wasn't as fancy as this one, though."

Coming over, he snapped it on and typed a few instructions on the miniature keyboard. A glowing, three-dimensional grid appeared on the screen. "You aim this detector," he said, moving the microphonelike device, "and it traces a map of the radioactive source on the screen. The intensity is color-coded. Blues and greens for the lowest-level radiation, then up through the spectrum. White's the hottest. Hmmm, this thing needs calibration." The screen was streaked with dashes and spots of blue.

Rankin tapped a few keys. "Damn, I'm getting a hell of a lot of background noise. The machine's probably on the fritz. Just like everything else around here."

"The machine is working just fine," said Bonterre evenly. "It is picking up radiation from St. Michael's Sword."

Rankin glanced at her, squinting his eyes. "What did you say?"

"The sword is radioactive."

Rankin continued looking at her. "You're jiving me."

"I do not jive. The radioactivity has been the cause of all our problems." Bonterre quickly explained while Rankin stared at her, his mouth working silently behind his thick beard. When she finished, she braced herself for the inevitable argument.

But none came. Rankin continued staring, his hirsute face perplexed. Then it cleared and he nodded suddenly, great beard wagging. "Hell, I guess it's the only answer that explains everything. I wonder—"

"We do not have time for speculation," interrupted Bonterre sharply. "Neidelman cannot be allowed to open the casket."

"Yes," said Rankin slowly, still thinking. "Yes, it would have to be radioactive as hell to be leaking all the way to the surface. Shit, he could fry us all. No wonder the equipment's been acting up. It's a wonder the sonar's cleared up enough to . , ."

The words died on his lips as his gaze turned back to the bank of equipment.

"Christ on a bicycle," he said wonderingly.

53

Neidelman stood motionless at the base of the Water Pit. Above his head, the lift hummed as it carried Streeter and Hatch up the array until they were lost from view in the forest of struts.

Neidelman did not hear the lift recede. He glanced at Magnusen, face pressed again to the hole in the iron plate, her breathing rapid and shallow. Without a word, he eased her aside—she moved sluggishly, as if exhausted or half asleep—grasped his lifeline, hooked it to the ladder, and lowered himself through the hole.

He landed next to the sword casket, knocking loose a dozen rattling streams of precious metal. He stood there, gazing at the casket, blind to the dazzling wealth that filled the chamber. Then he knelt, almost reverently, his eyes caressing its every detail.

It was about five feet long and two feet wide, the sides made of engraved lead chased with silver, the corners and edges decorated with elaborate gold work. The entire casket was strapped to the iron floor of the treasure crypt by four crossed bands of iron: a strangely crude cage to hold such a magnificent prisoner.

He looked more closely. The casket was supported by claw legs of pure gold. Each leg was formed as an eagle talon gripping an orb: obviously of Baroque origin and added much later. Indeed, it seemed the entire casket was an amalgam of styles, dating from the thirteenth century to the early Spanish Baroque. Evidently the lead casket had been added to over the ages, each decoration more sumptuous than the last.

Neidelman reached out and touched the fine metalwork, surprised to find it almost warm. He slipped his hand inside the iron cage and traced the workmanship with a slender fingertip. Over the years, no day passed in which he hadn't imagined this moment. He had often pictured what it would be like to see this casket, to touch it, to open it—and, in the fullness of time, draw out its contents.

Countless hours had been spent musing on the sword's design. Sometimes, he imagined a great Roman sword of beaten electrum, perhaps even the Sword of Damocles itself. At other times, he imagined a barbarous Saracen weapon of chased gold with a silver blade, or a Byzantine broadsword, encrusted with gems and too heavy even to lift. He had even imagined that perhaps it was the sword of Saladin, carried back by a knight from the Crusades, made of the finest Damascene steel inlaid in gold and set with diamonds from King Solomon's mines.

The possibilities, the speculations, filled him with an intense emotion, more overwhelming than anything he had known. *This must be how it feels to behold the face of God,* he thought.

He remembered there was not much time. Removing his hands from the silky metal of the casket, he placed them on the steel bands that surrounded it. He tugged, first gingerly, then with force. The cage that surrounded the casket was solid, immovable. Odd, he thought, that the bands went *through* slots in the iron floor and seemed to be attached to something below. The extraordinary security with which the casket was guarded confirmed its incalculable value.

Digging into a pocket, he drew out a penknife and gouged it into the rust that coated the nearest band. A few flakes came away, showing bright steel underneath. To free the chest, he would have to cut through the bands with the torch.

The sound of loud breathing disturbed his thoughts. He looked up to see Magnusen peering down through the opening. Her eyes looked dark and fevered in the swinging glow of the basket lamp.

"Bring down the torch," he said. "I'm going to cut this chest loose."

In less than a minute she landed heavily beside him. Falling to her knees, the torch forgotten, she stared at the sea of riches. She picked up a fistful of gold doubloons and fat louis d'ors, letting them slide through her fingers. Then she picked up another handful, more quickly; and then another, and another. Her elbow bumped against a small wooden casket and it ruptured into powder, spilling diamonds and carnelians. Then a momentary panic overwhelmed her and she scrabbled for them, stuffing the winking gems indiscriminately into her pockets, lurching forward and breaking additional bags in her haste. At last she fell facedown into the priceless mass, arms buried in the loose gold, legs spread, softly laughing, or crying, or perhaps both.

As he reached for the acetylene cylinder, Neidelman paused to watch her for a moment, thinking it was time she winched the bucket down into the chamber and began hauling the treasure to the surface. Then his eyes fell once again on the casket and Magnusen was instantly forgotten.

He wrapped his fingers around the thick brass lock that held the box shut. It was an ugly piece of work, heavy-looking and stamped with ducal seals, some of which Neidelman recognized as dating back to the fourteenth century. The seals were unbroken. *So Ockham never opened his greatest treasure,* he thought. *Strange.*

That honor would be reserved for him.

Despite its size, the lock held the box shut loosely; using the blade of his penknife, he found he was able to lift the lid a few millimeters. He removed the knife, lowered the lid, and again inspected the metal bands that were threaded through the lock, determining the most efficient places to make his cuts.

Then he twisted the cylinder's stopcock and struck the sparker: There was a small pop, and an intense pinpoint of white appeared at the end of the nozzle. Everything seemed to be happening with glacial slowness, and for that he was grateful. Each moment, each movement, gave him exquisite pleasure. It would take some time—perhaps fifteen minutes, perhaps twenty—before he could free the casket from its bands and actually hold the sword in his hand. But he knew that he would remember every second as long as he lived.

Carefully, he brought the flame to the metal.

54

Hatch lay in the bottom of the small stone well, half conscious, as if waking out of a dream. Above, he could hear rattling as Streeter drew the collapsible ladder up the shaft. The dim beam of a flashlight briefly illuminated the groined ceiling, forty feet overhead, of the chamber where Wopner had died. Then there was the sound of Streeter's heavy boots walking back down the narrow tunnel toward the ladder array, dying along with the light until silence and blackness fell upon him together.

For several minutes, he lay on the cold, damp stone. Perhaps it *was* a dream, after all, one of those ugly claustrophobic nightmares one woke from with infinite relief. Then he sat up, hitting his head on the low overhang of ceiling. It was now pitch black, without even the faintest glimmer of light.

He lay down again. Streeter had left him without a word. The team leader hadn't even bothered to bind his arms. Perhaps it was to make his death look less suspicious. But deep down, Hatch knew that Streeter had no need to tie him up.

There was no way he could climb thirty feet up the slippery sides of the well back to the vaulted room. Two hours, maybe three, and the treasure would be out of the pit and safely stowed aboard the *Griffin*. Then Neidelman would simply collapse the already weakened cofferdam. Water would rush back to flood the Pit, the tunnels and chambers . . . The well . . .

Suddenly, Hatch felt his muscles spasm as he struggled to keep panic from washing his reason away. The effort exhausted him and he lay gasping, trying to slow his pounding heart. The air in the hole was poor, and getting poorer.

He rolled away from the overhanging ceiling toward the base of the well, where he could sit up and rest his back against the cold stone. He stared upward again, straining for the least hint of light. But there was only blackness. He considered standing, but the very thought was exhausting and he lay down again. As he did so, his right hand slipped into a narrow cavity beneath a heavy stone slab, closing over something cold, wet, and rigid.

And then the full horror of where he was flooded through him, startling him to full consciousness. He released Johnny's bone with an involuntary sob.

The air was cold, with a suffocating clamminess that cut through his soggy clothes and felt raw and thick in his throat. He remembered that heavier gases, like carbon dioxide, sank. Perhaps the air would be a little better if he stood up.

He forced himself to his feet, hands against the side of the well for balance. Gradually, the buzzing in his head began to fade. He tried to tell himself that nothing was hopeless. He would systematically explore the cavity with his hands, every square inch. Johnny's bones had ended up in this chamber, victim of Macallan's fiendish engine of death. That meant the shore tunnel had to be nearby. If he could figure out how Macallan's trap worked, maybe he could find a way to escape.

Pressing his face against the slimy stone wall, he reached

his hands as high above his head as he could. This was where he would start, working his way down the stones systematically, quadrant by quadrant, until he had examined every reachable square inch of the chamber. Lightly, like a blind man's, his fingers explored every crevasse, every protuberance, probing, tapping, listening for a hollow sound.

The first quadrant yielded nothing but smooth stones, well mortised. Lowering his hands, he went on to the next section. Five minutes went by, then ten, and then he was on his hands and knees, feeling around the floor of the chamber.

He had scanned every reachable spot in the well—except the narrow crack along the floor into which his brother's bones had been pressed—and there was nothing, not a thing, that indicated an avenue of escape.

Breathing choppily, snorting the stale air into his nostrils, Hatch reached gingerly beneath the heavy stone. His hands encountered the rotting baseball cap on his brother's skull. He jerked back, heart thudding in his chest.

He stood again, face upward, striving for a breath of sweeter air. Johnny would expect him to do his goddamnedest to survive.

He yelled out for help; first tentatively, then more loudly. He tried to forget how empty the island was; tried to forget Neidelman, preparing to open the casket; tried to forget everything except his cries for help.

As he yelled, pausing now and again for breath, some last hidden chink of armor loosened within him. The bad air, the blackness, the peculiar smell of the Pit, the proximity of Johnny, all conspired to tear away the one remaining veil from that terrible day, thirty-one years before. Suddenly, the buried memories burned their way back, and he was once again on his hands and knees, match sputtering in his hand, as a strange dragging sound took Johnny away from him forever.

And there, in the thick dark, Hatch's yells turned to screams.

55

What is it?" Bonterre asked, her hand frozen on the Radmeter.

Rankin held up his hand for silence. "Just a minute. Let me compensate for any trace radiation." His head was mere inches from the screen, bathed in an amber glow.

"Jesus," he said quietly. "There it is, all right. No mistake, not this time. Both systems agree."

"Roger—"

Rankin rolled back from the screen and ran one paw through his hair. "Look at that."

Bonterre stared at the screen, a snarl of jittery lines underlaid by a large black stripe.

Rankin turned to her. "That black is a void underneath the Water Pit."

"A void?"

"A huge cavern, probably filled with water. God knows how deep."

"But—"

"I wasn't able to get a clear reading before, because of all the water in the Pit. And then, I couldn't get these sensors to run in series. Until now."

Bonterre frowned.

"Don't you understand? It's a *cavern*! We never bothered to look *deeper* than the Water Pit. The treasure chamber, the Pit itself—us, too, for Chrissake—we're all sitting on top of a goddamn piercement dome. This explains the faulting, the displacement, everything."

"Is this something else built by Macallan?"

"No, no, it's natural. Macallan *used* it. A piercement dome is a geological formation, an upfold in the earth's crust." He placed his hands together as if in prayer, then pushed one of them toward the ceiling. "It splits the rock above it, creating a huge web of fractures and usually a vertical crack—a pipe—that goes deep into the earth, sometimes several thousand feet, Those P-waves, that vibration earlier . . . something was obviously happening in the dome, causing a resonance. It must be part of the same substructure that created the natural tunnels Macallan—"

Bonterre jumped suddenly as the Radmeter in her hands chirped. As she stared, the blue shimmer on the screen turned yellow.

"Let me see that." Rankin punched in a series of commands, his large fingers dwarfing the keypad. The top half of the small screen cleared, then a message appeared, stark black letters against the screen:

**Dangerous radiation levels detected
Specify desired measurement
(ionizations / joules / rads)
and rate
(seconds / minutes / hours)**

Rankin hit a few more keys.

240.8 Rads/ hour
Fast neutron flux detected
General radiation contamination possible
Recommendation: Immediate evacuation

"*Merde*. It's too late."

"Too late for what?"

"He's opened the casket."

As they watched, the message changed:

33.144 Rads/hour
Background levels hazardous
Recommendation: Standard containment procedures

"What happened?" Rankin asked.

"I do not know. Maybe he closed it again."

"Let's see if I can get a radiation signature on the source."
The geologist began typing again. Then he straightened up,
still staring at the little screen.

"Oh, Christ," he muttered. "You won't believe this."

He was interrupted by a thump on the observation deck.
The door flew open and Streeter stepped in.

"Hey, Lyle!" Rankin said before seeing the handgun.

Streeter looked from Rankin to Bonterre, then back again.
"Come on," he said, motioning the gun toward the door.

"Come on where?" Rankin began. "What's with the gun?"

"We're taking a little trip, just the three of us," Streeter answered. He nodded in the direction of the observation porthole.

Bonterre slipped the Radmeter beneath her sweater.

"You mean, into the Pit?" Rankin asked incredulously.

"It's dangerous as hell down there! The whole thing's suspended over—"

Streeter placed the gun against the back of Rankin's right hand and fired.

The sound of the explosion was shockingly loud in the confined space of Orthanc. Instinctively, Bonterre looked away for a moment. Turning back, she saw Rankin on his knees, clutching his right hand. Thin streams of blood trickled between his fingers and pattered to the metal floor.

"That leaves you one hand to hold on with," Streeter says. "If you want to keep it, shut your hairy fucking mouth."

Once again he motioned them toward the door and the observation platform beyond. With a gasp of pain, Rankin hauled himself to his feet, looked from Streeter to the gun, then moved slowly to the door.

"Now you," Streeter said, nodding at Bonterre. Slowly, making sure the Radmeter was secure beneath her sweater, she stood up and began to follow Rankin.

"Be very careful," Streeter said, cradling the gun. "It's a long way down."

56

Hatch leaned against the wall of the chamber, his fear and his hope both spent, his throat raw from shouting. The memory of what had happened in this very tunnel, lost for so long, was now his again, but he was too exhausted even to examine the missing pieces. The air was a suffocating, foul-smelling blanket, and he shook his head, trying to clear the faint but insistent sound of his brother's voice: "Where are you? Where are you?"

He groaned and sank to his knees, dragging his cheek along the rough stone, trying to bring some clarity to his mind. The voice persisted.

Hatch drew his face away from the wall, listening now.

The voice came again.

"Hello?" he called back tentatively.

"Where are you?" came the muffled cry.

Hatch turned, felt the walls, trying to orient himself. The sound seemed to be coming from behind the stone that pressed his brother's bones into the stone floor.

"Are you all right?" it asked.

"No!" cried Hatch. "No! I'm trapped!"

The voice seemed to fade in and out of hearing. Perhaps, Hatch thought, it was himself, coming in and out of consciousness.

"How can I help?" he realized the voice was asking.

Hatch rested, thinking how he should reply.

"Where are you?" he asked at last. The rush of adrenaline had brought back a modicum of alertness; it would not last long.

"In a tunnel," the voice said.

"Which tunnel?"

"I don't know. It leads in from the shore. My boat was wrecked, but I was saved. Saved by a miracle."

Hatch rested for a moment, trying to suck in whatever air was left. There was only one possible tunnel the voice could mean: Johnny's tunnel.

"Where are you stuck?" the voice continued.

"Wait!" Hatch cried, breathing heavily, forcing himself to relive the old memories. *What had he seen?*

. . . There'd been a door, a door with a seal in front of it. Johnny had broken the seal and stepped through. A puff of wind from the tunnel beyond, blowing out the light . . . Johnny had cried out in surprise and pain . . . there'd been a kind of heavy dragging sound . . . he'd fumbled for a new match, lit it, seen the implacable stone wall before him, thick streaks of blood along its base and the joint where it met the left wall. The blood had seemed to almost weep from the cracks, rushing out and down like the leading edge of a red wave to creep around his knees and his sneakers.

Hatch wiped his face with a trembling hand, overwhelmed by the force of the memories.

A puff of wind had come down the tunnel when Johnny opened the door. Yet when Hatch had lit another match, there had been only a stone wall in front of him, and Johnny was gone. So the tunnel must have continued *beyond* the stone. Stepping into the room, or opening the door, or breaking the seal—something—had triggered Macallan's trap. A massive slab of stone moved across the tunnel, dragging Johnny with it, crushing him beneath, forcing his body into this hollow space, sealing off the rest of the watertight tunnel. There was no other explanation. The well, the chamber Hatch was trapped in, the vault room above, must all be part of the support mechanism for the trap. And Macallan—or perhaps Red Ned Ockham—hadn't wanted anybody interfering with the trap. So the vault room itself had been booby-trapped. As Wopner had learned at the cost of his life.

"Are you still there?" came the voice.

"Please wait," Hatch gasped, trying to follow the train of thought to its conclusion. The tunnel he and Johnny discovered must have been Red Ockham's secret entrance, the one Macallan had constructed for him—the back door to the treasure. But if a treasure hunter were to find the shore tunnel, Macallan needed a way to stop them. The trap that killed Johnny was obviously his answer. A massive piece of dressed stone, rolling in from one side, crushing any intruder who did not know how to disarm the trap. The stone was so expertly fashioned that, once in place, it would look like the end wall of the tunnel, preventing further exploration . . .

Hatch struggled to keep his mind focused. That meant once the Pit was drained, Ockham would have needed a way to reset the trap, to roll the stone back, and continue down the tunnel to reclaim his loot. Of course, Macallan had his own plans for Ockham once he reached the Pit itself. But the pirate had to *believe* he had a back door to the treasure.

So the trap had to work on a simple fulcrum mechanism, the stone delicately poised so that the slightest pressure would cause it to move . . . the pressure of a child's weight . . .

. . . But why, then, had nobody stumbled on the way to reset the trap, in that frantic search for Johnny, thirty-one years before—?

"Hey!" he cried out suddenly. "Are you still there?"

"I'm here. How can I help?"

"Do you have a light?" Hatch called.

"A flashlight, yes."

"Look around. Tell me what you see."

There was a pause. "I'm at the end of a tunnel. There's solid stone on all three sides."

Hatch opened his mouth, coughed, breathed more shallowly. "Tell me about the stone."

Another pause. "Big slabs."

"On all three sides."

"Yes."

"Any chinks or depressions? Anything?"

"No, nothing."

Hatch tried to think. "How about the ceiling?" he asked.

"There's a large stone lintel, some old oaken beams."

"Test the beams. Are they solid?"

"I think so."

There was a silence while Hatch strained to draw in more air. "What about the floor?"

"It's covered in mud. Can't see it all that well."

"Clear it away."

Hatch waited, willing his mind not to slip back into unconsciousness.

"It's tiled in stone," came the voice.

A faint glimmer of hope rose within Hatch. "Small pieces of stone?"

"Yes."

The glimmer became stronger. "Look closely. Does any piece look different from the rest?"

"No."

Hope slipped away. Hatch held his head in his hands, jaws agape, fighting for breath.

"Wait. There is something. There's a stone in the center, here, that's not square. It's tapered slightly, almost like a keyhole. At least, I think it is. There's not much of a difference."

Hatch looked up. "Can you lift it away from the others?"

"Let me try." There was a brief silence. "No, it's wedged in tight, and the soil around it is hard as concrete."

"Do you have a knife?"

"No. But wait, wait a moment, let me try something else." Very faintly, Hatch thought he could hear the sound of scratching.

"Okay!" the voice said, a thin tone of excitement carrying through the intervening rock. "I'm lifting it now." A pause. "There's some kind of mechanism in a cavity underneath, a wooden stick, almost like a lever or something."

That must be the fulcrum handle, Hatch thought drowsily. "Can you pull it up? Reset it?"

"No," came the voice after a moment. "It's stuck fast."

"Try again!" Hatch called out with the last of his breath. In the silence that followed, the buzzing returned, louder and louder in his ears; he leaned on the cold stone, trying to prop himself up, until at last he slipped away into unconsciousness.

. . . Then there was a light, and a voice, and Hatch felt himself coming back from a long distance. He reached up to the light, then slipped and fell, sending one of Johnny's bones spinning away. He breathed in the air, no longer stuffy and poisonous, faintly perfumed with the smell of the sea. He seemed to have fallen into a larger tunnel as the slab that crushed his brother had rolled back.

Hatch tried to speak but could only croak. He gazed up into the light again, trying to focus his blurry eyes on who was behind it. Raising himself on shaky knees, he blinked and saw Reverend Clay staring back at him, dried blood caked around his nose, flashlight in hand.

"You!" said Clay, disappointment huge in his voice. A large, thin cross of bright metal hung from his neck, one sharp edge covered in mud.

Hatch swayed, still breathing the delicious air. Strength was returning, but he could not yet muster the energy to speak.

Clay replaced the cross within his shirt and stepped closer, standing in the low doorway that Hatch himself had once stood in, more than thirty-one years before. "I took shelter near the mouth of the tunnel, and I heard your cries," the minister said. "On the third try I was able to shift the lever, and the end wall of the tunnel came away, opening this hole. What is this place? And what are you doing here?" He peered closer, shining the light into the chamber. "And what are all these bones that fell out with you?"

Hatch held up his hand in response. After a moment's hesitation, Clay reached down and Hatch staggered to his feet.

"Thank you," he gasped. "You saved my life."

Clay waved his hand in a gesture of irritation.

"This was the tunnel my brother was killed in. And those are his bones."

Clay's eyes widened. "Oh," he said, moving the light quickly away. "I'm very sorry."

"Did you see anyone else on the island?" Hatch asked urgently. "A young woman in a slicker? Dark hair?"

Clay shook his head.

Hatch closed his eyes briefly, took a deep breath. Then he pointed down the newly exposed tunnel. "This leads to the base of the Water Pit. Captain Neidelman's in the treasure chamber. We have to stop him."

Clay frowned. "Stop him from what?"

"He's about to open the casket that contains St. Michael's Sword."

A look of suspicion darted across the minister's face.

A series of racking coughs seized Hatch. "I've learned the sword's deadly. Radioactive."

Clay crossed his arms.

"It could kill us all, and maybe half the town of Stormhaven, if it ever got out."

Clay remained silent, staring.

"Look," said Hatch, swallowing hard. "You were right. We never should have been digging for this treasure. But it's too late for that now. I can't stop him alone."

A new look suddenly crossed the minister's face; a look Hatch found hard to interpret. Clay's expression began to change, brighten, as if his face was suffused with inward light. "I think I'm beginning to understand," he said, almost to himself.

"Neidelman sent a man to kill me," Hatch said. "He's become unhinged."

"Yes," said Clay, suddenly fervent. "Yes, of course he has."

"All we can hope now is that we're not too late."

Hatch stepped carefully around the litter of bones. *Rest easy, Johnny,* he said under his breath. Then he led the way down the narrow, sloping tunnel, Woody Clay following closely behind.

57

Gerard Neidelman knelt before the casket, motionless, for what seemed an infinity of time. The iron bands that surrounded it had been carefully cut away, one by one. As the precise white light of the acetylene torch freed each band, it had fallen away through the slots in the metal floor. Now only a single band remained, separated from the lock of the casket but clinging to its side by a thick coating of rust.

The lock had been cut, the seals broken. The sword was his to claim.

And yet Neidelman remained where he was, his fingers on the lid. Every sense seemed magnified. He felt alive, fulfilled, in a way he had never dreamed possible. It was as if his entire past life was now just a colorless landscape; as if he had lived but to prepare for this moment.

He inhaled slowly, then again. A slight tremor—perhaps the leaping of his heart—seemed to course through him. And then, with reverential slowness, he opened the lid.

The interior of the box lay in shadow, but within Neidelman could see a faint coruscation of gemstones. The long-hidden interior exhaled the warm, fragrant scent of myrrh.

The sword itself lay on perfumed velvet. He reached inside and placed his hand on the hilt, his fingers sliding smoothly between the beaten gold basket and grip. The blade itself was hidden, sheathed in a magnificent gold- and gem-encrusted scabbard.

Carefully, he drew the scabbarded sword from the box. The velvet on which the sword lay dissolved instantly to a cloud of purple dust.

He raised the sword—noting its heaviness with astonishment—and brought it carefully into the light.

The scabbard and hilt were of Byzantine workmanship, fashioned of heavy gold, dating to perhaps the eighth or ninth century, an exceedingly rare, rapierlike design. The repoussé and filigree were astonishingly delicate; in his vast studies, Neidelman had never seen finer.

He raised the scabbard and turned it to catch the light, feeling his heart almost stop as he did so. The face of the scabbard was thick with cabochon sapphires of a depth, color, and clarity that seemed impossible. He wondered what earthly force could bring such rich color to a gemstone.

He turned his attention to the hilt. The knuckle bow and quillion sported four astonishing rubies, each equal to the famous De Long Star, which Neidelman knew was considered the most perfect gemstone in existence. But embedded at the bottom of the pommel was a great double-star ruby that far surpassed the De Long in size, color, and symmetry. The stone, Neidelman mused as he turned the hilt in the light, had no equal on earth—none.

Decorating the ricasso, grip rings, and counterguard were a dazzling array of sapphires in a rainbow of colors—blacks, oranges, midnight blues, whites, greens, pinks, and yellows, every one a perfect double star. Once again, never had he seen such rich, deep colors. Not in his most febrile dreams had he imagined such gemstones. Each was utterly unique, each would command any price on the market. But to have them all set together in such a singular piece of Byzantine goldwork was inconceivable. Such an object had never existed in the world, nor could it exist again; it was without peer.

With an absolute clarity of mind, Neidelman could see that his vision of the sword had not been misplaced. If anything, he had underestimated its power. This was an artifact that could change the world.

Now, at last, the moment had come. The hilt and the scabbard were extraordinary: the blade itself must be beyond conception. Grasping the hilt in his right hand, and the scabbard in his left, he began to draw out the sword with exquisite slowness.

The flood of intense pleasure changed first to perplexity, then shock, then wonderment. What emerged from the scabbard was a pitted, flattened, deformed piece of metal. It was scaly and mottled, oxidized to a strange, purplish-black color, with inclusions of some white substance. He drew it to its length and held it upright, gazing at the misshapen blade—indeed, the word "blade" hardly described it at all. He wondered, remotely, what it could mean. Over the years his mind had imagined this moment a hundred, even a thousand, times. Each time, the sword had looked different.

But never had it looked like this.

He reached out and stroked the rough metal, wondering at its curious warmth. Perhaps the sword had been caught in a fire and melted, then refitted with a new hilt. But what kind of fire would do this? And what kind of metal was it? Not iron—it would have rusted orange—and not silver, which turned black when oxidized. Neither platinum nor gold oxidized at all. And it was far, far too heavy to be tin or any of the baser metals.

What metal oxidized purple?

He turned the sword again, and passed it through the air, and as he did so he recalled the Christian legend of the archangel St. Michael.

An idea formed within him.

Several times, late at night, he had dreamed the sword buried at the base of the Water Pit was, quite literally, the sword of legend: the sword of St. Michael himself, conqueror of Satan. In the dream, when he gazed upon the sword, he'd suffered a blinding conversion, like St. Paul on the road to Damascus. He had taken a curious kind of comfort in the fact that his rich imagination always faltered at this point. Nothing he could conceive was extraordinary enough to justify the veneration and dread that filled the ancient documents mentioning the sword.

But if St. Michael—the Archangel of the Sword—*had* fought Satan, his weapon would have been scorched and melted in the course of battle. Such a sword would be unlike any other.

As was the thing he now held in his hands.

He gazed at it anew, wonder and fear and uncertainty mingling within him. If this *was* such a sword—and what other explanation could there be?—then it was evidence, it was proof, of another world; of something beyond the material. The resurrection of such a sword would be a spectacular event.

Yes, yes, he nodded to himself. With such a sword, he could cleanse the world; he could sweep away the spiritual bankruptcy, give the fatal thrust to the world's decaying religions and their dying priesthoods, establish something new for a new millennium. His holding the sword was no accident; he had won it with his sweat and his blood; he had proven himself worthy of it. The sword was the proof he had been longing for his entire life: his treasure, above any other.

With trembling arm he rested the heavy weapon on the open lid of the casket. Once again he found himself astonished by the contrast between the supernatural loveliness of the hilt and the twisted ugliness of the blade. But now it had a kind of wonderful awfulness; a delicious, an almost holy kind of hideousness.

It was his now. And he had all the time in the world to consider—and perhaps, in time, comprehend—its strange and terrible beauty.

He carefully slid the blade back into its scabbard, glancing over at the casket as he did so. He would bring it to the surface, as well; the casket had its own importance, bound up inseparably with the sword's history. Looking over his shoulder, he was pleased to see that Magnusen had at last lowered the bucket into the chamber and was loading it with sacks of coins, slowly, like an automaton.

He returned his attention to the casket, and the one iron band that remained, rusted in place around one side. It was a strange way to strap down such a casket. Surely it would have been easier to bolt the straps to the floor of the treasure chamber, instead of running them underneath. What were they attached to below?

He backed up and kicked the last iron band, freeing the casket. The band broke away and shot down through the hole with amazing force, as if it had been attached to a great weight.

Suddenly there was a shudder, and the treasure chamber gave a great lurch. The right end of the floor dropping sickeningly, like an airplane plunging in violent turbulence. Rotten crates, canvas bags, and kegs tumbled from their positions along the left-hand wall, bursting upon the floor, showering gemstones, gold dust, and pearls. Stacks of gold bars leaned over heavily, then toppled in a great crash. Neidelman was thrown against the casket and he reached out for the hilt of the sword, ears ringing with Magnusen's screams, his eyes wide with astonishment.

58

The lift's electronic motor whined as it sank into the Pit. Streeter stood in one corner, gun in hand, forcing Rankin and Bonterre close to the opposite edge.

"Lyle, you *must* listen," Bonterre pleaded. "Roger says there is a huge void underneath us. He saw everything on the sonar screen. The Pit and the treasure chamber are built on top of—"

"You can tell your friend Hatch about it," said Streeter. "If he's still alive."

"What have you done with him?"

Streeter raised the barrel. "I know what you were planning."

"*Mon dieu,* you are just as paranoid—"

"Shut up. I knew Hatch couldn't be trusted, I knew from the moment I set eyes on him. Sometimes the Captain's a little naive that way. He's a good man, and he trusts people. That's why he's always needed me. I bided my time. And time proved me right. As for you, bitch, you chose the wrong side. And so did you." Streeter waved the gun in Rankin's direction.

The geologist was standing at the edge of the lift, good hand holding the railing, wounded hand held tight beneath the armpit. "You're insane," he said.

Bonterre looked at him. The great bear of a man, normally affable and easygoing, was filled with a rage she had never seen in him before.

"Don't you get it?" Rankin snapped. "That treasure's been soaking up radiation for hundreds of years. It's no good to anyone."

"Keep running your mouth and I'll put my boot in it," Streeter said.

"I don't give a damn what you do," Rankin said. "The sword's gonna kill us all, anyway."

"Bullshit."

"It's not bullshit. I saw the readings. The levels of radiation coming from that casket are unbelievable. When he takes that sword out, we're all dead."

They passed the fifty-foot platform, the dull metal of the titanium spars bathed in the glow of emergency lights.

"You think I'm some kind of idiot," Streeter said. "Or maybe you're so desperate you'd say anything to save your ass. That sword's five hundred years old, at least. Nothing on earth is that naturally radioactive."

"Nothing on earth. Exactly." Rankin leaned forward, his shaggy beard dripping. "That sword was made from a fucking *meteorite*."

"What?" Bonterre breathed.

Streeter barked a laugh, shaking his head.

"The Radmeter picked up the emission signature of iridium-80. That's a heavy isotope of iridium. Radioactive as shit." He spat over the side of the lift. "Iridium is rare on earth but common in nickel-iron meteorites." He rocked forward, wincing with pain as his shattered hand grazed the platform.

"Streeter, you must let us speak to the Captain," Bonterre said.

"That's not going to happen. The Captain's spent a lifetime working for this treasure. He talks about it, even in his sleep. That treasure belongs to him, not some hairy-assed geologist who joined the team three months ago. Or a French whore. It's his, all of it."

Raw anger flared in Rankin's eyes. "You pathetic bastard."

Streeter's lips compressed to a thin white line but he said nothing.

"You know what?" Rankin said. "The Captain doesn't give a shit about you. You're even more dispensable now than you were back in 'Nam. Think he'd save your life now? Forget it. All he cares about is his goddamn treasure. You're history."

Streeter whipped the gun to Rankin's face, jamming it between his eyes.

"Go ahead," Rankin said. "Either do me and get it over with, or drop the gun and fight. I'll kick your puny ass with only one hand."

Streeter swiveled the gun toward the lift railing and fired. Gore flew against the scribbled walls of the Pit as Rankin jerked his ruined left hand away. The geologist dropped to his knees, crying in pain and outrage, the index and middle fingers hanging by torn strips of flesh. Streeter began aiming calculated, vicious kicks at Rankin's face. With a cry, Bonterre threw herself at the team leader.

Suddenly, a throaty rumble roared up from the depths. It was followed a split-second later by a jarring blow that threw them all down onto the platform. Rankin reared back, unable to gain a purchase with his shattered hands, and Bonterre grabbed his shirt collar to keep him from tumbling over the edge. Streeter recovered first, and by the time Bonterre rose he was already gripping the rail, aiming his gun at them. The entire structure was shaking violently, titanium struts screeching in protest. Beneath it all was the demonic roar of rushing water.

The lift lurched to a shrieking halt.

"Don't move!" Streeter warned.

Another jarring shudder, and the emergency lights flickered. A bolt fell past, glanced off the platform with a clang, and went spinning down into darkness.

"It's begun," Rankin cried hoarsely, huddled on the floor of the lift, hugging his bleeding hands to his chest.

"What has begun?" Bonterre shouted.

"The Pit's collapsing into the piercement dome. Great fucking timing."

"Shut up and jump down." Streeter waved his gun at the gray shape of the hundred-foot platform, silhouetted a few feet below the lift.

Another jolt shook the lift, canting it crazily. A rush of chill air gusted up from the depths.

"Timing?" Bonterre shouted. "This is no coincidence. *This* is Macallan's secret trap."

"I said, shut up." Streeter shoved her off the lift and she tumbled several feet, landing hard on the hundred-foot platform. She looked up, shaken but unhurt, to see Streeter kicking Rankin in the abdomen. Three kicks and he was over the edge, landing heavily beside her. Bonterre moved to help but Streeter was already clambering catlike down the array to the platform.

"Don't touch him," he said, twitching the pistol warningly. "We're going in there."

Bonterre looked over. The bridge from the ladder array to the Wopner tunnel was trembling. As she stared, there came another violent shudder. The emergency lighting went out and the web of struts plunged into darkness.

"Move it," Streeter hissed in her ear.

Then he stopped. Even in the darkness, Bonterre could feel him tense.

Then she saw it, too: a faint light below them, rising quickly up the ladder.

"Captain Neidelman?" Streeter called down. There was no answer.

"Is that you, Captain?" he called again, louder, trying to make his voice heard over the thundering roar welling up from below.

The light kept coming. Now Bonterre could see it was pointed downward, its brightness obscuring the climbing figure.

"You down there!" Streeter called. "Show your face or I'll shoot!"

A muffled voice came up, faint and unintelligible.

"Captain?"

The light came closer, perhaps twenty feet below now. Then it snapped off.

"Christ," Streeter said again, bracing himself against the shaking platform, planting his legs apart and aiming downward, both hands on the gun. "Whoever it is," he roared, "I'm going to—"

But even as he spoke there was a sudden rush from the other side of the platform. Taken by surprise, Streeter spun around and fired, and in the flare of the muzzle Bonterre could see Hatch, slamming his fist into Streeter's gut.

Hatch followed the blow to Streeter's abdomen with a straight-arm to the jaw. Streeter staggered backward on the metal platform and Hatch came quickly after, catching a handful of Streeter's shirt and spinning him around. Streeter began to twist from Hatch's grip and Hatch pulled him forward, punching him twice, hard, in the face. On the second blow, there was a low crunching noise as Streeter's sinuses gave way with a splatter of mucus and hot, thick blood.

Streeter moaned and went limp, and Hatch relaxed his grip. Suddenly, Streeter's knee came up. Grunting in surprise and pain, Hatch fell backward. Streeter went for his gun. There was nothing he could do but shove the man, hard, toward the floor.

Streeter lifted his gun as Hatch dove for the far side of the array. There was a roar and a burst of light, and a bullet sparked off a titanium member to his left. Hatch ducked to one side, swinging around as another bullet whined between the braces. Then Hatch heard a gasp and a low grunt: Bonterre was grappling Streeter from behind. He lunged forward just as Streeter gave her a brutal backhand that sent her spinning toward the mouth of the tunnel. Quick as a cat, Streeter brought the gun forward again. Hatch froze, his fist hanging in midair, staring at the dim line of the gunbarrel. Streeter looked into his eyes and smiled, blood from his nose staining his teeth a dull crimson.

Then he lurched to one side: Rankin, unable to use his hands, had risen up and was butting Streeter toward the edge of the metal bridge with his body. For a moment, Streeter seemed on the verge of toppling. But he regained his balance and, as Hatch brought his arm back for a blow, turned the gun on Rankin and fired point-blank.

The geologist's head jerked back, a dark spray rising behind in the gloom of the tunnel. Then he slumped to the metal flooring.

But Hatch's fist was already in motion, connecting heavily with Streeter's jaw even as he wheeled backward. Streeter staggered heavily against the railing and there was a protest of metal. Instantly, Hatch stepped forward, shoving hard with both hands. The railing gave as Streeter sagged back. He toppled into space, scrabbling frantically for a purchase.

There was a gasp of surprise or pain; the crack of a pistol shot; the sickening sound of meat smacking metal. Then, more distantly, a splash that merged with the general rush of water far below.

The entire fight had lasted less than a minute.

Hatch rose to his feet, gasping from the exertion. He walked over to the inert form of Rankin, Bonterre already at the geologist's side. A single flash of livid lightning, reflected down through the tracery of struts, made it all too clear there was nothing he could do.

There was a grunt; the flashlight beam flared wildly; then Woody Clay heaved himself up onto the hundred-foot platform, sweat and dried blood mixing on his face. He had come up from below slowly, as a decoy, while Hatch had clambered quickly up the back side of the array to surprise Streeter.

Hatch was crushing Bonterre to him, his hands in the tangle of her dark hair. "Thank God," he breathed. "Thank God. I thought you were dead."

Clay watched them for a moment. "I saw something fall past me," he said. "Were those gunshots?"

Hatch's answer was interrupted by a sudden crash. Moments later, a large titanium spar came hurtling past them, raising fierce clangs as it bounced downward. The entire array quivered along its 150-foot length. Hatch pushed Bonterre and Clay across the shaking metal bridge into the nearby tunnel.

"What the hell's going on?" he panted.

"Gerard has opened the casket," Bonterre said. "He's set off the final trap."

Neidelman watched, paralyzed with shock, as a series of violent tremors shook the treasure chamber. Another sickening lurch, and the floor canted farther to the right. Magnusen, who had been thrown against the far wall by the first jolt, now lay partly buried in a great mass of coins, thrashing and clawing, crying out in an otherworldly voice. The chamber lurched again and a row of casks toppled over, bursting in a rotten spray of wood, filling the air with gold and jewels.

The shifting of the casket beneath him shook Neidelman from his paralysis. He shoved the sword into his harness and looked about for his dangling lifeline. There it was, just above him, rising through the hole in the top of the treasure chamber. Far above, he could make out the thin glow of emergency lights at the base of the ladder array. As he watched, they winked out briefly, then flickered into life once again. He reached for the lifeline just as another terrible lurch came.

Suddenly there was a screech of tearing iron as the seam

along the far edge of the floor split open. Neidelman watched in horror as the masses of loose gold slid toward the open seam, piling up against it, whirlpooling like water in a bathtub drain, pouring through the widening crack into a stormy black gulf below.

"No, *no*!" Magnusen cried, scrabbling through the hemorrhaging flow of treasure, even at this desperate extreme hugging and grasping the gold to her, caught between saving the coins and saving herself. A shudder that seemed to come from the center of the earth twisted the chamber, and a hailstorm of golden ingots buried themselves in the masses of coin around her. As the weight of the gold became greater and the whirlpool faster, Magnusen was sucked into the flow and pulled along toward the widening crack, her cries of *no, no, no* almost drowned by the roar of metal. She wordlessly stretched her arms toward Neidelman, eyes popping as her body was compressed by the weight of the gold. The vault echoed with the groan of buckling iron and the snapping of bolts.

And then Magnusen disappeared, sucked into the shimmering golden stream and down into the void.

Abandoning the lifeline, Neidelman scrambled up the shifting pile of gold and managed to grasp the swinging metal bucket. Reaching inside, he punched a button in the electrical box. The winch whined and the bucket began to ascend, Neidelman hanging beneath as the bucket scraped along the crazily angled roof of the iron vault before sliding up through the narrow cut.

As he slowly ascended the excavation toward the base of the ladder array, Neidelman hoisted himself into the bucket and glanced over its lip. He caught the last glimpse of a vast quantity of treasure—tusks, bolts of rotten silk, kegs, bags, gold, gems—vanishing in a great rattling rush through the crack in the treasure chamber below. Then the light, swinging wildly on its cord, smashed against the iron wall and was extinguished. The entire shaft went dark, lit only by the emergency lights from the array above his head. In the gloom, he saw—or thought he saw—the mangled treasure vault break free of the walls of the Pit and drop downward into a swirling chaos of water, sucked under with a final groan of iron.

A great tremor shook the shaft. Dirt and sand rained down, and the titanium bracings above gave a howl of protest. There was another flicker, and the emergency lights failed. The bucket came to a wrenching stop just below the ladder array, banging both sides of the narrow shaft.

Making sure the sword was secure, Neidelman reached up toward the winch rope, groping in the darkness. His fingers brushed against the lowest pilings of the array. Another terrible shudder twisted the Pit and he lunged upward with desperate strength, hoisting himself to the first rung, then the second, his feet dangling over the ruinous chasm. The entire support structure of the Pit was trembling under the strain, bucking like a live thing under his hands. There was a snapping sound in the darkness as one of the lower struts popped free. In the glow of a remote flash of lightning, he could see a broken body, bobbing in the watery ruin far beneath his feet.

As he hung from the array, gasping for air, the enormity of the disaster began to sink in. He dangled motionless for a second as his mind sought answers.

Then a vast black rage crept over his features and his mouth opened, wailing even over the roar of the void beneath him.

"Haaaaatch!"

60

What are you talking about?" Hatch asked, leaning against the wet tunnel wall, fighting for breath. "What final trap?"

"According to Roger, the Water Pit was built above a formation called a piercement dome," Bonterre shouted. "A natural void that goes deep into the earth. Macallan planned to snare Ockham with it."

"And we thought bracing the Pit would take care of everything." Hatch shook his head. "Macallan. He always was one step ahead of us."

"These struts of titanium are holding the Pit together—temporarily. Otherwise, the whole thing would have collapsed by now."

"And Neidelman?"

"*Sais pas.* He probably fell into the void with the treasure."

"In that case, let's get the hell out of here."

He turned toward the mouth of the tunnel just as another violent tremor shook the array. In the moment of silence that followed, a low beeping sounded from beneath Bonterre's sweater. She reached in, drew out the Radmeter, and handed it to Hatch.

"I got this from your office," she said. "I had to break a few things to find it."

The display was dim—the battery was obviously low—but the message displayed across the top of the screen was all too clear:

244.13 Rads/hour
Fast neutron flux detected
General radiation contamination probable
Recommendation: Immediate evacuation

"Maybe it's picking up residual radiation?" Bonterre suggested, peering at the screen.

"The hell it is. Two hundred forty-four rads? Let me see if I can bring the locator up."

He glanced at Clay, who obliged by turning the flashlight beam toward the machine. Hatch began stabbing at the miniature keyboard. The warning message disappeared, and the three-dimensional coordinate grid once again filled the screen. Standing, Hatch began to move the detector around. A blazing, rainbow-colored spot blossomed in the center of the screen, colors shifting as he turned.

"Oh, my God." He looked up from the screen. "Neidelman's not dead. He's on the ladder now, below us. And he's got the sword."

"What?" Bonterre breathed.

"Look at these readings." Hatch turned the Radmeter toward her. A ragged patch of white showed on its display, oscillating wildly. "Christ, he must be getting a massive dose from the sword."

"How much of a dose?" Clay asked, his voice strained.

"What I want to know is, how much of a dose are *we* getting?" Bonterre asked.

"We're not in immediate danger. Yet. There's a lot of intervening ground. But radiation poisoning is cumulative. The longer we stay, the bigger the dose."

Suddenly, the earth shook like a possessed thing. A few feet down the tunnel, a massive beam gave way with a loud crack. Dirt and pebbles rained around them.

"What are we waiting for?" Bonterre hissed, turning toward the depths of the tunnel. "Let's go!"

"Wait!" Hatch cried, the Radmeter buzzing in his hands.

"We *cannot* wait!" Bonterre said. "Can this tunnel lead us out?"

"No. The base of the well was sealed off when the reverend reset the trap."

"So let's climb out the Pit! We cannot stay here." She began walking toward the array.

Hatch pulled Bonterre roughly back into the tunnel.

"We can't go out there," he hissed.

"Why not?"

Clay was now at their side, looking intently at the screen. Hatch glanced at him, briefly surprised at the look of suppressed excitement, almost triumph, on the minister's face.

"According to this," Hatch said slowly, "that sword is so radioactive that even one second's exposure to it gives a lethal dose. Neidelman's out there now, and he's climbing toward us. If we so much as peek out into the main shaft, we're toast."

"Then why is he not dead?"

"He *is* dead. Even the most massive doses of radiation take time to kill. He was dead the moment he laid eyes on that sword. And *we're* dead, too, if we get within a sight line of it. Neutron radiation propagates through the air like light. It's vital that we keep rock and earth between him and us."

He stared at the Radmeter. "He's maybe fifty feet below now, maybe less. Go back down this tunnel as far as you dare. With luck, he'll climb right past us."

Over the uprushing of sound, Hatch heard an indistinct shout.

Gesturing for the others to stay back, he crept forward, halting just before the mouth of the shaft. Beyond, the web of titanium struts shivered and swayed. A low-battery alarm began sounding on the Radmeter, and he looked down to check the display:

3217.89 Rads/hour
Fast neutron flux detected
IMMEDIATE EVACUATION CRITICAL

Christ, he thought, *it's redlined.* They were still within safety limits, shielded by the rock and dirt of the Water Pit. But Neidelman was closer now, and soon not even the intervening earth would—

"Hatch!" came the hoarse, ragged voice.

Hatch paused.

"I found Lyle's body."

Still Hatch said nothing. Could Neidelman know where he was? Or was he merely bluffing?

"Hatch! Don't be coy, it doesn't suit you. I saw your light. I'm coming for you. Do you hear me?"

"Neidelman!" he yelled in return.

There was no answer. He glanced back at the Radmeter. The whitish blob on the screen kept ascending the grid, flickering in and out with the waning power of the battery.

"Captain! Stop! We need to talk."

"By all means. We'll have a *nice* little talk."

"You don't understand!" Hatch cried, inching even closer

to the edge. "The sword is highly radioactive. It's killing you, Captain! Get rid of it, *now!*"

He waited, straining to hear above the uprushing roar.

"Ah, the endlessly inventive Hatch," came Neidelman's voice, faint and unnaturally calm. "You planned this disaster very well."

"Captain, for Chrissakes, drop the sword!"

"Drop it?" came the answer. "You set this trap, wreck the Water Pit, kill my crew, deprive me of my treasure. And now you want me to drop the sword? I don't think so."

"What the hell are you talking about?"

"Don't be diffident. Take credit for your fine work. A few well-placed explosives did the trick, right?"

Hatch rolled onto his back, staring at the ceiling, searching for options. "You're a sick man, Captain," he called out. "If you don't believe me, ask your own body. The sword is a powerful emitter of fast neutron radiation. It's already stopped all cell mitosis and DNA synthesis in your body. Soon you'll be suffering from cerebral syndrome. The most severe form of radiation poisoning."

He listened. Except for the roar of the great gulf beneath, the only sound he heard was the dying chirp of the Radmeter. He took a deep breath.

"You're already in the prodromal period!" he called out. "First, you'll begin to feel nauseated. You probably do already, don't you? Next will come confusion, as inflammatory foci sprout up in your brain. Then tremors, ataxia, convulsions, and death."

There was no answer.

"For God's sake, Neidelman, listen to me!" he cried. "You're going to kill us all with that sword!"

"No," came the voice from below. "No, I think I'll use my gun."

Hatch sat up fast. The voice was closer now, very close: no more than fifteen feet away. He retreated down the tunnel to the others.

"What is happening?" Bonterre cried.

"He'll be here in a few seconds," Hatch replied. "He's not going to stop." As he spoke, he realized with grim finality that there was nothing they could do. They had no escape route. Another moment or two, and Neidelman would appear over the lip of the tunnel, sword in hand. And they would all be dead.

"Is there no way to stop him?" Bonterre cried.

Before Hatch could answer, Clay spoke. "Yes," he said, in a strong, clear voice. "Yes, there is."

Hatch turned. The look on Clay's cadaverous face was not only triumphant—it was ecstatic, beatific, otherworldly.

"What—?" Hatch began, but Clay had already brushed past him, light in hand. In a flash, Hatch understood.

"Don't do it!" he cried, grabbing for Clay's sleeve. "It's suicide! The sword will kill you!"

"Not until I've done what I came to do." Clay jerked his arm free and raced to the lip of the tunnel. Then—skirting Rankin's body—he leaped across the metal bridge to the array and descended quickly out of view.

61

Clinging to the rungs of the array, Clay climbed down a few feet, then paused to steady himself. A great roar was coming from the depths of the Pit: the sounds of collapsing caverns and thunderous water, of violent chaos churning in the unguessable depths. An uprush of damp air tugged and worried at the collar of his shirt.

He angled his flashlight downward. The ventilation system had shut down when the emergency power failed, and the air was heavy. The shaking spars were dripping with condensation, striped with clots of falling dirt. The beam licked through the fog, settling at last on the form of Neidelman, perhaps ten feet below.

The Captain was toiling painfully up the ladder, grasping each rung in the crook of his arm before hauling himself up to the next, his face contorted with effort. With every shudder of the ladder he paused, hugging the rungs in both hands. Tucked into Neidelman's back harness, Clay saw the flash of a jeweled hilt.

"Well, well," croaked Neidelman, staring up toward the flashlight. *"Et lux in tenebris lucet.* The light does shine in the darkness, indeed. Why am I not surprised to find the good reverend part of this conspiracy?" His voice dissolved into a hacking cough and he clung to the ladder with both hands through another nasty shudder.

"Toss the sword," Clay said.

Neidelman's answer was to reach into his belt and remove a handgun. Clay ducked to the far side of the array as the gun roared.

"Out of my way," Neidelman rasped.

Clay knew he couldn't confront Neidelman on these narrow rungs: he'd have to find a place with better footing. Quickly, he scanned the array with his flashlight. A few feet below, at the 110-foot mark, was a narrow maintenance spar. He put the flashlight in his pocket and used the darkness to descend one rung, then another. The array was trembling more violently now. Clay knew that Neidelman couldn't climb as long as he held the gun. But he also knew that the shaking came in waves, and as soon as the vibration ended Neidelman would put a bullet in him.

He dropped two more rungs in the blackness, feeling his way with his hands and feet as the shaking eased. A faint flare of reflected lightning showed Neidelman a few feet below him, hoisting himself toward the maintenance spar with one hand. He was already off balance and Clay, with a desperate movement, dropped another rung and with all his energy kicked out at the Captain's hand. There was a roar and a clatter as his foot connected and the gun fell away into darkness.

Clay slid down onto the spar, his feet slipping on the narrow metal grating. Neidelman, dangling below, howled with inarticulate rage. With a sudden flurry of energy he scrambled onto the narrow platform. Keeping the frame of the array between them, Clay took out his flashlight and shone it at the Captain.

Neidelman's face was streaked with sweat and dirt, skin frighteningly pallid, eyes sunken in the pitiless beam of the light. He seemed wasted, drawn, his body fueled only by the hard core of some inner will, and his hand trembled slightly as he reached behind him and drew out the sword.

Clay stared at it with a mixture of dread and wonder. The hilt was mesmerizingly beautiful, studded with huge gemstones. But the blade itself was an ugly, mottled violet, a pitted and scarred piece of metal.

"Step aside, Reverend," the Captain croaked. "I'm not going to waste my energy with you. I want Hatch."

"Hatch isn't your enemy."

"Did he send you to say that?" Neidelman coughed again. "I had Macallan soundly defeated. But I underestimated Hatch's treachery. Him and his operatives. No wonder he wanted Truitt on the dig team. And I suppose your protest was a ruse to distract my attention." He stared at Clay, eyes glittering.

"You're a dead man," Clay said calmly. "We're both dead men. You can't save your body. But perhaps you can still save your soul. That sword is a weapon of the devil. Cast it into the depths where it belongs."

"Foolish man," Neidelman hissed, advancing. "A weapon of the devil, you say? Hatch may have cost me the treasure. But I still have *this*. The sword I've spent the better part of my life preparing to claim."

"It's been the instrument of your death," Clay replied evenly.

"No, but it may be the instrument of yours. For the last time, Reverend, stand aside."

"No," said Clay, clinging to the shaking platform.

"Then die," cried Neidelman, bringing the heavy blade around and swinging it toward Clay's head.

62

Hatch tossed the now-dead Radmeter away and peered out into the darkness, toward the mouth of the tunnel and the vertical shaft of the Water Pit beyond. There had been vague sounds of voices; the flare of Clay's flashlight, silhouetting the metal skeleton of the ladder array; a gunshot, sharp and clear above the cavernous roar. He waited in an agony of uncertainty, the temptation to creep forward and take a brief look over the edge almost overwhelming. But he knew that even an instant's exposure to St. Michael's Sword meant lingering death.

He glanced back toward Bonterre. He could feel the tension in her body, hear her choppy breathing.

Suddenly, the sounds of a furious struggle erupted. There was the sound of metal striking metal, a hideous cry—whose?—followed by a strangled gibbering; then another great blow and clang of metal. Next came a terrible cry of pain and despair that receded until it, too, died into the roar of the Pit.

Hatch crouched, riveted in place by the horrifying sounds.

Then came more: ragged breathing, the slap of a hand against metal, a grunt of effort. A flashlight beam flared upward, searched the wall around them, then stopped, pinpointing the mouth of their tunnel.

Someone was climbing.

Hatch tensed, options racing through his mind. He realized there was only one. If Clay had failed, somebody else had to stop Neidelman. And he was determined it would be himself.

In the darkness beside him he felt Bonterre gathering herself to move, and he realized the same thought was in her mind as well.

"Don't even think about it," he said.

"Ferme-la!" she cried. "I will not let you—"

Before Bonterre could scramble to her feet Hatch jumped forward, half running, half stumbling toward the mouth of the tunnel. He poised on the brink, steeling himself, hearing her feet behind him. He leaped forward onto the metal bridge, ready to grab Neidelman and carry him into the roaring maw beneath.

Three feet down the ladder, Clay was struggling upward, his sides heaving, a large gash across one temple.

The minister wearily placed a hand on the next rung of the array. Hatch bent down, hauling him onto the platform as Bonterre arrived. Together, they helped him into the shelter of the tunnel.

The minister stood silently, leaning forward, head lolling, arms supported on his thighs.

"What happened?" Hatch asked.

Clay looked up.

"I got the sword," he said in a faraway voice. "I threw it into the Pit."

"And Neidelman?"

"He . . . he decided to go after it."

There was a silence.

"You saved our lives," Hatch said. "My God, you—" He paused and took a breath. "We'll get you to a hospital—"

Clay waved his hand wearily. "Doctor, don't. Please dignify my death with the truth."

Hatch looked at him a moment. "There's nothing medicine can do except make it less painful."

"I wish there was some way to repay your sacrifice," Bonterre said, voice husky.

Clay smiled, a strange smile that seemed partly rueful, partly euphoric. "I knew exactly what I was doing. It wasn't a sacrifice. It was a gift."

He looked at Hatch. "I have one favor to ask you. Can you get me to the mainland in time? I'd like to say good-bye to Claire."

Hatch turned his face away. "I'll do my best," he murmured.

It was time to go. They left the tunnel and crossed the shaking metal catwalk to the array. Hatch heaved Bonterre onto the ladder and waited as she began climbing into the darkness. As he looked up, lightning blazed across the sky and illuminated Orthanc, a dim specter far above, almost lost among the tracery of supports and beams. Curtains of rain, metal, and soil washed down, ricocheting through the complex matrix of the array.

"Now you!" Hatch shouted to Clay.

The minister handed him the flashlight, then turned wearily to the ladder and began to climb. Hatch watched him for a moment. Then, taking a careful grip, he leaned out over the edge of the platform and shone the flashlight down into the Pit.

He stared after the beam, almost dreading what he might see. But the sword—and Neidelman—were gone. Hatch could see a roiling cloud of mist cloaking the roaring gulf far beneath.

There was another sickening lurch, and he turned back to

the array and began to climb. All too soon he caught up with Clay; the minister was clutching a titanium rung, gasping for breath. Another great wave shook the ladder, shivering the remaining struts and filling the Pit with the protest of deforming metal.

"I can't go any farther," Clay gasped. "You go on ahead."

"Take the light!" Hatch shouted. "Then wrap an arm around my neck."

Clay began to shake his head in protest.

"Do it!"

Hatch started upward again, hauling the minister up each rung. In the gleam of the flashlight he could see Bonterre above them, concern visible on her face as she looked down.

"Go, go!" he urged, willing himself upward, one rung at a time. He gained the fifty-foot platform and continued, not daring to stop for a rest. Above, he could now make out the mouth of the Water Pit, dark black against the gray of the stormy sky. His muscles screamed as he forced himself upward, lifting Clay with each step.

Then the array gave another great lurch, and a blast of wet air and spray burst up from below. With a high-pitched tearing sound, a huge piece of the array came loose below them. Knocked against the metal railing, Hatch could see the cribbing on either side of the shaft begin to split and unravel. Beside him, Clay gasped, fighting to hold on.

Hatch scrambled upward again, fear and adrenaline sending new strength coursing through him. Directly above now, Bonterre was clambering up the array, her sides heaving. He followed, hoisting Clay along, sucking air into his lungs as fast as he could.

The rungs of the ladder grew slicker. Here, nearer the surface, the roar and shriek of the collapsing Pit mingled with the howl of the storm. Rain began to lash his face, warm after the foul chill of the tunnel. There was a violent tremor from deep within the Pit, and the array gave an almost human shriek as countless supports gave way. Torn from its anchors, the ladder swung violently from side to side, slashing through a forest of twisted metal.

"Go!" Hatch roared, pushing Bonterre in front of him. As he turned to follow he saw, with horror, the bolts along the central spine of the ladder begin to burst, unzipping like a jacket. Another massive tremor and the anchor supports of Orthanc began to buckle above their heads. There was a loud popping sound and one of the great observation windows dissolved into shards, raining down into the Pit.

"Look out!" Hatch cried, closing his eyes as the rain of glass and debris came crashing past. He felt the world begin to tilt and he opened them again to see the ladder array folding in on itself. With a lurch that brought his gut into his throat, the entire structure dropped several feet, accompanied by a chorus of twisting and snapping. Clay almost broke free, his legs swinging over the void.

"Onto the cribbing!" Hatch cried. He inched across a pair of struts, still supporting Clay. Bonterre followed. Grabbing Clay around the middle, Hatch hoisted him onto a titanium anchor bolt, then onto the old wooden cribwork that braced the sides of the Pit.

"Can you make it?" he asked.

Clay nodded.

Hatch clambered up below the minister, searching for handholds along the slimy, rotten face, urging Clay on. A piece of cribbing gave way beneath Hatch's feet, then another, and he scrabbled furiously for a moment before finding another purchase. He reached up, grabbed the bottom of the staging platform, and with Bonterre's help managed to haul the minister onto the platform and then to the grassy bank beyond.

Hatch clambered to his feet. To the south, he could see the dim shape of the rising tide pouring through a gap in the cofferdam. Bloated rainclouds scudded across the shrouded moon. All around the reefs the sea had been whipped white, the riptide carrying the line of foam as far as the horizon.

A thunderous clang from above spun him around. Freed from its foundations, Orthanc was twisting around, folding in on itself.

"To the dock!" Hatch shouted.

He grabbed Bonterre and they ran, supporting Clay between them, down the muddy trail toward Island One. Hatch glanced back to see the observation tower plunging downward, punching through the staging platform on its way into the Pit. Then the crash of a freight train gusted up from below, followed by a roar of water and a strange crackling sound: the snapping of countless wooden timbers as they pulled away from the loosening walls. A cloud of mist and water, mingled with yellow vapors and atomized mud, shot from the Pit and billowed into the night sky.

They moved as quickly as they could down the maze of trails to the deserted Base Camp and the dock beyond. The pier, sheltered by the lee of the island, was battered but intact. At its end, the launch from the *Cerberus* bobbed crazily in the waves.

In a moment they were aboard. Hatch felt for the key, turned it, and heard himself shout out loud as the engine roared to life. He flicked on the bilge pump and heard its reassuring gurgle.

They cast off and headed out into the storm. "We'll take the *Griffin*!" Hatch said, aiming for Neidelman's command boat, still stubbornly riding its anchors out beyond the reefs. "The tide's turned. We'll be going before the wind."

Bonterre nodded, hugging her sweater around her. "With a following sea and tide. Good luck, for a change."

They came alongside the *Griffin* and Hatch secured the launch, keeping it steady in the pitching surf while Bonterre helped Clay on board. As Hatch clambered up behind and ran to the pilothouse, lightning tore a jagged path over the island. He watched in horror as an entire section of the cofferdam collapsed. A great wall of water lunged through, pale against the dark sky as it enveloped the southern shore of the island in a mantle of white.

Bonterre brought in the anchors as Hatch primed the engines. He glanced toward the rear of the pilothouse, saw the bank of complex controls, and decided not to bother; he'd find his way back by dead reckoning. His eyes fell on the large maple table and he was irresistibly reminded of the last time he'd sat at it. Kerry Wopner, Rankin, Magnusen, Streeter, Neidelman . . . now all gone.

His gaze turned to Woody Clay. The minister sat in his chair, gaunt and wraithlike. He returned the gaze, nodding silently.

"All is secure," Bonterre said as she burst into the pilothouse, closing the wooden door behind her.

As Hatch eased the boat out of the lee, a great explosion sounded behind them, and a concussive wave rattled the rain-flecked sweep of windows. The heaving sea suddenly turned crimson. Hatch goosed the throttle, moving quickly away from the island.

"Mon dieu," Bonterre breathed.

Hatch looked over his shoulder in time to see the second fuel tank explode into a mushroom of fire that punched up through the low-lying fog, lighting the sky above the entire island and enveloping the buildings of Base Camp in a cloud of smoke and ruin.

Bonterre quietly slipped a hand into his.

A third roar came, this time seemingly from the bowels of the island itself. They watched, awestruck, as the entire surface of the island shuddered and liquefied, sending up vast plumes and waterspouts to violate the night sky. Burning gasoline spread a furious glow across the water until the waves themselves were on fire, breaking over the rocks and leaving the reef aflame.

And then, as quickly as it started, it was over. The island folded in on itself with a wrenching boom as the last section of the cofferdam gave way. The sea rushed into the open wound and met itself in the middle, rising in a great geyser whose top disappeared into the mist, falling back in a sluggish brown curtain. In a moment, all that was left was a great boiling patch of sea, worrying a cluster of jagged rocks. Plumes of dirty steam rose into the restless air.

"Ye who luste after the key to the Treasure Pitt," Bonterre murmured, *"shall find instead the key to the next world, and your carcase shall rot close to the Hell where your soule hath gone."*

"Yes," Clay said in a weak voice.

"It was a meteorite, you know," Bonterre added.

"And the fifth angel sounded," Clay whispered, *"and I saw a star fall from heaven unto the earth: and to him was given the key of the bottomless pit."*

Hatch glanced at the dying minister, afraid to speak, and was surprised to see Clay smiling, his sunken eyes luminous. Hatch looked away.

"I forgive you," Clay said. "And I believe I need to ask your forgiveness, as well."

Hatch could only nod.

The minister closed his dark eyes. "I think I'll rest now," he murmured.

Hatch looked back at the remains of Ragged Island. The fog was rapidly closing in again, enveloping the destruction in a gentle mist. He stared for a long moment.

Then he turned away and aimed the prow of the boat toward Stormhaven harbor.

63

The North Coast Realty Company had its offices in a small yellow cape across the square from the *Stormhaven Gazette*. Hatch sat at a desk in the front window, drinking weak coffee and staring idly at a bulletin board littered with photographs of properties. Under the headline "Great Fixer-Upper," he saw what could only be the old Haigler place: broken-backed and listing gently, but still quaint. "$129,500 steals it," he read off the card. "Built 1872. Four acres, oil heat, 3 bedrooms, 1½ baths." *Should have mentioned central air,* he thought wryly as he stared at the gaping chinks between the boards, the sagging sills. Beside it was a photo of a prim old clapboard on Sandpiper Lane, set between giant rock maples. Owned these fifty years by Mrs. Lyons, now deceased. "Not just a piece of property," read the accompanying card, "but a piece of history." Hatch smiled as he remembered the painstaking care with which he and Johnny had festooned those maples with toilet paper one Halloween more than thirty years ago.

His eyes traveled down to the next column of photos. "Maine dream house!" read the nearest card, burbling with enthusiasm. "Authentic Second Empire in every detail. Sunroom, bow windows, ocean views, wraparound terrace, waterfront dock. Original fixtures. $329,000." Underneath was a snapshot of his own house.

"Oh!" Doris Bowditch came bustling up. "There's no reason *that* should still be up there." She plucked the photo from the board and dropped it on a nearby desk. "Course, I didn't want to say anything, but I thought you'd made a mistake, not budging from a price as high as all that. But that couple from Manchester didn't bat an eye."

"So you told me," Hatch said, surprised by the regret in his voice. There was no reason for him to stay now, no reason at all. But despite the fact he hadn't even left town yet, he already found himself missing the weathered shingles, the clank of steel cable on mast, the resolute insularity of the town. Yet his was now a completely different kind of regret: a bittersweet nostalgia, better left to fond memory. He glanced out the window, past the bay, toward the few jagged upthrusts of rock that marked the remains of Ragged Island. His business—three generations of his family's business— was finished in Stormhaven.

"The closing will be in Manchester," the bright voice of Doris intruded. "Their bank wanted it that way. I'll see you there next week?"

Hatch rose, shaking his head. "I think I'll send my lawyer. You'll see that everything's crated and sent to this address?"

Doris took the proffered card and peered at it through rhinestoned glasses. "Yes, Dr. Hatch, of course."

Saying good-bye, Hatch stepped outside and walked slowly down the steps to the worn cobbles. This had been the last piece of business; he'd already shared a bottle of pop with Bud the grocer and called ahead to his housekeeper in

Cambridge. He paused a moment, then stepped around his car and pulled open the door.

"Malin!" came a familiar plummy cry.

Turning, Hatch saw St. John lurching toward him at an uneven trot, trying to keep numerous folders beneath his arms while maintaining his balance on the cobbles.

"Christopher!" he said with real pleasure. "I telephoned the inn this morning to say good-bye, but they told me you'd already left."

"I was killing the last few hours at the library," St. John replied, blinking in the sunlight. "Thalassa's sending a boat to take the last half dozen of us down to Portland. It should be here in the next half hour." He clutched the folders more tightly as a playful sea breeze threatened to spill his precious papers across the square.

"The Stormhaven Library?" Hatch said with a smile. "You have my sympathy."

"Actually, I found the place rather useful. It had just the kind of local history I'll need."

"For what?"

St. John gave his folders a pat. "Why, my monograph on Sir William Macallan, of course. We've opened up a whole new page in Stuart history here. And, you know, his intelligence work alone will merit at least two papers for the *Journal of the International Cryptographic Association*—"

The *basso profundo* blast of an air horn shivered the windows of the square, and Hatch looked in time to see a sleek white yacht turn into the channel and approach the pier. "They're early," St. John said. He balanced the folders awkwardly as he held out his hand. "Thank you again, Malin."

"There's nothing to thank me for," Hatch replied, returning the limp shake. "Best of luck to you, Christopher." He watched the historian teeter down the hill toward the dock.

Then he stepped into the Jaguar, closed the door, and cranked the motor.

He pulled out into the square and pointed the car's nose south, toward Coastal Route 1A and Massachusetts. He drove slowly, enjoying the salt air, the play of sun and shade across his face as he passed beneath the ancient oaks that lined the quiet streets.

He approached the Stormhaven Post Office and pulled over to the curb. There, balanced on the endpost of a white picket fence, sat Isobel Bonterre. She was wearing a thin leather jacket and a short ivory skirt. A large duffel lay on the sidewalk beside her. She turned toward him, stuck out a thumb, and crossed one leg over the other, exposing a shocking length of skin in the process.

"*Ça va*, sailor?" she called out.

"I'm fine. But I'd watch out if I were you." He nodded toward her tanned thighs. "They still burn scarlet women around here, you know."

She laughed out loud. "Let them try! Your town fathers are fat, fat to the last man. I could outrun them all. Even in these heels." She lifted herself from the post, walked over, and kneeled by the car, resting her elbows on the passenger window. "What took you so long?"

"Blame Doris the Realtor. She wanted to enjoy every last hard-earned minute of the sale."

"It made no difference." Bonterre pretended to pout. "I was busy anyway. Very busy, trying to decide what to do with my share of the treasure."

Hatch smiled. They both knew that nothing had been salvaged from the island; that the treasure could never, ever be reclaimed.

She sighed extravagantly. "Anyway, are you at last ready to drive me out of this *ville horrible*? I am looking forward to noise, dirt, panhandlers, daily newspapers, and Harvard Square."

"Then get in." Hatch reached over and opened the door.

But she remained leaning on the windowframe, staring at him quizzically. "You will allow me to buy dinner, yes?"

"Of course."

"And then we shall finally see how you Yankee doctors say good night to young ladies."

Hatch grinned. "I thought we already answered that."

"Ah, but this evening shall be different. This evening will not be spent in Stormhaven. And this evening, *I* am buying." With a smile, she dug her hand into the sleeve of her blouse and pulled out a massive gold doubloon.

Hatch stared in amazement at the oversized coin that filled her palm. "Where the hell did you get that?"

Bonterre's smile widened. "From your medical hut, *naturellement*. I found it there when I was rooting around for the Radmeter. The first—and last—of the Ragged Island treasure."

"Hand it over."

"*Désolée,* my friend," Bonterre laughed, holding it away from his reaching fingers. "But finders are keepers. Remember, it was I who dug it up in the first place. Do not worry yourself. It should buy us a great many dinners." She threw her duffel in the back seat, then leaned toward him again. "Now, back to tonight. I shall give you a choice. Head or tail?" And she flipped the thick coin into the air. It caught the sun as it turned, flashing brilliantly against the post office windows.

"You mean, heads or tails," Hatch corrected.

"No," Bonterre said as she slapped the coin against her forearm. "Head, or tail? Those are the correct terms, *non*?" She lifted her fingers and peeked at the coin, eyes widening salaciously.

"Get in here before they burn *both* of us at the stake," Hatch laughed, dragging her inside the car.

In a moment, the Jaguar's eager engine brought them to the outskirts of town. It was the work of two minutes more to reach the bluffs behind Burnt Head. Just as the car topped the brow of the hill, Hatch had one last glimpse of Stormhaven, a picture postcard of memory, caught in his rearview mirror: the harbor, the boats swaying at anchor, the white clapboard houses winking on the hill.

And then, in a flash of reflected sunlight, they were all gone.

Here is an excerpt from

Thunderhead

The Thrilling New Adventure
By Douglas Preston and
Lincoln Child

On a visit to her family's abandoned Santa Fe ranch, archaeologist Nora Kelly discovers an old letter, written from her father to her mother, now both dead. What perplexes Nora is that the faded envelope was postmarked and mailed only a few weeks before.

Her father vanished into the remote canyon country of southwestern Utah sixteen years ago, searching for Quivira, the fabled Lost City of Gold. Upon reading the letter, Nora learns that her father believed he had, in fact, located the lost city. But what happened to her father . . . and who mailed the letter?

In her quest for answers, Laura finds exhilarating adventure, unexpected mysteries, and deadly danger. Read on, for a sample chapter of THUNDERHEAD.

9

Nora stopped outside a closed oaken door labeled *Chairman of the Board, Santa Fe Archaeological Institute.* Clutching more tightly to the portfolio that now never left her side, she looked carefully down the hall in both directions. She was uncertain whether the nervousness she felt had to do with the events of the night before or with the impending meeting. Had word of her shenanigans at JPL somehow gotten out? No, that was impossible. But maybe this was going to be a dismissal anyway. Why else would Ernest Goddard want to see her? Her head ached from lack of sleep.

All she knew about the Chairman was what she had read, along with the rare newspaper photo and even rarer glimpse of his striking figure around campus. Although Dr. Blackwood might have been prime mover and chief architect of the Institute's vision, Nora knew that Goddard was the real power and money behind Blackwood's throne. And unlike Blackwood, Goddard had an almost supernatural ability to cultivate the press, managing to get the occasional tasteful and laudatory article placed in just the right venue. She had heard several explanations for the man's tremendous wealth, from inheriting a motor oil fortune to discovering a submarine full of Nazi gold—none of which seemed credible.

She took a deep breath and grasped the doorknob firmly. Maybe a dismissal would be a good thing at this point. It would free her to pursue Quivira unhindered. The Institute, in the person of Dr. Blackwood, had already passed judgment on her proposed expedition. Holroyd had given her the ammunition she needed to take the idea somewhere else. If the Institute wasn't interested, she knew she would find a place that was.

A small, nervous secretary ushered her through the reception area to the inner office. The space was as cool and spare as a church, with whitewashed adobe walls and a Mexican tiled floor. Instead of the imposing power desk Nora had expected, there was a huge wooden worktable, badly scuffed and dented. She looked around in surprise; it was the exact opposite of Dr. Blackwood's office. Except for a row of pots on the worktable, lined up as if at attention, the room was devoid of ornamentation.

Behind the worktable stood Ernest Goddard, longish white hair haloing his gaunt face, a salt-and-pepper beard below lively blue eyes. One hand held a pencil. A rumpled cotton handkerchief drooped from his shirt pocket. His body was thin and frail, and his gray suit hung loosely on his bony frame. Nora would have thought he was ill, except that his eyes were clear, bright, and full of fire.

"Dr. Kelly," he said, laying down the pencil and coming around the worktable to shake her hand. "So good to meet you at last." His voice was unusual: low, dry, barely higher than a whisper. And yet it carried enormous authority.

"Please call me Nora," she replied guardedly. This cordial reception was the last thing she expected.

"I believe I will," Goddard paused to remove the handkerchief and cough into it with a delicate, almost feminine gesture. "Have a seat. Oh, but before you do, take a look at these ceramics, will you?" He poked the handkerchief back into his pocket.

Nora approached the table. She counted a dozen painted bowls, all peerless examples of ancient pottery from the Mimbres valley of New Mexico. Three were pure geometrics with vibrant rhythms, and two contained abstract insect designs: a stinkbug and a cricket. The rest were covered with anthropomorphics—splendidly precise, geometric human figures. Each pot had a neat hole punched in the bottom.

"They're magnificent," Nora said.

Goddard seemed about to speak, then turned to cough. A buzzer sounded on the worktable. "Dr. Goddard, Mrs. Henigsbaugh to see you."

"Send her in," Goddard said.

4

Nora threw him a glance. "Shall I—"

"You stay right here," Goddard said, indicating the chair. "This will only take a minute."

The door opened and a woman of perhaps seventy swept into the room. Immediately, Nora recognized the type: Santa Fe society matron, rich, thin, almost no make-up, in fabulous shape, wearing an exquisite but understated Navajo squash blossom necklace over a silk blouse, with a long velveteen skirt.

"Ernest, how delightful," she said.

"Wonderful to see you, Lily," Goddard replied. He waved a spotted hand at Nora. "This is Dr. Nora Kelly, an assistant professor here at the Institute."

The woman glanced from Nora to the worktable. "Ah, very good. These are the pots I told you about."

Goddard nodded.

"My appraiser says they're worth five hundred thousand if they're worth a penny. Extremely rare, he said, and in perfect condition. Harry collected them, you know. He wanted the Institute to have them when he died."

"They're very nice—"

"I should say they are!" the woman interrupted, patting her impeccable hair. "Now, about their display. I realize, of course, that the Institute doesn't have a formal museum or anything of that sort. But in light of the value of these pots, obviously you'll want to create something special. In the Administration Building, I imagine. I've spoken to Simmons, my architect, and he's drawn up plans for something we're calling the Henigsbaugh Alcove—"

"Lily." Goddard's whispery voice assumed a very subtle edge of command. "As I was about to say, we're deeply appreciative of your late husband's bequest. But I'm afraid we can't accept it."

There was a silence.

"I beg your pardon?" Mrs. Henigsbaugh asked, her voice suddenly cold.

Goddard waved his handkerchief at the worktable. "These bowls came from graves. We can't take them."

"What do you mean, from graves? Harry bought the pots from reputable dealers. Didn't you get the papers I sent along? There's nothing about *graves* in them."

"The papers are irrelevant. Our policy is not to accept grave goods. Besides," Goddard added more gently, "these are very beautiful, it's true, and we're honored by the gesture. But we have better examples in the collection."

Better examples? thought Nora. She had never seen finer Mimbres bowls, not even in the Smithsonian.

But Mrs. Henigsbaugh was still digesting the grosser insult. "Grave goods! How dare you insinuate they were looted—"

Goddard picked up a bowl and poked one finger through the hole in its bottom. "This pot has been killed."

"Killed?"

"Yes. When the Mimbres buried a pot with their dead, they punched a hole in the bottom to release the spirit of the pot, so it could join the deceased in the underworld. Archaeologists call it killing the pot."

6

He replaced the bowl on the table. "All these pots have been killed. So you see they must have come from graves, no matter what the provenance says."

"You mean you're going to turn down a half-million-dollar gift, just like that?" the woman cried.

"I'm afraid so. I'll have them carefully crated and returned to you." He coughed into his handkerchief. "I'm very sorry, Lily."

"I'm sure you are." The woman spun around and left the office abruptly, leaving a faint cloud of expensive perfume in her wake.

In the silence that followed, Goddard settled onto the edge of the table, a thoughtful look on his face. "You're familiar with Mimbres pottery?" he asked.

"Yes," Nora replied. She still could not believe he had turned down the gift.

"What do you think?"

"Other institutions have killed Mimbres pots in their collections."

"We are not *other* institutions," Goddard replied in his soft whisper. "These pots were buried by people who respected their dead, and we have an obligation to continue that respect. I doubt Mrs. Henigsbaugh would approve of us digging up her dear departed Harry." He settled into a chair behind the worktable. "I had a visit from Dr. Blackwood the other day, Nora."

She stiffened. This was it, then.

"He mentioned that you were behind in your projects, and that he felt your tenure review might go poorly. Care to tell me about it?"

"There's nothing to tell," Nora said. "I'll submit my resignation whenever."

To her surprise, Goddard grinned at this. "Resignation?" he asked. "Why on earth would you want to resign?"

She cleared her throat. "There's no way, in six months, I'm going to be able to write up the Rio Puerco and Gallegos Divide projects, and—"

She stopped.

"And what?" Goddard asked.

"Do what I need to do," she finished. "So I might as well resign now, and save you the trouble."

"I see." Goddard's glittering eyes never left hers. "Do what you need to do, you say. Might that be searching for the lost city of Quivira?"

Nora looked sharply at him, and once again the Chairman grinned. "Oh, yes. Blackwood mentioned that, too."

Nora remained silent.

"He also mentioned your sudden absence from the Institute. Did it have something to do with this idea of yours, this search for Quivira?"

"I was in California," she replied noncommittally.

"I should have thought Quivira was somewhat east of there."

Nora sighed. "What I did was on my own time."

"Dr. Blackwood didn't think so. Did you find Quivira?"

"In a way, yes."

There was a silence in the room. Nora looked at Goddard's face. The grin was suddenly gone.

"Would you care to explain?"

"No," said Nora.

Goddard's surprise lasted only for a moment. "Why not?"

"Because this is my project," Nora said truculently.

"I see." Goddard eased himself off the table and leaned toward Nora. "The Institute might be able to help you and your project. Now tell me: what did you find in California?"

Nora moved in her chair, considering. "I have some radar images that show an ancient Anasazi road leading to what I believe is Quivira."

"Do you indeed?" Goddard's face expressed both astonishment and something else. "And just where did these images come from?"

"I have a contact inside the Jet Propulsion Laboratory. He was able to digitally manipulate radar images of the area, canceling out the modern tracks and leaving the ancient road. The course of this road matches the directions my father gave in his letter. It leads straight into the heart of the red rock country mentioned in the early Spanish accounts."

Goddard nodded, his face curiously expectant. "This is extraordinary," he said. "Nora, you're a woman of many surprises."

Nora said nothing.

"Of course, Dr. Blackwood had reasons to say what he did. But perhaps he spoke a little precipitously." He placed a hand lightly on her shoulder. "What if we make this search for Quivira *our* project?"

Nora paused. "I'm not sure I understand."

Goddard withdrew his hand, stood up, and walked slowly around the room, looking away from her. "What if the Institute were to fund this expedition of yours, roll back your tenure review? How would that sound?"

Nora gazed at the man's narrow back, absorbing what he had just said. "That would sound unlikely, if you don't mind my saying so," she answered.

Goddard began to laugh, only to be cut short by a series of coughs. He returned to the worktable. "Blackwood told me about your theories, about your father's letter. Some of the things he said were less than generous. But it happens that I, too, have long wondered about Quivira. No fewer than three early Spanish explorers in the Southwest heard these stories about a fabulous golden city. Cabeza de Vaca in the 1530s, Fray Marcos in 1538, and Coronado in 1540. Their stories are too similar to be fiction. And then in the 1770s, and again in the 1830s, more people came out of that wilderness, claiming to have heard of a lost city." He looked up at her. "There's never been a question in my mind that Quivira existed. The question was always exactly *where*."

He circled the table and came to rest on its corner once more. "I knew your father, Nora. If he said he found evidence for this lost city, I'd believe him."

Nora bit her lip against the unexpected well of emotion this comment generated.

"I have the means to put the Institute squarely behind your expedition. But I need to see the evidence first. The letter *and* the data. If what you say is true, we'll back you."

Nora placed a hand on her portfolio. She could hardly believe the turnaround. And yet, she had seen too many young archaeologists lose credit to their older, more powerful colleagues. "You said this would be our project. I'd still like to keep it *my* project, if you don't mind."

"Well, perhaps I do mind. If I'm going to fund this expedition—through the Institute, of course—I would like control, particularly over the personnel."

"Who did you envision leading the expedition?" she asked.

There was the slightest of pauses while Goddard steadily met her gaze. "You would, of course. Aaron Burk would go along as the geochronologist, and Enrique Aragon as the medical doctor and paleopathologist."

Nora sat back, surprised with the rapidity with which his mind worked. Not only was he thinking ahead to the expedition, but he was already peopling it with the best scientists in their fields. "If you can get them," she said.

"Oh, I'm reasonably sure I can get them. I know them both very well. And the discovery of Quivira would be a watershed in Southwestern archaeology. It's the kind of gamble an archaeologist can't resist. And since I can't go along myself—" he waved his handkerchief in explanation— "I'd want to send my daugher in my stead. She got her undergraduate degree from Smith, just took her Ph.D. at Princeton in

11

American archaeology, and she's anxious to do some fieldwork. She's young, and perhaps a little impetuous, but she has one of the finest archaeological minds I've ever encountered. And she's highly skilled at field photography."

Nora frowned. *Smith,* she thought to herself. "I'm not sure that's a good idea," she said. "It might muddy the chain of command. And this is going to be a difficult trip, particularly for a . . ." she paused. "A sorority girl."

"My daughter *must* go along," said Goddard quietly. "And she is no 'sorority girl,' as you shall discover." An odd, mirthless smile flashed briefly across his lips before disappearing.

Nora looked at the old man, realizing the point was nonnegotiable. Quickly, she considered her options. She could take the information she had, sell the ranch, and head into the desert with people of her own choosing, gambling that she could find Quivira before her money ran out. Or she could take her data to another institution, where it would probably be a year or two before they could organize and fund a trip. Or she could share her discovery with a sympathetic backer uniquely qualified to outfit a professional expedition, leading the top archaeologists in the country. The price of admission was taking the backer's daughter along for the ride. *No contest there,* she thought.

"All right." She smiled. "But I've got a condition of my own. I need to take the JPL technician who assisted me along as a remote imaging specialist."

12

"I'm sorry, but I'd like to reserve the personnel decisions."

Nora hesitated a moment. "It was the price of getting the data," she said at last.

There was a silence. "Can you vouch for his credentials?"

"Yes. He's young, but he's got a lot of experience." Nora was surprised at Goddard's ability to take a challenge, parry, and come to a decision. She found herself beginning to like him.

"I also think we have to keep this confidential," she continued. "The expedition has to be assembled very quickly and very secretly."

Goddard looked at her speculatively. "May I ask why?"

"Because . . ." Nora stopped. The real answer was *because I think I'm being shadowed by mysterious figures who will stop at nothing to find the location of Quivira.* But she couldn't say that to Goddard; he'd think her crazy, or worse, and rescind his offer in an instant. Any hint of a problem would complicate, maybe even wreck, the expedition. "Because this information is very sensitive. Think what would happen if pothunters learned about it and tried to loot the site before we could reach it. And on a practical matter, we have to move fast. The flash flood season will be on us soon."

After a moment, Goddard nodded slowly. "That makes sense," he said. "I'd like to include a journalist on the expedition, but I'm sure his discretion can be relied on."

13

"A journalist?" Nora burst out. "Why?"

"To chronicle what may be the most important find in twentieth-century American archaeology. Imagine the story the world would have lost if Howard Carter had not had the London *Times* covering his discovery. I actually have somebody in mind, a *New York Times* reporter with several books to his credit, including an excellent profile of the Boston Aquarium. I think he can be relied upon not only to be a good digger, but to produce a highly favorable—and highly visible—account of you and your work." He glanced at Nora. "You have no objection to *ex post facto* publicity, certainly?"

Nora hesitated. This was all happening so fast: it was almost as if Goddard had worked it all out before even talking to her. As she thought back over their conversation, she realized he must have. It occurred to her that there might be a reason for his excitement that he was not sharing with her.

"No," she said. "I guess not."

"I didn't think so. Now let's see what you've got."

Goddard pushed away from the desk as Nora reached into her portfolio and removed a thirty-by-sixty-minute USGS topo. "The target area is this triangle just to the west of the Kaiparowits Plateau, here. As you can see, it contains dozens of canyon systems that all eventually drain into Lake Powell and the Grand Canyon, to the south and east. The closest human settlement is a small Nankoweap Indian encampment sixty miles to the north."

Then she handed Goddard a sheet of paper: a

USGS 7.5-minute topographic map, onto which Holroyd had overprinted in red the final image from his computer, properly scaled. "This is an image taken from last week's Shuttle overflight, digitally enhanced. The faint, broken black line across it is the ancient Anasazi road."

Goddard took the sheet into his thin pale hands. "Extraordinary," he murmured. "Last week's flight?" Again he looked at Nora, a curious admiration in his eyes.

"The dotted line shows a reconstruction of my father's route through this country, following what he thought to be that road. When we extrapolated the road from the Shuttle radar image onto this map, it matched my father's route. The road seems to lead northwestward from Betatakin Ruin, through this maze of canyons, and over this huge ridge which my father labeled the 'Devil's Backbone.' It then appears to lead into a narrow slot canyon, ending up in this tiny, hidden canyon, here. It's somewhere in this canyon that we hope to find the city."

Goddard shook his head. "Amazing," he breathed. "But Nora, all the ancient Anasazi roads we know about, Chaco and the rest, run in absolutely straight lines. This road winds around like a broken spring."

"I thought of that, too," Nora said. "Everyone's always thought Chaco Canyon was the center of Anasazi culture, the fourteen Great Houses of Chaco with Pueblo Bonito at their hub. But look at this."

She pulled out another map, showing the entire Colorado Plateau and San Juan Basin. In the lower-right-hand corner, an archaeological site diagram of Chaco Canyon had been overlaid, showing the huge ruin at Pueblo Bonito surrounded by a circle of outlying communities. A heavy red line had been drawn from Pueblo Bonito, through the circle, through a half dozen other major ruins, and running arrow-straight to the upper-left-hand corner of the map, terminating in an X.

"That X marks the presumed spot of Quivira," Nora said quietly. "All these years we've believed that Chaco itself was the destination of the Anasazi roads. But what if Chaco *wasn't* the destination? What if, instead, it was the collecting point for a ritual journey to Quivira, the city of priests?"

Goddard shook his head slowly. "This is fascinating. There's more than enough evidence here to justify an expedition. Have you given any thought to how you might get in there? Helicopters, for example?"

Nora shook her head. "That was my first thought. But this isn't a typical remote site. Those canyons are too narrow and most are a thousand feet deep. There are high winds, beetling rimrock, and no flat areas to land. I've studied the maps carefully, and there's no place within fifty miles to safely land a helicopter. Jeeps are obviously out of the question. So we'll have to use horses. They're cheap and can pack a lot of gear."

Goddard grunted as he stared at the map. "Sounds good. But I'm not sure I see a route in, even on horseback. All these canyons box up at their sources. Even

16

if you used this Indian settlement far to the north as your jumping-off point, it would be one hell of a ride just to get to the village. And then, waterless country for the next sixty miles. Lake Powell blocks access to the south." He looked up. "Unless you . . ."

"Exactly. We float the expedition up the lake. I've already called the Wahweap Marina in Page, and they have a seventy-foot barge that will do the job. If we started at Wahweap, floated the horses up to the head of Serpentine Canyon, and rode in from there, we could be at Quivira in three or four days."

Goddard broke into a smile. "Nora, this is inspired. Let's make it happen."

"There's one other thing," Nora said, replacing the maps in her portfolio without looking up. "My brother needs a job. He'll do anything, really, and I know with the right supervision he'd be great at sorting and cataloging the Rio Puerco and Gallegos Divide material."

"We have a rule against nepotism—" Goddard began, then stopped as Nora, despite herself, began to smile. The old man looked at her steadily, and for a moment Nora thought he would erupt in anger. But then his face cleared. "Nora, you are your father's daughter," he said. "You don't trust anybody, and you're a damn good negotiator. Any other demands? You'd better present them now, or forever hold your peace."

"No, that covers it."

Silently, Goddard extended his hand.

About the Authors

Douglas Preston and Lincoln Child are the co-authors of the national bestsellers *The Relic, Mount Dragon, Reliquary,* and *Riptide*. Douglas Preston worked for the American Museum of Natural History in New York as an editor and writer. In 1989 he undertook a thousand-mile horseback journey retracing the Spanish explorer Coronado's search for the legendary Seven Cities of Gold. He is a regular contributor to *The New Yorker*. Lincoln Child was for several years a book editor at St. Martin's Press in New York. He has published numerous anthologies of short stories, including *Dark Company* and *Dark Banquet*.

The authors welcome reader e-mail at the following addresses: 102117.106@compuserve.com (Douglas Preston) and lchild@msn.com (Lincoln Child).